The
Flower
Shop

The Flower Shop

THE SEED TRADERS' SAGA

PETRA DURST-BENNING

TRANSLATED BY EDWIN MILES

amazoncrossing

Text copyright © 2008 by Petra Durst-Benning and Ullstein Buchverlage GmbH
Translation copyright © 2018 by Edwin Miles
All rights reserved.

Previously published as *Das Blumenorakel* by Ullstein Buchverlage GmbH in Germany in 2008, republished as *Floras Traum* in 2014. Translated from German by Edwin Miles. First published in English by AmazonCrossing in 2018.

Published by AmazonCrossing, Seattle

www.apub.com

Amazon, the Amazon logo, and AmazonCrossing are trademarks of Amazon.com, Inc., or its affiliates.

ISBN-13: 9781503950139
ISBN-10: 1503950131

Cover design by Shasti O'Leary Soudant

Printed in the United States of America

The Flower Shop

The Nymph of the Pond

The meadows surrounding the shimmering blue-green waters of the pond were more lush than most in the region, and a favorite among the goatherds who took their goats there to graze. The animals tugged sedately at the fragrant grasses and plants, and none were tempted to run away.

Satisfied with his choice of pasture, a young herder began to play his shawm, devoting himself to a pensive melody. But other sounds—far lovelier and finer—seemed to come from the pond itself and soon mixed with his dreamy tune.

Curious, the youth made his way down to the water's edge, and was surprised to spy, on a rock in the small pond, a beautiful water nymph with rippling black hair and sparkling green eyes. She plucked a golden harp and sang to it in a voice as clear as well water, a song the goatherd did not know, but which captivated him instantly. The nymph, with a gentle smile on her lips, glanced at the boy just once but did not interrupt her singing.

The goatherd had neither seen nor heard anything as lovely in his life. He felt as if he could sit there forever, and only when it began to grow dark did he return to his goats. After that, he visited the pond evening after evening to listen to the enchanted sounds.

One day, the nymph revealed to the youth that her name was Merline. But she told him he must never speak to her by that name, or call it aloud if he did not find her there, for if he did, something terrible would happen.

The goatherd nodded, but he was mystified.

One day, on his way to the pond, he came across an old pitch-burner who had been traveling in the region for as long as anyone could remember. The old man warned the goatherd to be on his guard. Many a young man had found his eternal grave in that pond because he could not resist the nymph's beguiling song.

The pitch-burner's warning fell on deaf ears, for the young goatherd had long ago fallen for Merline's charms. One evening, when he did not find the nymph atop her usual rock, he could do nothing other than call her name.

"Merline!"

Instead of seeing the nymph, the youth spied a blood-red rose that grew from the surface of the water and drifted to the bank. When he bent to pluck it, he tumbled into the water and was caught in the twining vines. In fear, he flailed his arms and kicked with his legs, but the pond did not release him, and instead pulled him down to its depths.

That night and the morning after, the goats bleated for their goatherd, to no avail. Then they wandered into the woods around the pond and were never seen again.

Chapter One

January 1871

"Baden-Baden! I already know I'm not going to like this place." Flora gazed grumpily out of the train window. The black coal smoke billowing from the locomotive mixed with the silently falling snow, creating an ugly, blurry veil that made everything gray and shadowy. The few people she saw had their noses hidden inside their overcoat collars or behind handkerchiefs to protect them from the bad air.

Flora pointed beyond the station building to a huge banner hanging from a hotel window. "Bayerischer Hof—look how they go on about their food and drink!"

"Don't worry. Our hotel is much closer to the center of town, and I can tell you now that it's far less exclusive." Hannah Kerner, who was sitting beside Flora, sighed. The last thing she needed was her daughter's carping.

"Well, that's one thing to be thankful for. Ugh! Everything looks so grim. And deserted. How are we supposed to do good business here?" Flora seemed unaware that her own countenance was at least as grim and unwelcoming as the face of Baden-Baden on that winter's day.

Hannah also peered dubiously at the snowed-in town. There were no soldiers in sight, although she was not sure if that was a good or bad sign. France had not yet officially surrendered, and the Franco-Prussian War continued despite the newspapers' exaggerated reports of a German victory. Apparently, King Wilhelm had had himself declared emperor just a few days earlier in the Hall of Mirrors at the palace in Versailles, and the papers were talking about it as a gesture of "complete subjugation." A German emperor in Versailles—that was something! Hannah's husband, Helmut, and the other men in the village had already lifted many glasses of beer and schnapps to the new emperor.

What if the French did not feel themselves to be "completely subjugated" after all? Was France perhaps on the cusp of a counterattack? And if it was, then Baden-Baden was a particularly unsafe place to be.

Although Hannah loved the town and knew it very well from earlier visits, she had an uneasy feeling. There had been far better times to visit Baden-Baden, and there certainly would be again, which only made Hannah even more resolved to put on a confident, carefree face for Flora's sake. She did not want fear added to her daughter's rancor and discontent.

Before their departure, Helmut had questioned everyone he knew who had been anywhere near Baden-Baden about the political situation. None of the travelers reported any fighting or dangerous situations, so Helmut felt it would also be safe enough for his wife and daughter, and Hannah had not said anything to contradict him. What could she have said? They could not afford to sit at home and wait for better times.

And now it fell to Hannah, in these extraordinary days, to instill in her daughter a taste for travel and trade. But until then, she had not had much success.

The train stopped. It was time to see what was waiting for them.

"Stop sulking!" said Hannah, with a glance at Flora. "You take the bag with the food and gifts, and I'll carry the seed sack and the traveling case." As she spoke, she wrapped her warm wool shawl around her shoulders and looked critically at her reflection in the filmy window. She straightened her felt hat and was satisfied with what she saw. She knew that the dark green of the matching hat and shawl showed off her nearly black hair and eyes to best advantage. The shawl and the small hat also marked her as a Gönningen seed dealer, who earned her living from the trade in flower and vegetable seeds and tulip bulbs. Not all the women in Hannah's village looked as good as she did in that attire: at thirty-nine, Hannah was still a very attractive woman.

Flora, too, wore Gönningen's dark green, although she wore the shawl as if it weighed on her shoulders like a half-ton yoke.

Oh, my girl, a seed woman's life is not so bad, Hannah thought.

A few minutes later, the two women were sitting in a coach and being driven toward the center of Baden-Baden. Hannah wanted to drop their luggage at the guesthouse before they visited their first customers.

As the coach rolled over the hard-packed snow that covered the long street, Hannah pointed out stately homes, mansions, and hotels—all residences of her esteemed Baden-Baden customers. Flora kept up her deliberately indifferent facade. Behind her sullen silence, Hannah could hear Flora loud and clear—she had no interest whatsoever in the "esteemed customers." But instead of being upset at Flora's behavior, Hannah felt as though her heart would break to see her daughter so unhappy.

How she loved her daughter! Of course, the twins—two years younger than Flora—were just as close to her heart. But her daughter was simply . . . her daughter.

Her Flora.

That she bore an uncanny physical resemblance to her mother was one thing. She had the same dark, wavy hair—although Hannah's was starting to show streaks of silver—and the same strong build. Perhaps a little too tall and well built for a woman, but certainly no beanstalk to get blown over with the first decent wind. Hannah's eyes sparkled like pebbles of coal, while Flora's were the brown of chocolate. Hannah considered her daughter to be pretty, but knew she was no ravishing beauty. And most of the time, at least, she was also a very nice young woman.

Twenty-one years earlier, if Hannah had not been pregnant with Flora, she would never have left Nuremberg for Gönningen, at the edge of the Swabian Mountains. She would very likely have spent her entire life as a maid at her parents' inn, or married to some Franconian grouch. Without this child, she would never have won Helmut, the man who loved her so much that it sometimes hurt. Admittedly, he had not been thrilled to see her when she first arrived in Gönningen on that cold December day, with her traveling bag in her hand, and told him the "good news." Still, he had done what an honorable man in such a situation was supposed to: he had married her. A great love? Not at the time. That came only through their years together. Today, Hannah could not imagine life without Helmut. Nor could she imagine living any differently than as a seed trader from Gönningen. She wanted that same happiness for her daughter.

Flora, the goddess of flowers . . . yet this Flora did not want to be a seed trader; she dreamed of something else and had nothing in her head but flowers. Could that foolishness be tied to her name?

It was Helmut who had suggested her unusual name. "A child born out in the open air, surrounded by nature, *must* be named after the goddess of flowers," he'd said. Hannah had not objected. In those days, she hardly had been able to form a single clear thought. Her water had broken out in the fields—to this day, she had trouble believing it! Flora's speedy arrival aside, she had not been a difficult child. She had been charming, in fact, and everyone in the village had a kind word for the little girl with her bouquets of flowers.

Hannah smiled at the memory, but sighed again a moment later. The way Flora had been behaving lately, no one in their right mind would call her "charming." And now she sat there with a look on her face as if she were being driven to the scaffold.

"I know you still dream of becoming a florist. Everybody has dreams. But you didn't like it at all when you worked at the Grubers' nursery in Reutlingen. You were no better off than a maid, slaving away for other people, while I had so much work at home that I didn't know which way to turn. It was very generous of your father and me to let you go to Gruber's. You wanted to learn something, and we didn't want to stand in your way. But what came of it? You dreaded the kind of work they did, and you practically begged your father not to make you go back. Please stop the coach!" she said, suddenly addressing the driver.

"Here? Now you don't want to go to Tausend-Seelen-Gass?" The man shook his head sourly, but he helped Hannah unload their luggage.

"That was not a proper florist's shop. It was more like a farm. I would have learned far more about floristry somewhere else," Flora said sulkily, scratching a hole in the snow with the toe of her shoe.

Hannah wanted nothing more than to take her daughter in her arms, but instead she said, "Be that as it may, now it's time for you to work with us, just as your friends are doing with their parents. Not that they all have it half as good as you. Think about poor Suse, for example, going off with her mother to the south of the Black Forest. Almost all their customers are poor. But Baden-Baden! Hardly anyone can boast a *Samenstrich* as good as this." Hannah hoped that Flora would become as enthusiastic as she herself was about Baden-Baden.

"Where are we going? I would have preferred to ride."

Hannah smiled. "I want to show you a little of the town. The train trip was not so tiring that we can't go on foot for a while."

"If we have to." With a sigh, Flora picked up the linen bag and the seed sack and Hannah took the traveling case, and they strode off across one of the bridges that crossed the Oos River.

"That is called the Conversationshaus," Hannah said as she pointed to a large building. "It's home to Baden-Baden's famous casino, and I've heard that there are dance halls and a fabulous restaurant and all kinds of things."

Flora screwed up her nose. "Bit pretentious, isn't it?"

Hannah decided to overlook her daughter's tone. "You'll see. Baden-Baden has many lovely aspects. Besides, it's a safe place to travel, and we'll be staying in a good guesthouse with a nice hostess. What more could you want?" Hannah shook her head. She could hardly believe that she was out in the icy weather trying again to show Flora the advantages of this trip. They had had similar talks through Christmas and New Year's. Sometimes she wondered if she and Helmut were not too good-natured altogether.

When Flora did not reply, Hannah continued, "Your father bought this *Samenstrich* from Martin Gsell for a great deal of money, as you know. He wanted you to have a particularly good territory to sell your seeds. Most of the customers in Baden-Baden are flower growers, so it's made for you! You can earn a very good living here. I admit that this war has made things difficult, at least for a while, but that makes it more important for us to be here this year. If we didn't come, our customers would go and buy their seeds somewhere else, and the money we paid for this territory would be thrown away."

Hannah shook her head.

"Flora, don't make this so hard for me. If I'd known how horridly you were going to behave, I'd have stayed home! Then you would have had to figure everything out by yourself." Hannah stamped her foot and involuntarily let out a groan. Although her boots had heavy leather soles, the cold had already crept into her bones. Since an accident many years before, in which her leg had gotten caught in a fox trap, she had been more vulnerable to cold weather.

Flora looked up, her face shocked and guilty.

"Oh, Mother, I'm sorry. Don't be mad at me. I *am* grateful to you and Father, really. I only wanted—"

Hannah took her daughter in her arms.

"Your dreams. I know, my child."

Chapter Two

Mother and daughter marched on, arm in arm. Flora had to admit to herself, if not her mother, that now that she was seeing Baden-Baden for the first time, she was quite taken with it. There was Lange Strasse, which was lined with beautiful hotels, and the Conversationshaus, and now they were on the pretty avenue called the Promenade, with one lovely little shop after another, left and right. Flora gazed in amazement at the colorful display in the window of a hatmaker's shop. And what was that? Flora lifted her nose in the air. Lavender. In the middle of winter? The fragrance emanated from a *parfumerie* in which golden chandeliers illuminated thousands of small bottles, jars, and crucibles— how splendid it looked!

"They call these shops the Promenade Boutiques," said Hannah. "I really wanted to go a little way along Lichtenthaler Allee and then turn back to the town center over one of the bridges farther down, but it is only a little longer to our guesthouse this way."

Flora nodded. So many beautiful stores—she could just imagine telling her best friend, Suse, about them. She pointed to the signs on the shops on the opposite side of the Promenade. "*Maison, confection, chocolatier*—don't you think all the French is a little, well, affected?"

"With all the French tourists, I'd call it good for business. But who knows if they'll be back in the future?"

"Mother, look, a florist!" Flora stopped short in front of the last shop in the row. The three large display windows were decorated with huge bouquets of roses set up in silver containers, and between the gold-framed windows themselves stood large pails, each with a fir tree. Everything looked very fine and exclusive.

This shop had nothing in common with Mrs. Gruber's nursery, where along the rows of flowers and vegetables one always found muddy shoeprints on the floor.

"These colors . . . where do they find blooming roses in the middle of winter?" Flora's voice had grown very quiet. Then she turned to her mother and asked vehemently, "Oh, Mother, can we go inside? Please? Just to look? Now that we're here."

"Child, we have to get on to—"

"Just for a minute? Look, there's a woman going in. She's so elegant."

"Maison Kuttner, hmm . . ." Hannah shook her head. "Certainly not one of our customers. They probably have their flowers delivered rather than grow them themselves." She looked from Flora to the flower shop and up to the large clock on the church tower on the other side of the street.

"All right, then. As long as you don't drag your feet too much when we come out."

"Oh, thank you, thank you!" After a quick kiss to Hannah's cheek, Flora was already halfway through the door.

The saleswoman's eyes roamed from Hannah's seed sack and shawl down to her heavy boots. Her expression tightened as if she were looking at something a dog had left behind. She pointed her finger toward the door.

"The delivery entrance is around the back."

Her two colleagues behind the counter also eyed Flora and her mother with disdain.

Flora was admiring the exotic flowers and plants in wide-eyed wonder and did not immediately realize the women behind the counter were addressing them. Passionflower, hollyhock, white myrtle . . .

"We just want to look at your flowers." Hannah's reply, spoken flatly, jolted Flora out of her reverie. She turned in confusion to her mother, who went on, "But I'm afraid that roses in winter are not really to our taste. We prefer . . . natural things." With her nose held higher than any of the women in the store, Hannah stalked out into the cold.

Flora followed, her head held high.

"What a bunch of sour old lemons," Flora hissed the moment they were outside. "And did you see those ridiculous ruffled dresses they were wearing? They might be just the thing for a confectioner but not a florist." With every word, a little white cloud puffed from Flora's mouth and hovered momentarily in the cold air before dissipating.

"And the roses! Forcing roses might be all the rage in Paris or Hamburg, but personally I find it terrible. Roses in winter is like Christmas in August!" Hannah scoffed. A horse passing by just then turned its head to them and whinnied enthusiastically.

Both women laughed.

Flora was surprised at how surely her mother navigated through the streets of the town. At the end of the Promenade they crossed a small square and reached Sophienstrasse, from where they had to keep their eyes open not to miss the turn into Stephanienstrasse.

"Look there. Grand Duchess Stéphanie from France had it built as her summer palace," said Hannah, pointing off to the right at a building that, despite its size and extensive lawns and garden beds, radiated nothing but charm. "I'm sure the street itself is also named after her. The gardener is also one of our customers."

Flora nodded, clearly impressed.

The farther they went along the street, the more its character changed. Here, too, the facades of the buildings were painted white, but the houses were taller and not as wide. The elegant show windows were gone, and the wares the shops sold—brooms, baskets, barrels, and more—were displayed on the sidewalk. This was no place to buy clothes or hats, but they passed a smithy, a tobacconist, and a grocery store. Beside the grocery was a bookshop, with its front window stuffed to overflowing with old books.

Flora frowned. "They could certainly make those lovely books look better than that."

Hannah gave her daughter a gentle nudge. "You and your attractive presentation. Come on."

Flora pressed her nose to the windowpane. "*The Language of Flowers*—what's that?" She pointed to the topmost book of a high pile.

"If you think we're going to spend time in this shop now, my dear, then you're mistaken," said Hannah emphatically. "Maybe we'll find a little time in the next few days."

Flora's annoyance at her mother did not last for long. So many different shops—were they the reason the coachman had called the street "*Tausend-Seelen-Gass*," "Thousand Souls Alley"? Or was it because so many people lived and worked there? *One could feel very much at home in this street,* Flora thought. It brought together city style with the kind of cozy familiarity she knew from Gönningen.

The end of the street—and with it, their guesthouse—was not much farther, Hannah informed her, and she grasped Flora's arm firmly as they approached another flower shop. This one was much smaller than Maison Kuttner had been. There were also no pretty potted fir trees outside, just an old man doing his best with a worn-out broom to sweep the snow off the front steps.

Flora gave the man a quick smile and glanced in the window as they went past. Apart from a vase of carnations and a few yellowing handbills, there was nothing to look at.

Hannah tugged at her sleeve. "The Gilded Rose guesthouse is just up ahead. Finally, I—"

Suddenly, they heard a dull thud followed by a cry of pain.

"Good heavens!" Hannah dropped their traveling case.

The old man was lying half on the sidewalk, half on the steps, the broom strangely wedged between his legs. Blood trickled from his nose and from the right side of his mouth. His tongue was protruding and looked as if it were starting to swell. Had he bitten it when he fell? He groaned.

"Can you hear me? Can we carry you inside?" Hannah shook the injured man's arm, looking over her shoulder for help, but the street was empty.

Flora could only stand and gape at the blood that was dripping onto the snow.

"Hello? Can you hear me?" Hannah repeated.

With an effort, the man lifted his head one more time and groaned. Then he did not move anymore.

Finally, Flora spoke. "He's dying! Mother, for heaven's sake, do something!"

Chapter Three

"And if you were thinking of something more modern, then may I suggest our beautiful zinnias?" Hannah opened a small linen sack and carefully shook a small pile of the seeds onto the table.

A fire roared in the wood-burning stove in the workshop at Flumm's Nursery. After the cold outside, the warmth was at first a welcome change, but both women soon began to sweat inside their woolen clothes. The earthy smell of the seeds—samples for the customers, with the delivery to take place later—mixed with the odors of sweating bodies and the dog that dozed in its basket by the door, its paws occasionally twitching.

For a moment, Flora felt herself transported back to the packing room at home, which had a similar smell. Not that she had any desire to be back there . . . weighing seeds all day, packing them into little sacks, stamping or writing on the packets, and then tying all of it into parcels that had to be carted off to the train station—it was always the same work, over and over.

Flora yawned. If only it weren't so stuffy. She could not stop her thoughts from wandering out through the misted window and away. She wondered how the old man was after his fall. He had been so weak, and at the same time so agitated! He had been weepy for a moment, too, for "causing so much trouble." Hannah and Flora had been relieved when he came to his senses. Someone had sent word to his son—had he taken his father to the hospital, or at least called a doctor? Flora and her mother had left the two men alone before that had been decided.

"Best quality, vigorous, and hardy." As Hannah spoke, she opened her price list and pointed to the zinnia line. "And the price speaks for itself."

Droplets of sweat trickled between Flora's breasts as she stood silently and watched her mother sell one type of flower after another to the grower. With every line that Hannah filled on the order sheet, her face relaxed more. But when it came to the zinnias, the man was undecided.

"Look at these colors! From pale pink to the deepest purple." Hannah closed her eyes for a moment with an enraptured expression. Then she snapped up a second book, leafed rapidly through its pages, and tapped on an illustration of zinnias in every conceivable color, painted in such detail that one could well imagine holding the velvety blooms in one's hand and breathing in their heady fragrance. "Aren't they wonderful?"

"All right, then," said Siegfried Flumm. "In the last few years, there hasn't been much demand for them. Everyone wants elegance these days, but who knows?" He shrugged. "Maybe rustic will be the order of the day again."

Hannah nodded eagerly. "I would absolutely recommend some of the more elegant varieties, too—our lovely larkspur, for instance. Would you like to look through our sample book for yourself?"

With an appreciative nod, the grower leafed through the book. He selected love-in-a-mist, garden cosmos, and China aster. Hannah quickly noted the details of the order.

The book had been the idea of Flora's aunt, Seraphine. Seeds by themselves, of course, were not particularly attractive, and colorful pictures would certainly help sales, Seraphine had argued. With her artistic talents, she had produced the first sample book many years earlier. Since then, she had completed a similar book for every member of the Kerner family who went out on the road to sell seeds. And Flora, too, could expect to get a copy for herself one day—Seraphine was already hard at work on the pictures.

Flora sighed softly. Everyone in the family seemed to have found their place in the seed trade, and they were happy with it. Everyone except her. No one could explain why that was so, least of all Flora herself.

"I want to be a florist. That's all, nothing else!" she had complained for so long that her parents had finally relented and allowed her to go to the nursery in Reutlingen the year before. They didn't consent out of any conviction that Flora had made the right choice, but because they had finally run out of arguments *against* her wish or her love of flowers.

Even as a small child, Flora had found nothing more interesting than spending hours wandering through the fields around town, picking flowers. Without any of the adults explaining it to her, she always knew exactly where and in which season she could find the different flowering plants. On the edge of the woods, she gathered willow herbs. Close to the cornfield she plucked daisies, poppies, and cornflowers, and along the creek she picked cowslips and cuckooflowers. She loved the delicate pale-purple cuckooflowers most of all.

Her time at the nursery in Reutlingen had been a letdown. They rarely did any flower arranging; instead, Flora spent most of the time planting seeds and looking after seedlings.

Of course, later half the village knew that Flora's apprenticeship had been a dismal failure.

"Always thought she was too good for the seeds, she did."

"All she has in her head is her own pleasure. She doesn't care one bit about how her parents are supposed to manage."

What the people had whispered when Flora slunk back to Gönningen like a whipped dog had hurt. Her brothers had laughed out loud; her parents had been half annoyed, half at a loss. And Seraphine had said something like "I once had dreams myself . . . The best you can do is to bury them as quickly as possible." Blast it, Flora was trying to do that, but—

"He fell? Good God! Old Sonnenschein has been suffering for quite a while. He's always down with a cold or dizzy spell or some other ailment. Not that he'd give you a word of complaint. He's always trying to convince the rest of the world he's on top of everything. His son, Friedrich, helps him out wherever he can, but he doesn't have much time to spare. He works at the Trinkhalle, but don't ask me exactly what he does there. There's hardly a true Baden-Badener who ever sets foot in the place; that's only for our esteemed guests." Flumm's tone was heavy with irony.

"Are you talking about the man from the flower shop?" Flora's question came so abruptly that Hannah and Mr. Flumm jumped. It was almost as if they had forgotten she was there.

Hannah glanced disapprovingly at her daughter. "I'm glad to see you haven't fallen asleep yet," she hissed.

"Kuno Sonnenschein used to be one of my best customers," said the nurseryman with a sigh. "But it seems money is in short supply in the Sonnenschein house these days. He only buys the cheapest varieties now."

"I suppose he is also a widower?" asked Hannah sympathetically.

"Oh, no. The good Mrs. Sonnenschein is as alive as you or I, but, well, how should I put it? She's of no use to her husband. She even has help in the house, like some sort of hoity-toity lady. Just let my Else try that with me!" Flumm let out a laugh.

Hannah cleared her throat, then said in her sweetest voice, "Believe it or not, I have a maid. My husband seems to think I'm much more useful helping with the business."

The nurseryman puffed his cheeks, nonplussed. "Well, if you look at it like that . . ."

"Aren't there any daughters in the family?" Flora asked. "I mean, if my parents ran a flower shop, it would be the most natural thing in the world for me to work there."

"There is one daughter, actually, but she's gone off to a nunnery," Mr. Flumm said.

Hannah took a deep breath. "Well, not everyone is as fortunate as you in having a thriving business where everyone lends a hand. Maybe we should complete this order form now," she said, lifting her pencil.

Chapter Four

When they returned to The Gilded Rose that evening, Hannah and Flora were tired and chilled to the bone, but they also had three sizable orders to celebrate. Besides Flumm's, they had visited two other nurseries on the edge of town, and all had placed generous orders. The following day was earmarked for their customers *in* town—hotel gardeners and the owners of private gardens, as well as the gardeners who worked for the town itself, the ones in charge of the extensive gardens around Baden-Baden's Kurhaus—with its casino, guest rooms, ballrooms, and more—and other local sites. Hannah was looking forward to doing good business with them.

Dinner would be on the table in fifteen minutes, their hostess promised when Hannah and Flora walked through the door. And she had already put hot water bottles in both their beds, she added with a kind smile.

A bed that was already warm! Flora hummed with pleasant anticipation as they ascended the narrow staircase. If the room was not too chilly, she could strip down to her underdress, curl up under the sheets—

"Don't think you're going to sneak off to bed too soon, child," Hannah said, as if she could read minds. "First, we celebrate the sales we've made today. That's as much part of this business as anything else. Just wait, I'll make you enjoy the seed trade yet!"

A decent meal, perhaps washed down with a pitcher of beer or glass of wine, then that warm bed—that was how Flora imagined the evening would be. She had not counted on her mother leading the entire tavern in a song.

> *A tailor went a-wandering*
>
> *One Monday in the morning*
>
> *And, lo, he met the devil*
>
> *With neither shoe nor stocking.*
>
> *Ho there, Mr. Tailor Man*
>
> *You'll come with me to hell*
>
> *And dress us wicked devils*
>
> *Which is just as well.*

"Sing with me, child!" Hannah encouraged her daughter as she had earlier, but Flora shook her head. Holding the handbag with the money they had earned that day firmly in her lap, she sat and listened as Hannah launched into the second verse of the travelers' song. The men who had joined them at their table sang along.

Hannah and Flora had not quite finished their meal—a hearty goulash made with vegetables and big chunks of meat—when the first of the other guests in the restaurant had asked if he might join them. It hadn't been long before more came along.

The newcomers quickly fell to trading stories, and Flora was amazed at how wholeheartedly Hannah joined in. After a day spent talking about seeds and sales, it would not have surprised Flora if her mother had been a little uncommunicative. Even for Flora, the men's tales bordered on being too much.

All but one of the men—who introduced himself as a trader in corsets and undergarments, which sent the others at the table into fits of laughter—bought a round of beer, schnapps, or wine. And when Hannah launched into the first song of the night, Flora was the only one who didn't sing along. She was surprised that every single one of the men knew the words.

At home, Hannah was always the first to get up to dance at the village festivals. It was a side of her personality that did not meet with everyone's approval. Dancing was decadent, or at least more than one old Gönninger thought it was—a point of view that neither Flora nor any of her friends shared. But sometimes even Flora found her mother's exuberance a little mortifying.

And now Hannah was singing and dancing around the restaurant to the rhythm of the song.

> *Once he'd done a-beating them*
>
> *He took his scissors honed*
>
> *And docked the devils' tails so short*
>
> *It made them yowl and moan.*
>
> *Ho there, Mr. Tailor Man*
>
> *Get out of our hell.*
>
> *We don't need our tails snipped off*
>
> *Which is just as well.*

Flora had to laugh. Then she noticed someone to her left, and she looked up. With a quick nod in her direction, a man slipped onto the end of the corner bench. Flora nodded back, returning his curt greeting. Hannah was already well into the next verse when Flora realized that the man who had just joined them was none other than Friedrich Sonnenschein, the son of the old flower seller who had collapsed. He gazed gloomily into his beer and was far away in his thoughts.

He seemed not to have recognized Flora, or he would certainly have said a few words to her—wouldn't he?—if only for the sake of politeness. From downturned eyes, she peeked across, studying him as surreptitiously as she could.

Friedrich Sonnenschein was not endowed with any exceptional physical characteristics, except perhaps for his eyes, which were a very pale blue and looked as translucent as a shallow pool. His nose was neither crooked, nor flat, nor too big; his hair was neither particularly neat nor particularly unkempt, and neither was he especially tall or short, but of average height. If anything, he was a little on the heavier side. Flora looked at her own arms and hands, which still bore the signs of the drudgery she'd endured at the Grubers' nursery. But wasn't it said that the calluses on a hardworking Swabian girl's hands were her prettiest jewels? Flora smiled to herself.

Despite his unremarkable appearance, however, there was something about Friedrich that made Flora think he was a nice man—friendlier, perhaps, and not as rough-edged as some of the other men there in the restaurant. And—

"Thank you again for helping my father."

So he *had* recognized her. "How is he?" Flora asked politely.

"He's up, but he's limping. And when he thinks no one is looking, he rubs at his hip." Friedrich Sonnenschein grimaced. "My father flatly refuses to admit that he's been getting weaker and weaker over the last year. It's as if he's aged a decade, but so quickly, almost from one day to the next, it seems. He tires quickly, and then he has these strange dizzy spells. But what can I do? I had to go out early in the morning, not for long, and I was going to clear the snow after that, but could my dear father wait that long? Never!"

Just then, Hannah returned to the table, laughing and out of breath.

"My goodness, my feet are killing me! Ah, the florist's son," she said, and immediately asked, "Flora, do you need another drink, too?" She raised her beer mug and gestured toward the bar.

Flora shook her head.

"Well, you two have a good time," said Hannah, and she grinned and danced away.

It made Flora smile to see her mother so relaxed and happy, so in her element.

Friedrich cleared his throat as if to draw her attention back to him. "You're not from here, are you?"

Flora shook her head. "We'd only just arrived and were on our way from the train station when we walked past your father's shop." Then she briefly explained the reason for their journey.

"Ah, so you're a seed dealer. There used to be an older gentleman who came to visit us—if I remember correctly, he also came from Gönningen. Back then, my father grew all his flowers himself, but he was also in much better health." Friedrich sighed.

"You work in a Trinkhalle, don't you? I'm sure that's very interesting," said Flora, to distract him from his concern for his father. Her mother had pointed out the building, which was close to the Conversationshaus. She could not begin to imagine what was inside its walls.

Friedrich looked up and replied with unexpected vehemence. "My employment means everything to me. In the last three years, I've worked my way up from a janitor's position to where I am now—the custodian of the entire Trinkhalle. The grounds are also part of my charge. Every bench, every gravel path, the barriers, the gardens—I have the privilege of taking care of all of it. Now that the war is over, there are some important decisions to be made, and they affect the future of the Trinkhalle and everything it stands for. What will become of Baden-Baden now that the French are no longer coming? Who will visit our spas? I hope very much that whomever we welcome here after the French will better appreciate the fine waters we have, and that they don't just come here for the casinos, but to try a curative bath and to take the waters. Oh, Baden-Baden has some exciting times ahead."

Curative baths? Take the waters? Flora did not understand a word of it, but she could feel the heat from the fire burning inside Friedrich. "And you want to be part of that," she said, hoping it was the right thing to say.

He nodded fiercely and took such a large swig of beer that some of it ran down his chin. He wiped his sleeve across his mouth and looked around as if to reassure himself that no one was eavesdropping. Then he said quietly, "Until now, whoever has leased the casino has also paid for the upkeep of the Trinkhalle. Now there are rumblings about developing a completely new management for the Kurhaus complex—the Conversationshaus with the casino, and perhaps the Trinkhalle. That could be a huge boost to its significance, but it could just as easily spell its doom. Am I supposed to water flowers in my father's shop instead of taking part in that process? That . . ." He fell silent and shook his head as if he could not even bear to think about it.

"And your sister can't help?" Flora asked, her heart pounding. Friedrich had no idea how much she envied him. *Let* me *help you at the shop!* she wanted to scream. But the words did not come out.

"My sister would rather follow God's call than look after our parents." Friedrich's voice was bitter. "When people talk about her, they talk about her 'calling,' and everyone is *so* understanding about how she *has* to follow it. With me, on the other hand—because I believe I can make a contribution to Baden-Baden's development—all they talk about is an 'obsession.' If you ask the people here, I'd be better off taking over my parents' business. The problem is that nobody can tell me how to get this 'obsession' out of my head. This is not a weed that you can just tear out by its roots!"

Unconsciously, Flora grasped Friedrich's hand. "You have no idea how well I understand what you're saying. They expect the same of me!" she said so loudly that several of the others at the table turned and looked at them. She felt herself blush and abruptly released Friedrich's hand. Then, in a whisper, she continued, "I'm being forced to work in my parents' business, too. And all I've dreamed of, all my life, is tying bouquets and arranging flowers. Even—"

"No . . . are you serious?" Friedrich interrupted her in disbelief.

"It's true!" Flora laughed out loud. "Even when I was a little girl, there was nothing I liked more than putting together bouquets. The seed business just doesn't interest me like the flowers themselves. I would love so much to change places with you! Life can be so unfair sometimes."

Hannah, who had been talking to their hostess at the bar, came back to the table.

"Isn't it a lovely evening? Didn't I tell you that a merchant's life was fun?" she said triumphantly.

Flora and Friedrich looked at one another. Then they burst out laughing.

Chapter Five

The rest of their trip proved to be as busy and successful as the first day had been. Wherever Hannah and Flora went, they were welcomed warmly. And the customers were buying. Because of the war, many of the gardens had lain fallow the year before, or the growers had made do with whatever leftover seeds they had. But now they were in a mood for billowing seas of flowers, for color and fragrance, for something to help drive out the memories of anxiety and terror.

None of their customers had deserted them, a piece of good news that Hannah could hardly wait to report to Helmut.

After ten days, they had ticked off every customer on their list. Mother and daughter were looking forward to getting home again, to sleeping in their own beds, to eating food cooked on their own stove. Helmut would not be there—he and his brother Valentin were expected back from Bohemia only around Easter—but at least the twins would already be home. Their *Samenstrich*—the territory where they sold their seeds—around Herrenberg was far less productive than Baden-Baden and did not require them to stay away as long.

Flora could not say that she had really enjoyed her first seed trading travels, but most of her hostility, at least, had evaporated. She found their talks with the various customers interesting, and she had not previously realized that the demand for different types of flowers was driven at least partly by fashion. This year, their customers were less interested in low-growing types, while long-stemmed flowers were highly sought after. Intense colors were also on the rise, pastels not.

As an experienced seed trader, Hannah was naturally able to accommodate all her clients' wishes. But would the customers buy just as much from her, Flora, next year? She resolved to spend the summer learning more about the traits of unusual varieties, so that she would be better prepared for dealing with the customers.

She saw Friedrich Sonnenschein only once more, on the morning after they had talked in the restaurant. She and her mother had just stepped out of The Gilded Rose when he came along the narrow street.

"That wasn't just talk, last night?" he asked without preamble after he had greeted them. "I mean, what you said about your greatest dream?"

"No, it really wasn't," Flora said, and laughed.

"Life is mean and skewed sometimes," he murmured to himself, and went on his way without another word.

"And what was that all about, may I ask?" Hannah said.

"Oh, nothing." Flora let out a little sigh as she watched Friedrich walk away.

How right he was . . .

The train started with a jerk, and as it rolled away, Hannah leaned back deeply into her seat. "Done!" With a smile, she held out her right hand to Flora, sitting opposite. "Congratulations. Your first sales trip. And you did really well."

Flora smiled back. "Do you really think so?"

Hannah nodded. "I do. And that's why . . ." She rummaged inside her traveling bag and produced a small package wrapped up in brown paper. "For you! A keepsake to remember your first time."

Frowning, Flora untied the string around the package.

"*The Language of Flowers*—oh, Mother!" Flora's delighted squeal made their fellow travelers jump. "I hadn't even thought of it again. When did you—"

"Our hostess went to the shop for me," Hannah interrupted her. "I thought you might enjoy it."

❦

Flora had thought that she might have a day or two's rest after the trip to Baden-Baden, but she was mistaken. The morning after their return to Gönningen, her mother called her into the packing room, where Gustav and Siegfried, the twins, were already at work. Flora was handed a pile of order sheets, and then she set to work weighing seeds, filling packets, and labeling them. For their bestselling seeds, they used special stamps with the necessary details, which Flora liked more than laboriously writing all the information by hand. Once an order was complete, she wrote the name and address of the recipient on the package. Now, for every name, Flora remembered a face, which made the work more interesting and, in turn, more bearable. Soon, the parcels were stacked high in the packing room and the hallway in front of it. Twice a week, they were picked up by a wagon and delivered to the train station, so that everything would arrive well before the planting season began.

"In the past, we took everything around ourselves by horse and cart," Hannah had told her children countless times. "It was a real headache in the snow and ice, not to mention dangerous." And Flora and her brothers rolled their eyes behind Hannah's back. Always the same story!

Flora thought often about Friedrich Sonnenschein and his father. She wondered how the old man was and whether his health had deteriorated even further, to the point where he could no longer run his shop.

As the weeks passed, her memories of the incident in Baden-Baden melted away like the snow with the arrival of spring. By mid-March, more and more green appeared in the meadows every day, and by the end of the month, winter seemed long ago.

Flora walked to the hills or the fields to watch nature's springtime advance as often as she could. The first flowers started to appear at the beginning of April—cowslips, daisies, and pennywort. One still had to look closely to discover the tiny flowers hiding among the faster-growing grass, but Flora was happy with every little bouquet she tied. She could not get enough of the delicate colors of the flowers, which looked as if brushed on with watercolors.

For the first time in her life, Flora did not simply give the bouquets she made to the first person to happen along, and that was because of the little book—almost forty years old, she discovered—her mother had given her. *The Language of Flowers*—what a lovely title, Flora thought every time she held it in her hand. And what an amazingly exciting subject to write a book about.

Flora found, for example, that giving someone cowslips could mean "How gladly would I win the key to your heart." It made her laugh now to think that just the year before she had given a bouquet of cowslips to the local butcher, a drinker of some renown!

As for the pennywort, she read that joy in springtime did not necessarily mean that a happy autumn would follow. It was therefore probably not a good idea to give a pennywort bouquet to the Widow Schlagenhöfer, who was in mourning from dawn to dusk for her beloved and prematurely deceased Eugen.

To Flora's surprise, Seraphine showed great interest in the book. Her aunt praised its beautiful flower illustrations, and she was interested in what it meant to present someone with certain flowers.

"Listen, Flora. Milkwort means 'I have to forget you, though it makes my heart bleed.'" With gleaming eyes, she had gazed at her niece. "Please never give me a bouquet like that."

Flora, who had no idea where to even look for milkwort and who was rather confused at Seraphine's request, simply nodded.

"Your aunt really is a bit strange," said Suse, when Flora told her about it.

It was a sunny spring day, and the two young women had both fled their mothers, who were constantly finding more chores for them. Now they sat together on a bank beside the Wiesaz River, the book open on Flora's lap.

"Just make sure you don't do anything dumb," Suse added, and elbowed Flora in the ribs. "Like giving that book to your aunt out of kindness. You'll never get it back. Come on, let's take a look and see what flowers I could give my dear Rolf."

"Young ladies *never* give flowers to young men," Flora replied, and sighed. Suse was doing it again: Rolf this, Rolf that! She used every opportunity she got to talk about "my Rolf," the son of a seed trader in the village, with whom she secretly met.

"Just yesterday, he told me again how very much he loves me. But can I believe him?" Suse looked doubtfully at Flora.

Flora grinned. "Let's ask the flower oracle!"

"Would you do it . . . please? The oracle is always kind to you."

With a sigh, Flora plucked a daisy growing beside her left foot, then began to pull out the petals, one by one. "He loves you, he loves you not, he . . ." At the end, she covertly removed two petals at once so that the outcome was good.

"He loves me," Suse sighed contentedly. "I knew it!" She turned a few pages in Flora's book, then looked up. "Here's something you could give me: watercress."

"And what would I be saying if I did?" Flora asked, giggling.

"'Follow the call of your heart.'"

"Oh, that would really be something for you! No, the most you'll get from me are—" Flora jumped to her feet, ran up the bank, tugged at something there, then ran back down to Suse and kneeled beside her, holding a stalk with green leaves in her hand. "Stinging nettles!" she said melodramatically.

"Nettles? What are they supposed to mean?"

"'Take care! Don't burn your fingers in your exuberance.' Catch!" Flora said, and she tossed the stalk spiritedly to her friend.

Suse shrieked and ducked, and Flora burst out laughing.

When both girls had calmed down again, Suse went back to the book. "Look, it says here that the language of flowers has been known in both the Orient and the Occident since days of old," she said. "And that the meaning attributed to a particular flower or plant originates either from its name or from its properties. Sometimes old legends or how the plants are used also play a role." Suse looked at her friend. "Well, then, let me ask you this, O gorgeous goddess of the flowers: What do you think burdock means?"

"Oh, that's easy. It means you stick to someone like a burr. Or like your Rolf!" Flora replied, and they burst out laughing again.

On the seventh of April, Good Friday, Helmut and Valentin finally returned from their long travels. Hannah cried tears of joy to see them safely home, and she and Helmut held on to each other as if they never wanted to let go. Gustav and Siegfried looked away in embarrassment, but Flora felt a trace of yearning. How must it feel to love someone so much?

The more spring advanced, the bigger and more varied Flora's bouquets became. She cut blooming forsythia twigs and added pussy willow and alder. And when the first daffodils and tulips finally sprouted in dense clusters in the garden behind the house, she sighed with relief. The previous autumn, she had planted more bulbs than ever before, and her father had grumbled at the expense—she counted herself lucky now to see that the bulbs had not been eaten by mice.

For now, she had pushed aside the thought that she would not be a florist after all. She still had her flowers in the meadows and the garden. And no one could forbid her from doing what she wanted with them in her free time.

When the letter came in mid-April, Flora was as stunned as every-one else.

Chapter Six

"'Dear Miss Kerner,'" Flora read aloud. "'Do you remember me? Friedrich Sonnenschein from Baden-Baden? I had the honor of meeting you and your esteemed mother in January, and the proprietress at The Gilded Rose was good enough to give me your address. She sends her greetings.'"

Helmut frowned. "Is she allowed to do that? Just hand out our address to anyone who asks?"

"Helmut," Hannah chided. "Keep reading, child."

"'I am yet grateful for the assistance you rendered my father on the occasion of his unfortunate fall on the steps of his shop.'"

"His writing's as stiff as an old shoe," said Gustav.

"Who did you push down the steps then?" Siegfried joked.

Flora glared at her younger brothers across the dinner table. Then she looked to her parents, who were watching her with pointed indifference as she read. Flora also noticed how Hannah reached for Helmut's hand and squeezed it, as if like that she could arm herself against any adversity.

Flora took a breath and forced herself to read on at a steady pace. She knew that the letter could change her life. No, that was not correct—it had already changed her life. It was her family who did not know that yet.

"'Unfortunately, my father's health has not improved. Several times a day, his vitality and strength desert him, and he has to rest, which of course is less than ideal for the business. I help where I can, but now that the spa season has begun, I am needed elsewhere.'"

Flora looked around. "Friedrich works at the Trinkhalle," she explained, but when no one said anything, she read on:

"'You are aware of the dilemma in which I find myself, and I do not want to bore you with that any further. But I would like to assure you of one thing: in all these months, I have not forgotten our conversation. Again and again, I am forced to realize how an accident—or should I call it fate?—brought us together.'"

Flora's brothers pushed each other around and were having trouble stopping themselves from laughing, but she decided not to berate them. And how angry her father looked! Did he perhaps think that Friedrich Sonnenschein had somehow been inappropriate? This was about something far more important. Her heart beat faster as she read on.

"'Allow me to come to the reason for this letter, which I have finally written after much hesitation. You mentioned that your dearest wish was to learn the florist's profession. Perhaps—'"

"A florist? Your dearest wish? What *else* did you discuss with him?" Hannah crossed her arms tightly over her chest, and her face wore an expression of dismay. "I'm completely at a loss."

"It's all very strange to me," said Helmut. "And where were *you* during this conversation? You didn't leave Flora alone with him, I hope?"

"Of course not! But I do not eavesdrop on every word of my daughter's conversations."

Flora continued reading to herself while her parents went back and forth. "Mother, Father! Friedrich Sonnenschein is asking if I would be interested in spending the summer in Baden-Baden, helping his father in the shop," Flora said before her parents could get themselves caught up in an argument. "In return, his father would teach me all he knows about floristry. But Friedrich also writes that I would have to go as soon as possible, or he'll be forced to find someone else."

Flora's announcement made all the others freeze.

"This is my opportunity to learn more about floristry! Food and lodging will cost nothing as I would be sharing a room with the maid, and you would not have to pay for my apprenticeship, either. Friedrich says that he hopes that his father will improve over the summer, so he does not want to take anyone on permanently. If I were to help out for the next few months, I would be doing his family a great favor, he says."

Flora looked from one to the other. "My *dearest* wish would come true . . . Now say something!"

Helmut stroked his beard thoughtfully several times. "If it is really just for this summer—"

"Tell me who's supposed to help me with the work in the fields? Don't think I'm going to slave away out there *again* all by myself while Flora is at the service of complete strangers." Hannah's voice was thick with irony, and carried some despair, too. She sounded like someone whose hopes were being dashed in front of her and who could do nothing to stop it from happening. "A young woman, alone, in a strange town! Really, Helmut, it's too dangerous."

"I'd be in good hands there, with the family." Wringing her hands, Flora looked back and forth between her parents. "Please . . ."

In the end, neither Helmut nor Hannah could deny Flora her wish. What good reason did they have? The twins offered to take over Flora's share of the work in the fields, and the family decided to leave the flower beds behind the house fallow—her absence would not leave too huge a hole.

"I can already hear what the people will say when they find out we've sent Flora away a second time to learn to be a florist," Hannah complained, but everyone in the family knew that she really did not care at all about the opinions of people in the village.

When, a week later, Flora packed her bag, Helmut and Hannah each had a heavy heart. Instead of letting it show, they wished her the best and gave her some pocket money, and a parcel of seeds as a gift for her hosts. Helmut, of course, would not let anyone tell him he could not carry his daughter's luggage to the station.

Besides Helmut and Hannah, Suse also came to say goodbye. She, too, did her best to hide her sadness at Flora's departure.

"What is wrong with us?" Hannah cried. "As seed traders, we should be used to saying goodbye. We do it every year, after all. You'd think we'd have some experience in it by now."

Helmut sighed. "There are some things you never get used to. They just get harder with the passing years."

Hands on hips, Suse looked Flora up and down with a critical eye. "I think you don't care about the flowers at all, really. You're only going to Baden-Baden because the Sonnenschein family has an interesting son."

"Who knows? Maybe I'll marry him and the whole flower shop will belong to me," Flora said, and she and Suse broke into a fit of giggling.

"Suse! Flora! Jokes like that are not appreciated," said Hannah, shaking her head, but in the face of the cheerfulness of the two young women, she and Helmut felt at least a little relieved.

With her head against Helmut's chest, Hannah watched the train roll away. Only when the last car was no more than a dark spot in the distance did she let her tears flow.

"It's just for a summer," Helmut murmured into her wind-tossed hair.

"We don't know that. Not yet," Hannah sobbed.

Chapter Seven

Although it was only midmorning, Ernestine Sonnenschein already felt as exhausted as if she had worked an entire day. With trembling knees, she settled onto one of the armchairs that faced the front window. Outside, the sun smiled down from a blue sky, reminding her that it was time she got to work in the garden. A good housewife, of course, started the garden work much earlier in the year. Could she really burden Kuno with turning over the garden beds on top of everything else? Or ask him to trim the hedge? So often lately, her husband had been too tired to do even the simplest things, a condition she could well understand herself. And his dizzy spells were a worry!

She could not take care of the garden. At least, not right at that moment. Ernestine's eyelids fluttered nervously when she saw the paper beside the inkpot. She had not yet put together the meal plan for the coming week.

She forced herself to close her eyes for a long moment, but instead of the calm and order she longed for, thoughts went scurrying through her mind like rowdy chickens. Three courses at lunch, at least two in the evening—any less would have been too meager for a decent shop-keeper's household, although Kuno and Friedrich often told her that she did not need to go to all the trouble. Kuno even said he would be satisfied with bread and cheese in the evenings.

Bread and cheese?

Ernestine could not recall her friend Gretel—the wife of Mr. Grün, the pharmacist—ever telling her about bread and cheese as an evening meal. She could not recall Gretel talking about her meal plans at all, which Ernestine took as a sign of good breeding.

Nor did *Die Gartenlaube*, the magazine delivered to the house each week, ever mention bread and cheese for supper. Its articles were always about housewives for whom putting the most diverse meals on the table every day was a priority.

What was she supposed to put on the table for lunch? Soup? A plate of vegetables with some ham? No, ham was too elegant for a Monday. Bacon was suitable for Mondays, and not too expensive.

Suddenly, it was there again, the thought that Ernestine hated so much, namely that it was *her* fault that money was in such short supply in the Sonnenschein household. Would not a more skillful housewife have found a better way to budget long ago?

Ernestine found the thought of money embarrassing. And a wife could not simply go to her husband and ask for more money. Nor could she count on Kuno or Friedrich to help when it came to dealing with the household. Both relied on Ernestine to keep everything sorted out, and they never bothered themselves with how she did it.

That apprentice girl that Friedrich had taken on was an excellent example. Was she, Ernestine, asked even once if she was prepared to take on this new burden? Or if there was enough housekeeping money to feed an extra mouth?

And of all the times he could have chosen, Friedrich brought the girl in when Kuno was doing so poorly. "Flora will help Father in the shop," he'd asserted. Oh, no doubt her son meant well, but what did

Friedrich know about real life? And—while she was on the subject—what did Kuno know about it?

Soup. They would have soup for lunch that day. Or a stew? Or plain broth?

Flora Kerner . . . Ernestine still did not know exactly how Friedrich had met the young woman. She was supposed to arrive on the midday train and would probably knock on their door sometime in the afternoon. That was good, because it meant Ernestine did not have to think about welcoming her with a meal.

"Flora Kerner wants to learn floristry. In return, she will take on some of Father's workload. You will thank me soon enough for this," Friedrich had said tersely.

Thank him? The things her son got into his head!

With a sigh, Ernestine looked out the window. The apprentice girl was not yet in sight, thank heavens, but she certainly had a wonderful view of all the horrible roadworks going on outside. Half the street had been torn up and turned into a huge ditch, and the coaches, street workers, and pedestrians had to share the other half. Workers shoveled piles of dirt from here to there and back again, or just stood around getting in the way. Everyone was cursing at everyone else. It was a madhouse.

Just then, Ernestine saw Sabine appear from around the corner with a shopping basket filled to bursting hanging from the crook of her arm. Her cheeks were red and her lips pursed as if she were whistling a tune like some street urchin. How could any human being be so untroubled?

Were those leeks in Sabine's basket? Ernestine could not remember writing leeks on the shopping list, so why had the maid bought them?

Though, a good leek soup with cream would not be the worst thing to put on the table for lunch. Or as a welcoming meal for the Kerner girl that evening. With a silver candelabra on the table . . . Then the girl would see that she had come to a good household. Suddenly, Ernestine's heart felt lighter. Time to put together the rest of the meal plan. With renewed energy, she dunked her pen in the inkpot.

Reluctantly, Ernestine interrupted her painstaking management of the household to have lunch with her husband, but her son did not come home, and without Friedrich the midday meal was a quiet and quick affair.

The moment the table was cleared, there was a knock at the door, and Ernestine looked up with a frown. Sabine was standing in the doorway and beside her was . . .

"The girl from Württemberg! My goodness, you're already here!"

Chapter Eight

Flora's arrival in Baden-Baden was so much different this time than the last.

The Hotel Bayerischer Hof, which had seemed so huge and grim to her in winter, now, in late April, had many tables and chairs set out on its expansive terrace and looked very inviting indeed. And people's facial expressions were no longer frozen by the winter cold, but, warmed by the sunshine, were relaxed and happy.

Instead of paying for a coach from the train station, Flora marched in high spirits into town, along clean, freshly raked gravel roads lined with blooming chestnut trees. Flaky white-and-pink petals rained down from overhead and landed on Flora's hair and shoulders. The air smelled of lilac and the first roses, and the sun sparkled through the trees along Lichtenthaler Allee—it was like walking beneath a miraculously lit green canopy.

Magnificent coaches rolled by as Flora walked along. Their gold fittings and beautiful paintwork were matched by the colors of the horses' harnesses.

The Conversationshaus was a hive of activity compared with how it had been in winter, and there, too, white-painted tables and chairs stood before its entrance. Many of the guests seemed to know each other, waving and calling out greetings to each other in languages that Flora did not understand. It was all so exciting!

Flora tried the door of the flower shop, but it did not open. "We'll Be Right Back," said a sign dangling at an angle from the door handle. No one came when she knocked, either. The shop was closed? In the middle of the day?

Flora tried to peer in through the window, which was covered by a gray film, probably dust and grime from the nearby construction. There was no sign of the shopkeeper. Was the old man so unwell that he could not be there to meet her?

With an uneasy feeling in her stomach, Flora picked up her luggage again. Then she walked around the side of the building, looking for the entrance to the Sonnenscheins' house.

Mrs. Sonnenschein sighed deeply. "My goodness, I really have no idea where my husband has gotten off to. There's always so much to do in one's own business. There are never enough hours in the day, are there?" Red flecks appeared on her cheeks, and she poked nervously at a few strands of hair that had worked their way loose, trying to push them back into her pinned-up hair.

"The master has retired to his bedroom. He was not feeling well," the maid said.

"Well, then . . ." Smiling helplessly, Mrs. Sonnenschein handed two hairpins—they had worked their way completely out of her hair— to the maid, then turned away from Flora so that the maid could pin it back up.

"From now on, you have me. I will certainly be able to take over some of the tasks your husband normally does." Flora tried to curtsy, but the lady of the house could not see the attempt because she still had her back turned.

"Finished," said the maid, patting Mrs. Sonnenschein once on the shoulder as if in confirmation. But the maid had pinned the hair back so carelessly, and not even in the right place! Still, Mrs. Sonnenschein's hair was not very neat at all, so the misplaced strands barely showed. Flora reached up reflexively to her own hair, artfully braided and pinned.

"Let me show you your room first. No doubt you would like to rest a little after your journey," said Mrs. Sonnenschein as she slowly climbed the narrow staircase.

"Rest? My mother would have more than a few words for me if I put my feet up on my first day here." Flora laughed as she turned to follow Mrs. Sonnenschein. "No, no. I'll just drop my things, and then I would very much like to see the shop . . . if I may."

"Sabine," said Mrs. Sonnenschein.

"Oh, no, really. I can carry my things myself." But before Flora could stop her, the maid, with a morose look on her face, picked up Flora's traveling bag and led Flora up the stairs.

Breathing heavily, the lady of the house finally pushed open a door on the right side of the landing at the top. "Here we are. You and Sabine will be sharing a room."

Flora looked first at the room—which was not large but looked brightly lit and clean—and then at Sabine, who did not look particularly pleased to have a roommate.

"I am so happy to be here! It's such a beautiful city. Is there a lovelier city than Baden-Baden anywhere in the empire?" Flora said to Sabine as she unpacked her things into the section of the wardrobe that Mrs. Sonnenschein had allocated to her.

"When the sun shines, it's a pretty sight wherever you look," Sabine replied. "But when it rains, it's as if the town dies, because all the fine ladykins strolling along Lichtenthaler Allee or riding in their fine carriages vanish into their fine salons, which the likes of us heat for them. And another thing," she added with a scowl. "Don't think I'm going to make your bed for you just because you'll be sitting at madam's table."

"Fine with me," Flora said, and she took the sheets that Sabine was holding. "I don't need a nursemaid." She sighed aloud. "What am I supposed to do now? I can't just sit here in the room for hours."

Dinner would be at half past six, at which time Flora would be expected in the sitting room, Mrs. Sonnenschein had said before retiring for her afternoon nap. Not a word about when her husband might be back on his feet. Not a word about the florist's shop, either, let alone about her duties, her working hours, or anything of that sort.

"My first day at work in the nursery in Reutlingen was completely different," said Flora, and she told Sabine about how she had pricked out hundreds of kohlrabi seedlings, turned over the compost heap, and rolled humus by the barrow load into the greenhouses.

Sabine giggled. "Before you die of boredom here, you can certainly help me in the kitchen." She took the pillowcase back from Flora and stuffed the pillow into it.

Flora glanced at her gratefully. "Am I mistaken, or are you also from Württemberg? Your accent . . ."

Sabine confirmed Flora's guess—she was from Leonberg and was the oldest of six siblings, all of whom envied her the position in the Sonnenschein household, she said.

"I get paid a few kreuzer plus board and lodging, and Mrs. Sonnenschein puts it aside for me. If I ever need a trousseau, I can use that money for it, she says." Then she screwed up her face. "If I ever need a trousseau . . . fingers crossed."

Flora sat down on her bed. "How long have you been here?" She patted the space beside her.

"A year," said Sabine, sitting next to Flora. "Ever since they shipped Miss Sonnenschein off to the nunnery. I heard Mrs. Sonnenschein say, "She's not pretty and not particularly bright—what else were we supposed to do with her?" while Sybille—that's the daughter—was standing right there. She looked terribly miserable."

A crease crossed Flora's brow. "I thought Miss Sonnenschein chose to go to the convent herself?"

Sabine shrugged.

"What about the son?" Flora asked curiously.

"Friedrich. We hardly see him. He leaves the house before breakfast. He works at the Trinkhalle, and usually doesn't get home till long after dinner's finished." There was a trace of regret in Sabine's voice. "He talks and talks, very serious, like the others, and he's a sturdy enough fellow. But he has no eye for the likes of us." Sabine sighed so deeply that Flora had to laugh.

"Well, life here can't be all miserable, can it?"

"Hmm . . ."

Sabine hesitated long enough that it seemed clear she was struggling with how much to tell Flora.

"As far as I'm concerned, I have enough work. The mistress is not what I'd call hardworking. When it comes to shopping, cooking, doing the laundry, and cleaning the house and the shop, I do the lot. All she does is peer over my shoulder. But I can't complain. It's better than being at home with my brothers and sisters and all the work in the stables. To be honest"—she lowered her voice—"sometimes I wonder why they took me on at all. The work here really just takes one. But madam is just, well . . ." Sabine shrugged. "Once we get the water piped straight into the house, everything will be easier. Then I won't have to haul it all the way from the spring, and what a blessing that will be! They say they'll be finished in a week. I'd like to get out there with a shovel and help the men myself so that they really get the job done!"

Both women laughed.

"So that's why it looks so horrible out on the street," said Flora.

"Did you think it was because of the French?" Sabine said, making Flora laugh again.

When, a short time later, they went down to the kitchen to clean the vegetables for dinner, each had the feeling that, beyond expectations, she had found a friend.

Chapter Nine

"Oh, believe me, it isn't easy running a business in Baden-Baden. That's how it was before the war and nothing is going to change about that now. If anything, it'll get harder, since the French aren't coming. They were good customers. Jewelry, clothes, flowers, didn't matter what. Always at the best restaurants, staying in the most expensive hotels, and they practically lived in the casino! Well, if you've got the change to spare . . . but I'll tell you, the business owners here didn't have any of that this year, of course." Mr. Sonnenschein swung his spoon out wide to add emphasis, then dipped it into his soup again.

"Not that we'll be missing the French money," said Ernestine. "We never saw any of it anyway. You were always against giving the shop a French name. 'Maison Du Soleil'—that would have sounded very nice, if you ask me. But it's too late now."

Kuno Sonnenschein glanced sideways at his wife. "This bowing down to everything French . . . if you look at it like that, the end of the French era is no great loss."

Flora was intrigued by the man who was to teach her the art of floristry. So far, she had not figured out much about him. Was he sorry that the French no longer visited the town, or was he pleased about it? Either way, it was about time that she took part in the conversation.

"But isn't the end of the war a blessing, too?" Flora asked. "In Gönningen, I've heard the men talking about how the emperor is going to use the money that the French have to repair the streets and build more of them. Traveling will be easier and more comfortable—that is a good thing. And luckily, we don't need a passport to travel inside the German Empire anymore. It was always such a lot of running around until you got one, and if you didn't have it on you when they checked, you were in trouble!"

"Oh, yes. The streets." Mr. Sonnenschein sighed. "But the real question is: Will the people still come here at all? Or will they suddenly decide to go to Karlsbad or Marienbad or some other spa town, or even head for southern climes? All those beautiful spots will be faster and easier to reach."

"Hmm. I hadn't thought about it like that," Flora said with a frown.

"Then you should, dear girl," Mr. Sonnenschein said solemnly.

Friedrich spoke up then. "Father, stop painting everything so black," he said. Then, turning to Flora, he added, "It's true, though. We miss having the French in town, but at least the Russians are loyal. And they're so filthy rich, it stinks to high heaven." He screwed up his nose in disgust.

"I know from my father that there are a lot of rich Russians. He used to do good business with them," said Flora, smiling at Friedrich.

"Well, our boy here would know. He deals with nobility and the rich every day at the Trinkhalle," Mrs. Sonnenschein said, and she patted Friedrich's hand. "He doesn't have to worry much about having enough guests, do you?"

"You're mistaken, Mother," Friedrich replied, pulling his hand out from beneath hers. "Even with us, it is much quieter than it was this time last year. There are fewer visitors in town. And it's no surprise at all that the hoteliers are complaining."

"But the hoteliers always find something to complain about," Kuno said. "And they don't look to me like they are starving."

Friedrich laughed. "You're not wrong, but you only have to look through the *Badeblatt* to see that their concerns are actually justified this year. Picture this:"—he turned now to Flora—"last year, fewer than thirty thousand guests were listed in the visitors' register. In 1869 it was around sixty-two thousand! But things will improve, I'm sure. They don't call Baden-Baden the summer capital of Europe for nothing, do they? This is where the wealthy of the world meet, and that can't change overnight."

Flora nodded uneasily. The way the Sonnenscheins talked, one could easily think Baden-Baden was on the brink of ruin. The war, which had all but ended just a few months before, seemed to have left its mark.

Flora looked down at her empty plate and realized she was far from full.

"Soup, soup, soup. And vegetables in between. We're all on short rations around here, and you'd do well to get used to it early," Sabine had told her when Flora was helping her in the kitchen. "Meat or smoked fish is a rare treat. They even skimp on *Speck*."

Flora found it strange that Sabine was eating alone in the kitchen at that moment. Back home in Gönningen, their elderly maid, Ursel, always joined them at the table. But Mrs. Sonnenschein obviously had her own views when it came to customs and decency.

"Can you tell me about the Trinkhalle? I've only seen it from a distance, and it looks quite magnificent, but I've never been inside. Is it a bar?"

Friedrich laughed. "No, the Trinkhalle is not a bar, but we certainly serve something! I'm talking about thermal waters, and from several different springs at once. The very best medicinal water there is, extremely beneficial for your health, whether you're suffering from an upset stomach or a gall bladder episode. Gout, a weak heart . . ."

Mrs. Sonnenschein looked at her son with motherly pride. "The Trinkhalle, the walking paths all around it, the pavilion—and our darling boy is responsible for all of it. But don't think for a minute that the casino leaseholder appreciates any of it. The only thing that matters is his gambling tables. He never thinks about the benefits of having the Trinkhalle next door."

"Oh, Mother," Friedrich said defensively. After a long silence, he turned back to Flora. "If you like, I'll invite you to try a glass of our outstanding medicinal water within our hallowed halls."

"I'd love to! I can hardly wait to find out more about Baden-Baden," Flora said. *Hallowed halls—so much fuss about a few glasses of water,* she thought to herself. And the way Mrs. Sonnenschein talked about her son, her *"darling boy."* Her own brothers would have slithered under the table in shame if their mother ever talked about them like that.

A wave of homesickness washed over Flora at the thought. To distract herself, she asked Friedrich, "That means you mostly deal with sick people, doesn't it? I'm not sure if I'd want to—"

"Oh, that's not the case at all. Baden-Baden is not a spa town in the sense of offering a cure for seriously ill people. Only rarely do the truly sick ever come to us."

Mrs. Sonnenschein's brow furrowed. "Your waters are so healthful! They take a little getting used to, perhaps, but they're very beneficial."

"But you can't go prescribing how the guests are supposed to spend their time. Most of them only have their own amusement in mind," Mr. Sonnenschein added.

Flora was dead tired. The long journey and the discussion at the dinner table had taken their toll. But when Sabine asked her if she felt like going for a walk that evening once she was done cleaning up in the kitchen, Flora spontaneously said she would. As long as it was light out, the maid was free to go out as she pleased, but she would be in trouble if she came back after nightfall. On that point, Sabine explained as they strolled along Stephanienstrasse, Mrs. Sonnenschein was unwavering. At that time of day, most of the businesses and workshops were closed, but the woman who ran The Gilded Rose, where Flora had stayed with her mother in winter, waved cheerfully to them as they passed.

Sabine had a tale to tell about every house and almost every inhabitant, and Flora's head was soon buzzing.

"This is Karl-Ottfried Schierstiefel's tailor's shop. He's an old crony of the master and drops in almost every day. You should hear them—they go on like old washerwomen! And . . ." Sabine seemed to be keeping a lookout for something.

"Is something wrong?" Flora asked.

The maid shook her head rapidly, but then changed her mind. She beckoned Flora closer. "Old Schierstiefel, well, there's this fellow Moritz who works with him . . ."

"Ah-ha, now you look like my friend Suse when she raves on about her Rolf."

"*You're* the one saying I've got a heartthrob, not me!" Sabine said, her face suddenly crimson. "Schierstiefel is an old miser. He never has any scraps of cloth left over. But there's also a woman with a tailor's shop a bit farther away, and you can often pick up a bit of leftover fabric from her. Enough for a hair band or two, certainly."

They strolled on.

"This is Grün's pharmacy. Gretel Grün is a friend of madam's and she is always very nice to me. Mmm, something smells good, doesn't it?"

The smell of sauerkraut and mashed potatoes wafted from the windows of restaurants.

Flora's stomach replied for her with a loud growl.

"Hungry?" Sabine asked with a frown.

Flora just nodded.

"Then I know just the thing!" With a loud laugh, Sabine pulled Flora onward. "This is Walbusch's general store. Mrs. Walbusch is a friend of madam's, and whenever she comes to visit the Sonnenscheins she always has to have a cup of coffee served instantly. And do the fine ladies care if I happen to be busy with the washing or cooking? Oh no! If you ask me, she's a crook. I think she charges madam far too much, but I won't let her do that to me!"

"Then why don't *you* just do the shopping at Walbusch's?"

"Because madam won't let anyone stop her from choosing her buttons and sewing thread herself. She spends hours and hours on something like that and comes home exhausted, because everything is, oh, such a strain . . ." Sabine theatrically wiped imaginary sweat from her forehead. The next moment, she grabbed Flora by the sleeve. "Here I am babbling away, and we hardly even know each other. You don't breathe a word of any of this to madam or the master, understood?"

"Do you think I'm some sort of tattler?" Flora said, affronted, but Sabine merely shrugged.

They had gone quite a way along the street when Sabine turned into a narrow side alley and from there into a courtyard.

"My little Württemberger girl!" she heard the moment they walked through the courtyard gate.

In front of Flora stood a giant of a man wearing a bloodstained apron, and she recoiled reflexively. Along the side of the courtyard were several slaughtered pigs, or rather half pigs, hung on large hooks from a balcony. Beneath one of the half pigs stood a large basin into which blood dripped. What in the world did Sabine want here? The huge man had already embraced Sabine and planted a kiss on her cheek. And the way he looked at her . . .

"Mr. Semmel—may I introduce Flora? She comes from Württemberg, too, and she'll be helping in the flower shop starting tomorrow."

For better or worse, Flora took the proffered blood-smeared hand. He was from the Swabian Mountains, he explained, but love had brought him to Baden-Baden many years earlier. The love, however, had long since flown, and now he was waiting for another, he added, looking at Sabine as he spoke. She stubbornly said nothing.

"Well? Can I interest two young women from Württemberg in a bowl of *Metzelsuppe*?" Mr. Semmel nodded toward the butcher's shop.

Flora and Sabine exchanged a glance. "You bet!" they said, at the same time.

"You really know this town backward and forward, don't you?" said Flora as they went on their way again after a rich bowl of the broth left over from making sausages. For the first time that day, her stomach felt warm and full.

"And side to side." Sabine laughed. "One has to know where one is, right? We won't go to bed hungry tonight."

"Um . . . do you think we could still take a look at the Trinkhalle where Friedrich works?" Flora asked.

Sabine frowned. "Do we have to? I can tell you right now that it's too late to get in, and even if it was open, the water tastes just awful! I tried it once—just once. It doesn't cost anything, after all. But who would pay for stuff like that? No one! Let's go for a walk along by the hotels, where all the high-and-mighty spa guests stay."

Sabine suggested getting there via the Promenade so that they could look in the windows of all the lovely shops, and Flora readily agreed.

"I know this place," Flora said when they found themselves in front of Maison Kuttner. "I was even in there with my mother." With a deep crease between her eyes, she told Sabine about their reception in the flower shop.

"They pinch all the good jobs and customers from the master. But it's no surprise. They're in the middle of everything here, and the Sonnenscheins are in the middle of nowhere.

Flora shook her head. "Now you're really exaggerating. You can get to the Sonnenscheins' shop in a few minutes at a brisk walk. It's only a few streets."

"But for the spa guests, even a few streets is too far. Personally, I wouldn't set foot inside that place," said Sabine as she tried to move Flora along. "The likes of us aren't good enough for them."

Flora stopped abruptly and planted her hands on her hips. Angrily, she asked, "Does our money stink? Are we worth any less than the fine ladies and gentlemen here?" She swept her hands out wide, including the other people out walking with her gesture.

Sabine, somewhat embarrassed at the scene Flora was making, tried again to pull Flora on. "We're servants, no more. Other laws apply for us. That's how it's always been."

Flora bit down on her lip. That was not how she saw things at all. What had her father always told her? "Child, some of our customers like to treat traveling traders like the dirt under their feet. But as a Gönningen seed woman, you're the equal of anyone on this earth. If we've got something to say, we don't let anyone tell us to be quiet."

Dusk was slowly beginning to settle by the time they reached the shores of the Oos. Flora looked at the hotels with fascination. They stood side by side along the river like pearls on a string. And on their terraces, in the dining halls, in the fire-lit lounges and salons, everywhere she looked, she saw glittering chandeliers and flickering candles, like countless fireflies on a summer night.

"We should be getting back. We really have to be home again before dark," said Sabine.

Flora could not drag herself away from the magnificent sight. "Look, they are dancing over there. I think it's a ball," she said reverently, and she nodded in the direction of the Englischer Hof, on the terrace of which elegantly dressed ladies and gentlemen were standing in small groups. "I'd love to take a closer look." Musical notes drifted through the evening air, which was already saturated with the fragrance of lilac and lily of the valley.

Sabine sniffed dismissively. "It's nothing special. The guests there have a party every night of the week. I know a chambermaid, Konstanze, at the Englischer Hof, and the tales *she* has to tell . . ." Sabine paused meaningfully. "Just imagine, the guests there eat foie gras for *breakfast*! With the finest white bread! And caviar, too. They bring it all the way from Russia in golden tins, says Konstanze."

Foie gras . . . Flora knew how fine that tasted. Her father had once brought home a small tin of it himself.

"The spa guests . . . I still don't know what that's all about. The master said earlier that they spend a lot of money in the local shops, but they can't just do that the whole day long, can they? And certainly not for the whole summer. They have to work sometime, don't they?"

Sabine laughed. "That's what you think. Konstanze will tell you otherwise. After breakfast, they go for a walk, and if you have a little free time, you should see that for yourself. You have *never* seen lovelier clothes in your life." Sabine's eyes gleamed longingly. "Sometimes they'll return to their hotel rooms throughout the day, and Konstanze says that the women change their clothes up to five times in a single day, and that they have maids just to help them get dressed. They meet other guests for lunch or a drink. Or they go shopping, or to the casino. And starting early in the afternoon, all the gracious nobles have to start prettifying themselves for the balls and parties of the evening. I think we can safely say that none of them actually work."

Chapter Ten

The next morning Sabine dragged herself, grumbling and groaning, out of bed. "Six o'clock, and not even properly light yet. You've got it good. You can lie in like a lady while I'm off to light the stove, boil water, set the table, bring in the milk, and a whole lot more besides." She spat on her hands and ran them through her hair, which she then began to weave into a braid.

Flora, furrowing her brow, looked toward the window. From outside came a chorus of loud twittering. The birds seemed impatient for the sun to brighten the day.

"Believe it or not, I'd much rather come down with you now, but I'm not supposed to show my face before breakfast."

"Be grateful for what you've got," Sabine mumbled, her lips full of hairpins.

"I'll do your hair for you if you like," said Flora, who could hardly bear to watch Sabine fumbling clumsily with her braid.

A look of delight appeared on Sabine's face. "Gladly, but on my day off, when we have more time. Maybe you can even weave in a flower. But now . . . enjoy your well-earned rest, young mistress!" She made an exaggerated curtsy in front of Flora, then thumped off down the steps.

What now? thought Flora, stretching her arms and legs so far that they made an assortment of cracking noises. Should she perhaps go for a morning walk? She could cut some apple and pear blossoms for the store—she had seen several trees heavy with blooms on her way from the train station. And she would be making herself useful on her very first day in the shop.

But perhaps Mr. Sonnenschein was up early and had already gone to get fresh flowers and branches?

As she lay there wondering what to do, her mother's words suddenly came back to mind. "I don't mean to dampen your enthusiasm for a moment," Hannah had said as she ironed her daughter's blouses and skirts the day before Flora left Gönningen. "But don't let it carry you away. *We* are used to keeping ourselves busy, and for me personally a hard worker is worth ten times any lazybones. But too much hustling and bustling can upset other people. You don't have to always do everything differently. Many things can simply be left as they have always been."

"You sound like you think I'm a permanent pest. Don't worry, I'll behave myself," Flora had said, feeling quite outraged at Hannah's remark.

"Oh, child, I just want to give you a little useful advice to take with you," Hannah had replied. "In Reutlingen, your enthusiasm did not just make you friends. When we came to fetch you, Mrs. Gruber said she was happy she no longer had to hear a thousand ideas from you every single day." Hannah had looked up fondly from the iron to her daughter. "There's a difference between working hard and being a know-all. If you're clever, you'll take a step back and watch how the Sonnenscheins do things for a while. And even if the way they do things is not always to your taste, well, keep that to yourself. *You* are the newcomer, and *you* have to get used to your new surroundings, not the other way around. Believe me, I've been through it myself . . ."

But surely her mother would have no objections if she just went out to pick a few flowers, would she?

Flora leaped out of bed.

At nine o'clock, with breakfast behind them, Kuno Sonnenschein and his new apprentice went into the store. Finally.

Her new workplace! Her first day! Hannah could hardly wait to get her hands on something. She put the present she had brought with her—a parcel of flower seeds—on a shelf to one side and looked around expectantly.

The shop was bigger than she'd imagined from seeing it from the outside on her first visit in January. While there was only one front window, it was large and divided into three panes. It was also rather dirty, and so densely plastered with handwritten notes and handbills that most of the morning sunlight was blocked.

Flora frowned. Wouldn't it be better to get rid of all of that and put a few flowerpots in the window?

Beside the window was the door, also with panes of glass, over which hung a doorbell. When Kuno opened the door, the bell tinkled melodiously. *How charming,* Flora thought, and she smiled and breathed in deeply. With the door open, a little more light streamed in with the fresh air from outside.

Opposite the front door and large window, the shop counter stretched across the entire breadth of the sales room. Flora ran her hand over the decades-old wood, felt its grooves, saw the stains left behind by water and flowers—it felt warm and full of life. She pushed aside a few small bulbs and leaves, no doubt left over from the day before.

There was the long counter, two chairs behind it, a large cupboard to the right of the door that opened into the hall that connected the shop with the Sonnenscheins' house, shelves on all the other walls, a few small tables topped by potted plants—and that was the extent of the furnishings. Most of the space was taken up by buckets all around the counter, with rhododendrons, viburnum, some green stems and foliage, carnations, and pale yellowish roses. The selection of flowers was not particularly broad, Flora thought. And it didn't smell terribly good in there, either. She screwed up her nose and quickly located the cause of the bad odor: the cut flowers urgently needed fresh water.

"So? Is it how you imagined it would be?" Kuno stood in the front doorway, his arms crossed over his chest, unmistakable pride in his voice. "There never used to be any flower shops like mine here. Twenty years ago, Josef Kuttner—his shop is down on the corner of the Promenade—and I were the first to take the risk. When I was young, people used to go to the farmers directly or to a nursery if they wanted flowers. Or they cut them in their own garden. But then the municipal authorities started buying the land that belonged to the nurseries and using it for shops and business buildings, and the nurseries moved out to the countryside. People didn't want to go all the way out to the country just to buy a few flowers. That was when I saw my opportunity."

Flora nodded, impressed. "We don't have a single florist at home in Gönningen. Not yet, at least. It's so lovely here!" Flora lifted one hand, her gesture taking in the entire shop. "I like your shop much more than Maison Kuttner. When Sabine and I walked past there yesterday evening, we couldn't see any flowers at all because of all the porcelain and silverware and whatnot. It all looked so terribly congested." *At the same time,* she thought, *a little more of everything certainly would not hurt this place*—everything looked so sparse, somehow.

Kuno shrugged. "Josef Kuttner's customers seem to like all that. But the people who come here don't have the money for that kind of thing."

The old man looked so dejected that Flora felt obliged to cheer him up. She trotted outside to collect what she had picked early that morning and deposited by the front door.

Kuno gaped at the huge bundle of greenery and wildflowers that Flora laid on the counter. "You've already been out this morning? Well, whoever trains you in the future will be happy to have someone with that kind of enthusiasm, I'm sure."

Flora was puzzled. What did he mean by "*whoever trains you in the future*"?

"Now don't look so surprised. Friedrich told me about your little secret." Kuno gave Flora's hand a fatherly pat.

Little secret? "What . . . what did your son say, exactly?" Flora croaked.

"Not much, really. He said that you're due to start a real floristry apprenticeship in Reutlingen this coming autumn. But that your parents fear that you lack the necessary, let's say, manual dexterity, and you want to get some practice in the basics first. Of course, I'm only too happy to help, but . . ." The fleeting smile that had appeared on his face disappeared and he looked even more concerned than before. "My customers tend to buy just one or two flowers at a time. Very few of them can afford a proper bouquet. Looking at it like that, you could probably learn more at Maison Kuttner. Also, I'm a little wobbly at the knees these days—not that I'd make a big thing of it, God forbid." He let out a hefty, sudden sneeze, dug in his pocket for a handkerchief, and dabbed at his nose and eyes.

Slowly, Flora realized what had happened. Hadn't Friedrich mentioned in January how stubborn his old father could be? And that he accepted help only with the greatest reluctance? Apparently, Friedrich had resorted to a trick: rather than convince his father that he needed help, he had convinced *him* to help someone else—Flora. She had not thought that Friedrich Sonnenschein would do something like that.

"Well, I must say I'm very grateful for the opportunity to be able to look over your shoulder a little," she said stiffly, but then she blurted, "Oh, you have no idea how happy I am to be allowed to work here! Just to think, the first customer could come in at any moment."

"Well, these things take time. First things first. Let's get what you've picked into some water." He lifted the bundle from the counter. "What in the world is all this? And where did you get it?" He scrutinized the feathery-looking, branching stems of one plant in particular.

"Don't they smell wonderful? I thought a bouquet would smell just as lovely if we bound some of that into it . . . wouldn't it?" Suddenly, Flora was no longer so sure of herself. The scent of the strange flowers made her nose tickle.

And it seemed to have the same effect on Kuno, too, because he sneezed again.

"And this one? I can honestly say I've never seen anything quite like it. Oh my, what have you brought us here?" he mumbled into his handkerchief.

"Unusual, aren't they?" Flora smiled as she looked over the branches with the tiny flowers that she had cut from a bush. They were quite distinctive, and had cocoon-like balls attached to the stems. Were there flowers maturing inside? "I just went for a walk through the meadows beside Lichtenthaler Allee. There are so many strange plants there. Trees with red bark, and bushes unlike anything I've ever seen. I really just wanted to pick a few daisies, but I soon forgot all about that."

Kuno smiled. "Ah, I see. Lichtenthaler Allee is like a gigantic botanical garden. In the last twenty years, Monsieur Benazét—he was the leaseholder of the casino—spent a great deal of money having exotic trees, shrubs, and flowers brought in from all over the world and planted along there. Although I'm fairly sure he did not intend for you to come along and cut them all down. Let's hope no one saw you, or we could find ourselves in trouble."

Flora suddenly felt a little wobbly at her own knees. All she had wanted to do was help, and she had done it all wrong!

Kuno placed the spoils of Flora's plundering in a bucket of water. "Come, come. You couldn't have known. I, for one, would be very happy to have you pick flowers for the shop in the future, too. But please, just the usual kinds. You know, when I was younger I used to go out collecting in the meadows myself. The only problem was that while I was out wandering across the fields and floodplains, the shop stayed closed. And the customers here are not the kind inclined to wait in front of a closed door."

"But—" Flora had been on the verge of saying that one could go out early in the morning. Or that the woman of the house could have looked after the shop. She stopped herself, though, afraid of offending him.

Instead, she picked up the parcel of seeds she had brought with her and placed it on the counter. "My father says that in case you don't get all your flowers from Flumm's Nursery and you grow some of your own, then these seeds might be welcome."

Kuno tried to answer, but his words were lost in a bout of coughing.

My God, the man is really not well at all, Flora thought. She looked on with concern as Kuno lowered himself onto a chair, and in a short while his coughing subsided and he was able to examine the parcel of seeds.

"Zinnia, lobelia, poppy—so many different kinds! Your father is a generous man, and I will write him a thank-you letter today." He looked out the window then, pondering. "Maybe I really should try my own flower beds again . . . You know, until the year before last, I had rows and rows of flowers in the garden out back. For a city garden, it's quite large. They were beautiful to look at, and much cheaper than having them delivered. But last year I was hit by a bad cold just when I should have been pricking out my seedlings to give them more room— it was frustrating, I don't mind telling you. Now the flower beds are overgrown with weeds." He shrugged. "Well, Mr. Flumm has to earn a living, too. By the way, he comes every Mo . . . Monday, and . . ." His last words were swallowed by wheezing, and he whipped out his handkerchief and spat into it.

Flora turned and looked at the various buckets of flowers. They had been delivered only the day before? They looked very tired for being only a day in the shop.

"Heavens above, there must be something in the air today. But enough of that!" said Kuno, resolutely stuffing his handkerchief back in his pocket. "Maybe you'd be interested in helping me lay out a decent flower bed? I'm sure you'd learn quite a lot in the process."

Flora groaned to herself. She had not traveled to Baden-Baden to grub around in the earth again. "And what about my training here in the shop?" she asked delicately.

"Your training, yes . . . well, why don't we start with you just watching how I do things for a while?"

At that, Flora nodded eagerly.

"Before you start, make sure you have everything you need for the job at hand. The flowers, the greenery, various scissors, raffia for tying. Once you've started a bouquet, you won't want to put it down just because you can't find the scissors you need or because the binding wire is still in the drawer." As he spoke, he began placing flowers together.

"A bouquet has to look attractive from every side. And it is important to make sure everything is bound tightly—so better a little more greenery than too little. You start with one flower in the center, you see. Like this. And then you work around it in a circle. Of course, you have to think ahead about how you want to arrange the flowers within the bouquet."

Enthralled, Flora watched as Kuno combined a variety of flowers and greenery into a perfectly formed bouquet. It certainly looked different from her impulsively picked and assembled bunches.

"Is that bouquet meant for a particular customer?"

"Well, it could be given to someone on their birthday, but it could as easily grace a dinner table for a fine meal. It would be just as good for a young woman as for a more mature lady. Of course, there are special occasions for which a hand-tied bouquet like this really is not what you want. When . . ." Kuno furrowed his brow, as if he was having trouble thinking of a suitable example. "When a man, for example, wants to give flowers to an actress at the theater. After the show, you know? The good lady would not want to be hidden away behind a ball of flowers, of course. She'd much rather use the flowers to complement her own allure! For that, I would tie a sheaf bouquet, which can be carried over the arm." He plucked a handful of carnations from a bucket and began to arrange them over each other in a staggered pattern. Then he trimmed off the overlong stems and laid the bouquet across the crook of Flora's arm.

Flora tried to catch her reflection in the window. "It's amazing. The effect is completely different, isn't it?"

Kuno nodded appreciatively. "That's the art of it. You must look at the flowers you have and see what you can do with them and what not. With carnations, you have quite a few options, but with long-stemmed flowers like roses or lilies, for example, you can't tie them into a perfectly round bouquet. At least, not without using thirty or forty blooms. And who has the money to pay for that?" Kuno stepped in front of the counter and held his hands out toward the buckets. "Flowers for us are like fabric for a seamstress. A seamstress would not even consider sewing a headscarf out of heavy velvet, right? She'd probably choose a light linen."

Flora beamed at her teacher. *Thank you, Mama, Papa. Thank you for letting me come here!*

But her smile quickly gave way to horror when Kuno untied the raffia around his bouquet. The flowers and greenery dropped onto the counter, and one of the carnations snapped off at the top of its stem. Why was he destroying his creation?

Kuno pointed to the tangle of flowers on the workbench.

"Your turn. We want your future floristry masters in Reutlingen to be happy with your work, don't we?"

Chapter Eleven

The training for the day was over by ten in the morning—and Kuno was already at the end of his strength. When Flora's bouquet looked almost identical to his own, an achievement that seemed to take him by surprise, he opened a newspaper and told Flora to look around the shop and learn where everything was. Flora had not even opened the first drawer when Kuno was racked by an attack of coughing.

"A glass of water," he gurgled, "and I'll be fine." His face had turned as red as fire.

Flora held out the requested glass of water to him, but all Kuno could do was hold on to the counter tightly. His knuckles were white with the strain.

"Mr. Sonnenschein? What's the matter?" Flora frantically opened the front door and used the newspaper to fan some fresh air over him, but he seemed to be getting worse by the second.

Flora supported him under both arms and pulled him onto a chair.

"I'm coming right back!" she cried, and she ran through the door-way that led into the hallway.

Mrs. Sonnenschein. Or Sabine. They would know what to do. Or should she send for a doctor right away?

In the hallway, she spotted a shadow on the stair landing. "Mrs. Sonnenschein, your husband! He . . . he can't breathe—" In her excitement, Flora began to cough herself.

Drawn by Flora's cries, Sabine now appeared at the kitchen door. "It's probably just the muggy weather," she said.

"The weather, yes," said Ernestine, too. "I'm feeling rather queasy myself. Sabine, could you . . . ?

Sabine wiped her hands on a small towel and sighed. "Let's get the master into the house. Flora, can you give me a hand?"

"Strange, he's never had a coughing fit like that before," said Sabine after they had gotten Kuno to the chaise longue in the front room. Small beads of sweat had dotted his brow, and he was as pale as death, but after a while the coughing stopped and his breath came more easily.

"Don't you think we should go and get his son, just in case?" Flora asked uncertainly.

Sabine laughed at the idea. "The young master would just *love* it if I went and dragged him out of the Trinkhalle every time his father felt ill. No. I just have to keep an eye on Mr. Sonnenschein, that's all there is to it."

She twisted her mouth to one side. "Go now. If that 'We'll Be Right Back' sign hangs on the door permanently, even our last customers will abandon us."

Flora had not been in the house more than ten minutes altogether, but in all the excitement she had forgotten to close the front door of the shop. When she returned, she was shocked to see two women leaning over the flower buckets in front of the counter. One of them lifted out a large bunch of roses.

"Finally! We were starting to think we'd have to help ourselves," said the woman with the roses. "I'd like these." She held the flowers up to Flora.

"Certainly, madam." Flora hurried behind the counter, opening all the drawers as she went. Was there paper somewhere for wrapping? What did a bunch of roses like that even cost? Where was the money kept? Help! Why did Kuno have to come down ill today of all days, on her very first day?

Flora wrapped the roses in pages from Kuno's newspaper, then named a price that was clearly far too low, because the woman said, "Then I'll take twice as many."

Flora gave her a pained smile.

"You must be the new apprentice, right? From Württemberg? Where is Kuno?"

"Uh, yes. I'm Flora. The master is—" She abruptly stopped herself. What business was it of this nosy woman what was going on with Mr. Sonnenschein?

"I'll add a little greenery to the bunch, if you like," she said, and she quickly trimmed off two of the stems of the fragrant plants she had picked that morning. That seemed to please the woman.

"Maybe I can get served sometime today, too?" the other woman said impatiently. "I need flowers for a birthday. Goodness, it takes forever here."

With a hint of a curtsy, Flora smiled at the second woman. "I'll be with you in just a moment."

An hour later, Flora had served four women, and to each of them she had given one of the aromatic stems.

"It's rare to be given anything, just like that. Normally, all you get for nothing is sorrow and pain," one woman had murmured. She had bought a single tulip, and Flora watched as her fingers, red and chapped like those of a washerwoman, stroked the petals tenderly. She had to dig in her purse for a long time to find the few kreuzer to pay for it. "I really can't afford luxuries like flowers anymore. But when I look at the tulips, they make me think of my Berthold. He loved them very much . . ."

Flora had then pressed a few forget-me-nots into the woman's hand as well. "These flowers mean that someone will carry you in their heart always," she said, and the woman smiled.

Not all the customers were so poor, but with one or two others, Flora had wondered if anything besides the flower or two they bought would find its way to the table. Flora sighed.

She would, of course, tell Mr. Sonnenschein about the small bunch of forget-me-nots she had given the old lady.

Since her first two customers, Flora had discovered not only where the money was kept—in a wooden case in the top drawer behind the counter, tucked away beneath a few old rags—but also a price list. At least, she hoped that's what it was, and not a list of what Mr. Sonnenschein paid his suppliers.

A fleeting sense of pride came over her then. She'd held up quite well, all things considered, hadn't she? But her mood clouded over again a moment later. Where was Mr. Sonnenschein? Was he feeling better? And why hadn't Sabine come to tell her how he was?

This was certainly not how she had imagined her first day on the job: standing all alone in the shop and having to make the best of things. So much for "*take a step back*," as her mother had advised her. When she wrote about this to her parents . . .

But, if she were honest with herself, she had taken a great deal of pleasure in all of it.

Flora was watering the potted plants when the doorbell tinkled anew.

"It's getting harder and harder to get along this street every single day, let me tell you!" Still in the doorway, the man took off his shoes and knocked the right against the left, letting a fine rain of dust fall just outside the door. "Kuno?"

"The master isn't here just now. Can I help you?" Flora curtsied.

The man looked her up and down. "You must be the new apprentice girl. Pleasure to meet you. Schierstiefel's my name, gentlemen's outfitter. My shop is a little farther along the street. I always come in on Tuesdays for carnations for my wife. But if Kuno isn't—"

"Oh, that's no problem at all," Flora said hastily, coming out from behind the counter. So this was the man with the apprentice of his own, the Moritz that Sabine had mentioned. "A bouquet every week, and carnations—*the* symbol of deep friendship. How lovely! May I add a stem of this, too? No charge, of course."

When Sabine came in at six o'clock with the key to the store and the news that the master of the house had retired completely for the day, Flora was so exhausted that all she could do was nod. Why were her eyes so red and teary? She hoped she had not caught something from Mr. Sonnenschein.

Her first day at work . . . She was pleased with what she'd done, even if she felt more tired than she'd ever felt in her life.

Chapter Twelve

Evening came, and Kuno had not completely recovered. His eyes were no longer teary and his cough had disappeared, but his throat was so raw that he could not speak beyond a quiet croak.

The doctor they had finally called in looked puzzled. "Strange. Normally, I'd suspect it was a reaction to something, like a bad hay fever, but . . ." Pondering, he tugged softly at his beard.

"But?" Ernestine said breathlessly.

The doctor looked up. "I've had several patients today with similar complaints, all here on this street. I've just come from the Schierstiefels, in fact. Perhaps it's a virus going around?" He looked at Flora, who was standing in the doorway, listening to their conversation. "If I may be allowed an observation, young lady, you look to be rather strained yourself. Red eyes, runny nose."

"Heavens, don't say that! The girl's only been with us a day. The last thing we need is her getting sick, too. If her parents hear that . . . well, it doesn't bear thinking about." Ernestine pressed both hands to her breast. "Doctor, I've been feeling rather ill myself."

The next morning, Kuno was feeling a little better but not well enough to get out of bed. Flora, apart from her runny nose, felt fine and convinced Friedrich and his mother that she would be able to watch the shop by herself for the day.

Preparing herself for the day ahead, she was so filled with excitement and anticipation that she could barely stop herself from grinning constantly. She twisted the key energetically in the lock as plans for the morning turned over in her mind. The previous day, the morning hours had been relatively quiet. If today was the same, she would use the time to mop the floor and—

Flora had not even made it to the counter when her scream filled the room and she ran out again in a panic.

"You can't be serious," Sabine said, shaking her head vigorously. Stretching her neck, she peeked around the doorframe and into the shop, without setting a single toe over the threshold. "That is disgusting, just horrible! No, I'm sorry, I can't do it!" She lifted both hands defensively as she stepped back. "You'll find cleaning things in the little room off the hall."

"Please, I'm begging you, don't desert me now!" Flora held on to Sabine's sleeve tightly. The fine hairs on her arms were standing on end. "Maybe with a broom?" she whispered. "Please?"

On the floor, on the walls, across the counter, on the flower buckets—everywhere she looked scuttled hundreds of small, almost transparent spiders.

"Where did they all come from overnight?" Flora whimpered. What a terrible shop she was in. "Have you ever seen anything like it?"

"No! If madam sees those things, she'll drop dead on the spot. Which I could understand, actually." Sabine screwed up her face as if she'd bitten into a lemon. "All right, look: first, we'll bash them with the dustpan. And then I'll sweep and you hold the dustpan—*not* vice versa!"

Flora ran off toward the closet to get a bucket, dustpan, and broom. Anything was better than having to deal with that horror alone.

The two women beat at the little creatures for several minutes without much success. The spiders were quick on their feet and clearly quite determined to go on living. But after a while, Flora's and Sabine's aim improved. The floor was already covered with many spider cadavers when Flora's gaze froze for the second time that morning.

"Sabine," she whispered. "There!" She pointed toward the twigs that she had cut the day before, the same ones she had thought were particularly lovely.

Where the cocoon-like white balls had been, there were only open shells. From some of them, the little spiders were still emerging.

"Oh my God." The maid slapped her hand over her mouth.

"What in the world did I bring back with me?" A shiver ran through Flora, and she let out a hysterical laugh.

The spider-eradication campaign was still in full swing when there was a rapping on the shop door. The two young women jumped.

It took a moment for Flora to recognize the silhouetted figure standing in the doorway as one of her customers from the day before. Just behind her stood a man in uniform.

"She's the one!" the woman snapped as Flora opened the door for her. "She's the one who gave me that terrible stuff! 'A gift' indeed—that Württemberg girl was trying to kill me! And my Otto, too."

The policeman behind her cleared his throat. "Nothing's been proven, ma'am. We are simply in the process of establishing the facts of the matter and—"

"The *matter*?" the woman interrupted him scornfully. "Just look at the girl, standing there like innocence itself. I tell you, it was an attempt on my life. She tried to suffocate me in the night. Just wait. The doctor will be here any minute, and then you'll have your *matter*!"

The officer looked meekly at the floor, where a few spiders were still scurrying around.

"It's Else Walbusch, the lady from the general store. What's she talking about?" Sabine whispered to Flora, and she surreptitiously flattened a few more spiders underfoot.

"I have no idea." It took a few moments for Flora to recover from her surprise. She was beginning to feel as if she had landed in a nightmare. An attempt on her life?

"The police are here?" Ernestine, attracted by the turmoil, entered the shop and looked from the officer to Flora to Sabine to Mrs. Walbusch. "Holy Mary, Mother of God!"

"Oh, that's made you prick up your ears! And I'm not the only one your apprentice tried to kill with her greenery. The shoemaker's wife, Berthold's widow, and Gretel as well—all of them coughing and wheezing and having to call in the doctor. And they all have the same green fronds in a vase, and all of them got the stuff here!" Else Walbusch looked around the small assembly in triumph.

"My heavens, Kuno . . ." Ernestine's breast heaved and fell.

"I don't understand." Flora's voice was filled with incomprehension, and she was grateful when Sabine squeezed her hand reassuringly.

The officer cleared his throat again. "Mrs. Walbusch believes the flowers you sold her yesterday are extremely poisonous. Where did you get them?" he asked harshly.

"There it is, back there in that bucket!" Else Walbusch replied before Flora could say anything. "But there's hardly any of it left now. Yesterday that was quite a fat bundle. I hate to think who else she gave that poison to."

"Flora, what does this mean?" Ernestine staggered and had to hold on to the counter.

"It looks as if the plants I picked yesterday morning are poisonous. And I gave some of it to everyone who came in," Flora said, her voice flat. "It smelled so good."

Sabine, frowning deeply, looked at the bucket holding what was left of the spoils of Flora's collecting expedition the day before. "You mean that could be where Mr. Sonnenschein's coughing spells have been coming from?"

"So you admit the charge?" the officer said sternly.

Flora bit her lip. A nightmare. She would wake up any moment, would wash the bad dreams away with cold water on her face and laugh—

"Flora?" Ernestine said, then held her breath.

Flora was speechless. The spiders' nests, and now poisonous plants—apparently, the day before, she had gone straight for the plants that could do the most damage.

"I didn't mean to hurt anyone . . ."

"I think now would be a good time for me to fetch the young master from the Trinkhalle," Sabine murmured to Flora, and she ran out of the store.

Flora was banished to her room while the family discussed her future in the Sonnenschein house. But she could not put up with being shut away in the dim room for long. The notion that she would have to pack her things and go home again was horrible. What would her parents say? Maybe she could explain everything to the Sonnenscheins one more time.

Flora tiptoed down the stairs and discovered another eavesdropper listening at the dining room door: Sabine.

"Am I being sent home?" Flora whispered.

Sabine shrugged. She stepped to one side so that Flora could also press her ear to the door.

"I can't imagine what the people are saying . . ." ". . . our last customers, gone . . ." ". . . she only meant well . . ." ". . . a know-all! And dangerous, too . . ." ". . . it was *not* meant that way!" ". . . she was supposed to *help* Father, not . . ." ". . . a menace to life and limb . . ."

"That's enough!" Friedrich's voice was suddenly so loud that Sabine and Flora jumped. "Flora is certainly *not* out to take anyone's life or their limbs. This was a series of unfortunate events and no more." Friedrich seemed to be standing directly in front of the door now. At least, Flora and Sabine could clearly understand every word he said. "Do you really want to send her away because of this?"

"Yes. No!" Kuno's voice sounded almost agonized. "I also think the girl meant no harm—"

"No harm! And what about the people along our street? How am I supposed to show my face among them after this . . . this catastrophe!"

"Oh, Mother," Friedrich said, and sighed loudly. "I'll think of something to make it up to them—if Flora is allowed to stay."

Flora and Sabine exchanged a glance. "He's certainly looking out for you," said Sabine.

Flora was too dismayed to say anything, and merely nodded. Friedrich also had stood up for her in the shop earlier. He had managed to convince the police officer and Else Walbusch not to take the matter any further.

"Mother, what do you think of this? We'll go together from house to house, explain everything calmly, how Flora did not know the plants and therefore did not know that they could cause adverse reactions like that? After all, even the doctor was not familiar with them or their symptoms. If you—"

"Me?" Ernestine cried in horror. "Why me? I did not do a thing to—"

Without thinking, Flora opened the door and rushed into the dining room.

"If you will allow me to, I will go and visit all the neighbors myself. An apology is the least they can expect from me."

Friedrich looked at his parents with his eyebrows raised, but all they gave him in reply was a shrug of the shoulders.

"And will *you* allow me to accompany you?" he said to Flora, who felt instantly relieved at the suggestion. Of course she would.

"Well, that's done," said Friedrich hours later as they sat drinking a glass of beer in The Gilded Rose. Flora's error of judgment, of course, had become the talk of the entire street, and when they entered the bar at The Gilded Rose, they were met with a barrage of generally good-natured jokes until the proprietress put a stop to it, then treated Friedrich and Flora to beer.

Friedrich raised his mug in a toast. "To better times."

"I'll gladly drink to that," said Flora with a tired smile. "Thank you very much for coming along with me. I would have felt very uncomfortable by myself."

"Most of them were very understanding, don't you think?" Friedrich said, and he wiped the beer from his moustache. "Apart from Else Walbusch, almost all of them could laugh about it, at least. And everyone knows that Else loves to stoke a little strife."

Flora sighed. "I don't imagine I'll ever be friends with her. But everyone else here seems to be very nice. And your poor parents, the trouble I've caused them. If my mother knew, she'd probably give me a good slap in the face."

Friedrich laughed. "When I saw her, your mother seemed quite harmless."

Flora managed a little laugh herself. "She is, really. It's just that I'm always hearing from her how my eagerness makes me put my foot in it or makes other people uncomfortable. And, I'm sorry to say, this time she was right."

Chapter Thirteen

On Sunday morning, a few days after Flora had arrived, Friedrich searched the house for her, but she was nowhere to be found. Had she gone out with Sabine, perhaps? Friedrich could have sworn the maid had left the house by herself. Puzzled, he stood in the hallway. Flora wouldn't be in the store, would she? He would not put it past her.

"Cleaning windows, mopping the floor, clearing up, watering . . . Flora is practically falling over herself to help. And any brown leaf she sees—snip!" his father had said to him just the day before.

"She's probably trying to make good for the incident with the poisonous plants," Friedrich had replied. "She said she'd never forget that you forgave her. And also that she's so grateful for everything she learns from you."

His father had waved it off. "The girl is naturally talented. I'd like to know who got it into their heads that she was all thumbs."

Friedrich had been delighted at his father's words, as if they had applied to himself. Flora was so likeable and unaffected, so very different from the women who visited the Trinkhalle. Often, he caught himself thinking that he would like very much to get to know her better.

Blast it, why does there have to be so much to do at the Trinkhalle just now? he thought in annoyance as he unlocked the door to the store.

But Flora was not in there, either.

Disappointed, Friedrich went into the kitchen to get a glass of water, and he happened to glance out the window—and there she was. He pushed the curtain aside to see better.

Flora was digging in the garden with a trowel. In broad daylight on Sunday! If his mother saw her doing that! A smile flitted across Friedrich's face. Luckily, his parents had announced that they wanted to visit some friends after church.

He was already at the door out to the garden when he saw Sabine coming from the street and heading in the same direction. Friedrich turned and went back inside. He hoped Sabine would not keep Flora too long.

I know I did not *come to Baden-Baden to start digging around in the dirt again,* Flora thought as she supported herself on the spade and rubbed her aching back. The perspiration ran down her back, her face was grimy and itchy, and her hair clung to her scalp.

At least all the effort was getting her somewhere. The garden beds were finally free of weeds and stones, and the earth itself was wonderfully crumbly.

The church bells rang eleven times when Flora, filled with anticipation, untied the linen sack holding the packets of seeds. She had to hurry if she wanted to be finished by lunch.

A familiar, spicy fragrance rose when Flora opened the first packet, which contained tiny poppy seeds, so easily blown away by the first breath of wind that came along. The smell called to her mind an image of the packing room at her parents' house.

Next came nasturtiums, marigolds, zinnias, and the delicate seeds of echinacea. Carefully, Flora planted the seeds in the moist earth.

Let's hope those birds in the pear tree don't peck them out of the ground first chance they get, Flora thought. It would be good if Friedrich could build a scarecrow.

"Are you out of your mind? Slaving away like that on a Sunday?"

Flora looked up in surprise. Sabine was standing in front of her with a handful of strawberries, holding them toward her. "I was just given these. Want one?"

Flora crushed one of the strawberries in her mouth, savoring its delicious sweetness. She would rather not know from which big-hearted benefactor Sabine had received the fruit or if, as with the butcher, she had had to pay with a kiss . . .

"Well? What do you think?" she asked.

"I don't see anything but a square of brown earth, but I must say that *that* looks very neat," Sabine replied. "I can't really picture flowers growing there yet."

Flora laughed. "Every year at home, I'm taken by surprise. What do you think? Should I trim back that overgrown hedge a little?"

"Now listen, God did not make the earth in a day. Besides, the Sonnenscheins will be back soon, and if madam sees you like that, you'll be in for it. Come inside and I'll warm some water so you can wash. You look worse than me during spring cleaning."

Flora looked down at herself. Her skirt was damp and brown at the knees, and her hands were filthy, too. Her hair had come loose and flopped in a tangle over her right shoulder. Would one bowl of hot water be enough to fix all that?

"But what if Mr. Sonnenschein falls ill again in the next few days? Then I'll have to look after the shop and won't have any time for garden work."

"So what?" Sabine said. "Why are you worried about the garden at all? The young master should be the one out here breaking his back." She turned and strode off toward the kitchen.

Flora watched her go.

"Flora! For heaven's sake, what are you doing out here?" she heard, but this time it was Friedrich.

"Isn't it obvious?" she replied with a laugh, and she swung her arm around toward the garden bed. "I know it is better to prepare the soil in autumn, and it is very late for most of the summer-blooming flowers. But I didn't want the seeds my father gave me to bring along to go to waste. And your father will be happy to see this, I'm sure. Won't he?" A sudden wave of doubt struck Flora. Would they call her presumptuous for this, too? Then all she would have achieved was the opposite of what she wanted.

"Father will be thrilled," Friedrich said hurriedly. "Until the year before last, he was a keen gardener, but then . . . his health, you know."

Flora nodded. "I think the customers will appreciate a wider choice of flowers, too. The flowers that bloom here in a few weeks will be as freshly picked as they can possibly be. And they won't cost a cent, unlike the flowers from Flumm's Nursery."

"Their quality leaves something to be desired, doesn't it?" Friedrich grimaced. "When I see the half-wilted flowers in the buckets . . ."

"I wouldn't really say that," said Flora slowly. The nurseryman certainly dealt in high-quality flowers—he purchased his seed from Gönningen, after all—but he probably kept the best he had for the customers who had the money for them. In the Sonnenschein flower shop, they could not afford any more than second-grade blooms.

"Here I am gaping like a fool!" said Friedrich abruptly. "I came out here to ask you if you'd like to go for a stroll. I think, after such a tumultuous week, you've earned a change of scenery and some time to rest and recuperate. But I see you're happy to work even on Sundays. I suppose I could have helped you."

"It's all right," Flora said. "I'm done with the garden bed anyway. I just wanted to trim the hedge a little—"

"The hedge?" Friedrich cut in. "I'll help! Just wait, I'll get a second set of shears. It's always better with two." He took off his vest and rolled up the sleeves of his white shirt.

Flora watched him, feeling rather doubtful about their joint enterprise. Mrs. Sonnenschein would certainly not be happy to come home and find her son at work in the garden.

Friedrich was right: with two of them, the work went faster and was a lot more fun. After an hour, they had trimmed back the overgrown hedge considerably. The garden looked not only bigger, but also brighter and more orderly. The more branches that fell, the more surprises awaited them. Flora discovered a rhododendron bush, patches of lily of the valley, and a few shrubs that neither she nor Friedrich was familiar with.

"As long as it's not poisonous," Friedrich teased.

"Or a spider's nest," Flora added, and they burst out laughing.

"The garden desperately needed this," he said as they packed up the spade, hoe, garden shears, and other tools. "But I've had hardly any time to spare this year. Every day, the leaseholder of the casino asks for something new. One day it's a list of all the maintenance costs, the next it's an estimate of how many water bottles I fill for the guests." He shook his head. "I guess the town demands these lists of him. And I'm happy to help, of course, but I already have enough to do with the guests themselves. One of them will want to hear a presentation about the healing benefits of the waters, then comes another asking for directions, and so on, and so on." He sighed, but waved one hand dismissively. "But I'll gladly make time for you. How would you like me to show you the town after lunch?" Friedrich smiled. "You won't find a better guide than me. I know every corner of Baden-Baden."

Flora shooed away a bee that was trying to crawl into the sleeve of her jacket.

"I don't know. My feet are rather sore," she said as the little creature buzzed away. "Would you have time next Sunday, instead?"

Friedrich nodded, smiling broadly. Then they went to the summerhouse, which had pretty decorated windows and a glass-paned door. It stood at the back of the property and had a small shed against one side where they stowed their garden tools. *Perhaps they used the summerhouse on warm days in the past,* Flora conjectured, but the cast-iron furniture stacked in one corner inside was now quite rusted.

"Please spare me any commentary. I know well enough that everything here has fallen into some disrepair," said Friedrich, whose eyes had followed hers.

Flora laughed. "I think it probably looks far worse than it really is. A few buckets of soapy water and a scrubbing brush, maybe a fresh coat of paint for the garden furniture, and it would be really very nice. It would be worth it, I think." Flora pulled one of the chairs over to prop open the door. "Could you help me get these chairs outside? Then I'll wash them down and—"

"Flora? Friedrich? Thank goodness. I thought I heard burglars out here for a moment." Ernestine looked the two of them up and down and clapped her hand over her mouth. "Oh, my heavens, Friedrich, your trousers!" She pointed at Friedrich's right trouser leg—there was a long tear where a thorny rose tendril had caught it.

"I . . . I can sew that up again," Flora squeaked. "Friedrich just wanted to help."

Ernestine turned to Flora. "Sabine will take care of Friedrich's trousers. You'd do better to look after your dress. It's filthy! Oh, I hope no one saw you." Ernestine looked left and right as if to reassure herself that they were really alone. "On a Sunday, too. It isn't proper."

Friedrich pointed to the freshly dug flower bed. "Look at how industrious Flora has been, Mother. In a few weeks, we'll have the most beautiful summer flowers here. Isn't that wonderful?"

Ernestine's eyes fluttered back and forth like two insects. "Well, the garden was a little . . . overgrown, I'll grant you." She looked at the flower bed. "You did that all by yourself?"

Flora nodded. Was the mistress of the house unhappy about what she'd done?

Ernestine sighed. "It does look very neat and tidy."

A smile flashed across Flora's face, but a moment later she saw Ernestine's expression darken again.

"But before you know it, the weeds will be back. I used to try to help Kuno in the garden, but I think you have to be a born gardener or not even try. And the summerhouse! I'm afraid to look at it nowadays. There was a time I had friends over for coffee here. They always found it so elegant to take coffee in the garden." Ernestine shrugged. "It was terribly much work, preparing for a little party like that, but I was happy to do it. Well now, those times are in the past, like so much . . ." She sighed deeply.

"But why?" Flora asked. "If this summer is as nice as last, you could enjoy your garden again. We were just about to carry the garden furniture out. If we spruce it up, paint it—"

"Carry the furniture out—now?" Ernestine cried. "What would the neighbors say to see you two hauling furniture around like hired hands? I mean, really, Friedrich, at least *you* should know better." Ernestine looked reproachfully at her son.

"Of course, I can do it by myself, and—" Flora began.

"Nothing of the sort!" Ernestine said, cutting her off. "Work like that is not seemly for a young woman, now really!"

Chapter Fourteen

"Work like that is not seemly *for a young woman!"* Flora was still angry at Ernestine's outburst. If that were true, then her own hardworking mother was an *uns*eemly person.

What was wrong with good, honest work? But Flora pushed her anger aside. Now that the garden was looking so nice, the next thing to do, obviously, was to get the summerhouse in order again, she had argued to Friedrich.

"A fresh coat of paint—where am I supposed to find the money for that?" he had groaned, but two days later he came home carrying a pail of white paint.

"You're mad," said Sabine when Flora told her she was going to stay and paint the garden furniture with Friedrich instead of going out for a walk with her. "You spend all day in the shop, then break your back in the evenings, too. No one's going to thank you for it, you know."

"That's not why I do it," Flora replied. "I enjoy the work. I always have. Back home, I can't just sit by when something's . . . ugly. Often it's enough to brighten a dull corner with a pretty posy, or to throw a colorful blanket over an old chair. When things look nice, everyone is happier, aren't they?"

Sabine shook her head. "You're starting to sound like madam with her magazine stories. Everything is pretty and lovely in those, too. As if that's all that matters in life! I, for one, am happy when everything is more or less clean and I don't have to go to bed hungry. Whether something is pretty or not doesn't interest me at all." Sabine frowned. She really could not comprehend Flora's creative urges.

"Oh, it was never this lovely before!" Ernestine cried when Friedrich fetched her and his father. The snow-white table on which Flora had arranged a bowl of lilies of the valley now stood in the center of the summerhouse, the chairs around it in an inviting circle. "But all the work . . ."

Friedrich laughed. "For me, it was a welcome change. Who knows, maybe I'll find the time to chop down the old fir trees in the next few weeks. That would brighten the whole garden wonderfully, wouldn't it, Flora?"

It troubled Ernestine that a complete stranger would show such an interest in their garden—and could talk her son into helping with all the work. In the past, whenever *she* had tried to get Friedrich to help in the garden, she had had to keep at him for weeks before he would lift a finger. But he helped Flora without so much as a bleat.

Else Walbusch still had her reservations. "Yesterday evening I saw your Friedrich fixing that garden gate alongside your apprentice girl, oh yes. And they were having a good laugh while they were at it!" she said, when Ernestine visited the general store in search of a replacement button.

Gretel also happened to be there when Ernestine arrived. "Could there be romance in the air?" she asked archly.

"Romance, my foot! The girl from Württemberg is just angling for a husband," Else replied brusquely.

Ernestine, of course, could not think of anything else after the brief exchange in Else's store. Was Flora really on the hunt for a husband? Did she really believe she had found a good candidate in Friedrich? Flora was, admittedly, pretty, hardworking, and friendly. Ernestine could not say a word against her. On the other hand: a love affair, under her very roof? Good heavens, that would certainly not do!

"So what if it's true?" Kuno replied sullenly when she told him her fears that evening in bed. He hated it when Ernestine chose to speak to him just when he finally began to feel as if he was drifting off to sleep. He would have preferred to just pull his nightcap over his eyes and not reply at all, but instead he said, "If you ask me, she wouldn't be a bad choice at all. But I think you're imagining things. Flora Kerner has nothing but flowers in her head, unfortunately."

"How can you be so certain? And what is 'unfortunately' supposed to mean?" Ernestine sat straight up in bed. The braid she had woven before getting into bed was already unraveling. "Would you honestly approve of a love affair under our own roof? And wouldn't something like that be against the law? Do you even know if Friedrich is in his room? Or is he still sitting downstairs with the girl? My heavens, I think I'd better go see what those two are—"

"Don't you dare!" Kuno interrupted. "If you happen to be right—and I stress *if*—then it would be the first time that Friedrich has taken a real interest in any girl. About time, too, I'd add." He let out a deep sigh and pushed his head deeper into his pillow. "For my part, I've got nothing against bringing Flora into our family one day. Quite the contrary, in fact."

"Kuno!"

Flora had no idea that her abundance of energy was causing Ernestine to lose sleep. And her own mother's warnings not to stick her nose into everything were long forgotten. To Flora, the Sonnenscheins seemed overjoyed at her enthusiasm and commitment. Ernestine was even planning a coffee afternoon in the summerhouse, which certainly surprised Sabine—she had never known the mistress of the house to be so active. When Ernestine asked her to bake two cakes in addition to the usual *Hefezopf,* Sabine grumbled a little. Deep down, however, she was happy to see a little life in the house for a change.

The laying of the water pipes had just been completed and the street once again made passable for pedestrians and vehicles when Flora dug small cypress trees out of the back garden and set them out to the left and right of the shop entrance. In their plain terra-cotta pots, the trees certainly were not as spectacular as the ornamental cherry trees now at the front of Maison Kuttner, but Flora hoped they would draw more attention to the shop. The front window, which she thought was particularly unappealing, was next on her list: while Kuno buried himself in his newspaper, she discreetly removed the faded advertising. Then she set up a small table just inside the window and covered it with a slightly moth-eaten tablecloth that she had dug out of a cupboard.

"A table? There?" Kuno asked when he finally noticed what Flora was doing.

"I'd like to put the potted plants on it to show them off a little more."

"I don't know. People might think we're selling furniture," Kuno murmured. But he let Flora finish the job. That same day, they sold six of the potted violets that had previously gone unnoticed inside the shop.

"Ernestine, our Württemberg girl has ideas that you and I can't keep up with," Kuno said to his wife that evening, with admiration in his voice. Ernestine's forehead rippled.

"You don't think she's overdoing things a little? She's been here barely longer than a week, and she's turning the whole shop upside down."

Kuno simply shrugged. "Maybe it's high time something around here got turned upside down."

Ernestine silently wondered if her husband was coming down with something. His newfound wit worried her.

Although Flora inspected her flower bed every day, she knew that it would be weeks before the first flowers appeared. So in her second week in Baden-Baden, she once again went out walking before breakfast to pick wildflowers. With the aid of maps that Kuno sketched for her, she discovered more and more meadows and stretches of riverbank along Lichtenthaler Allee where she could cut all the geraniums, dandelions, bird's eyes, and wild rose she could carry—all flowers she knew and none that would lead to another poisoning scare or spidery fiasco.

When she returned from these walks, her arms filled with flowers and her feet wet with morning dew, most of the houses in town were only just waking for the day. Shutters swung open, and on balconies she would occasionally see a man stretching in the morning air or smoking a cigar. From the hotel terraces came the clattering of porcelain and silver cutlery as the tables were being set for the day.

Flora gazed longingly at the pure-white linen tablecloths, in the center of which there was invariably a bouquet of beautiful flowers in a vase. She would have loved nothing more than to provide the flowers for the fine hotels personally—she would have put out fat bunches of snapdragons or white roses tied with bright ribbons.

Fantasies, she chided herself, swinging her load of flowers from one arm to the other. Fancy customers like that were hardly likely to allow their flowers to be arranged by an apprentice in a flower shop where even Kuno's regular customers insisted on being served by the boss himself.

"Don't worry over it, Flora," Kuno said when yet another woman had refused to allow Flora to serve her. "The people would rather go to an old hand than a newling. That's how it's always been. It's not something to take personally."

Flora did not find Kuno's words particularly consoling. How was she supposed to learn to tie a bouquet if no one ever wanted one from her? Or did their customers still secretly harbor a grudge over the affair with the poisonous plants?

Luckily, such grim thoughts came up only rarely when Flora went out for her morning walks. Some days, she marched up the steps to the marketplace and down again just because she felt like it. Once, feeling particularly exuberant, she followed a sign that read *"Pferdebad"*—a horse bath—and found herself behind the Palais Hamilton, standing in front of a huge hall, but she did not find the courage to venture inside. Baden-Baden really seemed to have many fascinating secrets, and she could hardly wait for Friedrich to show her more of the town.

Usually, Flora chose a route that took her along the Promenade, where she could gaze wistfully in the windows of the boutiques. Such lovely hats! And gloves. And silver jewelry. And sweets. And . . .

The only shop she snubbed was Maison Kuttner. The snotty young women who worked there could go to the devil, as far as she was concerned.

The women in Maison Kuttner, however, took a very good look at Flora: whenever she walked past with her meadow flowers, one of the saleswomen was always outside, sweeping the sidewalk and steps vigorously. And the moment she spied Flora, she called to her colleagues, who hurried out.

"Just look what she's got today!"

"She'll empty the meadows before you know it."

"The poor customers. All they get to buy is weeds."

"What customers? Old Sonnenschein doesn't have any left!" And they all cackled like geese.

For the first few days, Flora gritted her teeth, put on her most stoic expression, and ignored the young women. She did not want trouble, and their chatter was too childish altogether. But one morning, when she heard them call her a "vandal" behind her back, she had had enough. She was picking flowers, not vandalizing anything!

Furiously, she stopped in her tracks, turned around, and glared at their leader, who stood among the others with her arms crossed and a hateful look on her face.

"I don't know what I ever did to you, but if you think your stupid chatter makes any difference to me, you're sadly mistaken! Your *maison* here with all its trinkets and trumpery is no more than a junk shop—at least we sell real flowers. And your candy-colored aprons might be just the thing for a sweet shop, but certainly not for a florist. They look ridiculous, simply ridiculous."

Flora screwed up her nose and stalked away, her head held high.

She was still boiling when she arrived back at the Sonnenscheins' store. Kuno was so engrossed in his newspaper that he did not even manage a few words of praise for what she had plundered from the meadows. *And I put up with those miserable cows for this,* Flora thought angrily, and she stomped out to the garden to get the watering can she had left there the evening before.

"Child, you're not going to dig another flower bed, are you?"

Flora jumped. She had not heard Ernestine coming. *And what if I am?* she almost said.

Ernestine stood there in her nightgown with tousled hair, and Flora realized why Kuno did not insist on her helping in the store.

"You certainly look grim this morning," Ernestine said, frowning. "That's not like you at all. What's got you so upset? Not Kuno, I hope?"

Flora shook her head vehemently. "No. It was . . ." And before she could think better of it, she burst out with the entire story. "It's no wonder Maison Kuttner does better business, being where they are. The really good customers don't stray to Stephanienstrasse, and they don't know that your husband can make such beautiful bouquets," Flora said. She looked uncertainly at Ernestine, who had listened to her litany stoically. Had she said too much? Was it indecorous to speak so openly?

Ernestine sighed loudly. "Oh, child, when it comes to flowers, Kuno can measure up to anyone, I'll allow. But when it comes to running a business . . ." She bit her lip. "You know, there was a time when I truly believed we could hold our own against Josef Kuttner. Back then, Kuno turned my father's plumbing business into the flower shop. I had an idea or two of my own then, too. If it had been up to me, we would have sold a few knickknacks and ornaments from the very start. Porcelain figurines, maybe candleholders and small vases. Those things go well with flowers, don't they? And then I had my embroidered tablecloths, which everyone admired. I would have loved to make a few of those for the shop and sell them. But Kuno . . ." She shrugged. "He thought a woman should not get mixed up in a man's work."

"Then your husband should come and take a look at my village. In the seed trade, the women *have* to work." Flora was quietly surprised to discover that the building that now housed the shop had once belonged to Ernestine's family.

"I am astonished that he lets you do as you like. And Friedrich also uses every opportunity he gets to help you, too," Ernestine said in a less friendly tone.

"Oh, they both know it isn't for the long term. I'll be going home in autumn," Flora said hurriedly. But as she spoke, she noticed that the idea of leaving again burned like a bushel of nettles. As much as she missed her family, leaving Baden-Baden was not something she wanted to think about now.

Ernestine tapped thoughtfully at her chin, and it seemed to Flora that the mistress of the house had suddenly forgotten all about her. She picked up the watering can and was about to return to the shop when Ernestine took a deep breath.

"Do you think Kuno needs you right now? Or do you have a moment for me? I . . . I've just thought of something. It's probably a silly idea, but . . . come with me!"

A short time later, both women were in the cellar, and between them stood a large stale-smelling crate that Ernestine, after much hunting around, had discovered on one of the rearmost shelves.

"And this here is what they call a five-finger vase." She held the strangely shaped vase in the light of the candle she had gotten from Sabine before they had descended into the cellar. "You only need a few flowers for one of these."

Flora stared in disbelief at the mountain of newspaper, from which more and more porcelain appeared: vases, bowls, platters.

"That's made you open your eyes, hasn't it? All Baden-Baden porcelain, and very old! The factory that this came from closed down long ago," said Ernestine, her cheeks red with excitement. "My father took the crate in payment when one of his customers couldn't pay an outstanding bill. But my mother didn't want to have anything to do with any of it, so the crate came down here. I talked to Kuno years ago about maybe selling these things, but he said he was a florist, not a junk dealer."

"But . . . this is fine porcelain. A real treasure! I could decorate the shop window with it. I'm sure you could earn good money with this," Flora cried enthusiastically. She felt like hauling the crate upstairs and getting Sabine to help her wash every single piece.

"Well, I'm happy that at least one person around here agrees with me." An uncertain smile appeared on Ernestine's lips. "Do you really think this could be something for the shop? If you do, you'll have to convince Kuno. He won't listen to me."

"I'll manage it!" said Flora, and laughed.

Chapter Fifteen

Konstantin Sokerov had hardly slept a wink, but he felt more awake and refreshed that morning than he had in a long time.

It was still quiet in the town, with hardly a soul to be seen around the Conversationshaus in Baden-Baden, just an old man reading a newspaper a few benches away. In front of a café, a young man unloaded milk cans loudly from a wagon. A woman with her arms full of flowers stopped and exchanged a few words with him, and when the wagon-driver's horse tried to take a bite from the flowers in her arms, she laughed and hurried away.

Konstantin watched her go, noting the lightness in her step. He had not seen her face behind all the flowers, but he was certain that she was young and pretty.

It was not hard for him to find in the flower girl a good omen. He was in the right place—he felt it with every fiber of his heart.

Konstantin stretched until his joints cracked. The long journey from Paris had shaken him thoroughly from head to foot. He had no lack of opportunities to ride on wagons or in carriages, and to his surprise he had discovered that many French people still traveled to the German Empire, for business and for money. Is that why the customs officers' checks at the border had taken such a long time? Was every wayfarer a potential French rebel unwilling to accept the outcome of the war? The portfolio containing Konstantin's paintings was examined several times, but the landscape watercolors and pencil portraits had finally convinced the border guards that they were dealing with no more than a harmless art student.

Konstantin drew a comb from his pocket and began to battle his tangle of hair. He ran his hand over his cheek, and it was like running his hand over coarse sandpaper—he urgently needed a shave. On top of that, he was hungry and thirsty, the morning's chill had crept into his bones, and he had to empty his bladder soon.

All discomforts aside, the smile would not leave Konstantin's face, and in the nearby trees a few birds had begun their morning chorus. He would go to the café as soon as it opened; it was not as if he could not afford *petit-déjeuner* and a newspaper. Konstantin's hand moved to the inside pocket of his jacket. The cigar he'd pilfered from his traveling companion was still there, and the roll of bills as well.

The man would get over the loss of the cigar, and likely the money, too. When Konstantin had climbed up to join him in the coach, he had noted instantly that the man was not about to go hungry. The carriage was well made and well kept, the horses healthy and strong. And the way the man had spoken, the things he had said . . . Konstantin was all too familiar with people like him.

Indeed, stealing was not how he usually got by, but considering the emergency he found himself in, he could not be particular.

He shook his head, as if trying to drive away his memory of the last few days like some bothersome insect. Paris was far away, and he had to forget the trouble with Claudine, his fellow student, as quickly as possible. Impoverished students dedicating their lives to art that did not pay? He'd had enough of that, more than enough.

He would smoke the cigar while he read the newspaper. No doubt, in a spa town like Baden-Baden, there was a local *Blatt* that listed all the visitors and the hotels they stayed at, and maybe even a report or two about the concerts they attended and the plays that were currently *à la mode*.

The first thing he would do was find out who was who and what was what. He would get to know the right people—people who knew how to enjoy life, and who possessed the necessary cash to do so.

Adieu, Paris! Bonjour, Baden-Baden!

Konstantin's gaze surveyed the long, elegant facade of the Conversationshaus. He wanted to see what lay beyond the massive entrance. The glorious ballrooms. The casino—especially the casino.

"The Baden-Baden season—there's nothing to match it. Anyone looking for an exciting time finds his way to Baden-Baden." How many times had he heard those and similar sentiments in recent months? Baden-Baden—after a while, it had sounded to him like an earthly paradise.

He went into the bushes behind the Conversationshaus to relieve himself and found his thoughts turning homeward. Was his mother already awake? Had his father come home from his nightly spree at all? And what about his sisters?

Home was Veliko Tarnovo, a pretty, medieval town in Bulgaria, its buildings huddled on steep hillsides, while in the valley below, the Jantra River meandered along. In the past, Veliko Tarnovo had been the capital of the Bulgarian Empire, and even today its inhabitants were proud of its history.

The Sokerovs lived in a large house high on the most prestigious hill in the city, a hill called Trapezitsa. A house . . . it was closer to a small palace. Apart from his family, the only other residents on Trapezitsa were the clergy and a few rich landowners.

When Konstantin and his siblings had been children, their family was among the wealthiest in the entire region. His father's father had been a trader under Turkish rule, and his business had flourished. It was only after his grandfather's death that things began to decline. Konstantin was five at that time, and his father had taken over the family business, trading in silk, linen, and cotton. Elin Sokerov was a good-looking man, a charmer, and an arrogant good-for-nothing. Through his own folly, he quickly lost all favor with the Turkish authorities, who threw every obstacle imaginable in the path of his business.

Why had his mother not deserted her husband? Konstantin wondered as he lifted his bag onto his shoulder. The milk wagon trundled away around the corner. Perhaps the café would open now.

Dana Sokerova had once been a beauty and was well educated. Even today, Konstantin was sure that when the business had begun to fail, his mother could easily have found a more capable breadwinner—one who could have provided for her and her children. Instead, she had found a thousand excuses for her husband's failure.

Konstantin once had asked his mother why his father didn't do anything to improve his lot, but she never answered. And he had to watch as his mother, her face streaked with tears, sold her jewelry and treasures piece by piece so that she could feed her children.

He stepped into the café, sat at a table by the window, and set his case of pictures on the chair beside him.

A waitress stepped up to Konstantin's table. When she saw him, she began to giggle a little, and her face turned a shade of red.

Konstantin grinned. Even unshaven and sleepless, he seemed not to have lost his effect on women. He ordered breakfast and asked for a newspaper. Luckily, he spoke not only French but also reasonable German, for which he thanked his mother's mother, who was Austrian.

Why had his mother always believed his father's claims that soon, soon, things would turn for the better? Nothing ever came of it, and Dana Sokerova resigned herself to her fate.

Love had allowed his mother to forgive, to accept, to suffer everything. Since that realization, Konstantin had felt only contempt for his mother. But the lesson she had taught him with her behavior was one he would never forget: women would sacrifice everything for love. In particular when that sacrifice was made for the benefit of a good-looking, charming man who understood how to build castles in the air with words.

And there was a second discovery he had carried with him: poverty was terrible, and something he never wanted to experience again.

Breakfast came. The waitress curtsied coquettishly and asked if she could bring him anything else.

She could, he replied: a glass of champagne.

They sold champagne only by the bottle, the waitress said, to which Konstantin responded that if that was the case, he would take a whole bottle.

The champagne bubbled nicely in the goblet that Konstantin raised in a toast to himself. A city where champagne could not be bought by the glass, but only by the bottle—that was his kind of city. So it was good that he had chosen Baden-Baden over Rome, after all. The newly won capital of Italy had indeed been high on his list of potential destinations, one of many . . . Oh, there were so many places he wanted to see in his life!

When, the year before, it had become clear that there was no future in the family business, Konstantin had said to his mother, "I want to see the world!" although he knew they did not have the money for him to travel. He had not, however, reckoned with Dana Sokerova's ingenuity. After a two-day journey—where and to whom, Konstantin still did not know—she surprised him with a scholarship to a university close by that had connections to an art academy in France, not far from Paris. Konstantin's travel costs to France would be covered along with his board and lodging for a yearlong course of study.

A year in Paris among painters, writers, sculptors, all paid for . . . Konstantin would never have dreamed that fate could be so good to him. He wished he knew how his mother had obtained the scholarship for him. It had nothing to do with his talents with charcoal or brush, which were average at best.

Dana Sokerova, wearing a frozen smile, had told him that she felt certain that time abroad would provide interesting opportunities. That was his goal, too, Konstantin thought as the street outside the café filled with passersby. Women, mostly, he realized—one of the women, her brown hair pinned high on her head, looked very nice indeed. She wore a dress of glistening silver silk and several strings of pearls. As if sensing his gaze, the woman turned toward the café.

Konstantin raised his glass to her through the window.

Soon after his arrival in Paris, it became clear to him that he would never be successful as a painter. Though he had truly enjoyed playing with color and form, he resigned himself to finding his calling elsewhere.

He would find a way into the right circles. Money would be no object for him, never again in his life. Paris had been a debacle, but he had learned from it. He'd lost all interest in silly girls. And getting involved with married women brought nothing but trouble. Widows, on the other hand . . .

The woman in the silver dress had slowed her step, and it seemed to Konstantin that she was considering entering the café. Konstantin flashed her a smile. Widows . . .

He would continue to be Konstantin Sokerov, aspiring painter, from Veliko Tarnovo, which had long been known for its icon painting. He would not mention Paris.

The woman in the silver dress continued walking. A pity. Should he present himself as an icon painter? No, that was too specific. In his experience, most people were satisfied with a vaguer description.

The champagne bottle was empty, and Konstantin turned it upside down in the ice bucket.

Who would have any interest in his painting? People wanted to be entertained—that's what it was all about. They wanted to feel flattered and liked. And when it came to that, Konstantin Sokerov was perhaps the greatest artist of them all.

Chapter Sixteen

"Do you know the maid of a painter who has a summer residence somewhere not far from here?" Flora lisped. She took a hairpin out of her mouth and pinned another strand of Sabine's hair firmly at the back. "Franz Xaver Winterhalter, I think that was the name Mr. Sonnenschein mentioned."

As she did every second week, Sabine had this Sunday free, and she wanted to meet—in secret, naturally—Mr. Schierstiefel's apprentice. Flora had offered to style her hair for her.

"Of course I do. Greta. I see her often at the market. She travels with her famous employer all over Europe, just imagine! They're only here in Baden-Baden in summer." It was the answer Flora had expected—the maids from the private households all seemed to know each other very well. "Did Greta come in the shop? She used to buy bouquets here for the women that Mr. Winterhalter was always painting."

Flora nodded. "She was in yesterday. She was my first 'real' customer, so to speak. Her master wanted a pastoral bouquet for a certain picture he's painting. I could hardly believe it, but Mr. Sonnenschein let me put it together all by myself. I used cornflowers and ears of wheat and red poppies, and it came out very pastoral looking, if I may say so. Mr. Sonnenschein himself had nothing but praise for my work."

"Well, that's wonderful. So why do you look so down in the mouth?"

"Oh, it's silly . . ." Flora wrapped a strand of Sabine's hair around her finger until it fell in a pretty curl over her cheek. "It's about the language of flowers." She pointed with her chin toward her bed, where the book that her mother had given her lay. "Of course, I explained to Greta what the individual flowers stood for. I think it's fascinating. But when I was alone again with Mr. Sonnenschein, he really gave me a telling off. He said there's nothing more likely to be misunderstood than the language of flowers. One person will say one thing about a flower, and the next will say something completely different. He said all you do is let yourself in for a lot of trouble."

"Well? Is that true?" Sabine asked as she probed gingerly at her newly styled hair.

Flora pinned a flower into Sabine's hair as a finishing touch. Then she gave a little shrug. "I don't know. I used to think my little book was the only one of its kind, but the master says there are many just like it. Then he told me I shouldn't say another word in the future about what flowers mean."

"It's not so bad. You should be happy that your bouquet is going to be immortalized in an oil painting," Sabine said, trying to sound consoling. "How do I look?"

"Far too beautiful," said Flora with a grin. "The boys out on the street will be whistling at you the whole way."

Sabine looked at her slyly. "Your Friedrich certainly knows how to behave better than that, doesn't he? The way he dances around you, I'm sure he already sees you as the future Mrs. Sonnenschein."

"Don't talk nonsense! Friedrich just wants to show me the town, that's all. He probably feels obligated because he was the one who brought me here in the first place." Flora looked dubiously at her cardigan. With its worn sleeves and the darned hole on the back, it no longer looked as pretty as it once had. On the other hand, it was good enough for a stroll.

"And I suppose that's why he's always looking at you so rapturously, too? Because he's obligated," Sabine said, and grinned. "So tell me, has he tried to kiss you yet?"

"Are you mad?" But at the look of disbelief on Sabine's face, Flora had to laugh. "I mean, really. You're starting to sound like Suse in her last letter. She thinks Friedrich is the reason I came to Baden-Baden in the first place."

"Well, his behavior is not normal, take it from me. Think about it: he has an important position at the Trinkhalle, and he still finds time to help you in the garden and ruin his best trousers in the process. Which *I* then have to patch up. In all the time I've been here, he's never lifted a finger to help me, and do you think he's ever offered to take *me* traipsing around town? I'm telling you, if he's not in love with you, I'll eat a broom."

"Compared to the fantasies blooming in your mind, the garden in the backyard is a desert. Friedrich is a first-class friend, that's all," Flora said. But Sabine looked no less skeptical. Flora braced herself for another remark, but her friend simply sighed.

"You're right. What do I know about men? I don't even know if Moritz really loves me. He says he does, all the time, but . . ." Sabine gave a little shrug and suddenly looked downright lost.

Flora put her arm around her friend's shoulders. She could not stay mad at Sabine for long. "Let's ask the flower oracle!" Without waiting for an answer, Flora plucked a daisy from the little vase on the windowsill.

"He loves you, he loves you not, he loves you, he . . ."

Sabine watched, spellbound, as Flora tugged off one petal after another. The oracle, Flora noted with a practiced eye when there were still a few petals left, was not going to end well.

"He loves you, he loves you not, he . . ." And again, as she had for Suse, she covertly tugged off two petals at once. Now it would work. "He loves you!" Flora looked triumphantly at Sabine. "Rest assured, the flower oracle never lies!"

Sabine sighed with relief.

※

"If your guide may be so bold . . ." Just after they had turned the first corner, and with a small bow, Friedrich crooked his arm for Flora. And when she took his arm and held it lightly in her hand, he felt her trembling gently.

"My esteemed guide, may I perhaps be permitted one request? I would dearly love to pay a visit to the *pferdebad*. I have walked past that very building several times already and still don't have the slightest idea what a 'horse bath' is all about." Flora's cheeks were red with anticipation.

"I must say, of all the places I could show you, I would not have thought of the *pferdebad* at all." Friedrich smiled to himself. That was typical of Flora—other women would have asked about a hat shop, but Flora Kerner was more interested in wet horses.

He sneaked a glance across at her, saw her hair shining in the sunlight, and noted how prettily her brown skirt swayed with every step. For him, Flora was far more beautiful than all the women who were preoccupied with showing off the latest Paris fashions at the Trinkhalle.

As luck would have it, the *pferdebad* was open, and just as they entered, a brown stallion was being led to the pool inside. Flora watched in astonishment as it stepped into the water-filled stone basin; then she crouched and dipped her fingers in the water. "It's hot!" she exclaimed, and the stallion whinnied as if in agreement.

Friedrich smiled and handed her his handkerchief.

"The temperatures of our hot springs are all between one hundred thirty-three and one hundred forty-five degrees, and they benefit not only our rich guests' beautiful horses, but of course the guests themselves," he explained as they left the *pferdebad*. "Most of the hotels here have a bathhouse where the guests can enjoy a bath in marble pools. And then we have the steam bath beside the market square. Many years ago, hunters and gatherers used the region's hot water, and the salt, too, of course. Later, the Romans came. They say that the young emperor Caracalla was the first guest of honor in our city. That was in the year 197. At least, that is the year chiseled into a kind of stone commemorative plaque."

"Baden-Baden has existed so long? Incredible."

Friedrich nodded. "It was from Caracalla that our city earned its second name of Aquae Aureliae, which one could loosely translate as 'Emperor's bath.'"

Flora sighed. "A real bath in gloriously hot water. Or a sweat bath! I'd like to try both, I think. Are ladies also allowed to use the baths, or are they only for gentlemen?" Flora looked wistfully toward the steam bath at the market.

"The fairer sex are allowed to enter the baths as well, of course. But first we'll go to the Trinkhalle," Friedrich replied, though he had noted the direction of her gaze.

As he and Flora made their way toward one of the bridges over the Oos, he continued with his history of the town. "Just a few years ago, they carried out excavations beneath the market square and actually discovered the remains of Roman baths. For archaeologists and people like me who would like to be an archaeologist, it was an exciting find." He paused for a moment, and was about to tell Flora about the hypocaust heating system they had uncovered, about the sweat rooms and changing rooms, but Flora stopped at the end of the bridge, a stone's throw from the Conversationshaus. "Could we see that, too?" Flora asked, looking up at the stately building. "Or do they only let rich people in?" She glanced in the direction of three elegantly dressed gentlemen approaching the entrance just then.

Friedrich's countenance clouded over—Russians, probably on their way to squander money that was comparable to several years' wages earned by their average countryman.

He cleared his throat. "Why don't we save that for a bad-weather day? I would very much like to show you the Trinkhalle. I'm sure you'll like it." He patted Flora's hand lightly and drew her onward. "The leaseholder of the casino also pays for the splendid grounds around the Kurhaus . . ." Friedrich's gesture took in the crunching gravel paths, the whitewashed benches, the copious flower gardens, and the small ornamentally trimmed trees. "As the custodian of the Trinkhalle, I am his employee. Having the Trinkhalle and Kurhaus so close together is, of course, ideal for our visitors. They come to us first for a glass of water, and then they head for one of the roulette tables at the casino in the Conversationshaus. Or vice versa: first they lose a lot of money, and then they're happy that they don't have to pay for our therapeutic water." He stopped in front of the long, substantial building. "And here we are!"

"When you're standing right in front of it, it looks much bigger than from a distance," Flora murmured. "And you're really the manager of all this?"

Friedrich laughed. "Manager—that sounds so grand. When it comes down to it, I'm the 'man Friday' around here. Keeping things clean and in good shape are as much a part of my job as filling water bottles for visitors who want to enjoy our water at home."

They climbed the few steps leading up to the colonnade, and at the top Flora let out a little cry of delight. "How lovely!"

Friedrich smiled, watching Flora turn in a circle, her head tilted back, entranced by the architectonic play of form, light, and color that made the Trinkhalle what it was.

Suddenly, it was as if he were seeing the building again for the first time. The elegant columns that lined the arcade along the front gave it a feeling of boundlessness. In that moment, every thought of how difficult the pale stone was to clean was forgotten. All Friedrich saw was the lively contrast between the columns and the colorful walls, the facade worked in brick and terra-cotta and marble. He did not think about how much work it was to keep the rough surfaces free from dust and spiderwebs, but saw instead how everything merged into a stream of colors in the sunlight.

"It's magical . . . ," Flora said, her eyes wandering across the fourteen frescoes that decorated the arcade.

"Each one of these scenes—horse and rider, castles and ruins, landscapes and mythical figures—illustrates a legend from this region. This one here is Merline, the nymph of the pond." He pointed up to the image of a young woman.

She was naked, and under her left arm she held a harp while a deer nuzzled against her at her right side. The nymph looked to be sitting on the bank of a pond, and in the background, among the bushes, were a handsome youth and a white-bearded old man, the latter appearing to be holding the younger man back.

"The look on her face!" Flora exclaimed. "It's as if she wants to tempt the young man to jump into the water with her!" Flora reflexively stepped back from the painting.

"That is exactly what the picture is supposed to convey," said Friedrich. "Here I am, trying to show you something new, but you already know the legend of 'The Nymph of the Pond.'" He had been looking forward so much to regaling her with that particular tale, which was always a highlight for the Trinkhalle's female visitors. Now he found himself slightly disappointed.

"I don't know the story at all, and I love listening to stories. We have many of our own back home in the Swabian Mountains. The tales my grandmother used to tell me—I could have listened to her forever.

I was only describing what the painting made me imagine. Perhaps my guide could tell me a little about this nymph?" Flora bobbed in a polite little curtsy and smiled.

Friedrich did not need to be asked twice. "She told the young goatherd who came to visit her at the shore of the pond that her name was Merline, but also that no one was ever allowed to call for her by name. It was a warning often forgotten, however, and young men were willing to throw away their shepherding lives to catch another glimpse of the beautiful nymph. There were many times that a young man was heard crying out the name Merline. But instead of the nymph, a blood-red rose appeared on the surface of the water. The young goatherd reached for it, but as he grasped it, he was pulled into the depths of the pond and was never seen again. Which is how we humans are sometimes, always wanting what we cannot have."

Flora looked up at the fresco with fascination.

"What about the poor goats?" she abruptly asked. "How could they get along without the goatherd to look after them?"

"The goats?" Friedrich, hot from the bright sun, wiped the sweat from his forehead. "Actually, no one has ever asked me about the goats before. I honestly don't know."

Flora waved it off. "It doesn't matter. Merline wouldn't get anywhere with us, would she? You're happy and content here in your beautiful Trinkhalle, and I have the flower shop . . ."

Chapter Seventeen

How the girls strolled along in their Sunday best! How their hands—hands that spent the week dusting, scrubbing floors, doing laundry—gripped the cheap parasols that, beneath the lush, green canopy of leaves, were not even necessary. How their eyes, otherwise clouded with dust from the coal ovens and cleansing powder, gleamed with Sunday.

His fingers laced at the back of his neck, his legs stretched in front of him, Konstantin gazed down the small boulevard, while the conversation at the long table where he and Irina sat bubbled along quietly.

Soon, soon he would shine again, would pay unaccustomed compliments and be merry.

How the pedestrians looked toward them, with envy in their eyes! There—you could practically see it inscribed on that one young fellow's face, try as he might to conceal it. How he strutted along in probably the only suit he possessed.

The woman beside him was pretty. The fellow would have done well to whisper a few sweet words in her ear instead of letting his envy of others get the better of him.

But no. And now the fool was off and running, chasing a child whose governess was too lazy to keep her eye on her young charge. Oh dear, now *he* was confronted by an angry swan and doing his best to save the child, and in the process ruining his only suit. Well, if he wanted to play the hero . . . and yet, the young woman was looking at him now with newfound admiration.

Konstantin turned away. Oh, he had not forgotten that he himself, just a few days earlier, had also possessed only one decent set of clothes. But thank heavens, and thanks to his own talents, that had changed.

As he had so often lately, he burst into ringing laughter. His light-heartedness was infectious, and some of the others at the table began to laugh with him, without knowing why. But the reason was obvious: there he was, Konstantin Sokerov, Bulgarian art student, rubbing elbows with the crème de la crème of Russian spa society beneath the *arbre russe*, "the Russian tree," in Baden-Baden, a small town in the German Empire. He could as easily have sought out new friends from Persia or South America here—wasn't the world just one big, crazy party? At least, when you were among the wealthy.

Oh, Mother, if you could see me now!

Getting to know Irina had not been difficult. Princess Irina Komatschova, to be more precise. And all the others. An evening or two in the casino, a couple of generous gestures in the Hotel Badischer Hof—taking care, of course, that those gestures did not overstretch his resources—and strolling up and down Lichtenthaler Allee a few times, looking vaguely lost. And then the first conversations. Yes, he was new in the town, but for a painter, Baden-Baden was practically a paradise, *n'est-ce pas?*

Irina, the widow of Nikolajev Komatschov, was experienced and clever enough to realize very quickly that Konstantin's yearning to be part of the good life was very great, but his purse very small. Not that that would necessarily always be the case for an aspiring artist. Everyone knew the prices that true works of art brought in, and that the prices rose constantly.

"Let's call it an investment in the future. When you are rich and famous, you can pay back every pfennig of my . . . advances," she had said in an encouraging tone when she invited Konstantin to move into her rooms in the Hotel Stéphanie les Bains. That he would become her lover had been acknowledged between them for some time, if not stated outright.

And Konstantin was content with that.

Irina, who could chat away like a farm girl, was ten times more preferable to him than Matriona Schikanova, who lived separated from her husband. Matriona was certainly a few years younger than Irina, but her moods changed faster than the weather on an April day, and Konstantin found her rather a strain.

Irina, with her endless strings of pearls and her penchant for thrift—which, considering her immense wealth, was nothing more than petty—was also preferable to Princess Nadeshda Stropolski, who was known simply as Püppi and who was immediately the bosom friend of everyone she met. At their very first encounter, she had confided in Konstantin the most intimate details of her various illnesses. Strangely, Püppi was very popular, and even her miserable little dog was tolerated, licking plates clean and leaving its filthy paw prints everywhere it went.

Although Püppi traveled with an entourage of more than ten—including two lady's maids, two drivers, and a groom for her horses—an air of loneliness constantly surrounded her. She had been a widow, immensely rich and exceptionally generous, for most of her life. Did that contribute to her popularity? Or was she so loved by all because she could party night after night away? She had to sleep, of course, but that's what the days were for—when the sky brightened, she went to bed.

"She has been this way for years," Irina had explained. "Ever since the day a soothsayer prophesied that death would take her at night, in her sleep, Püppi has turned the night into day."

From the corner of his eye, Konstantin glanced down at the widow, dressed in green silk. Somehow, the lonely old woman touched his heart.

If only she did not dress so youthfully! The intensely green dress with the deep-cut neckline might have been something Matriona could wear, with her considerable and flawless décolletage, but it did Püppi's wrinkled neck and drooping breasts no favors.

Konstantin squeezed Irina's arm fondly. Yes, he had chosen well.

He turned his attention to the men: Count Popo, who always laughed loudest at his own jokes; Piotr Vjazemskij, the gambler, whose only love in life was the casino, and who was nobody's partner, but stayed conspicuously close to Püppi; and then honorable Count Nikajew, Sergej Lubelev, and all the others.

Konstantin had quickly seen through all of them. It was always the same circle, and they always talked about the same topics. And if an outsider to their circle joined them, their pleasure was great, something that Konstantin himself had experienced. They had willingly taken him in, soaking up his youth and beauty, listening to his stories about Bulgarian cities and towns. And his wistful sighs whenever the talk turned to art.

Konstantin was well aware of the danger of being chewed up by this circle of friends and spat out again. But he would not let things go that far.

"Irina," he whispered, his voice raw and throaty. The legs of his chair crunched in the gravel as he pulled it in closer to the table.

The princess turned around to him, her cheeks reddened by the wine and the delicate tidbits melting away on large platters in the sun. So soon after lunch, nobody really had any appetite. But Count Popo had ordered for everyone, and so they occasionally reached apathetically for a morsel.

"I don't have the words to tell you how beautiful you are . . ." His words trailed away almost bashfully as he stroked Irina's cheek, the touch as light as a breath of wind. In his peripheral vision, he saw that two or three of the other women at the table were observing them in that moment. Püppi, especially, was watching them openly, while the little dog on her lap stood on its hind legs and clawed at her chest for attention.

Irina's laughter rang across the table like a small bell. She, too, was aware that the others were watching them, and she seemed to enjoy it at least as much as Konstantin. She pinched his cheek as one might with a young child.

"Kostia, why so shy?"

"It is your eyes." The words seemed to force their way out of him, louder this time so that the others could also hear him. "Once, years ago, Mama, Papa, and we children were traveling. We came to the Dunaj, the river they call the Donau or Danube here. There had been a thunderstorm the night before, but in the morning the weather was beautiful again, the air perfectly clear." He looked into Irina's eyes. "I will never forget that sight . . ."

Irina frowned. "Go on."

Konstantin now had the attention of almost everyone at the table. Even Count Popo was looking in his direction. Only Piotr Vjazemskij, at the other end of the table, seemed to have no interest in Konstantin's story. He had taken a pack of cards out of his pocket and was shuffling them so quickly that the eye could barely follow his movements. Konstantin had to suppress a smile. Piotr—mentally, at least—had probably already been at the casino for hours.

"The Dunaj seemed to me to be a rainbow of colors, emotions, and textures. It was passionate and wild one moment, then smooth and calm, as harmless as a dove."

Irina's eyes clung to his lips like a wasp to a marmalade jar, and Püppi's sighs were music to his ear.

"Your eyes remind me of that day. When I look into your eyes, I see my homeland."

"Home. Perhaps the greatest yearning of them all." Even Count Popo's voice was emotional.

"Oh, Kostia." Irina beamed. "Isn't he sweet?" she asked no one in particular.

"Only an artist pays compliments like that. Just wait, he'll be wanting to paint you next, Irinotschka," said Matriona, and she stuffed a piece of duck foie gras into her mouth.

"There's nothing I'd rather do." Konstantin raised his hands regretfully. "But without an atelier . . ."

"Irina, darling, didn't you want to take a look at that house today, the one that was for sale? They say it's a real gem." Püppi gestured vaguely up the hill with her chin.

"And isn't a house like a piece of home in a foreign land?" Konstantin asked before Irina could reply. "Perhaps there would be a small room in which I could paint. Besides, I could make myself at least a little bit useful. Looking after the garden, or . . ." He left his sentence unfinished.

"Kostia is worried that he's living off me. Isn't he sweet?" Irina said to Püppi.

"But, Irina, painting is the only way I can earn a living. I—"

Püppi's long, thin fingers, which reminded Konstantin of a bird's claw, reached toward him.

"Konstantin Sokerov! Irina can certainly afford a little Don Juan like you, so don't go worrying your pretty head about it."

Konstantin smiled at her. Her and all the others.

"I have an idea," he said in an enthusiastic voice. "Why don't we all go and look at the house together? We'll take a case of chilled champagne and act as if we live there and have something to celebrate. Wouldn't that be a wonderful bit of fun?"

Chapter Eighteen

With a great deal of pomp and ceremony, Friedrich served Flora a glass of water.

"Drink it a sip at a time, please," he said, watching her expectantly. "A drinking regime needs a certain degree of leisure."

Flora sipped courageously at the water in the glass—and it tasted disgusting! Hot and oily and salty. Sabine had really been right.

The other visitors to the Trinkhalle—primarily pale-looking women of advanced age—seemed to find the water quite palatable. Some, she noticed, were going back for a fresh glass.

I suspect the "leisure" part is not for me, Flora was about to say when, behind her, she heard a loud woman's voice.

"Mr. Sunshine! How nice to see you!" A tall woman with broad shoulders came striding toward them in an unladylike fashion. She wore a rather austere-looking blouse over a black skirt, and her unadorned gray hair swung in a single braid over her shoulder.

"Lady Lucretia—the pleasure is all mine." A smile lit up Friedrich's face as he took the woman's proffered hand and shook it vigorously. "You arrived yesterday, didn't you? I read your name in the *Badeblatt*," he said. "And as I can see, you have found your way back to the daily routine without any trouble at all." He indicated the oversized glass that the woman held in her hand.

While the woman drank a large swig of the medicinal water, with Friedrich benevolently looking on, Flora used the moment to empty her glass unseen behind her back. How could anyone voluntarily swallow so much of the stuff?

"My dear Mr. Sunshine, you would not believe how happy I am to be back here after the miserable English winter," the woman said, and her red-veined cheeks grew a shade redder as she spoke.

Mr. Sunshine—it sounded so funny that Flora had to bite her lip to stop herself from giggling. The woman was from England, then. *Friedrich could introduce us, couldn't he?* Flora thought to herself. But he was just standing there, listening to the woman as if spellbound.

"My day begins with a robust march," the woman was saying. "That is followed by a number of exercises designed to promote one's physical well-being. After breakfast comes my daily visit here to the Trinkhalle, then it's back to the bathhouse at my hotel, then—"

"And the Kneipp hydrotherapy?" Friedrich interrupted her. "Have you decided to do without those this year?"

"Oh, no! I save that for the end of the day, along with a decent glass of brandy. You'll see—by the end of the summer, I'll be practically reborn," she said, and they both laughed.

Feeling rather confused, Flora joined in their laughter. What were they talking about?

"Lady Lucretia O'Donegal is one of the Trinkhalle's long-standing visitors," Friedrich explained when they were outside and alone. "She has a weak heart, for which her doctor long ago prescribed her a course of hydrotherapy. She has been coming to Baden-Baden every year since. And unlike most of the others here, her therapy really is all about her health. Some years ago, she asked for an analysis of our spring, and once she was convinced of the quality of our medicinal water, her drinking regime became a fixed part of her daily life at the spa. Lady Lucretia is a wonderful example of just how beneficial our waters are."

They were walking along one of the gravel paths, and Friedrich plucked a few leaves from a bush and absentmindedly rubbed them between his fingers.

A weak heart? Flora's impression had been of an exceptionally robust woman.

Friedrich abruptly tossed the crushed leaves aside. "We need more guests like her! But most of the people who would benefit from a course of treatment here can't afford it. Poor factory workers who tend a machine for twelve hours at a time. Or miners whose lungs have been damaged."

Flora looked sideways at Friedrich. She had never heard him sound so bitter. Poor factory workers . . . she could not imagine people like that at the Trinkhalle at all.

"There are some seats free just now," she said, and she pointed to the chairs that were arranged in a semicircle around a small stage outside the Conversationshaus. Friedrich had told her that, several times a day, open-air concerts for the spa guests took place, and Flora, walking with Sabine in the evenings, had passed by several times when a concert was under way, but the young women had not found the courage to sit down with the paying guests. Now, a band was playing a march, and they sat and listened for a few minutes, during which Flora covertly used her handkerchief and a little spit to try to remove the white rim around her shoes caused by the dusty paths. She would have liked to sit a little longer, but Friedrich was already on his feet again—there was so much more he wanted to show her.

"It looks as if the people who come here still have money to throw away." Friedrich nodded in the direction of the street cafés, their tables all occupied now, at midday.

She had wanted to ask Friedrich if they might stop and enjoy a cup of coffee, but after his last remark she did not dare. The disparaging undertone in his voice was clear.

Was he fundamentally against such pleasure? Or could he simply not afford it?

Since her arrival in the Sonnenschein house, she had not seen an open bottle of wine, or any other delicious distractions. Sabine had enough trouble just filling the family's bellies with the money she had for groceries.

Flora glanced at Friedrich. He looked pale, perhaps even a little ill. It seemed his "medicinal waters" did little to stave off hunger.

By contrast, life back home was far more luxurious. Her father was always bringing fine things home from his travels—nougat, honey, candied violets, and more. No one had to fear going hungry in their house, that was certain.

The aroma of fresh coffee wafted across the gravel path they were walking along. And the cakes that the serving girls brought out on white plates looked delicious. Flora's mouth watered.

While Friedrich led her onward, Flora turned her head back for a final, almost envious, look. On the outermost edge of the many tables, she noticed one party of guests at a single long table. Three waitresses bustled around the group, carrying heavily laden trays. The women at the table wore brightly colored garments and raised their glasses with bejeweled hands for a toast to the gentlemen. One elderly woman was feeding her little dog a spoonful of whipped cream—how unpleasant!

Flora touched Friedrich's arm and drew his attention to the group. "Where are those people from? They seem to be speaking several different languages."

"Russians, most likely. Many of them speak excellent French," he said.

Flora raised her eyebrows. Her guide really seemed to have an answer to everything.

Her parents would have felt at home among all the vibrant activity. Flora pictured her father sitting beneath one of the huge chestnut trees, drinking beer, while her mother sipped a glass of wine. Her parents would not have begrudged themselves that.

"Your visitors all seem so cheerful—it makes you want to talk and laugh along with them. And they're all so beautifully dressed. Just look!" Flora pointed toward three little girls trotting along clumsily beside their governess. Their dresses were made of layers of lace, with countless colorful glass beads sewn on. But in such elaborate outfits, they could not jump puddles, shoot marbles, or even dance in a circle properly.

Flora was still caught up in that thought when the smallest of the three girls suddenly pulled free of the governess's hand and charged off toward one of the swans that had settled on the grass some distance away.

"Lebed! Lebed! Lebed!" the child cried over and over while the governess seemed rooted to the spot in sudden fright. She had both hands pressed over her mouth and watched wide-eyed as the other two girls joined in the chorus of "*Lebed!*" and ran toward the swans.

Why didn't the governess run after them? She must know that swans could easily turn aggressive. Flora quickly moved to block the two other girls while the swan suddenly rose to its feet and hissed anxiously.

"Friedrich, the swan has cygnets!" Flora pointed urgently in the direction of the small flock that had appeared from beneath the swan's spread wings.

Friedrich was already running.

Beating its wings wildly and with its beak open wide, the large bird launched itself at the smallest child, while its babies peeped and waddled away in all directions.

The little girl stopped in her tracks, and not another sound came from her lips. For a moment, Flora hoped that the bird, confronted by the child's defenselessness, would change its mind. But it was not to be: the swan was already pecking at the girl, who instantly curled up on the ground, squealing.

The next moment, Friedrich snatched the girl up and set her down on her feet; the governess, who had finally broken out of her daze, picked her up and carried her to safety.

Flora could only watch helplessly as Friedrich became the target of the swan's ire.

"At least it wasn't my fault this time," said Flora in a squeaky voice, pointing to Friedrich's trouser leg. Where the swan had attacked him, there was a new tear. A little blood seeped through the fabric, but he assured Flora that the injury was nothing.

Flora realized that her knees were shaking. She knew well that an attack by an angry swan could have had far worse consequences than a torn trouser leg. Relieved that nothing more serious had happened, she took Friedrich's arm again.

"I would say that your act of heroism has earned us a little rest."

A short time later, they were sitting on the terrace at the Englischer Hof hotel. Friedrich's eyes were bright with the excitement of his wrangle with the bird, and his cheeks were red. To Flora he no longer looked sallow and unhealthy, but very manly indeed.

While Friedrich ordered the light lunch and a half carafe of wine, Flora inconspicuously stretched her legs beneath the table. Finally!

All the impressions of the morning, capped by the incident with the swan, had worn her out more than any day's tramp across fields and meadows.

When the waitress had poured the wine, they clinked glasses.

"I don't really fit in here at all," she said, turning to take in all the tables with their white tablecloths, the fine chandeliers inside, and all the elegantly dressed patrons.

"The Englischer Hof is certainly among Baden-Baden's better hotels. I don't normally come here myself, but today is a noteworthy day, isn't it? Besides, I would like to take the opportunity, in this special place, to thank you for all you have done with Father's shop in such a short time. The trees in front of the door, the nice porcelain—my mother would never have thought to bring that up from the cellar on her own. Practically every day, I hear from people on the street how much lovelier everything looks now."

"I'm happy to hear it." Flora took a good mouthful of the wine. "But—" She broke off, because the waitress had just brought two plates of the finest-looking bread she had ever seen: slivers of hard-boiled egg delicately garnished with a pink mayonnaise covered two slices of bread with the crusts trimmed off, and on the side were tiny flowers carved from radishes.

"My goodness, *this* is the 'light lunch'?" Flora whispered when the waitress had left again. "This is very different from a slice of bread topped with a bit of sausage or *Speck*," she said. "Even the bread is special in Baden-Baden . . ."

"Try it!"

Flora followed his lead and bit hungrily into the bread.

"What do you mean by special?" Friedrich mumbled, his mouth half-full.

"From what I've seen today, it seems to me that there are two worlds here. There's our world, where the people do their daily work and eat bread and *Speck*," *or bread with no Speck at all*, she thought to herself. "And then there's the world of the rich, who give their horses baths and eat fancy light lunches." Flora shook her head.

As she spoke, Friedrich picked up his napkin and dabbed mayonnaise from one corner of his mouth.

"You're absolutely right. And I believe that in other spa towns, like Karlsbad and Marienbad, the visitors and the locals also lead very different lives." He picked up his glass and looked at her over the rim. "Would you prefer it if a few of the people around us came to our front room at home every evening and played cards?"

"That would be something new, wouldn't it?" said Flora with a laugh. "But they could at least find their way to the shop."

Friedrich sniffed. "They've got eyes for nothing but Maison Kuttner with all its pomp and—"

"Maison Kuttner! I can't hear that name anymore," she said so loudly that a lady at the next table frowned and turned toward them. Flora gave her an apologetic smile and went on more quietly, but with no less insistence.

"Our shop is nothing for them to turn their noses up at! It's roomy, it's bright—if only the location were a little better. There are just a few hundred steps separating us from . . . from wealth."

Friedrich's brow furrowed. "You're right, of course, but what can we do about it? And besides, it isn't so bad. Father says that business was good last week, and his customers have been very happy with their meadow flowers. And when the flowers from the garden come in summer, all the better."

All well and good, but what the shop brings in is far from enough to live a decent life, Flora thought. Then her mother's words came back to her: *"In Reutlingen, your enthusiasm did not just make you friends . . . And even if the way they do things is not always to your taste, well, keep that to yourself."*

"I'm sorry. Forget what I said," she murmured with an embarrassed shrug. But then she blurted, "It just makes me mad that all the spa guests run to Maison Kuttner and your own father has no well-to-do customers at all."

Friedrich reached between the bread plates and wineglasses for Flora's hand. "I don't have the slightest idea what we could do to change that. Perhaps I could ask if I could put up an advertisement for the shop at the Trinkhalle? I must say I would feel a little uncomfortable with it, but . . ."

Flora was surprised when he held her hand, but she found his grasp pleasantly warm. "That's not a bad idea at all. Though even if we succeeded in getting the spa visitors into the shop, I don't know what rich people want. I realized that very clearly today. Since I've seen all of this"—Flora looked left and right, acknowledging everything around them—"I feel like more of a stranger than ever. The Englischer Hof, the Holländer Hof, the Französische Hof—Baden-Baden has just the right place for any traveler to feel at home. The Russians have their favorite places, the English too; every group has its idiosyncrasies."

"Is our Swabian girl feeling apprehensive?"

"You're making fun of me!" she snapped.

"Not in the slightest," Friedrich said with a smile. He held her hand more firmly. "But I wonder if we shouldn't at least *try* to find out what our honored guests might like? I mean, it doesn't matter where you buy them, flowers are flowers, aren't they? There can't be that much difference."

"Well, we're not going to impress the rich with the wildflowers I pick. They're more likely to be interested in unusual flowers," Flora said. "But that aside, your father would be horrified to hear us talking like this. It's *his* shop."

Friedrich was still holding her hand. *Isn't it unbecoming, him doing that among all these people?* Flora wondered. She pulled her hand free and reached for her wineglass.

Friedrich exhaled loudly. "It's important to me, too, that Mother and Father earn a better livelihood than they have so far. Mother would be a lot happier if she didn't have to count every kreuzer twice. She doesn't complain about it, but . . ." He waved it off. "It's certainly worth a try, don't you think?"

Flora felt a light flutter in her belly. Could they really get new customers into the shop in the short time she would still be there? Or to put it another way: What did they have to lose?

And Friedrich would help her . . . The fluttering in her belly grew a little more intense.

She set her wineglass down, reached across the table, and took Friedrich's hand in hers. "All right, it's worth a try!"

Chapter Nineteen

As much as Friedrich enjoyed the time he spent with Flora, he could not clear his mind of all the worries that beset him during the summer of 1871. Though the streets and cafés of the town were still very lively, it was easy to see that since the war, there were fewer visitors to the spa complex, and that meant less income. And while the guests might not notice that cuts were already being made, Friedrich, who was intimately familiar with the town, saw the signs: here a moldering park bench that had not been replaced, and there, flower beds that were not being planted. The leaseholder of the casino had also reduced Friedrich's budget for the maintenance of the Trinkhalle for the season. He could still get by, but what if, one day, someone decided the Trinkhalle was no longer viable and simply closed it?

Friedrich's anxiety only increased when a rumor started circulating that the new government in Berlin was planning to close all the gaming houses in the empire. He silently regarded everyone who threw their money away at the gaming tables with cynicism, but what would Baden-Baden be without its casino? Some claimed that it would be just another forgotten Black Forest village, but others believed it would become a town on its way to becoming a true spa destination. With sick people, too—or rather, with their hopes for a cure—there was also good money to be made.

Friedrich had not yet formed his own opinion on the matter. If there was no more leaseholder for the casino—and therefore also for the Trinkhalle—then what would become of him? Would he really go onto the town payroll now that municipal funds were so short? Questions were already being raised about how the fund that had supported the spa since 1850 would be replenished in the future.

Many of the big names in German politics also stayed away that year, although the artists still came, at least: painters, writers, and musicians, even Johann Strauss, "the Waltz King" himself, gave concerts in Baden-Baden that year.

Still, anyone whose livelihood depended on the town's spa and casino spent the summer worried that their jobs might suddenly disappear.

Although he did not normally get out of the Trinkhalle before eight, Friedrich and Flora had gotten into the habit of going for a walk in the evenings.

"Are you really sure you're not too tired?" Flora asked the first few times. "I could go out with Sabine, too."

But Friedrich insisted that it would be a great pleasure for him to go out with her for a stroll, and thus began a ritual that, soon, neither of them wanted to do without.

As the summer advanced, instead of the activity of the tourist areas, they sought the quiet of the small area of parkland behind the Trinkhalle, where the birds in the sequoias twittered their evening songs, the bees buzzed, and they felt as if they were far out in the countryside.

In the evening hours, everything there had a special radiance. The wooden backs of the park benches still held the warmth of the day. The air carried the fresh scent of forgotten laundry hanging on a line in a garden, which mixed with the perfume of the well-dressed women out for their own evening strolls. And Friedrich put his arm around Flora and told her the names of the more exotic trees and bushes in the park.

Flora would have liked to go to the Conversationshaus with Friedrich and drink a glass of wine, or go to one of the open-air concerts more often. How was she supposed to find out more about the wealthy visitors and what they might be looking for if she was never able to get close to them?

But at the end of the day, Friedrich was often so tired that he wanted nothing more than to get away from all that turmoil, for which she could hardly blame him. She, too, some evenings, felt utterly exhausted, although at the start she had no idea *why* she was so tired. Every day, there were long periods when not a single customer came their way. It took some time for Flora to realize that it was those times when no one was there that were wearing her out so much. She would have been a thousand times happier if the shop was crowded and noisy as a dovecote. But so far, neither she nor Friedrich had had an idea about how to attract more doves.

It was not only Flora's closeness to Friedrich that grew from day to day, but also her attachment to Baden-Baden. Soon she felt very much at home in the town.

Thanks to the seeds her father had sent along, the Sonnenscheins' garden was in full midsummer bloom, and as a result the shop offered an abundance of flowers. Lavender-colored bellflowers, deep-purple zinnias, colorful coleus, petunias, and more—the Gönningen seeds had lived up to the promise made by the seed dealers to their customers.

She could have made the most beautiful bouquets for the spa visitors, flower baskets for their children, and floral decorations for their magnificent coaches as well. But the spa visitors and their staff continued to go to Maison Kuttner, and Flora doubted they were aware that the Sonnenschein shop even existed.

One hand pressed to her breast, Ernestine wandered through the house. Her heart was beating so hard that she thought it might burst out of her chest.

Today was the big day. They would be arriving in an hour. One after the other.

Heavens! What had she let herself in for? Didn't she have enough to do already? She could no longer imagine at all that it had been her idea to invite some friends for an afternoon of coffee and cake.

Gretel, Luise, and the other women were looking forward to it so much—because, of course, *they* did not have to do any of the work. For days, whenever she bumped into one or the other of them in Else Walbusch's store or on the street, the talk was always about the coffee afternoon. Gretel had even asked if she could bring her sister, who was visiting Baden-Baden just then. And Luise's newly married daughter wanted to come, too.

Strangers. Two guests more than originally planned . . . and they all would walk through the main house. She had to sleep in the bed she had made.

She had already been out to check the summerhouse. Sabine had set the table very nicely, and pitchers of lemonade were prepared. She would bring the coffee and cake from the kitchen once the women had taken their places around the table. That was how Ernestine had planned it.

Now, in the front room of the main house, the flower arrangement on a lace doily in the center of the sideboard caught her eye. Blue cornflowers and some pink blooms she did not know the name of and white baby's breath.

More of Flora's handiwork. Did Kuno have any idea how often the girl pilfered flowers from the shop for their house? Weren't they losing sales like that?

Ernestine's nostrils flared. It smelled so good in here! And the sideboard looked lovely with the bouquet of flowers. But where did that vase come from? She did not recognize it at all . . .

With a frown, Ernestine pushed the flowers aside a little. Flora had actually put the bouquet in a soup tureen—had anyone ever seen anything like it?

It was the one with the chipped rim, probably the result of some inattention by Sabine. Ernestine had been quite annoyed when she had discovered the damage a few days before. The tureen was an old piece she had inherited from her mother.

A smile crept over Ernestine's face, and then she let out a little laugh. The mass of flowers that formed the bouquet hung over the edge of the tureen in such a way that the damage was out of sight.

She relaxed a little. Everything looked somehow brighter and more welcoming than it usually did. Was it the tablecloth? Or the bouquet? Or was it the fragrance of verbena and mallow wafting in through the half-open window? Maybe it was just the beautiful weather.

Ernestine let out a deep sigh. If she were to be honest with herself, she was looking forward a little to her coffee circle. Everyone was sure to like Sabine's nut cake, and the little tartlets she had baked were lovely to look at.

When her guests began to arrive, Ernestine's heart once again began to beat a touch faster, but this time less from anxiety and restlessness, and more in anticipation.

"Do you hear all that cackling?" Kuno jabbed his chin in the direction of the garden. "It's always the same. You get two women together, and they natter on like you've never heard before." He shook his head and laid aside his *Die Gartenlaube*, the magazine that the mailman had brought earlier. Once he had read the chapter of the serialized novel that he looked forward to every week, the other members of the family could read whatever they wanted.

"It sounds as if the ladies are having a nice time. Your wife—" Flora stopped talking when the doorbell to the shop tinkled. It was Gretel Grün, the pharmacist's wife.

"Kuno—can you imagine?" Gretel began. "My sister called your garden a 'wellspring of calm'! She was quite amazed at how stylishly we can do things here in Baden-Baden. Living in Stuttgart, she seems to think she's the only one in the world with good taste." She pursed her lips in an expression of such extreme disapproval that a thousand tiny creases formed above them.

"I'm pleased to know everyone is enjoying it," said Kuno.

"I don't remember your garden ever looking so lovely, to be frank. As I said to Ernestine earlier, we need to make this coffee afternoon a regular weekly thing. And now I'd like to have a bouquet just like the one you have in your summerhouse." She was already taking out her purse.

Kuno's face lit up. "Flora tied that bouquet, you know. I'm sure she'd be glad—"

"And it's really very lovely," Gretel interrupted him. "But I would still prefer *you* make my bouquet."

Although Ernestine was thoroughly worn out afterward and swore she would not be inviting anyone again soon, the women returned to the Sonnenscheins' garden for coffee the very next week—her friends had simply talked her into doing it again!

It was the end of July, and the garden looked gorgeous. The sun-warmed air was heavy with the scent of the different flowers. The almost aphrodisiac aroma of the phlox clusters mixed with the delicate perfume of the old rosebushes, while peppermint and thyme lent the air a slightly peppery note.

Ernestine's friends were intoxicated by it all. "This air!" they cried. "These colors! The abundance of it all!" Almost every one of them marched into the flower shop afterward and went home with a fat bouquet.

For Flora, the stream of new customers had a bitter taste: hardly any of Ernestine's friends were willing to let Flora bind a bouquet for them. How was she supposed to develop as a florist?

At least Kuno let her get all the practice she wanted when they were alone. Spherical Biedermeier bouquets, decorative vases, posies—over time, she learned more and more techniques. Her finished works were then placed in water and sold. No one needed to know that Flora was the one who made them.

Flora was overjoyed to see the painter's maid, Greta, come to the store again. Her master, Mr. Winterhalter, had found the first bouquet quite lovely, and a picture commissioned by the noblewoman was taking shape, but until it was finished several bouquets were going to be required.

Flora set to work eagerly each time the painter sent for a new one—if it had been up to her, his painting would have been a monumental work that would take decades to complete, for which dozens and dozens of bouquets would be needed.

Chapter Twenty

"I'm telling you, nothing will come of Flora and the young master . . ." Sabine sighed lavishly. Then she raised her beer glass and clinked it against her friend Minka's.

At eight in the evening, it was still unusually hot in the town, and the two young women had agreed spontaneously to treat themselves to a refreshing glass of beer at The Gilded Rose. They had spent the entire day sweating—Sabine in the kitchen at the Sonnenschein house and Minka in the laundry at the Englischer Hof—so they enjoyed even more the luxury of a free hour and a bit of gossip. Because the waiter at The Gilded Rose was an old friend of Minka's, they had high hopes for a free refill of beer. But so far the proprietress had kept an eagle eye on the women and the waiter.

"Really? You really think Flora and Friedrich won't amount to anything? Can't you already hear the wedding bells ringing?" Minka looked up from her glass with disappointment. "You can't just rob me of all my illusions! I mean, that a fine young man like Friedrich Sonnenschein would take one of us as his wife, it's what we all dream about, isn't it?"

Sabine nodded grumpily. "But it doesn't look like that particular dream is going to be fulfilled. Flora always says that I read too much into their evening strolls, but . . ."

Minka nodded. "The poor thing! I'm sure she's inconsolable not to have her love returned—"

"*Her* love? Don't be ridiculous! Flora acts as if none of it has anything to do with her. I asked her whether the young master had already kissed her, and she just about throttled me. If you think she'd go out of her way to win him as a husband, then you'd better think twice. She hasn't got even an ounce of coquette in her, that one. Doesn't even bother to dress herself up when the young master takes her out. She does my hair up beautifully whenever I meet Moritz, but she doesn't go to any trouble with her own."

As expected, Minka shared Sabine's disapproval. "Well, I for one would be making eyes at him all day if I had half a chance, I'll tell you that. And I'd do it until he had no choice but to fall in love with me."

"But if Friedrich was serious about Flora, he would have to court her at least a little, wouldn't he? Bring her a little gift now and then, like Moritz does for me. Look, he sewed together this flower for me." Sabine proudly puffed out her chest, where a flower made of leftover shirt silk was pinned to her dress.

When Minka had admired it sufficiently, Sabine went on with her litany. "But Flora has never received a thing from Friedrich. When he takes her out, all they do is walk through town. Or sit in the garden. Flora said just yesterday that she can practically greet every blade of grass out there by name. If it were up to her, the young master would at least invite her out for an occasional glass of wine. Or maybe for a dance. And she wants to visit the casino, too, before she goes home."

"The casino?" asked Minka in disbelief. "And dancing? Is she completely mad? That's for the finer types around here."

"Oh, Flora has no fear of the rich. A few weeks ago, she had a squabble with the snobby witches at Maison Kuttner, and left them looking very dazed indeed, apparently."

Minka giggled. "That just makes me like your Flora more. I'd love to get to know her. Why didn't you bring her along?"

Sabine shook her head. "I asked her if she wanted to come tonight, but she said she had other plans. She's got a bee in her bonnet about getting more *distinguished* customers into the shop," she said, and the two friends laughed loudly at that bit of lunacy. "Flora is currently going around visiting one *distinguished* shop after the other, and she went out again tonight, too. She's been to the *parfumerie*, the glovemaker's, and even to the hat shop beside the Palais Hamilton. Everyone knows that the saleswomen in those shops think they're better than us just because of where they work."

Minka nodded. "They'll shoo you away if you so much as look in their window for too long. But how can Flora afford to go to all those expensive places? Does she have a donkey that craps ducats for her?"

"Oh, she doesn't buy anything. She just wants to see how other businesses deal with their customers, for ideas for the flower shop." Sabine shrugged. "That's just the way Flora is. Whatever she does, all she has in mind is the business."

"Then she shouldn't be surprised if nothing ever comes of finding a husband," Minka said. It was a thought that had crossed Sabine's mind, as well.

"It's strange. I really can't imagine that Flora won't be here anymore in just a few weeks." Kuno rustled the newspaper loudly as he lowered it.

"Neither can I. I've grown very used to having her around," Ernestine agreed without looking up from her embroidery at Kuno. She eyed the basket of thread critically—should she do the next tendril in a lighter green or a somewhat darker tone?

"Schierstiefel talked me into going for a beer with him at lunchtime. When I shilly-shallied a little, he told me the shop was in good hands with Flora."

Now Ernestine looked up. "You, drinking at lunchtime?"

Kuno shrugged. "Why not? It was very interesting in The Gilded Rose, too. You would not believe how excited some of the people there get when they talk about Bismarck and the emperor. Flora says her father would go off for a drink like that all the time. And also that, now that the war is over, one has to enjoy life a little bit." He reassembled his newspaper elaborately.

Ernestine reached for the bowl of raspberries that Flora had picked that morning. The fruit was deliciously sweet and a real treat. Oh!— despite all her care, a drop of raspberry juice landed on the handkerchief she was embroidering for Flora.

"When Flora's gone, I can forget about taking my midday naps, though they've done wonders for my health," said Kuno.

"You'll still be able to take your naps. Just close up the shop, like you used to," said Ernestine, and glared at the damaged piece in her hands. Should she try to wash it out right away or finish embroidering the flower first?

"But I can't just close up the shop anymore." Kuno gave his wife a reproachful look, which she did not see because she was concentrating on embroidering a pink flower over the spot of raspberry juice.

"People really do seem to be getting over the war, gradually," Kuno added. "My own spirits are very good! And I hope the people around here manage to hold on to their taste for beautiful things for a while."

"You can mostly thank Flora for that 'taste for beautiful things,' you know," Ernestine replied. "When I look at how she's transformed your old junk room out front . . . I just think about the porcelain." She held her breath. Would Kuno finally find the words of praise she had hoped for? Many of the vases, bowls, and figurines had been sold, after all, and at good prices, too.

Kuno proved himself full of praise, in fact, but not for Ernestine. "The girl certainly has a wonderful imagination, though I'm not saying I like everything she comes up with. A little more reserve would certainly be more appropriate now and then. But I can't understand her parents' fears that she might embarrass herself in front of her Reutlinger master. She's a natural talent. I just hope the people there know to appreciate it." He paused for a moment. When he spoke again, his voice had a somewhat abashed tone.

"There's something I've been meaning to ask . . . Do you think that Flora likes it here, in our family?"

If she likes it? In the family? What was Kuno going on about? "Of course she does," said Ernestine. "Just today I let her borrow my favorite painting from the dining room. She wanted to re-create the still life of flowers and fruit for the front window of the shop. Has she done that?"

Kuno nodded. "Friedrich thinks it's a little overwrought."

Ernestine's brow furrowed as she put her needle and thread aside. "Well, now, if it had been *me* who came up with an idea like that, you would have packed me off to an asylum. But that girl can do whatever she likes with you." She shrugged. "Our Friedrich is sometimes more old-fashioned than you."

They both laughed. Kuno then asked, "What is going on with Friedrich and Flora?" He now had the bowl of raspberries on his lap and was popping them into his mouth with gusto.

"If you're afraid that Friedrich would behave at all disrespectfully toward Flora, I can put your mind at ease," said Ernestine. "I admit I had certain fears myself, at the start. All those long walks, his helping out in the garden . . . Luise and Gretel have been teasing me constantly about church bells ringing soon. But I think they're wrong."

There was a touch of disappointment in her voice. If she were to be honest with herself, the thought of her son tying the knot with Kuno's apprentice was far less unsettling than it once had been. On the contrary . . . Of course, one had to make sure that common decency was preserved, but the one did not preclude the other, did it?

She took the bowl of raspberries that Kuno held out to her and sought out a particularly delicious-looking specimen. "The boy's been the very picture of respectability."

Kuno's expression darkened noticeably at Ernestine's last words.

"The picture of respectability—I think I'd find another way to put it. If Friedrich lets that girl go, he's a damn fool!"

※

"My beloved Flora!" Friedrich's voice was no more than a croak. He opened the top button of his shirt—it felt as if something was cutting off his air. He cleared his throat. *Start again.*

"My dear, esteemed Miss Kerner." No, that sounded far too stilted. He took a deep breath and opened the left door of the wardrobe, where a mirror was affixed. With one hand on his chest, he lowered himself onto one knee.

"Dearest Flora . . ." No, going down on one knee felt contrived. He sighed and stood up again.

Standing, then. "Dear Flora . . ." Yes, that would work. "You and I . . ." He bit his bottom lip. What came next?

Blast it, why was it so difficult to admit his feelings to Flora? He found her delightful beyond measure, but why could he not simply tell her that? She was so pretty and natural and almost always had a smile on her lips. Of course, she could get quite furious at times, too, but he was enthralled by her even in those moments . . . and the way her brow furrowed when she was concentrating on something!

He was probably approaching the whole thing wrong. It would be better to give her a few compliments instead of just blurting out what he felt.

"Dear Flora, when I'm around you, I feel like the happiest man in the world." That didn't sound bad at all, and it was the truth.

What if she just laughed at him? She hadn't heard anything of that nature from him at all. For her, he was most likely just a good friend.

But that had to change. He wanted to marry her, and before too long. He was twenty-five, after all. If he did not find the courage to admit his feelings to Flora soon, she would return to her village and all would be lost. No kisses and no embraces.

Panic overcame Friedrich, and he paced back and forth in his room like a caged tiger. It was not only that he could not find the words, but also that he had no idea *where* he should propose to Flora. Women usually had a rather pronounced sense of romance, so . . . what would be romantic?

Friedrich stopped his pacing and gazed out the window.

Why was this so hard for him? Was it too early for a proposal of marriage—was that it? Wouldn't he be better off just asking Flora if she would like to stay on awhile longer? Then, over time, everything would happen more or less by itself.

And it was not as if he hadn't already suggested that to her.

They had been in the garden, and Flora had been pulling out weeds. He had watched her as he smoked his pipe. And somehow, their conversation—as so often—came back to the store. Flora had told him that she still had so many ideas flying around in her mind for decorating the front window, and that her time there was running out. And she had looked so sad that Friedrich had simply had to ask her, "Then why don't you just stay? Write to your mother and tell her that my father is not completely back on his feet yet, and . . ." He had taken Flora's hand in his and squeezed it as he spoke. "Wouldn't that be a good idea?"

"No." Flora had shaken her head fiercely. "I won't lie to my parents."

And Friedrich, embarrassed, withdrew his hand. "You're right. Please excuse my stupid suggestion. What I actually wanted to say . . . well, I—"

"Stupid?" Flora laughed hoarsely. "Do you think I haven't already thought of doing just that a dozen times already? The thought of leaving almost breaks my heart."

It's the same for me. I can't imagine and don't want to imagine a life without you in it! Friedrich had wanted to say, but all he had managed to get out was "It is not as if you'll be gone forever. You'll come back to our lovely town in the future, I'm sure. As a seed trader."

He slammed the wardrobe door, furious at himself. As if that was anything like the same thing! He did not want to have Flora in his memory as a brief acquaintance. He wanted to love her.

In good times and in bad, forever and ever.

Chapter Twenty-One

Princess Irina Komatschova gazed out the window of her suite at the Hotel Stéphanie les Bains.

Three more days and August would be over. How the days flew past, faster than the horses at the racetrack.

After the first cooler nights, the leaves of the enormous chestnut trees were slowly changing from green to yellow. Here and there, a single leaf was already sailing earthward. It had rained overnight. The small tables on the hotel terrace were abandoned, and she knew the proprietor of the restaurant would not be putting out tablecloths or cutlery that day. On mornings like these, the guests preferred to take breakfast inside, where it was warm. But Irina had no appetite, either for an omelet or anything else.

She hated these days, no longer part of summer but not yet truly autumn. They spread a strange kind of melancholy that was not good for her. Irina shook herself like a bird shaking water from its feathers.

At fifty-three, the princess was still an attractive woman. And she was shrewd and spirited, too—as a simple country girl, would she ever have landed the great Nikolajev Komatschov otherwise?

It had, admittedly, been a loveless marriage. When it became clear that she was not able to give her husband any children, he had quickly lost all interest in her. Tokens of affection? Compliments? She had only ever received those from other men.

Life at Nikolajev's side had been hard. Her wealth helped, of course. Nikolajev's death five years earlier and her inheritance of half the Crimean Peninsula had made her one of the richest women in Russia. At least in death he had been generous.

Wealth bestowed security. Money was good against fear.

And yet . . .

If only there wasn't the constant talk of rebellion in her homeland! Of rampaging serfs, of farmers who, instead of doing their work, demanded more money, more rights—who had ever heard of such a thing?

Every day, Irina went to her mailbox in the hotel, and every time, she held her breath as she flicked through the letters and cards. She was able to relax only if she found no bad news from home, neither a fire in her gem mines nor a revolt on one of her estates.

What if the seemingly endless river of money dried up one day? *That* was what instilled in her a fear of falling back into the poverty that she remembered only too well from her childhood.

She stared as if numb at the pile of bills on the small table in front of her. So many! And the season was not even over.

Some of them were silly, little bills from a restaurant here or there, a hairdresser, or the confectionery store with the wonderful pralines. There was a rather grimy invoice for the coach that she had rented for the entire season, and now the man, a farmer with a leering grin, wanted part of his payment in advance.

"Poshel k chertu!" He could go to the devil! Irina sniffed with contempt. He could stand on one leg and dance and make his two old nags do the same, but he would get his money only at the start of October, when the season drew to an end.

Irina was shocked to see how much money she had lavished this season on the excursions that she and Kostia had made in the Black

Forest. And then there were the bills for the countless gifts they had taken along! When one was invited to visit Prince Menshikov, one could not merely take along a *bonbonnière*, oh no. One had to take a gift more appropriate to the prince's station. The same was true for the visits to Matriona Schikanova, or dear Anna or the Gagarins—Princess Isabella appreciated receiving expensive French porcelain from her guests, though the cabinets at her villa in the city were already overflowing with the stuff.

Invitations, naturally, also meant return invitations.

For years, Irina had gotten into the habit of setting herself up as a hostess at the start of each new season. The last thing she wanted was a reputation as a sponger, happy enough to enjoy a party at someone else's cost, but never arranging anything herself. Her summer party that year, in fact, had been celebrated in grand style on the terraces of the Hotel Stéphanie—Konstantin had persuaded her to hire a band, and that invoice, like all the rest, had not yet been paid.

On the other hand—Irina scratched a wavy pattern into a misted window with one fingernail—it would be even worse not to get invitations at all anymore. To be cast out from the upper reaches of the Russian aristocracy. A nobody, unrecognizable.

She and her charming young companion, however, were welcome wherever they went. Everyone liked Konstantin—his laugh, his mad ideas, his perpetual good mood.

Irina frowned with confusion when she noticed a bill for her suite. Hadn't she agreed with the hotelier to pay for everything at the end of the season? Were installment payments some kind of new fashion?

"Durák!" The simpleton!

There were rumors that the Hotel Stéphanie was not doing well at all. There was talk of a frantic search for a buyer to renovate and modernize the crumbling building. Irina could only hope that the rumors had no substance. The hotel was still affordable. She had to admit that, if one looked carefully, it was easy to find places that needed attention, and the water was almost always ice-cold from the spigot, although the hotelier boasted of being an adherent of the so-called curative baths—what a travesty!

Irina's hand flicked through the air as if she were chasing away an annoying insect. Who cared about such trivial things? When it came down to it, they were in the hotel only to sleep, and sometimes not even that. So why did she have to pay such horrendous sums?

Yes, she brooded over everything she spent. But was it any wonder, with the constant fear that gnawed at her?

It was a mystery to Irina how Püppi and the others could live for the moment. Almost every day she heard stories about Russian farmers who burned down their master's barn, or ran off, or stole the livestock, and whose bad behavior was stirred up by political rabble-rousers—cretins who sat around in universities and came up with idiotic ideas just to keep the commoners from doing their work.

"But that's what we have our overseers for," Püppi had said in bewilderment the one time that Irina had dared to air her fears. "That's why we pay them to pull out their whip if they have to."

Irina laughed bitterly. And what happens if those overseers also start getting funny ideas in their heads?

Thankfully, she had not let anyone talk her into buying the house up on the mountain. In her present state, it would have been just another thing to worry about.

Konstantin had liked the house, and she found it moving that he really wanted to have a "nest" for the two of them.

She looked over toward the bedroom, and for the first time that morning, her expression softened.

Dear, sweet Konstantin . . .

She would never have thought that life might still have a great love in store.

He slept so soundly! Like an infant that has drunk its fill at its mother's breast. *He* had no sense of fear at all. Dear, dear Konstantin—only youth could be so guileless and carefree.

"You're right, dear Irina," he had said, when she turned down the house. "So high up on the hill, we would be quite far away from everything. From the Hotel Stéphanie, everything is close and easy to reach, even at your age . . ."

For a moment, Irina had been uncertain whether she should find his remark insulting. Did Kostia really think she was no longer strong enough to walk up a hill? But then she had seen the look in his eyes, full of love and concern.

Irina had not told Konstantin the true reason for saying no to buying the house. Nor had she informed him that, if the situation did not deteriorate, she was planning to buy a house the following season, but a far larger one. *If* she was going to keep a home in Baden-Baden, then it would have to be large and appropriately stylish. Konstantin would then have not only a room of his own, but the entire *bel étage* for his art. He gave most generously of his feelings, and she did not want to be petty in return.

But it was an undeniable fact that her young lover was already an expensive luxury. He loved roulette almost as much as he loved cards. But could she deny him those small pleasures, especially as he neglected his painting for her sake? Everything in life had its price.

"Around four weeks from now—on September thirtieth, to be exact—Kaiserin Augusta will be celebrating her birthday, and I have been invited again as I am every year," said Irina when she and Konstantin were sitting at breakfast two hours later. While Konstantin wolfed down a plate of eggs, Irina's gaze kept wandering out through the window into the late-summer garden. "Have I ever mentioned that the kaiserin and I are related? Far, far removed, of course, but I still like to be a little more extravagant with a gift." Irina pushed the cup of now-cold coffee away in disgust and reached for her champagne glass. "But I would also be only too happy not to go to the party, because it signals the end of the season, which means 'adieu, Baden-Baden.'"

"Why are you so gloomy today?" Konstantin asked. "There will be a new season next year! It's up to us to make the most we can of the winter, too! Irina, *mon amour*, what do you feel like doing? Would you like to go to the sea? What about London? You know I will go anywhere with you. Or what about Monte Carlo? Piotr says that the casino there has been open again for a long time now that the war is over. Irina, when I picture you strolling along the promenade at Monte Carlo in a frilly snow-white dress, a parasol in your hand, the silver handle shining in the glow of the setting sun, the sea, so blue . . . turquoise and azure, and almost green in places—what a sight for a painter!"

Irina laughed, interrupting his raptures. "Now stop it. You're making my mouth water! Monte Carlo . . . not this year. I fear you won't much like my next destination." Irina let out a deep sigh. *Now don't make yourself sound like an old mourner,* she reproved herself silently, and she straightened her back. It was better for Kostia to know. "Konstantin, my dear, I want to pay my estates a visit this winter, and make sure that everything is in order."

"You want to go to . . . Russia?" His eyes were as round as marbles; he looked as bewildered as a child who has just been told that a long-promised outing won't be taking place.

Irina shrugged apologetically. "Crimea in winter has little to recommend it. So I will be much happier knowing you are there with me. With a man at my side, the unpleasant inspections I have to make will, I hope, be a little faster and a little easier. And there will be a few bright spots, too. Visits to relatives and—"

"Visits to relatives," said Konstantin in a tone of voice he might have used for "criminals" or "lepers." He frowned. "Irina darling, when are you planning to pull up stakes?"

"I haven't set an actual date yet," she said, taking out a diary bound in white leather. "What about October second? The Saturday before that is Kaiserin Augusta's birthday celebration. We could have everything packed on Sunday and leave on Monday."

Konstantin chewed on his lip for a moment, then took a deep breath and nodded slowly. "So about four weeks until we leave. Well, we'd better make good use of the time," he murmured.

Irina laughed. "Oh, we will, my darling!"

Chapter Twenty-Two

At the end of August, on one of her walks through the meadows alongside Lichtenthaler Allee, Flora noticed a bright splash of violet for the first time—the first autumn crocuses. She quickly turned her back on them.

They were the only flowers that Flora had never liked. Ever since she was a little girl, her mother had drummed into her never to pick the harmless-looking but highly toxic flowers.

That was not the only reason Flora did not find the flowers very lovely. The sight of them was enough to awaken a wistfulness in her, because they were a sign that summer would soon fade. Then the wind would blow across the stubble in the fields, and the land would look barren and dull where cornflowers had stood just a few weeks before.

Flora put the final weeks—before nature gave itself over to hibernation—to good use. Like a squirrel stocking up its supply of nuts, she went out every day and gathered supplies for winter: nicely formed branches, rose hips, thistles, and all sorts of berries and aromatic herbs. She even collected empty snail shells and took them home with her. Soon, from hooks in the shed that was built on to the summerhouse and from the ceiling in the shop itself hung not only many, many bundles of herbs to dry, but hundreds of different flowers and grasses.

"Child, what am I supposed to do with *these*?" Kuno asked, picking up one of the striped snail shells. But all in all, he was overjoyed at the booty Flora brought back with her from her expeditions, because he had decided to try again with dried flowers that winter. Of course, he also planned to order fresh flowers from more southern regions, but those were sinfully expensive, making a good supply of dried plants and flowers very helpful indeed.

Flora thought it a wonderful idea, and as much as she'd enjoyed gathering all the raw materials, she would also have loved to be there when Kuno's skilled hands created art from a few thistles and leafy vines. By then, though, she would be long gone, and once again standing in her parents' packing room, filling seed orders.

"Just look what she's humping around today—more thistles!"

Flora pressed her teeth together. She did not want to spoil her last Saturday in Baden-Baden by getting into a fight with the brainless little witches at Maison Kuttner. "Thistles! Oh my god! As if she wasn't prickly enough already."

"And look—she's been snipping bits off fir trees, too. Is it Christmas already?" asked one.

"I can't wait to see what she drags home in winter—ice flowers, most likely," their ringleader sneered, sending her colleagues into fits of giggles.

Enough! Flora was already several steps past the pretentious shop when their needling finally became too much. She wheeled around.

"You want to know what we're planning for winter?" She glared angrily at the young women from behind her armful of fir sprigs. "I can tell you this: Great things! Things the likes of which Baden-Baden has never seen before! Our customers' eyes will be as big as dinner plates.

They'll be breaking down our door, and you and your forced roses will be roundly snubbed in favor of our marvels!"

Flora enjoyed the look of confusion on their faces; then she turned on her heel and stalked off triumphantly, smiling broadly to herself.

She'd shown them! They'd spend ages wondering what might be behind her claims of "*great things*" and "*things the likes of which Baden-Baden has never seen before.*" But Flora's high spirits evaporated as quickly as they had appeared, and left no more than a bitter aftertaste. The only "novelty" would be that, beginning Monday, she would no longer be there.

Because the first of October fell on a Sunday, Flora's departure was planned for the following day, the second.

On Saturday evening, Sabine accompanied her on her final stroll through their quarter of the city, a neighborhood she had grown very fond of. They visited Semmel, the butcher, who gave her a few sausages as a going-away present, and said farewell to the proprietress of The Gilded Rose and many others she had come to know. Even Sabine, usually so brisk and self-assured, was dejected, and Flora was relieved when they got back to the house.

She spent Sunday packing and digging over the flower bed, now empty, in the backyard. Although she kept looking for Friedrich, he did not show his face at all in the afternoon. He was probably on duty at the Trinkhalle, thought Flora, and she could not protect herself from the feelings of disappointment that weighed on her like a heavy, wet coat.

That evening, a bottle of wine was opened in her honor, and the entire family drank to her health. Ernestine shed a few tears at her impending departure, and even Kuno seemed deeply moved, swallowing hard to contain his emotions. Only Friedrich sat there stonily. Flora had expected more from him, frankly: Could he not have conjured an invitation to the theater or some other memorable moment? They had become good friends in the past few months. At least, Flora assumed that they had.

But with the general mood so gloomy, she was almost happy when Monday finally came.

The light, drizzling rain that had been falling all weekend had evolved into a steady downpour by Monday morning.

"Look, even the sky is crying to see you go. Maybe we should have taken a carriage after all," said Sabine, stomping along beside Flora.

"I still prefer to walk. I get to see the town one more time. You can go back if you want," said Flora, switching her traveling bag from her left hand to her right.

"Nonsense!" the maid replied. "If none of the others can bring themselves to accompany you, then I'm not going to leave you in the lurch, too. I'm going to miss you, Flora, even if I find all your energy exhausting."

"I'll miss you, too," Flora murmured. "Nearly half a year! It's gone by so fast. It was wonderful here, with you." A lump was forming in her throat again.

Sabine ducked beneath some low-hanging branches. "I was actually expecting the young master, you know . . ."

"Well, that's what you get for all your wild speculations. So much for Friedrich being madly in love with me." Flora could not keep the bitterness out of her voice. She could understand Kuno not wanting to close the shop to go with her to the station, and also that a farewell on the platform would have been far too upsetting for Ernestine. But that Friedrich would not see it as appropriate to accompany her to her train and say a proper goodbye, well . . . she would not have thought that of him at all.

The two women walked on in silence.

Around them, the streets were empty. None of the businesses along the Promenade had opened, no tables stood in front of cafés, and everything gave an impression of desolation.

Flora shivered. The mood reminded her of Gönningen. In September, or October at the latest, when the work in the fields was done, most of the seed traders went off for months at a time to visit their customers all over the world. Days before their departure, the whole village was frantically busy with preparations. Children cried more often and clutched at their mothers' skirts, knowing well that they would soon be sent off to Grandmother or a distant aunt. But no bawling or tears made any difference. The day of departure came as it did every year, and afterward, for many weeks, Gönningen was like a ghost village.

When Flora arrived home, she knew, her father and Uncle Valentin would already have left. She hoped that her father had received the letter she had sent, in which she wished him a safe and successful trip.

The station was a confusion of spa guests, their servants, and mountains of luggage, all of it blocking the platform, stairs, and passages. Sabine and Flora were constantly being bumped in the side or pushed out of the way, and Sabine cursed loudly at their treatment.

They managed to find a spot a little away from the chaos, where they could wait for Flora's train. From the corner of her eye, Flora noticed the tall figure of Lady Lucretia, surrounded by a profusion of luggage. The Englishwoman, too, cut a melancholy figure.

"Half the town seems to be leaving. Baden-Baden will feel quite deserted by tomorrow." Flora pointed with her chin toward the departing visitors. "I hate goodbyes!" she suddenly said, from deep in her soul. "I always have, even when I was a child, even—" And before she could stop herself, she threw both hands over her face and began to sob.

Flora still had her face buried in her hands when she suddenly felt consoling arms embrace her. The warmth felt good, and her sobs subsided. At least Sabine had some sympathy.

"Flora . . . you can't say goodbye. You . . . you can't go at all!" she heard a male voice say beside her.

Only then did Flora realize that the consoling arms did not belong to Sabine.

Chapter Twenty-Three

"Well? What's going on?" Ernestine whispered in Sabine's ear.

The maid shrugged. "They're sitting facing each other. I think the young master, I mean, your son, he's . . . holding Flora's hand." She squinted through the keyhole into the front room, a task not made any easier with Ernestine leaning on her back.

Flora, of course, had pestered Friedrich all the way home in the carriage. What was the matter? Why did she have to return to the house? Was something wrong with Kuno? Had there been an accident?

And she had become furious when Friedrich would not tell her anything. She had even shouted at him because, for his sake, she had now missed her train.

Friedrich took no apparent notice of any of it. "Soon," he had said all the way home. "We'll talk soon." And he had laughed as he said it.

"He's holding her hand? But . . . that can only mean that he's summoned up the courage after all. And at the last moment, literally—my heavens! Better late than not at all, though, right? My one-and-only . . ."

"Now he's kneeling in front of her. How romantic!" Sabine could already picture herself telling Minka all about it. She'd been right all along thinking that Friedrich had fallen for Flora.

"He's kneeling? *Mon Dieu!*" Ernestine was so animated that she broke into French, which was really not like her at all. "I can't believe my boy had to make this all so exciting—he certainly doesn't have that from me."

Sabine gave her mistress a sideways look. She would never have believed that Ernestine Sonnenschein would be so thrilled about a daughter-in-law.

Sabine turned her attention back to the keyhole, and her train of thought was rudely interrupted. "Oh! Flora is shaking her head. It looks like he's said something that she doesn't agree with."

"Doesn't agree with? Any woman would count herself lucky to call my one-and-only her own."

I don't know what's going on any more than you! Sabine felt like saying. "Oh! Now—" she began, but quickly fell silent again. Let madam squirm a little longer. It was not necessary for her to know how passionately her son was kissing Flora just then.

Sabine turned away from the keyhole with a smile on her face. "I think their conversation might still take a little while. Maybe it's better if we leave them to it. Besides," she said, doing her best to look decorous, "listening at keyholes is really *not* what a well-bred woman does, is it?"

"I've been losing sleep for weeks, lying awake agonizing over how I can say to you what I *want* to say to you. With every passing day, my insecurity only grew. And when your departure was truly imminent, I thought all was lost . . . I could have kicked myself for my inability to speak my mind."

Flora let out a confused laugh. "But we've been talking our heads off to each other every day." *What is this all about?*

"But I don't want just to talk. I'd much rather . . ." Friedrich did not finish his sentence, but lifted his hands in the air, as if in exasperation. The self-assertiveness he had shown at the train station had vanished, and he abruptly dropped to one knee in front of Flora. "My God, I really wanted everything to be more romantic. I wanted to come out with a thousand pretty words and . . ." He took a deep breath. "Flora, dear Flora, will you be my wife?"

"Your . . ."

"You see? You find the very idea bewildering! That's what comes of all the camaraderie we've shared. But . . . we *do* like each other. At least, *I* like *you*, from my heart. I could say nice things about you day and night, because I find you so enchanting, so fascinating, so pretty. I admire your courage, your energy, your . . . everything! Of course we're friends, but there's nothing wrong with being friends in a marriage, is there?"

Flora nodded silently. She felt as dazed as if someone had hit her on the head with a hammer.

"I've never actually thought about marriage," she said. Which was an understatement, she realized. She had never really paid any serious attention to her feelings for Friedrich at all. Oh, she had certainly been aware that their relationship had changed over the months, and that she perhaps found him more than just "good company." But Flora had not found a name to use for those changes.

Friedrich let out a deep sigh. "Dear Flora, say something, please!"

"I'm speechless," she said plainly.

"Don't you think you might come to view my proposal . . . favorably? The two of us—would that be so unthinkable?"

She shook her head. "I like you, I do, very, very much! You know that." Her lips trembled and her voice sounded somehow metallic. Good heavens, Friedrich was actually proposing to her!

"The two of us, together forever. That would also mean that you could bring all your ideas to life. Father already gives you a free hand. And one day, the shop will belong to us anyway. With Flora Sonnenschein in charge."

"Oh," Flora breathed. Her shop? Friedrich, her husband? What would Kuno and Ernestine have to say about that? And what about her parents? Her mother was counting on her being home that same day.

Flora's head was spinning as wildly as leaves in an autumn wind.

Her silence prompted Friedrich to speak again. "Even though you might only harbor friendly feelings for me right now, love can still grow. I will do everything in my power to be a good husband. Love *can* grow. Don't you think so, too?"

Flora nodded. That love could come from friendship, well, wasn't that how it had been between her own mother and father?

"Love is like a seed," she murmured, more to herself than to Friedrich. "Only when you tend it and nurture it can it thrive."

Friedrich's brow furrowed. "You can think about it, of course. Take all the time you need. I mean, if you want to return to Gönningen first, the next train leaves at twelve. It doesn't mean that . . . I mean, we both know that—"

"Friedrich, hush. If you aren't quiet for a moment, I won't be able to think at all."

"Hmph." Friedrich looked at Flora for a long moment, then stood up and went to the window.

The only sound in the room was the ticking of the clock on the wall, but from the door to the hallway came the usual soft Monday-morning noises: Ernestine's raised voice somewhere in the house, the occasional tinkling of the bell over the front door of the shop, a wagon rolling to a stop in the street outside.

Flora smiled. The voices of the family members, the daily routine, the house, the garden, and the shop—she had become so intimately familiar with all of it. And she had felt at home there since she had first arrived, had been able to accept the small quirks of Kuno and Ernestine without a problem. She had enjoyed her life in the Sonnenschein household. And as far as Friedrich was concerned . . .

Now she knew what difficult questions had been weighing so heavily on his mind in recent days and weeks.

She smiled. He was a good man, and she would probably never find a better one.

Friedrich had actually proposed to her, and had essentially kidnapped her from the train station to do so. She would never have expected him to do that!

Flora's smile turned into a small laugh, and Friedrich turned around immediately and came to her.

"If I . . . if I really were to . . . say yes," she began, and her heart was pounding. Should she really?

"Yes?"

"Then there is something that you would have to do urgently." She smiled mischievously at Friedrich.

"What? Tell me!" Friedrich's face was so full of concern, as if he were expecting the worst.

"You'll finally have to kiss me!"

Chapter Twenty-Four

The whole house was in a state of excitement.

Sabine was the first to congratulate Flora. "I'd given up hope, I have to say," she whispered to Flora while Friedrich went to fetch his parents. "Oh, I'm so happy for you! But don't think you can start ordering me around now like the mistress does," she added with a wink.

Kuno's cheeks were flushed red as the four of them sat around the table. He clapped Friedrich jovially on the shoulder. "Congratulations, my son! It took you long enough. There were a few times I wanted to give you a good kick in the rear!"

"Kuno!" Ernestine hissed. "Watch your language. What's our future daughter-in-law going to think?"

Flora and Friedrich held hands and laughed.

Ernestine plucked nervously at her hair, which was tied into a bun, and it soon looked like a battered bird's nest. "Good heavens, well, this changes everything. Where is Flora supposed to spend the night now? As the future Mrs. Sonnenschein, she can hardly keep sharing a room with Sabine, can she? Should we set up Sybille's room for her? Oh, someone has to tell her, too."

"Mother, settle down," said Friedrich, and he laughed again. "Flora has only just accepted my proposal. Now that you and Father know, the most important thing is that we make the midday train to Gönningen so that Flora's mother does not worry unnecessarily. I will go along, of course, because I would also like to ask her father for her hand."

"Do you really want to come along to Gönningen?" Flora asked in some disbelief. "What about your work?" She had never known Friedrich to be so spontaneous.

"My work isn't going anywhere. What's more important is that I don't let my bride-to-be out of sight, or she might decide to change her mind!"

Flora gave Sabine, who was standing in the doorway, a furtive wink.

"You won't meet my father, I'm afraid. He and Uncle Valentin have already left for Bohemia, on their usual sales trip. They won't be back until Christmas."

Friedrich kissed first Flora's hand, then his mother's, making them both giggle bashfully.

"Then we'll write him a letter. Your mother is sure to know an address where it will reach him," he said energetically.

"But . . . but . . ." Kuno looked first at his son, then at Flora. "What about Flora's new floristry master? What's he going to do if she doesn't take up her post as planned?"

Flora and Friedrich giggled like two schoolchildren. They had forgotten all about Flora's invented apprenticeship in Reutlingen!

The closer their train got to Flora's home village of Gönningen, the more restless she became. What would her mother say? Would she feel that Flora had left her to fend for herself with all the work? Or would she believe, perhaps, that the whole thing had been planned like this from the start?

"Mother is going to fall off her chair, I swear. I never even hinted at anything like this in a single letter I wrote," she fretted as the autumn landscape rolled past. "She'll probably think I've been hiding it from her for months."

Friedrich squeezed her hand and tried to reassure her, but it was not an easy task.

"What about my seed selling in winter and our customers in Baden-Baden?" Flora asked despairingly.

Friedrich frowned. "I thought you wanted to suggest to your parents that you continue to serve the customers in your Baden-Baden *Samenstrich*, didn't you? There's very little to do in the shop in winter, and you would have plenty of time to carry on with the seed business. Maybe we could even put up a rack of seeds and sell them directly."

"Of course, but . . ." Flora's thoughts tumbled on and on.

"You're starting to look as worried as my mother," Friedrich said.

Flora glared at him. "I've never had this many things to worry about before!"

And Hannah very nearly did fall off her chair. The newly engaged couple were sitting at the dinner table with her, the twins, Seraphine, and Suse when Flora made the announcement. After a stunned moment of silence, everyone started talking at once.

"You're marrying a stranger, just as I did!" was the first thing Hannah said. She was on the verge of tears.

Suse let out a high-pitched squeal. "I knew it! I knew it!" She jumped up and threw her arms around Flora.

The twins made some unintelligible sounds that could be interpreted as congratulations, and then they clapped both Friedrich and Flora on the shoulder.

Hannah stood up and busied herself with the coffeepot at the stove. A minute for herself, just a minute to . . .

Her little Flora was getting married. And leaving Gönningen forever. Just as she herself had once left Nuremberg to go in search of Helmut.

She looked back over her shoulder, scrutinizing her daughter. It was all so sudden. Had Flora thought this through? The way she held Friedrich's hand, she seemed almost childlike, naïve. Or was she perhaps pregnant? But Hannah instantly rebuked herself for her suspicions: not every woman gets married because she *has* to.

So many memories came at once. It had been bitterly cold when she arrived in Gönningen just before Christmas in 1849, the snow knee-deep. And she had been so worried about whether Gönningen might be a new home for her at all. Admittedly, the situation she found herself in back then was not comparable to Flora's. The way Friedrich seemed to idolize Flora left his love in no doubt. But in 1849, Hannah had had to fight to win her husband's love. It was not always a fair fight, but what was it they said? All's fair in love and war . . .

Since then, she and her rival, Seraphine—Helmut's fiancée when Hannah arrived in Gönningen—had come to terms with how things were, and they even lived under the same roof, albeit on different floors. Seraphine had been married to Valentin almost as long as Hannah had been married to Helmut. And sometimes Valentin even managed to make his wife smile, although most of the time he tried in vain. Helmut had no interest at all in his sister-in-law, and Hannah would not have stood for any less! The bond between the brothers continued to be very close, and the two women had their work to do, so they did their best not to get in each other's way.

Yes, many things had changed. And many things had stayed the same.

"If you like, I'll give you my wedding dress. It's hanging in my closet, as good as new," said Seraphine to Flora just then.

Something felt as if it were pressing at the back of Hannah's eye. The old times were forgotten. Her little girl in a wedding dress—it was hard for her to imagine.

Oh, if only Helmut were here. He would no doubt whisper to her that she should not be so sentimental. Or would he be even more sentimental than her? It was not easy for a father to let a daughter go, after all.

Oh, Helmut . . .

He would like Friedrich, Hannah was certain of that.

Friedrich hung on Flora's every word, nodding almost reverently at everything she said. He was head over heels for her, that was obvious. He seemed a little quiet, but she was sure he was a decent fellow. Even the twins, lounging against the kitchen cabinets, seemed to think that; they also seemed to have forgotten that they had announced earlier that they were going off to meet their friends at The Sun. And Suse, who had just planned to pop in for a moment to welcome her friend home, also made no signs of leaving, although it was now well after dark.

Hannah set the pot of freshly brewed coffee on the table, then sliced a fruit loaf. It was really time for her to be thinking about getting dinner started, but she did not want to disturb the wonderful mood with too much bustling around. When was the last time they had all been gathered so pleasantly at the table? How often did happy news like this come along?

At some point, the last crumb of fruit loaf was gone, and the coffeepot empty. The twins took Friedrich off to the inn with them—his engagement to their sister had to be duly celebrated, after all. Suse put on a shocked face at the late hour and hurried away. Seraphine retired to her room with a headache.

Finally, mother and daughter were alone.

Hannah opened a bottle of red wine.

"Why only now?" Flora asked, indicating the bottle.

"I'm not going to waste good wine like this on your brothers," Hannah replied with a laugh. "Well? Are you happy, my child?" she asked over the rim of her wineglass.

Flora sipped the wine thoughtfully. "Of course I'm happy. But I've never really been *un*happy in my life, so I don't feel much different from usual."

Hannah frowned. "Hmm. But if you're in love . . ."

"What do I know about being in love? Oh, Mother, I feel so stupid sometimes," Flora suddenly said. "All summer, I've been going walking with Friedrich. We've talked and told stories and laughed together. And in all that time, it never occurred to me that we might be in love with each other. Whenever Sabine teased me about it, I actually got rather angry at her. I was firmly convinced that all we had was a remarkably close friendship." She looked at Hannah with an almost despairing look in her eyes. "Can a person really be so naïve?"

Hannah smiled. Her Flora, her own little know-all in everything but matters of the heart.

"Being a little slow to understand the state of your own feelings is not uncommon. I'd go so far as to say it's probably true of most of us."

"Really?" Flora looked at her mother hopefully. "You know, my mind was really on the flower shop most of the time."

Love doesn't happen in your mind, Hannah almost said, but kept it to herself. "You wanted to learn something, and your training came first. Your father and I expected nothing else of you. We knew you didn't go to Baden-Baden to flirt with men."

"Of course, but . . ." Flora still looked depressed. "But, well, Friedrich and I . . ."

"Yes?"

"It's just that, somehow it seems strange to me that we will soon be husband and wife. And when I think about us, well . . ." Flora's concentration was trained on her fingernail tracing a crack in the tabletop.

Hannah sighed inwardly. *Oh no, here come the questions that every mother dreads.* The questions about the wedding night, the questions . . . and answers for which every word was a strain.

She suddenly felt old and tired and far removed from all of that. What could she tell her daughter to take away with her? Who was *she* to give good advice?

"Don't worry, child, everything will fall into place. There are things between a husband and wife that don't need to be discussed ahead of time. They simply happen. And despite what you might imagine, it won't be bad, believe me," said Hannah with as much determination as she could muster. Then she straightened her back, slid open the drawer beneath the tabletop, and took out paper and a pencil. "Why don't we write to your father? He will be as surprised as any of us to hear the happy news."

Chapter Twenty-Five

Baden-Baden, November 2, 1871

My dearest Flora!
We have been apart for three weeks now, and my desire
to see you again is so strong that I have a mind to board
the next train to Gönningen.

Flora looked up from Friedrich's letter. "He misses me . . . Oh, I miss him so much! What a stupid idea for me to stay here until the wedding."

"What do you mean, a stupid idea?" said Seraphine. "Don't we have enough work to do before the big day?"

"Of course." Flora's gaze drifted wistfully out the window in the direction of Baden-Baden.

It was a dreary November day, and the fog hung so low over the Swabian Mountains that Gönningen was engulfed in a damp, cool pall. "If only the wedding wasn't so far off."

Suse and Seraphine were with Flora in her room. Seraphine was doing her best to alter her beautiful but far-too-small wedding dress to fit Flora. Again and again, she pinned layers of material into place at the neckline, at the back, and around the skirt, and Flora then had to turn and bend and sit. Either the top would fit and the skirt would billow unattractively, or the skirt hung nicely but the fabric stretched uncomfortably across Flora's chest.

Throughout the fitting, Flora would not let anyone stop her from reading Friedrich's letter, which had come that morning. She was hungry for news from Baden-Baden. And, of course, she had to tell Suse and Seraphine everything.

"'I am using every free minute to connect my room and Sybille's,'" she read aloud. "'The door is already out, although I still have to fix the parquetry in the connecting section and then rearrange the furniture. I hope you like the little nest I am preparing for the two of us.'"

Suse sighed. "A little nest! How romantic."

Flora's brow furrowed. "It's hard to imagine going back to Baden-Baden and not sharing a room with Sabine but living with Friedrich instead."

"So tell us, where are your rooms, exactly? And what do they look like?" Seraphine asked.

"On the second floor, just beside his parents' bedroom. I hope they don't snore too loudly." Flora giggled. "But I can't tell you what Friedrich's room looks like, because I've never seen it. Sybille's room is really just a small room with a window. You'll have to come and visit me as soon as you can, so I can show you everything." She turned to the next page of the letter. "But what's this? 'Mother wants me to tell you that she agrees to having the wedding on January thirteenth in Gönningen. And she approves of the seating arrangements your dear mother went to such a lot of trouble to sketch out and enclose in your last letter. The same goes for all the other suggestions your mother put forward—I do believe the two of them will get on very well.'"

Flora looked up. "January the thirteenth has been officially sanctioned, thank God. If I think about dragging this all out any longer . . . The thirteenth is a Saturday, and the flower shop is normally closed from midday Saturday until Monday morning, so it makes sense to have the wedding on a weekend. But I honestly did not think that Ernestine would be so willing to have the wedding here in Gönningen."

Suse laughed. "Usually, the groom's parents are happy if they have as little to do with the arrangements as possible. All the work, you know, not to mention the money."

Flora shrugged. "There will only be a dozen guests coming from Friedrich's side, no more, but we'll have more than two hundred. Getting all of them to Baden-Baden would have been expensive." She turned back to her letter.

"'Mother is terribly excited. She's starting a thousand things before she finishes even one. By the time January thirteenth arrives, her nerves will be completely shot, and mine and my father's to boot! Darling, you can be happy that you don't have to be here right now.'"

Flora grimaced. "He goes on to say that unfortunately his sister can't come to the wedding. I'm not really sad about that. Just before I left Baden-Baden, Friedrich and I went to the Lichtenthal Abbey on a Sunday, where I met Sybille."

"So what's she like? Not everyone can claim a nun in the family," said Suse.

"She wore a martyred look on her face, and I found her rather boring. She kept making snide remarks, as if she was somehow envious of Friedrich. In any case, we only stayed for an hour, and I was quite happy to leave again." Flora frowned. "It's strange, actually. The nunnery is situated very close to the town, but it is its own world, very different from the town."

Then Flora's thoughts had moved on, and she turned to the next page of the letter. "Flora, please," Seraphine mumbled, and she tugged a pin from between her lips. "Stop fidgeting. If you don't hold still, we're not going to get anywhere with this dress."

The wedding preparations progressed with every passing week, and Seraphine actually managed the miracle of refashioning her old wedding dress so that it fit Flora perfectly.

Hannah dedicated herself to organizing the celebrations at The Eagle, the biggest inn in the village. It had not only a large hall, but also many rooms where the Sonnenschein family and others from Baden-Baden could stay on the night of the wedding. Besides, her own wedding celebration had taken place there many years before, and Hannah's mood turned sentimental at the memory. If only Helmut would finally get home—she would have loved to sit and reminisce with him.

If you think the guy is the right one for our Flora, then tell them both they have my blessing, he had written to Hannah once Flora and Friedrich had written to him to tell him of their plans. *Flora chose him herself, so he will be the right one,* Hannah had written back, and in his next letter Helmut had replied, *Let's hope our Flora has the same knack in picking husbands as her mother did back then.*

"Oh, Helmut, my darling! Finally!" Sobbing with joy, Hannah threw herself into her husband's arms. "I was really starting to fear that you wouldn't make it back in time." Hannah covered his face with a thousand kisses.

Helmut, who still had his seed sack over his shoulder, smiled from ear to ear and tried half-heartedly to free himself from his wife. "Christmas Eve is not until tomorrow, so we're more than on time, aren't we?"

Valentin, still standing behind Helmut in the doorway, cleared his throat. "Uh, perhaps I could get inside, too?" He was looking off over Helmut's shoulder toward the stairs.

Where is Seraphine? Flora wondered, waiting impatiently herself for her chance to embrace her father. The men come home from weeks spent in distant lands, and there was no sign of her aunt. It was, admittedly, not necessary to be as effusive about it as the two turtledoves—as her parents called themselves—but a heartfelt "Welcome home" when her husband returned after so long away was not too much to expect.

How sad her uncle looked . . . Flora threw her arms around him and hugged him tightly. "I'm so happy to see you home again."

Helmut, who had finally managed to escape Hannah, laughed loudly. "And you don't know how happy we are to be here! I could not have stood another day on the road. Now it is time to celebrate. Good business behind us, Christmas ahead—"

"And New Year's Day," Hannah threw in. "With big New Year's pretzels—"

"And a wedding!" said Flora and Helmut, as if from one mouth, and they exchanged an affectionate look.

"My little girl is a bride now," Helmut murmured.

Hannah clapped her hands. "Oh, life can be so wonderful!"

The day after Christmas, Hannah had had enough of cooking, clearing the table, and washing dishes, so the family was at The Sun inn. The twins went off to sit with their friends in one corner; Hannah went to the kitchen to join Käthe, the proprietress of the inn; while Helmut, Valentin, and Flora made a beeline for the table where the seed traders regularly met.

"Sit, sit," said Klaus Müllerschön, a neighbor, and he slid across to make room for Flora.

"Anyone hungry?" asked Käthe, coming to the table just then with a tray laden with mugs of beer, but Helmut, Valentin, and Flora were the only ones who took her up on the offer. The rest were there only to talk and catch up. Most had not seen each other since autumn, after all, and many of them, in the meantime, had many miles in many lands under their belts. All were happy to be home again.

How had the business been? What was the latest news from Russia, France, England, and Switzerland?

Klaus Müllerschön had almost been the victim of a robbery in Alsace, but the police had happened to come along just in time. And Fritz Sailer, an imposing man of sixty, reported that one of his horses had perished in a snowstorm. He and his son had become bogged down in a snowdrift. Half-frozen and weakened themselves, they had had to abandon the beast to its fate to get themselves to safety.

Flora listened in rapt silence. Although she had heard such stories for years, she had the feeling that she was only now actually conscious of much of what was said.

How brave the Gönningers were. How courageous and—

Flora jumped when Klaus laid a hand on her shoulder.

"But enough of the trade! Girl, tell us about Baden-Baden. Does anyone there want your flowers?"

"Some, certainly . . ." Flora had been so engrossed in the men's stories that she had to gather herself. She drank a swig of beer, then told them about the flower beds she had laid out in the Sonnenscheins' garden. "Things in the shop are actually going quite well, but . . ." She trailed off uncertainly, not wanting to bore anyone. But when she looked around, she saw only interested faces, so she straightened her shoulders and went on. "The problem is that we are too far from the center. There are wealthy spa guests from everywhere there, and I wish so much that they would come to us. The Russians like to throw their money around, but they simply don't find their way to our side street."

The men at the table laughed. Käthe, bringing plates of stew to the table, looked at Helmut. "You and your brother went off to Russia once, and you know the country and the people. Can't you give Flora some advice?"

"Yes, exactly! You dealt with enough rich Russians on your travels there, didn't you?" Fritz Sailer said.

"I remember now, too," Klaus added. "You went on for years about how magnificent everything was."

Käthe laughed. "And at the end of the trip, someone robbed you and stole almost everything you'd made."

Helmut looked around the table. "You've got good memories, I must say." Then he turned to Flora. "Doing business with the Russians is not so hard. You just have to—"

"But you were there so long ago," Flora interrupted him.

Helmut put down his spoon and frowned. "I wouldn't call it 'so long,' exactly. You make it sound like I'm ready for the scrap heap."

"Brother dear, I don't think the youngster wants to hear our stories anymore," Valentin said with a laugh.

"Of course I do!" said Flora, not very convincingly.

"What I have to say is as true today as it was then." Helmut looked around, making sure he had everyone's attention. "If the Russians won't come to your shop, then you have to go to them. Just like we did, back then. Or do you think a single Russian has ever strayed as far afield as Gönningen?"

"So you think I should take my flowers door-to-door?" Flora asked, somewhat perplexed.

"Don't say a word against door-to-door selling," said Fritz. "There's nothing dishonorable in it."

Helmut nodded. "What's stopping you from approaching the spa guests in their hotels?"

"Maybe one of the hoteliers would be prepared to sell your bouquets to his guests. With a small addition to the cost, of course," Fritz added. "Or you might be allowed to set yourself up in a corner of the lobby."

"You all have some ideas," said Flora, taken aback.

"You just have to ask the right people," said Fritz.

"But that's only the first step, my girl. Once you've made the first contact, that's when the work really starts," Helmut said. "You can't just offer a run-of-the-mill posy to the rich. They want huge bouquets, stunning arrangements, unusual varieties. Crazy things, basically. Of course, it all has to be the very finest quality, and even that won't be enough. The rich want to be entertained well for their money, which means you have to play a kind of court jester. You have to give them the feeling that they are the finest, most elegant, most important people in the world. You have to put on a show! We learned that very fast back then, didn't we, Valentin?"

"It's no different with my rich customers in Zurich," Fritz said with a dry chuckle. "What did you call it? Playing the court jester? I couldn't have put it better. But every time has to be opening night! Don't think for a minute that the rich will be content with just *one* performance."

Flora shook her head. "I don't know what to say. That's a lot to digest." She looked around the group. "I'll do what you suggest with the hotels at the start of next season, certainly. I'm curious about what Kuno and Friedrich will have to say about it, but . . ."

"What is it? Just ask," said Fritz, and the others nodded vigorously. They clearly felt very much in their element as advisers.

"The 'show' you say you have to offer the rich—what would that look like, coming from me?"

The seed traders around her laughed. Helmut put an arm around Flora's shoulders and gave her an encouraging squeeze.

"That, my child, is something you will have to find out for yourself."

Chapter Twenty-Six

Konstantin Sokerov judged it the right decision to travel to Monte Carlo. There could hardly be a more pleasant way to spend the winter.

It had not rained a single day since their arrival, and even today, New Year's Eve of 1871, the sun shone over the Mediterranean coast. Konstantin was certain that the sun would continue to shine on him in the new year.

He paused for a moment, with his hands on the sun-warmed wall of the quay, and looked out over the sea.

It was a perfect day to go out sailing, in fact. But it would also be ideal for a gallop along the coastal strip. Sergej had told him just the day before that the stables beside their hotel possessed a pair of Arab stallions that loved to run and which one could rent by the hour.

"What a glorious day!" Laughing, Konstantin turned around to his companion. "A day to celebrate and indulge and make love." Yes! That was perhaps the best of all the possibilities that lay before him.

"Not so loud, you old charmer," she replied, patting him on the arm. "I feel the green-eyed glances from the other ladies enough already. They would be only too happy to take my place, and I am quite sure that flippant comments like that from you will only make things worse, darling."

"If you think so." Konstantin's thoughts were already drifting again.

No doubt Crimea would be in the grip of snowstorms, with an icy wind blasting across the land, freezing people and animals. Crimea—who could think of going to such an inhospitable place of their own free will? A slight shudder ran through Konstantin at the thought.

He swept his eyes across the bay and the harbor toward the casino. In the mild sunlight, it looked as if a baker had covered a cake with too much frosting. The casino in Bad Homburg in Prussia was supposed to be just as grand, François Blanc had told Konstantin a few days before. François would know: he and his brother had founded the Prussian casino, and he now ran the gambling rooms in Monte Carlo.

It was really no surprise at all that the casinos of the world were overflowing with pomp and splendor, not if one thought of the money gambled away every day in their merry rooms.

They would have to pay a visit to Bad Homburg, and the sooner the better, François Blanc had urged him, because a rumor was circulating that the German emperor wanted to close down every casino in his realm—what a catastrophe that would be!

And what would become of Baden-Baden then? Konstantin wondered. He had felt quite at home there, and would gladly go back. But the next summer season was still a long way off.

Konstantin straightened his shoulders and breathed in the mélange of odors that was so typical of Monte Carlo: freshly fried fish wafting from the fishermen's huts, the scent of winter jasmine mixed with the scents worn by the women who paraded along the promenade by the water, and over all of it the green traces of the seaweed washed up constantly by the waves and from which the women recoiled in such disgust.

Konstantin laughed. "It's true—I feel as if I could hug the world today! The world and you." He blew an extravagant kiss to his companion.

"You look so beautiful. Your white dress with all its frills, the silver pommel of your parasol that gleams so wonderfully in the sunlight. And the sea itself, with all its blues, its turquoise, its deep azure. A painter could hardly wish for a more enchanting motif. How lovely you are, Püppi."

His compliment was met with a coquettish giggle. Konstantin rolled his eyes mentally—the old clichés still worked the best, and it made no difference if the woman's name was Irina, Püppi, or something else.

"You're very charming today, as ever. Does this dress really suit me? You don't think it makes me look a little pale?"

A white dress, in fact, was far from flattering for a woman of a certain . . . maturity. All those frills really looked far too youthful.

"If anything, the only thing wrong with that dress is that it is perhaps a little light for the fresh breeze off the water." He thoughtfully laid his companion's fur stole across her shoulders, then lifted his arm for her to take. "What do you say, my dear? Shall we look in quickly on Marie and François? Marie said just yesterday evening that it had become a tradition for her to open her house on the last day of the year, with a glass of champagne for every guest."

"Are you really just after a glass of champagne? Or are you more interested in the red and the black?" Püppi replied.

Konstantin smiled. "I'm an open book to you, aren't I? Would it be all right if I were to leave you alone for an hour or two? Piotr told me that I absolutely cannot deny him a final game to salute the old year."

As expected, she patted his arm fondly. "Go, go! I'd like to rest for a little while, anyway. I *do* want to be fresh to properly celebrate the last night of the year, after all."

Konstantin's eyes shone. "Oh, Püppi, what have I done to deserve a woman as kind and considerate as you?"

Chapter Twenty-Seven

On the eleventh of January, Friedrich and his parents arrived in Gönningen, and his guests the next day. Flora's family greeted them all warmly, and although the two sets of parents were very different, they quickly found common ground. While Ernestine looked around rather pleadingly for Kuno when Hannah led her away to the kitchen for a chat, just an hour later the two women were setting the table together for dinner, and Ernestine was proudly telling her about her "garden parties," which had been possible only because Flora had fixed up their garden so prettily.

While the women were occupied with each other, Helmut and Kuno discussed the outcomes of the war—Kuno listened with concern to Helmut's tales of the many new routes that had opened up. "Do you think any tourists at all will find their way to us in Baden-Baden now?" he asked.

Helmut replied, "No doubt. Baden-Baden is still the number-one spa town in the entire empire."

Under the watchful eyes of their parents and relatives, the prospective bride and groom managed no more than a fleeting embrace. They had no opportunity to be alone; everybody wanted their piece of the happy couple.

"As excited as I am to be marrying you, I'll be glad when all the wedding hubbub is over," Flora said in a rare quiet moment with Friedrich. "After all the chaos, I think I'm going to need some time in a spa myself."

"Then you should take the waters, as well," Friedrich said, his arms around his bride-to-be. "Our excellent waters are wonderfully invigorating!"

"Well? What do you think?" Hannah and Flora stood arm in arm in the doorway that led into the main hall at The Eagle. It was the morning of the thirteenth of January, and the wedding was to take place in a few hours. Friedrich and his parents were at breakfast.

Although she had sat up half the night creating the flower arrangements for the hall, Flora was not tired in the slightest—more elated and nervous, in fact. Hannah was the first to see her finished handiwork, and Flora was excited to hear what she thought.

"I've never seen anything so lovely in my life," Hannah said reverently.

Flora smiled proudly. Considering that it was winter and that she had almost no fresh flowers to work with, everything looked quite outstanding.

"What a wonderful idea, to decorate the chairs as well."

"That was most of the work. Suse and I thought we would never get through it all," Flora said with a laugh.

They had adorned each of the more than two hundred chairs with a small ensemble of fir sprigs, rosemary, and a dried red rose, and attached them to the back of the chairs so that they would not be crushed by the guests.

"In the language of flowers, rosemary means 'Soon I will be yours forever.'" Flora found the sentiment especially appropriate for the occasion.

Suse had asked her what the fir sprigs meant, and Flora had rolled her eyes and replied, "'Don't be so grumpy all the time.' Not really what you want for a wedding, is it? But it's about the only greenery you can find right now."

Flora had even decorated the table intended for gifts with garlands of fir and roses. If it held no gifts, at least it would not look so empty.

In an uncertain voice, she asked her mother, "What if no one gives me anything? Maybe the people here don't like it that I'm marrying someone from outside the village . . ."

Hannah looked sideways at her daughter. "Ah. I think your nerves are getting to you." She took Flora by the arm and turned her toward the door. "Let's go home. It's high time we dressed our bride up a little. Maybe that will get your mind onto other things."

The parish priest's sermon was particularly moving. He had known the bride since she was a baby, and on his strolls through the village she had given him one of her handmade bouquets many times. He quoted from St. Anthony:

> *Oh curious one, you who toil and turn your hand in many fields, go not to the ant, but to the bee, and learn wisdom there . . . Leave not one flower to fly to another, as triflers do . . . Gather what you need from a single book, and keep it in the hive of your memory.*

Hannah sniffed so loudly that Helmut had to elbow her in the ribs, and Suse and some of the other young women from the village sighed wistfully. How lovely Flora looked in her beaded dress. One could hardly see the fabric that had been added when Seraphine had let it out. And how gorgeous the bride's bouquet was—composed from white orchids, myrtle, and white roses—and the bridal wreath, also of orchids. Kuno Sonnenschein had brought the bridal flowers with him from Baden-Baden, and the guests agreed unanimously that he certainly knew his craft.

The party that followed in The Eagle was also a success. The guests were amazed at Flora's floral contributions, and the food, comprising both Swabian and Baden dishes, tempted both the Gönningers and their Baden-Baden visitors to have seconds. When everyone had had their fill, the proprietor of the inn, with two of the kitchen hands, carried in a triple-layered wedding cake. The expensive ingredients—marzipan, chocolate, and sugared almonds—and the sight of the cake itself drew gasps on every side. A moment later, several of the women let out little squeals of delight when small bowls of candies were distributed to every table. Helmut had brought it all back with him from Bohemia. He went around and handed each of the men a fat cigar.

So many presents! Ernestine's eyes were the size of apples.

Silver candlesticks, fine linens, a mother-of-pearl toiletries kit with gilded handles, and even a sewing machine were on the gift table.

And the guests were all wearing their finest—Ernestine would never have suspected that a small Swabian village could dress with such style, and certainly not that their apprentice-girl's family was so well-to-do. The thought bothered Ernestine enough that her cake lay untouched on her plate for some time.

Kuno, by contrast, dug into all the food with gusto—no doubt he would suffer for it the next morning. And he laughed and laughed, as if he had no cares in the world at all. And to think, that morning he had hardly been able to drag himself out of bed because of the weight of all the new impressions.

"Don't you like the cake, Mother? Would you prefer a few pralines instead?" Friedrich asked in passing.

"My heavens, I feel I'm going to burst any second," Ernestine said. "Look, you're expected." She pointed her son in the direction of the dance floor.

With embarrassed smiles and a little awkwardly, the bride and groom began to waltz around the dance floor. It made Ernestine dizzy just to watch. But with every turn they took, her heart grew lighter. Maybe one should simply enjoy a day like this, and not brood so much?

"Makes you want to be young again," sighed Gretel Grün, also sitting at Ernestine's table. She looked expectantly at her husband as she spoke, a look he studiously ignored.

"I don't think I've ever seen your Friedrich show so much energy before," said the pharmacist, then added, "Lovely party, too!" He drew luxuriously on his cigar.

Finally, Ernestine stabbed her fork into her slice of cake. With her lips still sticky, she smiled at Gretel. "Isn't the chocolate just marvelous?"

"Flora's family haven't spared any expense at all," said Gretel, impressed. "Chocolate in a cake . . ."

Ernestine shrugged. "Friedrich would not have entertained the notion of marrying a girl from a poor family. He knows what suits us. I mean, the girl is marrying into a thriving business, after all. That's something we can be proud of, isn't it, Kuno?"

Chapter Twenty-Eight

If it had been up to Flora, the party would have gone on and on. One more song. One more dance. And one more toast to the bride and groom. Before the wedding, she never imagined that getting married could be so much fun.

At some point the ranks of guests began to thin—it had been a long, exciting day for everyone. "Goodbye, Mrs. Sonnenschein!" many said as they left. And every time, it took Flora by surprise.

Some could not resist an insinuating remark, and while Friedrich only grinned, Flora's face flushed crimson. When she thought that everyone there knew what would happen later that night . . . it was embarrassing, terribly embarrassing.

When Kuno and Ernestine went up to their room, it was already two in the morning. Ernestine, with a mixture of astonishment and horror, said she had never stayed up so late in her life.

Hannah watched them depart, a wistful expression on her face. "I think I've had enough for one night, too," she said to Flora. "Today of all days, my leg is especially painful. Maybe I've just been dancing too much."

"Stop complaining," said Seraphine, sitting with them at the table. "Getting married only happens once. Prost!" She raised her wineglass with a laugh.

Mother and daughter shared a look. Was that really Seraphine? They had never seen her so cheerful.

"You can laugh," said Flora. "When I think about . . . what's still to come, it makes my knees go weak. I wish it was already tomorrow." She bit her bottom lip and looked over to the table where the men had taken Friedrich into their midst.

Hannah and Seraphine exchanged a knowing look. "Stay calm, child. Nothing bad will happen," Hannah whispered. "Your Friedrich is a fine young man; just let him do what he wants. Oh, look, there's—" Before Flora had a chance to say anything, Hannah was scurrying off toward the kitchen, calling over her shoulder, "I'll be right back!"

"Where's she off to?" Seraphine asked, shaking her head. Then she turned to Flora. "You lucky thing! I'd give anything to experience an all-consuming love one more time. A love so intense it hurts. A love you would die for if you can't have it in life."

All-consuming? Die? Flora gave her aunt a lopsided look. Did Seraphine always have to be so terribly theatrical?

She took another mouthful of wine, although it had lost its flavor long before. She felt ill and dizzy. Why had her mother run off like that? She was probably telling The Eagle's proprietor what he was supposed to do with all the leftovers.

Flora suddenly felt lonely and tired and frightened and . . . just terrible. With all the excitement, she was finding it hard just to breathe properly. Or did that have more to do with the tight dress? On the one hand, she could hardly wait to undo the dozens of eyelets and peel herself free of the top. On the other, she could think of nothing more terrifying.

At least Hannah had had the foresight to reserve a room for her and Friedrich at The Sun, the inn run by her friend Käthe. They would not have to spend the night under the same roof as Friedrich's parents at The Eagle. Just a wall between them, and everyone able to hear what . . . Flora shuddered.

Friedrich waved to her from the table where he sat with the other men. She smiled back. He looked so happy and relaxed, her husband . . .

"By the way, something occurred to me about how you can attract those rich Russians," said Seraphine so suddenly that it took Flora a moment to realize what she was talking about.

"What?"

"I'm talking about the advice your father gave you. The show one has to put on for one's pampered clientele. I've had an idea for how you might do that . . ." Seraphine paused—clearly only to pique Flora's interest—before going on. "It's to do with the book about the language of flowers that you showed me last winter," she said, when she was sure of her niece's attention. "Have you read any more about the subject since then?"

Flora frowned. "What do you mean by more?"

"Oh, there are many more books about flowers. Have you read Balzac's novel *The Lily of the Valley*? Or do you know Goethe's marvelous flower poems?"

Flora shook her head and laughed. "You were always the big reader in the family. To be honest, for a long time I thought the book about the language of flowers that Mother gave me was the only one of its kind." This could not be happening, she suddenly thought—here she was on her wedding night, sitting with Seraphine and blathering away about flower books. Was this Seraphine's attempt at distracting her from all her fears? If that was the case, Flora could not say for certain that her aunt would have any success.

Seraphine raised her eyebrows dubiously. "It doesn't look as if you're as interested in the topic as I thought. Just a few months ago you couldn't talk about anything else. I remember clearly how you constantly told us about the meaning of this or that flower."

"That's true, but . . ." Flora could only shrug. What did her aunt expect of her?

"I, for one, have not been able to get the subject out of my head," said Seraphine, her voice heavy with disappointment. "But here in the village, no one has any interest in painting or flower poems. I thought you, at least—"

Flora raised her hands defensively. "Don't look at me like that! Believe it or not, I was so busy with all my work that I hardly had a moment to spare for the language of flowers. You say there are more books about it? Then I definitely want to read them."

At Flora's words, Seraphine's expression immediately grew more positive again. "If you ask me, the symbolism of flowers will appeal greatly to the Russians—people say they are a particularly Romantic people. And while it's true that you can buy flowers anywhere, flowers that tell stories or that appear in poetry, well, that would be something out of the ordinary, I'm sure of it."

"You may be right," said Flora, but she sounded skeptical. "I had the same idea not long after I went to Baden-Baden, but my dear father-in-law has no interest in the language of flowers. Actually, it was the opposite: he made it very clear to me that he did not appreciate me bothering the customers with it. He thinks that the language of flowers is too ambiguous altogether, and misunderstandings happen."

"He's not wrong, of course. Flowers have a very different symbolic meaning in the Orient than they do here in Europe, and the connotations are probably different in every country. I have, however, discovered that the symbolism attached to a particular plant is also connected to the time in which a writer lived. The ancient Egyptians, for example—" Seraphine stopped abruptly. "I don't want to bore you. It was just an idea. It's just that, since you came home with that little book . . . for me, it was like the key to a new world. Dealing with seeds all the time can be a little monotonous."

Flora laughed. "You don't have to tell me!"

Seraphine leaned closer. "Right now, I'm reading a wonderful French book about the language of flowers. It's over fifty years old. For the first time in a long time, I'm glad I learned French." The corners of her mouth crept into a smile.

"When I told Friedrich that they teach French and even English in our village school, he didn't want to believe it. I explained to him that it's because we go off to sell our seeds all over the world." Flora shook her head. "I did not think that you would also be interested in the language of flowers."

Seraphine laughed. "There are simply a lot of people who love flowers more than anything else, although most of them can't live out their love the way you can."

Chapter Twenty-Nine

At some point in the evening, it had begun to snow. Flora and Friedrich stamped hand in hand through the snow-covered streets to The Sun, and in the light of the occasional streetlamp, falling flakes danced, silvery, through the air.

"As if we're the only two people on God's earth," Flora whispered, looking back at their footprints in the snow.

"Whoops! Careful," said Friedrich when Flora slipped and almost fell. He let go of her hand and held on to her arm firmly. "It's not a good night to break a leg, after all. The teasing would never stop."

Friedrich carried Flora over the threshold of The Sun. He had heard somewhere that it was supposed to bring good fortune to the marriage. No sooner were they inside than he put her down and leaned back against the closed door.

"Well, that's behind us," he said, and puffed his cheeks. "I would not have thought it would be such a strain."

Flora gave him a playful push. "Do you mean the carrying, the party, or slipping and sliding all the way here?" she asked, and both of them broke into laughter.

She was happy to see that the room that had been reserved for them was warm. Candles stood ready, and beside them a box of matches. Käthe had also put out a plate of cookies and a carafe of wine on the small table by the window.

Everything looked cozy, and Flora sighed. Perhaps it would not be so bad after all.

"As if we hadn't already had enough to eat and drink tonight," said Friedrich, shaking his head.

"But you'll still drink a little wine with me, won't you?" Flora held up the carafe inquiringly. When Friedrich shrugged, she said, "It's silly, really, but you and I have seen less of each other today than everyone else. There was always someone wanting something of us. But that's over now . . ." As she poured two fingers of wine into each glass, Friedrich wrapped her in his arms.

"What a marvelous party that was! Flora, you know, I'm the happiest man in the world. And so . . . here, for you."

Flora frowned and looked at the small packet that lay on Friedrich's open palm. "Another present?"

"What do you mean, *another*? I haven't given you anything at all yet. Open it!"

In the candlelight, Flora pulled at the thin paper until a small container appeared. Carefully, she opened the lid. Inside, on pale tissue paper, lay a silver brooch in the form of a letter *F*, studded with small sparkling stones.

"They're marcasites," Friedrich explained. "Not as valuable as diamonds, to be sure, but they shine very prettily. I know you love to wear flowers on your dress. Well, now you can pin them in place with the brooch.

"How beautiful. Thank you," Flora whispered. She had never seen a brooch quite like it. While she moved it back and forth in the candlelight, studying the way the stones glittered, she suddenly noticed the silence that had forced its way between her and her husband.

"I think we should slowly be . . ." Friedrich began after a long moment.

Flora laughed, feeling embarrassed. "You're probably right. Maybe you could undo the loops?" She turned her back to him.

Friedrich went to work awkwardly. "You're so beautiful," he said, when Flora stood before him in her underdress. "Honestly, I'm a little excited. It . . . it's the first time for me, too. I didn't want to . . . do it with just any . . . I wanted to wait for the right one."

"Oh, Friedrich," Flora said hoarsely. The first time for him, too? Was that good or bad? *It won't be so difficult,* she told herself bravely. But how was she supposed to get into her delicate pink nightdress without Friedrich watching her?

The next moment, Friedrich drew her toward the bed.

"You would not believe how much I've been looking forward to this moment," he whispered as he took off his trousers. "I don't want to hurt you. You have to tell me if I am, all right?" He lay on top of her cautiously.

Flora was unable to say anything. In the candlelight, their bodies formed one large, moving shadow on the wall.

"How lovely you are . . . so beautiful . . ." Friedrich's breathing was warm with red wine, and it tickled her ear. His lips were firm, and for a brief second Flora thought she felt his tongue, but then the moment passed.

"Just let him do what he wants," her mother had said. Flora opened her legs a little. She felt his knee between her thighs. Then something else. Something . . . hard. Flora knew what *that* was. She had grown up with two brothers, after all.

"Should I?" Friedrich looked at her inquiringly. "Is it all right if I—"

Flora let out a small laugh. "Oh, Friedrich, of course you should."

He laughed with her then, and kissed her lips softly.

After that, everything happened very quickly. Friedrich moved up and down, and Flora's back ached a little as he did so. He whispered a few more endearments in her ear, how lovely, how beautiful she was. Then he groaned and rolled off her.

"My angel, you have made me very happy!" He gazed at her from shining eyes.

"And you have done the same for me," said Flora, her voice husky. *That was everything? It couldn't be. Could it?*

She snuggled close to Friedrich, pulled at the bedcover that he had wrapped around himself. "I'm going to need a corner of that if I don't want to freeze to death on my wedding night."

"Should I get another blanket? Or something to drink? A towel? I saw a whole pile of hand towels on the chair by the door." He was already climbing out of bed.

Before he got back, Flora lifted the bedcover. Why hadn't she thought to lay a towel down first? She was sure that's what the pile on the chair was intended for.

She prodded carefully at herself with one hand and felt a slight twinge beneath her fingertips, but it did not really hurt. Nor had it hurt just a minute before, when Friedrich . . .

Her mother had been right, again—it had not been so bad.

So now she was a real woman. Although, she had to admit, she did not feel so much different from before.

Flora took the hand towel from Friedrich, then lifted the bedcover for him. When his now cooled body touched hers, she flinched.

"What a day," said Friedrich, and yawned. "I am terribly tired."

Flora smiled. "Don't you think the twins went a little too far with that drinking song of theirs? I don't know what your mother must have thought. Friedrich?"

But a snore was all the answer she got that night.

Chapter Thirty

Two days after the wedding, the young couple returned to Baden-Baden with Friedrich's parents. Of course, there were tears during the goodbyes.

But Helmut and Hannah were already halfway to Bohemia in their minds. Hannah was overjoyed to go away with her husband and talked to Flora at length about the closeness between herself and Helmut that developed anew every time they went on their adventurous and never entirely safe journeys. Valentin, however, was happy to be able to stay home and give his sore back—which had been plaguing him—a little rest.

The arrangement, however, was possible only because Flora would tend to the Baden-Baden *Samenstrich* by herself that year, which secretly made her very anxious indeed. Would the customers be as willing to buy from her as they were from Hannah? Despite the impending customer visits, however, Flora was looking forward to getting back to the town. She could hardly wait to see the nest that Friedrich had created for the two of them.

Now that Seraphine had reminded her about the language of flowers, Flora was also dying to collect more material on the subject. Friedrich, whom she had already let in on her plans, wanted to accompany her to the library at the first opportunity, but he also advised her not to say a word about her ideas to the ever-skeptical Kuno, at least for the time being. That was fine with Flora—she was far from certain that they would go anywhere, after all.

Could she attract the spa guests to the shop, assisted by the language of flowers? Or were Seraphine and her father—with their talk about "putting on a show" for the rich visitors—oversimplifying things?

In Baden-Baden, Flora was thrilled to see the two rooms that she would be living in with her husband in the future. The marriage bed and a large wardrobe stood in what had once been Sybille's room, and Friedrich had turned his old room into a kind of sitting area, with a patchwork rug on the floor and two flower pictures on the wall above an old sofa.

"A bit of peace and quiet again, finally!" said Sabine grimly as she helped Flora get her clothes into Friedrich's wardrobe. But Flora knew Sabine well enough to realize that she was not comfortable with the thought that Flora was now her "mistress."

She put one arm around Sabine's shoulders. "The only thing that is changing between us is that I'll be living one floor lower down. You'll be in trouble if you start calling me Mrs. Sonnenschein! For you, I am and I will always be just Flora."

"Really? I can't just—"

"Oh, yes, you can! Let's just not make a big production of it, all right?"

Relieved by Flora's words, Sabine returned to the kitchen, and Flora—just as relieved—went to the shop.

Even after getting married, Flora and Friedrich remained the best of friends, and their life together worked well. Now that it was winter,

Friedrich did not have to be constantly available at the Trinkhalle, and while he checked in several times a day to make sure everything was fine there, he had more freedom than during the spa season. If it had been up to him, he and Flora would have been in bed much of the time. With every passing night of love, their awkwardness faded, and with each act of love they grew a little more familiar and assured in their motions. Before long, Friedrich knew that although Flora enjoyed the feel of his hands stroking her breasts, she fended him off when he tried to kiss her there. And Flora quickly learned that Friedrich could use a little assistance in reaching his goal, and that afterward it was best if she lay very still.

So this is what it felt like to be husband and wife . . .

They enjoyed the tender hours they shared on those long, dark winter nights, but at the crack of dawn Flora swung herself out of bed, ready to tackle the day. On the streets of Baden-Baden, she encountered many of the gardeners and nurserymen that she had met the winter before with her mother. They acknowledged each other, said hello, and exchanged a few words. Before long most of them knew that she had married into the Sonnenschein family and, of course, the flower shop. That she continued, simultaneously, to be a daughter of the Kerner seed family from Gönningen did not seem to bother them at all.

"The main thing is that I'm still able to order my seeds as I always have," said the gardener from the Holländer Hof hotel.

And Mr. Flumm, once he had placed his annual order, remarked, "I've got a dozen particularly nice orchids on offer. I actually had Maison Kuttner in mind, but if you want them, they're yours."

Flora glanced wistfully at the pots containing the exotics. "I fear we can't yet afford something quite that exclusive."

Still, her seed trade in Baden-Baden thrived. At the end of a busy week, she packed a pile of order forms into an envelope and sent them off to Gönningen.

When Flora had left Baden-Baden at the start of October, the town had been filled with all the chaos and frantic hustle of the departing guests.

Now, early in the new year, it was as if the streets had been swept clean. Few gave any thought to flowers. Enough potatoes in the cellar, wood and coal for the stove—those were the essentials, and a visit to the flower shop was far down anyone's list of priorities.

Flora would never have believed that a day could drag on so long. She spent hours tidying drawers and sorting bits and pieces out of sheer boredom. Or she cleaned the windows. Now that it was cold outside and cozy and warm inside, the windowpanes fogged over faster than Flora could wipe them clear. How were they supposed to lure passersby into the shop if they could not even see through the window?

Kuno, suffering from a range of minor maladies, came to the store only rarely, much to Flora's annoyance. She hoped that Friedrich would find the time to make good on his promise and take her to visit the library soon. With a stack of books, she could pass the long hours in the shop much better, she was sure.

Kuno's day usually started with him appearing in the morning to collect his newspaper and ended with him returning at five to close up. In the hours between, he took regular naps, but still often retired for the night before dinner.

How can one man sleep so much? Flora wondered. It wasn't normal. But no one other than her seemed particularly concerned. Apparently, his ailments in the winter months were a given.

The meager income of the winter months made itself felt at the dinner table. Ernestine went to great lengths to come up with new, economical dishes. It was not as if the family went hungry, but they were often close to the edge.

It's this blasted seasonal work! Flora thought many times while she waited in vain for customers. It was no different for them in Gönningen. For the seed dealers, too, the money they made on their annual sales trip in autumn had to last the whole year. And woe betide anyone who didn't manage to put at least a little aside.

On one particularly gloomy January morning, Flora suddenly heard giggling in front of the shop. Several shadows appeared on the other side of the fogged window; then the shop door was opened so energetically that the little bell almost came out of its fitting.

The girls from Maison Kuttner in their *oh-so-gorgeous* aprons!

Flora's pulse sped up and shivers ran down her spine when she recalled what she had boasted so pompously to these same young women shortly before her departure for Gönningen. She couldn't have suspected back then that she and Friedrich—

"There she is, dear Mrs. Sonnenschein, surrounded by all her *marvels*! I have to say, I'm impressed," said their leader, looking around the store with her eyes open wide.

Flora could only follow the other young woman's gaze to the buckets holding a few lonely bunches of carnations, the fir sprigs, and a few forced apple twigs that, so far, had steadfastly refused to bloom. From the ceiling hung the bundles of dried herbs and flowers, and their sparse offerings of potted plants were scattered around the room. In the dim light cast by the oil lamp, it all looked rather shabby.

"Perhaps I'm a little slow on the uptake," said the leader to the two girls accompanying her, "but there's one thing I'm not completely clear on. With what amazing business ideas does our little forest marauder here plan to please her clientele this winter?"

Flora held her tongue. So this is what she got for all her big talk! She would have thrown all three of them out of the shop if she could have.

"It's really very simple," one of the other girls replied. "Flora Sonnenschein is demonstrating a particularly involved method of twiddling her thumbs."

Giggling maliciously, the three saleswomen from Maison Kuttner ran out of the shop, leaving the door open behind them.

Flora inhaled deeply. That did it!

It was bad enough that she had to put up with such silly chatter at all. But it was far worse to know that the Kuttner girls were right.

In a few steps, Flora reached the door of the shop, closed it, and locked it. Then she ran through the back of the store into the house.

She found Friedrich in the kitchen, where he was stuffing old newspaper into wet leather boots.

"Friedrich, we have to do something. It's high time we took a stand against those arrogant witches from Maison Kuttner."

"You can borrow whatever you like and take it home or read it in the reading room at the library—we'll go there first. If you especially like a particular book, we can buy it, if it's not too expensive," said Friedrich, pushing open the entrance door to the Conversationshaus.

As they made their way in the direction of the reading room, Flora cast a surreptitious glance through the glass panes of the door that led into the casino. What magnificent chandeliers! And the walls practically shone—she was certain they were covered with pure silk.

They were here for the books, of course, but now that they were inside . . .

"Um, Friedrich," she whispered, "what would you think about, well—"

"Visiting the casino?" he interrupted her, laughing. "And squandering my hard-earned money at the roulette table instead of spending it on a book for you? Oh no!"

Obediently, Flora padded along behind her husband.

Moments later, she was left standing in wide-eyed amazement. D. R. Marx's library and reading room played second fiddle to the casino in almost nothing. The atmosphere was one of substance and high-mindedness, and the entire room smelled of perfume and *eau de cologne* and the fragrance of the large bouquet of roses that stood in a silver champagne bucket beside the cashier and that clearly bore the hallmark of Maison Kuttner.

Flora was thrilled. This place had nothing at all in common with the dusty bookshops she knew from Reutlingen.

"Up ahead there is one of the two sisters who run the reading room," Friedrich said, pointing with his chin. "You can ask them for whatever you want. In the meantime, I'll be back there looking at the books on archaeology."

When Flora asked if the library had books about flowers, the woman looked at her questioningly. What kind of book did Flora have in mind . . . botanical identification guides? Novels? Goethe's flower poems? Or would the young lady prefer to read something of an edifying nature, the story of vain Narcissus, for example, whose name was synonymous with spring daffodils? Of course, they also had books with pretty flower pictures, the woman added.

Flora was speechless.

The librarian swept away almost silently on her soft-soled shoes, and returned a minute later with a stack of books in her arms. Flora would no doubt be able to decide for herself what she wanted.

She let out a little hysterical laugh. If Seraphine could see this . . .

*Every year, from April 28 to May 3, the Romans cel-
ebrated "Floralia," a lively spring festival in honor of the
keeper of gardens . . .*

It was all so exciting! Flora was so deep into her book that she
barely noticed the raised voices outside, in front of the Conversationshaus. Only when most of the library visitors were already at the windows did she look up.

A male voice could be heard, loud and upset, perhaps also a little
drunk, bemoaning something. A second man seemed to be trying frantically to talk to the first.

"Russians, probably," murmured a woman by the window. "I wonder what it's about?"

"It's about money, of course," said the woman next to her. "They
both just came from the casino. I saw it with my own eyes."

"He's got a pistol!" another woman suddenly screamed. "*Mon
Dieu!* He wants to kill himself!"

Flora practically leaped to the window.

"Can you see why I am so ill-disposed toward games of chance? Some
of the spa guests are so addicted to roulette and cards that they stay
here through winter just to be near the casino. And then this kind of
thing happens," said Friedrich as he and Flora made their way back
toward Stephanienstrasse with a pile of books. "The poor devil probably gambled away everything he had in the world."

Flora said nothing. She had been deeply affected by what had played
out in front of the window, the way the man had taken out his pistol
and waved it around in the air. Had he really planned to kill himself?

After a period of time that felt to Flora like an eternity, the fellow
had allowed his friend to lead him away unhurt, but he had kept a firm
grip on the pistol.

"You don't think he'll try it again, do you?"

Friedrich shrugged. "He would not be the first."

If someone had told Flora six months before that she would one day become a passionate reader, she would have laughed out loud. In her family, evenings were spent playing cards or singing together, working on a handicraft, or going to one of the village inns. Seraphine was the only one who read very much, and most of the time it was boring poems that didn't interest anyone else.

Now, however, Flora spent long hours in the shop working her way enthusiastically through a stack of books from the library. Whenever she found a passage that she really liked, she quickly added it verbatim in her notebook. Poems, wise and witty commentary, unusual flower meanings—with every passing day, she filled more pages of her notebook.

The evenings, too, were reserved for reading. Flora had thought that she and Friedrich would be able to sit on the sofa in their room for that purpose. She would have loved to snuggle in his arms while she read. But Friedrich said that having candles burning in two rooms was a waste of money.

Instead, almost every evening saw all four Sonnenscheins sitting together amiably, each with his or her favorite reading material. Friedrich read books about archaeology and excavations, while Kuno and Ernestine turned to *Die Gartenlaube*.

In the current issue, the serialized novel that Kuno enjoyed so much concerned a prisoner whose court case was dragging on. Kuno found the story thrilling and took great pleasure in telling Friedrich and Flora the latest developments in lurid detail, but he left out important pieces of information in his retelling: even after several weeks, Flora still had no idea why the man had been locked away in the first place.

Flora had never imagined that *she* would bore other people with excerpts from *her* reading material.

"Friedrich, did you know that even in ancient Greece the people decorated rooms with flowers? They believed they could sense the presence of the gods in the scent of the flowers."

"Ah, hmm," Friedrich murmured without looking up from his own book.

Flora continued: "Even the Egyptians had an exceptional relationship to flowers. Florists were highly respected among them. Can you imagine? It says so right here." She tapped on the open page in front of her.

"Now you've got those old Egyptians in your head, too . . ." Ernestine shook her head almost disapprovingly, then pointed to a calendar on the wall. "February second. Today is Candlemas. Finally! Now, we will really be able to see the days getting longer. Soon we'll be able to have dinner in daylight again."

"Candlemas day, put beans in the clay; put candles and candlesticks away. That's the old rhyme, isn't it?" Kuno said, smiling at his wife.

Flora looked from one to the other. "You don't seem much interested in my discoveries!"

"Oh, child," Ernestine replied, "when you go on all the time like that, I can't concentrate on my own reading. To be quite candid, I find the endless flower stories a little tedious after a while."

Flora looked at her mother-in-law in annoyance. How could anyone have so little sense of poetry?

Friedrich just grinned.

Kuno took off his reading glasses. Barely stifling a yawn, he said good night.

"You're going up already? I wanted to tell you what I read yesterday," said Flora.

"And that would be . . . ?" Kuno asked, suppressing a sigh. He glanced toward the stairs as if he could hardly wait to get into bed.

Flora took a deep breath—now or never! "It's about the language of flowers. Did you know that in the past, especially in Paris, florists gave their customers small booklets with their bouquets, explaining something of the symbolism of the flowers? They did it to *avoid* misunderstandings. Wouldn't that be something we could do, too?"

Kuno grimaced. "Are you starting with that again? Honestly, I don't understand what you see in that old stuff. You're so progressive otherwise."

"Romantic sentiments are not 'old stuff,'" Flora said vehemently.

Kuno waved off her objection. "Call it what you like, but don't start bringing all of that"—he flailed one hand in the direction of Flora's books—"into the shop. We want to sell flowers, and that's all. Our customers have no interest in Goethe and Balzac and all the rest! And you already know what I think of the language of flowers."

"Yes, but . . ." Flora looked plaintively toward Friedrich, but he only shrugged and said, "Not everyone is as thirsty for knowledge as you are."

"If we start making the symbolism and the little stories known, we'll set ourselves apart from the others. Maybe, with the language of flowers, we'll be able to bring in some new customers in the coming season. Maison Kuttner—"

"Enough!" Kuno interrupted her, his expression suddenly stern. "I'll say it one last time: I don't want to hear another word about it. As if I didn't have enough to worry about. All the invoices, the housekeeping money, taxes, heating, etcetera, etcetera—*those* are things to worry about. And you come to me with all that fanciful stuff." He glared at Flora.

"But—" Flora wanted to say that if business were better, all those worries would fall by the wayside, but Kuno cut her off again.

"No buts. And now, good night."

Chapter Thirty-One

Kuno Sonnenschein went to sleep that night for the last time, and for all time.

Ernestine's scream the following morning rang through the hallway, and it was not long before all the residents of the house had gathered at Kuno's bedside. Bewilderment, horror, disbelief. Ernestine shook her husband's lifeless arm, telling him not to make such undignified jokes. Flora promised that she would never, ever mention the language of flowers around him again if he would please, please wake up.

Only when the doctor that Friedrich sent for confirmed the death of the master of the house—heart failure, nothing unusual in men of Kuno's age, sadly—did the terrible truth begin to seep into the consciousness of the family.

In the days that followed, the bell over the shop door did not stop ringing. Else Walbusch, Gretel Grün, and many other neighbors came to express their condolences.

Flora's hands trembled as she tied the wreath for Kuno's funeral. The winter sun gleamed through the window, its rays falling directly onto the counter where Flora worked. For a moment that went on uncannily long, it seemed to Flora that Kuno was watching her from heaven as she worked. Just as he taught her to do, she checked that every little twig was cleanly tied to the one beside it.

She was in the process of attaching a bouquet of white roses to the wreath when the mailman arrived with the latest issue of *Die Gartenlaube*. The moment the mailman was gone, Flora broke down sobbing. Kuno would never know what became of the prisoner in his beloved serial.

Sabine stared at the mountain of potatoes she still had to peel. Potatoes for lunch, potatoes for dinner . . . if it went on like this, she'd have potatoes growing out of her ears. But better that than nothing to eat at all. She sighed deeply. As she picked up her knife again, a shadow appeared in the doorway.

"Flora!" A sudden jolt ran through Sabine. Good gracious, was it so late already? She hadn't even put on the potatoes to boil.

"I closed up early," said Flora, dropping onto one of the chairs. "There aren't any customers anyway."

Sabine gazed at the potatoes. Another one of those days . . .

In the time following Kuno's death, Flora had felt that the reticence of his old customers was a sign of piety. But now three weeks had passed and still no one came.

"No customers, no income, it's that simple. And I don't have any more money to buy flowers." Flora sighed. "When the first flowers start to bloom, which won't be all that long now, then I'll probably have no choice but to sign on at Flumm. I might as well close up the shop now and look for work as a maid somewhere."

Sabine raised her eyebrows. "What does your husband have to say about that?" She nodded toward the front room.

As he had every evening, after returning from the Trinkhalle, Friedrich had gone straight in to see his mother. Since her husband's death, madam had lost her voice. It made no difference what any of them tried; so far they had been unable to rouse the widow from her cocoon of grief. And while it was very nice of Friedrich to lavish so much care on his mother, Sabine wondered whether his wife didn't deserve a little attention, too?

"Friedrich . . . hasn't been much of a help to me at all." Flora laughed sadly. "When spring is here, the people will be more interested in flowers again, he says." Her eyelids fluttered as she stared at Sabine. "And what if they aren't?" She threw her hands over her face, and her body shook with sobs.

Helplessly, Sabine stroked her friend's back.

"What kind of silly creature am I? Since when did crying make anything any better?" Flora gulped.

Sabine held out an apple for her. "Eat something. When I see how pale and wretched you look, I get truly scared."

When Flora just shook her head, Sabine picked up a knife and sliced the apple into chunks. Then she fed Flora as she would a small child. After a little while, she saw some color return to Flora's pallid cheeks.

"I think it's about time you began to tell your mother-in-law about your concerns. I mean, doesn't she have a right to know how serious things are?" Time to recover from the shock of her husband's death was one thing, but couldn't Flora and Friedrich see that Ernestine was only sinking deeper and deeper into her grief with every passing day?

"When money was tight in the past, madam at least helped me to bring some variety into what I serve. But right now, she doesn't seem to care how I get by with the little bit of money your husband gives me." Sabine heaved the pot of potatoes onto the stove.

"Ernestine is grieving so deeply. How can I burden her with anything else? And quite apart from that, how could *she*, of all people, help me with the shop? As for the housekeeping money, I can give you something. My mother gave me a bit of money when I got married. Friedrich doesn't know anything about it, and my mother said I should put it away for a rainy day."

"Well, today is looking rather rainy, I must say!" said Sabine, and laughed. "I hope you really can spare a little."

A smile crossed Flora's face, and then she jumped up and returned a short time later with a large leather drawstring purse. When she had given Sabine a few coins to bolster the housekeeping money, the maid returned to the stove in a lighter frame of mind and speculatively stabbed a potato.

"It's always the same worry: money, money, money! You need a goose that lays golden eggs, or to win a million marks in the casino. Then I'd bake a chicken for you every day, and ham and pies as well. No more turnips and potatoes every day." With a sigh, she replaced the lid on the pot.

Instead of answering, Flora stared at the purse in her hands.

"The casino . . . it would be worth a try."

"Are you out of your mind? Good gracious, Flora, I was making a joke! Please tell me you're not seriously thinking about taking your good money and—" Sabine broke off abruptly when she saw the look in Flora's eye. She knew that sparkle only too well: it appeared whenever Flora got an idea into her head that nothing could shake out again.

Wearing one of Ernestine's hats with the brim pulled low over her eyes, and with Ernestine's black shawl around her shoulders, Flora hurried through the narrow streets in the direction of the casino, her purse held firmly in her hand.

She had only two hours. If she could be back home again for dinner, Friedrich would not even know she had left the house.

She peered along the alley ahead. The weather was bad, and most people were indoors. Only Sabine's friend, the butcher Semmel, was in sight, carrying a bucket across his courtyard. Two stray dogs were jumping around him. *I hope he doesn't recognize me,* thought Flora anxiously.

Just then, he looked over in her direction. He nodded a curt greeting, then turned away to deal with the persistent dogs.

Had he realized who she was?

Two hours. After that, she would either be a well-off woman without a worry in the world, or . . .

Two hours to make her fortune in the casino. It would be enough just to double her money. She would, of course, give part of it to Sabine, and she would use the rest to buy beautiful flowers.

The Conversationshaus came into view, and Flora's daydreams dissipated in the wintry air.

Two hours. And she had never even seen the inside of the casino.

Summoning all her courage, Flora pushed open the door to the gaming room.

For a while, she simply drifted aimlessly around the cigar-smoke-filled room. There were no more than two-dozen guests present, primarily older men, although there were also several women drinking sparkling wine and waggling fans.

Relieved not to see a familiar face among them, Flora found herself behind one of the roulette tables. The game did not appear particularly complicated. While the players were busy placing their *jetons*, the croupier set the roulette wheel spinning. Then he flicked a small ball in the opposite direction. *"Rien ne va plus!"* he called to no one in particular, and the players gathered around the table seemed to hold their breath. The ball rolled and rolled, then hopped and jumped for a few seconds. Only when it finally settled into one of the small compartments did the croupier call the winning number and its color.

After she had watched for a while, she decided to try her luck. Guessing the right number in advance seemed to her a great risk, but she was willing to try her luck with choosing a color.

Red was the color of the most beautiful tulips in Gönningen, and her favorite roses as well. Red was also the color of love.

"*Faites vos jeux,*" said the croupier, his expression impassive.

With trembling fingers, Flora opened her purse and laid all her *jetons* on . . .

"Red!" She was so excited that her voice almost broke.

Dear God, please, please . . .

With her hands clasped as if praying, Flora held her breath and stared at the rolling ball.

Dear God, please, please . . .

Black, red, black . . . The ball slowed down, popped into a black, jumped on, clattered its way over several numbers until finally settling on . . . red!

"*Numéro trois, rouge!*" The croupier pointed his rake at the number three.

Flora could hardly believe her luck. She gaped in disbelief at the *jetons* that the croupier pushed her way. She could exchange them for cash at the cashier at any time, he said helpfully.

It was as simple as that? A few breathless moments and she had doubled her money.

After all the sadness and all the worry, luck was finally smiling on her. Flora felt it deep inside. She'd be stupid not to try one more time . . .

"Red!"

It worked again. The ball dropped into twenty-three red.

"The girl has a lucky touch," remarked the man beside Flora, clapping his hands appreciatively.

"Beginner's luck," murmured a man across the table.

Flora beamed. So much money all at once! When she told Friedrich . . . but of course she could not do that.

While the other players were busy with their own bets, Flora thought feverishly. So much money, so easily earned. But easy come, easy go, they said . . . Should she really risk it a third time?

"Mesdames et messieurs—faites vos jeux, s'il vous plaît!" The croupier was already setting the wheel in motion.

Flora took a deep breath. Why not? Red *was* her lucky color.

"Red!"

Either God was not a gambler or he was not present in Baden-Baden that day.

The ball stopped on black.

Chapter Thirty-Two

Ernestine never had considered seriously that she might one day have to go on living without her husband. If she ever found herself drifting into such grim thoughts, she had always pictured Kuno at *her* grave: the way he laid flowers, and the way he used a small hoe to keep her last resting place free of weeds.

Kuno's death, therefore, came as even more of a shock to her. He was not young, of course, and not in the best of health. And Kuno had always been somehow *old*. Even when he was courting her, there had been something wooden about him, and he had been sickly back then, too. At the start, she had been sympathetic toward him for his weak constitution, but at some point she had stopped paying it much attention. Instead, she ran his household as best she could.

And this was the thanks she got . . .

Ernestine bit her teeth together hard.

She was sitting in the dining room, as she did every morning. Not because she felt particularly at home in there. The opposite, in fact, was true. The sight of Kuno's empty chair was almost more than she could bear. But it was no better in the bedroom, where it still smelled of him, or in the ironing room, where his suits hung beside the door.

Ernestine stroked her fingers tenderly over the arrangement of dried flowers. Even in these cold months, Flora thought to decorate the table with flowers. It was also Flora who tended Kuno's grave—since the funeral, Ernestine had not been back to the graveyard. Others believed her grief was too great, and Ernestine let them believe it.

The truth was that her anger was too great. She did not want to lay eyes on Kuno ever again, not even on his grave.

How dare he leave her alone?

Ernestine glared in fury at the chair on which Kuno had sat for years.

He had not even left a will. The lawyer that she and Friedrich had visited, however, had told them that even without a will, not much would change for them.

Sneaking away like that, without a word—that was no way to behave!

When she thought about it, though, hadn't he spent his life in much the same way? Always wanting his peace and quiet to read his newspaper. Bismarck and the emperor—oh, Kuno knew all about them. He could talk about all that with Schierstiefel for hours at a time. But other conversations were far less important to him. Couldn't he have spoken to the manager of the Conversationshaus just once? Perhaps *their* flower shop could have been the one to decorate its halls.

When they were first married and had opened the shop, many ideas of that sort had gone through Ernestine's mind. She would gladly have brought a little momentum into the new business. But all Kuno wanted, even then, was his peace and quiet.

"Don't worry your head needlessly! Don't interfere!" His words from that time still echoed in her ears.

And at some point, Ernestine had bowed to his will and spent the subsequent decades under the assumption that as a woman, it was only proper to stay in the background when it came to business matters. But when she had visited Gönningen, she had begun to have her doubts—Flora's mother and the other women most definitely *did* worry about the business! They *did* interfere. They did not let their men drown in despair and apathy . . . as she had done.

Ernestine gave herself a shake, as if someone had dropped ice down her back. She had never had much interest in wealth, but a little more money would have been nice.

Her eyes automatically turned to the drawer in which she kept her housekeeping money. She did not need to open it to know how little was inside. But no, "*don't worry your head!*"

How were things supposed to go on? What were they supposed to live on?

With her head propped on her hands, she watched Sabine come in to set the table for lunch. One soup bowl for each of them, no more.

She knew that Friedrich meant well, sitting with her for hours and holding her hand, but it was not helpful. He was a good son, but his salary was not enough to feed an entire family, a fact that he seemed unaware of, just as he seemed unaware that Flora was consumed with worry. She moved through the house like a shadow of herself.

It was not Flora's fault that the business was doing so poorly. The blame for that lay squarely with Else Walbusch and the other women, all indifferent to their plight, none of them willing to trust the girl to tie a beautiful bouquet.

And all Friedrich had to say was "Things will turn for the better."

Ernestine sniffed. That was the kind of talk she would have expected from Kuno.

If there was one thing she had learned in her life, it was that absolutely nothing would turn for the better if no one lent an active hand.

She had to speak to Friedrich. And to Flora and Sabine. Ernestine prayed to the Lord above that she would not start to rail against Kuno when she did.

As if to practice, she cleared her throat.

A short time later, the family sat together for lunch. Without warning, Flora blurted, "If something doesn't change soon in the shop, we'll be forced to close."

Friedrich went on spooning his soup into his mouth without looking up.

Flora went on. "Now that Kuno's regular customers have deserted us, we have only one chance. We must win the tourists as customers! And the only way to do that is with the language of flowers. I know Kuno had no interest in that because he was afraid he would just be confusing our customers. But—"

"And he was right, wasn't he?" Friedrich interrupted her.

"Just listen to what I have in mind first. You know the notebook I've been keeping. I've got so much information in there now that it will be easy for me to go through and choose the loveliest symbolic meanings. If I write my own flower primer, so to speak, and have it printed . . ."

Friedrich slapped one hand against his forehead theatrically. "Now I understand. Today is April first!" He laughed out loud.

Ernestine looked at him reproachfully. Couldn't he see how serious Flora was?

"Friedrich, this is not a joke!" Flora cried. "Not at all. I've already written home about it. Seraphine would be prepared to help me and would even come to Baden-Baden. Of course, it would not be a real book, but more of a booklet. But with Seraphine's illustrations, it will certainly be very lovely. And it won't be a problem to fund it. Uncle Valentin wants to pay for the printing. He says we should print more than I had in mind, because they would also be a useful aid for selling seeds. Friedrich, I'd finally have something special to offer the people who come here for the season."

Friedrich laid his soup spoon aside with a loud clack. "You seem to have thought this through very carefully. But did it occur to you to talk your plans through with me before you started getting everyone else you know involved? And, if I may be so bold, I daresay that the language of flowers might not be as special as you seem to think. And that you are willing to hurl us into debt for it . . . well, I don't think that's good at all."

Flora looked at her husband with embarrassment. "Debt? But—"

"Enough!" Ernestine shouted.

Flora's and Friedrich's heads jerked around.

Ernestine glared angrily at her son. "It's shameful how little trust you put in your wife! If Flora thinks her flower booklet is the right thing to do, and if her family is willing to support her with it, then *we* will certainly not set any obstacles in her path. Or do you want to take over the running of the shop yourself?"

Friedrich shook his head in confusion. "That's out of the question, of course. I just meant—"

"Then good," Ernestine interrupted him. She turned to Flora. A smile played on her thin lips.

"Your aunt Seraphine is welcome here anytime, if she doesn't mind that things are a little basic just now."

"But, Mother! Father would never have wanted Flora—"

"Your father is dead! But we must go on," Ernestine said, cutting him off again. "Flora, if your flower primer has to be ready for the start of the season, then you will have to hurry. Who knows? Maybe I might even be of some use to you and your aunt, at least a little?"

Chapter Thirty-Three

As she did every year, Princess Nadeshda Stropolski, known to her friends as Püppi, had rented a suite with a balcony at the Europäischer Hof for the season in Baden-Baden.

She pulled her wrap closer around her shoulders and gazed out from the balcony at the surrounding parks and buildings, all of it silvery in the light of the moon and stars. She loved the view from so high—even in the hours when everyone else was asleep, there was something captivating about it. The enormous trees that marked the course of the Oos River looked like monsters angling for human sacrifices. Soon—when the dawn fog thinned and a pale sun crept above the meadows—the morning concert of the birds would ring from those same trees. Püppi would have been pleased to see how the moon-silvered landscape transformed into a brilliant watercolor, as if a painter had managed to cover his canvas with every shade of green there was, all at once.

By then, though, she would be going to sleep. As she did every day once dawn had broken. Because then she was safe.

From the balcony, she slipped quietly back into the sitting room of her suite. She glanced toward the bedroom, where Konstantin was sleeping—he had no need to fear the kiss of death at night. That was *her* prophecy. Even after all these years, she heard the voice of the wart-faced gypsy woman in her ears.

Isa, Püppi's little dog, had curled up beside Kostia's head as she did every night. Soon, both would awaken, rested and ready to take on the world, while she was old and tired and could finally go to bed.

A shudder went through her. She drank a mouthful of tea and pulled a face. The girl had brought the tray an hour earlier, but until now Püppi had ignored the sharp aroma of the brew in the hope that Konstantin might wake and join her for a cup of tea. The tea was cold, and Kostia still asleep.

It was not so long ago that, drunk with sleep, he had called her to him in bed and they had made love. Love . . .

Püppi's gaze was drawn to the crackling fire in the fireplace. The maid had kindled it when she had brought the tea. Did she feel so cold because she was tired? Or was it because she was afraid? Fear could feel as cold as ice, too. Püppi knew that better than anyone.

They had arrived in Baden-Baden just the day before. Piotr had traveled with them, which had made the long drive less tedious, at least for Konstantin. That same evening, Count Popo hosted a welcome dinner—nothing big, though, because not all of their friends had arrived yet.

They had all been so overjoyed to see each other again! Prince Gagarin had been so carried away at their return to Baden-Baden that he proclaimed that he was contemplating having a church built in the town. And Matriona Schikanova had announced that in a few days her husband and four sons would be arriving—much to the pleasure of Popo and Piotr, because the Schikanov men were considered outstanding riders and cardplayers whose presence had been sorely missed the previous season when business had kept them in Saint Petersburg. Her dear friend Anna had told the guests about an opera premiere that she had attended in Cairo of Giuseppe Verdi's *Aida*.

Irina Komatschova had not talked about it, but Püppi knew that she had spent the winter visiting her estates on the Crimean Peninsula.

When Konstantin talked about the marvels of Monte Carlo, Irina's expression had turned dour, and she had asked if he had at least managed to do a little painting, since the Mediterranean coastline, unlike Crimea, certainly had no shortage of scenes worth immortalizing in watercolor.

Püppi had hurriedly changed the subject. The thought of Konstantin and his painting always made her a little sad.

Dear Konstantin! The urge to go in and embrace him was almost overwhelming. She loved him so much! And he seemed to love her in return, for he had put aside his plans for painting just to be with her through the winter. And, she knew, he had wanted to paint so very much. The winter jasmine. Monte Carlo harbor with all its boats. She herself with her parasol in one of the many parks. But no, for her sake, he had buried his dream of one day being celebrated as a great artist.

Konstantin was still extremely affectionate with her, yet there were moments when Püppi sensed that he paid less attention to her than he did at the start of their travels together the previous October. Sometimes she believed that she even sensed a trace of impatience in him.

As she had the previous evening.

Gagarin's nephew had begun to play his violin, and Kostia had danced. With Anna. With Matriona. He had even asked Irina to dance, which had softened her sullen expression. The only one he had not danced with was her, Püppi. "I'm sure you must be tired after the long journey," he had said, and told her that she should look after herself.

Püppi swept a strand of gray hair out of her eyes. She had not been tired, but whenever Konstantin talked like that, she suddenly *felt* tired. And old. And worn out.

And yet she would have given anything to be young! For Konstantin. For their love . . . or in the end he would regret that he had chosen her over his art after all.

Frowning, she looked at the small bouquet on the table in front of her. Flowers were the favorite subject of many painters, but did

Konstantin paint them, too? Or was he more of a portrait artist? Or interested in landscapes?

The truth was that she did not know. She had never asked him to show her his portfolio.

Why hadn't she become some kind of benefactress for him, a patroness of his art?

So far, she had done nothing—absolutely nothing—for him in that regard.

Someone must have put the bouquet in the room the evening before. Konstantin? No, the pretty arrangement of buttercups, willow herbs, and yellow twigs that Püppi did not recognize did not carry his signature at all. When he gave flowers, it was usually opulent arrangements with roses and lilies that were meant to impress but did not last long. The hotelier, perhaps?

Püppi's heart suddenly began to beat faster, and she let out a little giggle. Did she perhaps have a secret admirer?

Then she saw the leaflet attached to the bouquet: *Sunshine from Sonnenschein's*, it said. Advertising for a florist's . . . Püppi grimaced. So much for her secret admirer! She'd do better to think about how she could promote Konstantin's paintings.

Beneath the leaflet she discovered a small booklet: *Flora's ABC of Flowers*.

Püppi flipped through the pages curiously. Everybody knew that a four-leaf clover meant good luck, but she was intrigued to see that lavender could be read as a symbol of love and devotion—how very interesting! She went on until she came to the buttercups that made up much of her bouquet, and read: *Give buttercups if you can recognize beauty even in old age, and if you love change.*

Püppi was taken aback. She loved beauty, and she had no objection to change if it was in her favor.

The illustrations of the flowers were certainly very lovely. In fact, the entire booklet was lovely . . .

Without warning, Püppi had an idea, one that was so thrilling that she grew quite dizzy. A *vernissage*! An exhibition of Konstantin's pictures! And this florist would supply symbolically fitting flowers for it.

Dear Konstantin, he should know what it felt like to be a celebrated artist.

The sun was rising slowly into the sky when Püppi finally went to bed. When she woke up, she would seek out the florist behind the bouquet. Change? She was more than ready!

Chapter Thirty-Four

As so often in the late afternoon, the end of the street where the flower shop was located felt all but deserted. The housewives who had done their shopping in the morning were now busy cooking or doing laundry. And the tradesmen and merchants whose workshops and establishments lined the same street as the flower shop were all inside, at work.

Or they're cleaning all the pollen off their clothes and furniture, Flora thought grumpily as she wiped the window clean for what felt like the fiftieth time that day. As pretty as she found the chestnut flowers, she could certainly do without the mess of pollen that came with them.

What she needed was a miracle. She would have been happy with a moment of epiphany, something to explain why her ideas had not brought in any new customers.

The shop was filled with potted lilies of the valley that no one wanted to buy. She had sold no more than half a dozen. In the past, Flora had always found their unique fragrance intoxicating. But now, amid a sea of them, she found the smell merely pungent and pervasive.

She had dug dozens of the flowers out of the garden behind the house, but most of them she had bought from Flumm's Nursery.

"'Lily of the valley and the nightingale's song herald the joy of love and the coming summer'—that's all well and good, but are you sure you want to put all your money on one horse? Why not buy some other flowers, too, like before?" Flumm had not been enthusiastic about her idea.

Lily of the valley was also considered a harbinger of a new age, which was exactly what the Sonnenschein shop needed urgently, Flora had replied.

Ernestine and Friedrich had pleaded for her to buy a wider range, too—and why hadn't she listened to them? What was she supposed to write to her parents, from whom she had borrowed the money to pay for the plants? She had had no money of her own now for weeks.

Everything was going wrong. Her ideas were simply not good enough to save the shop. Why didn't she go off in search of a position as a domestic or a chambermaid in one of the hotels?

Flora's eye fell on the tall stack of booklets that she had collected proudly from the printer just the week before. *Flora's ABC of Flowers.* The lilies of the valley were not the only lame horse she had banked her money on.

And yet the booklet had turned out so beautifully. Seraphine and Flora had selected more than a hundred different flowers for it, from simple meadow flowers to expensive nursery varieties. She had agonized over every word of the meanings. The texts were splendid, and Seraphine's illustrations were lovely. Flora had been thrilled to hand over her work to the printer a little farther up the street. And the printer had made a huge effort to have the job completed by mid-May—he looked on the work as a service to another local, he'd said.

The day after collecting the finished booklets, Flora had gone to the hotels and handed out more than fifty of them as welcoming gifts for the incoming seasonal visitors. And each booklet was accompanied by a bouquet of meadow flowers. But for what? Since then, not one of the visitors had come in to show any kind of appreciation for the *ABC*, although her address was printed very clearly on the handwritten leaflet she had appended to each one.

She had copied the names of the new arrivals and hotels they were staying at from the guest list in the *Badeblatt*. Friedrich had pointed out that this was where the names of the newly arrived guests were listed, and Flora had been scrupulous in spelling each guest's name correctly. *Princess Nadeshda Stropolski*, she had written on one. *Prince Vladimir Menshikov, His Highness Nikolaj M. Romanov . . .*

If she was being so generous toward people she had never met, Friedrich suggested, then she should certainly give one of the booklets and a bouquet to Lady O'Donegal—the Englishwoman had also arrived for the start of the season. Ernestine, however, wrung her hands and asked if this kind of petitioning was even proper.

Proper? When your stomach is growling with hunger . . .

Flora banged the palm of her hand hard onto the shop counter. She felt like curling up in a ball and crying in anger and disappointment.

Perhaps the booklet would at least go over well with her parents' customers. A hundred and fifty copies had been sent directly from the printer to Gönningen—Helmut and Valentin wanted to take *Flora's ABC of Flowers* with them on their next journey.

In the meantime, Baden-Baden had filled with people visiting the spa. Some days, Lichtenthaler Allee was so crowded, it was almost impossible to get through. But no one walked as far as their shop.

Flora abruptly jumped to her feet. Out! She needed to get out before the fragrance of lilies of the valley made her sick.

"Excuse me, I—" Taken by surprise, Flora let go of the door, on the opposite side of which was an older woman wearing a bright-pink dress.

"Am I in the right place? Sonnenschein's?" the woman asked in broken German.

Flora nodded. The woman's sudden appearance had given her quite a shock. Or was it the woman's perfume making Flora dizzy? It smelled of cinnamon and other spices, and it was so penetrating that it overwhelmed even the scent of the lilies of the valley.

"Good, good. I don't have much time." The woman waved a copy of Flora's little book in the air. "I am planning a *vernissage* for a Bulgarian artist, and of course I am going to need flowers. The artist loves grand gestures, so I picture something opulent—roses, lilies, orchids. What can you offer me?"

Flora's heart felt as if it might burst out of her chest at any moment, it was beating so hard. Opulent flowers? She didn't have anything like that! And what the devil was a "*vernissage*"?

"That's a . . . sensitive matter," Flora said, just to reply with anything at all.

Her first foreign customer, and from her accent Flora guessed she was Russian. And all Flora could do was stammer out meaningless words.

The woman fiddled with the dozen or more strings of pearls around her neck. "What is so *sensitive* about a few flowers to go with some paintings?"

Paintings! So a *vernissage* was an exhibition of paintings.

Flora gulped nervously. In her mind, she heard her father, in a singularly Swabian way, say, "The woman *fernelet*!" And this woman in her pink dress truly was a classic "distant beauty"—she looked youthful and attractive from far away, but close up her face was as wrinkled as an old turtle's. And her makeup did nothing to alter that.

Flora cleared her throat. "First and foremost, the pictures themselves need to be allowed to open up to the observer. Flowers can only help the beauty of the art to unfold, no more." Considering that she had no idea where she was going with her words, she sounded quite certain of herself. "Opulent varieties like roses and orchids would only be a needless distraction for the eye."

The woman frowned.

Flora hastily picked up her thread. "I would recommend something white. White is the color of purity, and white is also the color of the artist's canvas before the first stroke of a brush." She picked up a particularly pretty lily of the valley and turned it lovingly in all directions. "In the language of flowers, lilies of the valley are a sign of the joy that recurs every year, and they are also the herald of a new age." As she talked, she tried to puzzle out how she would integrate the tiny flowers into an exhibition of paintings. Beside the enormous canvases painted by Franz Xaver Winterhalter, no one would even notice the lilies of the valley. White lilies, callas, or orchids, those would be just the thing—the "distant beauty" was right about that. "Which is why we have lilies of the valley, symbolizing so perfectly the start of the new spa season. But they are also the ideal flower to accentuate the beauty of art."

The woman clapped her hands together. "I like this language of flowers very much," she said. "All right. The *vernissage* is to take place this coming Saturday." She gave Flora the address and told her what time she would expect her there. "Bring two hundred of these . . . lilies of the valley, you called them? Or no, let's say five hundred."

When the woman left, Flora quickly hung the "We'll Be Right Back" sign on the door and ran off toward the Trinkhalle. She found Friedrich in the middle of explaining the frescoes on the wall to a group of older English women.

"Friedrich, we have a problem!" Flora cried breathlessly, ignoring the astonished looks from the English guests. "Where in the world can I find another four hundred lilies of the valley at short notice?"

Chapter Thirty-Five

"Oh God, I don't have the slightest idea what happens at a *vernissage*! Is it just invited guests or can anyone walk in? Do they hang the pictures on the wall, like you'd expect? And where am I supposed to put my flowers? What do you think—is this dress all right?" Flora babbled away without waiting for answers and held up her dark-blue dress in front of her for Sabine to inspect.

The maid, who was sitting on the bed in Flora's bedroom and eating a wrinkled apple, shrugged. "It's been sewn up once along the hem, but what difference does that make? The guests won't see you."

"But what if they do?" Flora rummaged on through her wardrobe. She had never put much store in clothes. All her skirts, blouses, and dresses were either dark brown, dark green, or black, and were chosen for practicality rather than looks. She had not given much thought at all to the fact that she would need "fine" clothes for "fine" customers.

"Maybe the *vernissage* is a kind of art market. Like a normal market, but with paintings instead of vegetables. Friedrich should know this sort of thing," said Sabine.

"He's never been invited to anything like this, either," Flora replied distractedly. Of course, her favorite blouse just *had* to be missing two buttons. "But he knows about Princess Stropolski, he says. She spends every season living in the Europäischer Hof. But he's never heard of a painter named Konstantin Sokerov."

"He's probably an old-timer like that Mr. Winterhalter," said Sabine between bites of her apple.

"At least it's not starting until the afternoon. I'd feel bad having to close the shop on a Saturday morning," said Flora.

"Madam could have filled in at the counter in an emergency. Or me."

Flora did not seem to be listening to her. Her hands planted on her hips, she mumbled angrily to herself, "What kind of fool am I! Every child in Gönningen knows that you must present yourself well if you're going to get anywhere in business. The seed merchants always look after their appearance. I don't even have a good dress to put on." Like a damp sack, Flora plopped onto the bed beside Sabine.

"I've got an idea. Here's what you do." Sabine sprang to her feet and rummaged through Flora's wooden jewelry box. "Put on the dark-brown dress. That's at least reasonably all right. And with your *F* brooch you pin a little nosegay to the collar as an eye-catcher."

Flora let out a relieved sigh. "Oh, Sabine. What would I do if I didn't have you?"

"You'd find someone else," Sabine replied drily, but she was smiling broadly.

Flora stood and took her by the hands and turned her in a circle. "You know what? When I have the money for this job in my hand, we'll go out shopping."

The family, of course, was speechless when Flora told them about the visit from the Russian princess.

Five hundred lilies of the valley? For an exhibition of paintings?

For a moment, Ernestine had looked as if she were going to pass out. "Well, that's the Russians for you," she said in the tone of someone who would know. Then she fixed her son with a sideways gaze and added that the woman would certainly not have come to the shop at all without *Flora's ABC*.

"Then you can pay your parents back the borrowed money right away. I'm not comfortable being in debt," Friedrich had said.

Flora had nodded absently. Her parents would not be knocking at the poorhouse door if she took some time to pay them back. But first and foremost, she had to make sure the princess was satisfied. And then . . . could such miracles happen more often?

Flora toyed with her provisional corsage as she stood just inside the back door of the exhibition hall at the Europäischer Hof. As long as no one was bothered by her presence or threw her out, she had no intention of giving up her place. Oh no! She wanted to remember every detail so she could tell Friedrich and Ernestine all about it later.

Pictures and guests admiring them—that was as far as she had envisioned a *vernissage*. But all the rest . . .

Just the pictures! Flora had imagined enormous oil paintings, perhaps impressive, life-size portraits of noblewomen or arresting landscapes painted in saturated hues.

But here, the pictures on show were rather pale watercolors, painted almost childishly she thought. People, landscapes, houses—it seemed the painter took as his subject whatever was in front of him. The pictures of houses were very pretty, and Flora thought she recognized one or two.

Reluctantly, and with much grumbling, one of the servants at the Europäischer Hof had set out small tables beneath each of the paintings of houses. Flora positioned her lilies of the valley on each table so that it looked as if the flowers were growing in the front garden of each house. The effect seemed to be well received by the guests; at least, most of the people were standing at those paintings.

Flora would not have said that any of the pictures were outstanding. For her taste, Seraphine did a much better job. She had also been unable to spot the artist himself, and did not know if that mattered to her or not.

She could hardly take her eyes off the guests, all dressed as if they had been invited to a royal wedding. The men wore tailcoats sewn from gleaming cloth, or uniform jackets heavy with gold braid and epaulets, and their trousers were decorated with piping in contrasting colors. While the men went no further than heavy gold watch chains and signet rings, the women glittered in tiaras, necklaces, and elaborately beaded jewelry. The dresses they wore were stunning, each lovelier than the next, lined with lace and studded with pearls and precious stones, and fashioned from countless layers of the finest fabrics. Flora also noted some made of gleaming velvet, and realized that she had not known that one could use the heavy material to fashion such artfully conceived clothing as what she saw in front of her.

If only Ernestine could see this, Flora thought with excitement. Just then, she saw the Russian woman who had commissioned her coming in her direction with another woman at her side.

Suddenly, her excitement gave way to anxiety and worry. She hoped the princess was happy with the flowers.

As she had when she visited the shop, the Russian was wearing a bright-pink silk dress. Now, her hair was pinned up into an artful tower atop her head, the hairpins themselves gleaming with precious stones. Across her arm lay a small dog that panted loudly and drooled strings of saliva onto the pink fabric.

"Here is my flower girl!" said Princess Stropolski to her companion. "Flora Sonnenschein. Isn't she just a wonder, darling?"

"A wonder, indeed." The other woman smiled.

Flora had no idea how one was supposed to greet such women—or even *if* one was supposed to—but she tried a small curtsy.

"That *ABC of Flowers* is from her. You must have received one as well, Irina?"

"Utterly delightful!" said the woman, who seemed a little friendlier now. "Yes, I've glanced through it."

"If madam has anything floral in mind, the language of flowers is exceptionally versatile," Flora said.

The woman named Irina leaned conspiratorially close to Flora. "Is there a flower that will take away all a person's worries?"

Flora's brow creased. The woman seemed to have misunderstood the point of her *ABC of Flowers* completely.

When Flora did not answer immediately, Irina turned back to the princess. "Do you still remember that wise man that Anna brought along to meet us last year?"

"Wasn't he able to read the future in pieces of bark? There was something strange about that whole business, if you ask me. The way he sat and stared at his bits of wood . . ." Princess Stropolski gestured as if wanting to wipe away the memory—after her own death had been foretold, she did not take kindly to fortune-telling.

"I found him amusing. Do you still remember? He predicted that Matriona would get pregnant again when she gets old!" Irina's laugh rang out loudly.

The princess shook her head. "No, no, I prefer to follow the advice of my flower girl. Her white blooms do show off Kostia's pictures to their best advantage, don't you think? And the *vernissage* seems to be quite the sensation among my guests."

"Oh, definitely. We will be so grateful for every little bit of distraction this season. Baden-Baden has become such a crashing bore," said Irina, with a thin-lipped smile. "Perhaps the flower girl can tell us more about talking flowers one day?"

Flora looked from one woman to the other in confusion. They were talking about her as if she were not even there!

Princess Stropolski suddenly turned and peered across the room toward the door. "Oh, look, Konstantin has finally arrived." Her wrinkled face stretched into a smile that only made it more wrinkled.

Flora's gaze followed the princess's.

That tall young man who was making his way slowly through the throng of guests was the artist? If that was so, then he was considerably better looking than his pictures.

In contrast to most of the other men, he wore neither uniform nor tails, but a slim-cut, peplumed jacket of the style one saw more often among hunters. His hair was long and tied back loosely with a black velvet band. Flora had never seen hair like that on a man before, though she thought it looked very masculine and dashing.

Flora looked down at herself and her plain brown dress, and took a step backward.

Chapter Thirty-Six

When Konstantin first heard that Püppi had organized an exhibition of his pictures, he would have liked nothing more than to slap her face. Instead, he had acted surprised and put on his most modest smile. An exhibition? For him? But he had not yet matured as an artist, not at all . . . and in his mind, he called down fire and brimstone on Püppi's head. He had been doing so well as a "would-be artist," but where would he stand after this exhibition?

In the end, he had no choice but to put on a brave face, because the portfolio containing his pictures was already at the framer's, after which the hotel concierge would get to work hanging his works in the ballroom.

Anyone witnessing Konstantin's charming smile at the *vernissage* would never have suspected just how much the event disgusted him.

"As is so often the case with true art, we laymen do not have to understand everything that we see . . ."

He tilted his head almost reverently in the direction of the speaker—Count Popo—as if the man's words were the most moving he had ever heard.

"As these white flowers are the herald of a new age, so will the painter of these works proclaim a new age to us, and . . ."

What an old windbag Popo could be! Konstantin had no intention of proclaiming anything to anyone, because this damned exhibition had not been his idea at all.

"And the transience of nature moves us much as does the transience of glorious art."

Glorious art? His hastily splashed watercolors had never been intended to go before any kind of audience. And why was Popo rattling on about flowers and nature?

Konstantin turned and looked toward the back door of the ballroom. The flower girl, admittedly, was a pretty thing, and she probably found the whole affair terribly exciting. Maybe he would exchange a few words with her later. She'd probably turn pale with awe at being able to talk to the artist in person.

Konstantin smiled. Perhaps his *vernissage* might be amusing after all.

Püppi nodded at Popo's words, visibly moved, along with the rest of them. Even Piotr Vjazemskij acted as if he were listening to the count, although in spirit he had more likely wandered off to the casino long before. Matriona, who had been at a party all through the previous night with Püppi and him, tried to stifle a yawn behind her hand, and Konstantin noted that she was swaying with weariness.

The sight abruptly made him laugh out loud.

What a mad crowd he was part of! They would do anything for a bit of fun and distraction. They were even willing to see him as an artist and were not above applauding his "work."

So why should he spoil their fun? Who was he to curse Püppi for her crazy impulse? His job here was to play along, with a solid dose of self-mockery and humor, not to turn tail and run like a thief caught in the act.

He waved over one of the serving girls and plucked a glass of champagne from the tray she carried.

"My friends!" he called loudly, with a sweeping gesture to take in everybody around him. The guests all turned from Popo to him. "Let us drink to the health of our speechmaker, who is able to compare my pictures to *art* like no other man on earth!" Accompanied by the assenting murmur from the crowd, Konstantin drained his glass and immediately accepted another. "And a toast to you all, dear friends, for taking note of my amateurish attempts with such benevolence." Those standing around him laughed and lifted their glasses to him, and he returned the gesture in kind.

"And I would like to propose another toast to our most beloved Püppi, to whom alone all credit must go for the idea for this exhibition— I would never have dared to bore you with my pictures." Konstantin noted with satisfaction that not one single person there seemed bored. On the contrary—they all seemed to find the event extremely entertaining. "Unfortunately, I have been neglecting my painting of late, which I am sure everyone in this room can attest to." He shrugged nonchalantly, then kissed Püppi's hand for a provocatively long time. "But what does one's own career matter when one has been given the love of a wonderful woman?"

His words were met by a storm of applause. Konstantin smiled.

An artist? Oh, he was certainly that. But in which métier, he wondered . . .

Chapter Thirty-Seven

Konstantin Sokerov's *vernissage* was the start. While Flora's lilies of the valley were not exactly *the* talking point of Baden-Baden, word about the clever placement of the flowers in front of the pictures—Count Popo had even mentioned it in his speech—certainly did get around. Afterward, those who had heedlessly put their copy of *Flora's ABC of Flowers* aside rediscovered the little booklet. Word quickly spread to spa visitors who were not on Püppi's guest list, and soon everyone had heard about the "talking flowers." Many were taken with the idea—Seraphine was right that it appealed to the Romantic nature of the Russian soul.

And so, in the 1872 spa season in Baden-Baden, Flora and her flowers were suddenly *en vogue* among the visitors to the beautiful town.

"I have a very special . . . concern," a pimply young Russian man said to Flora one morning. He had introduced himself as Igor Salnikov after he came rushing into the store. Excitedly, he told Flora about the girl he was courting, a girl so arrogant that she did not even notice how intensely he was trying to court her.

"She simply ignores my existence! For her, I'm no more than air. How am I supposed to declare my love to her?" The young admirer ran his hands through his hair despairingly. "I'm afraid my situation is so hopeless that not even your famous language of flowers can help."

Flora was amazed at how perfectly he spoke German. She had been worried, at first, that the meanings she had attached to the flowers in her *ABC* would not be understood by the foreign visitors, but Friedrich had reassured her. "Anyone with that much money can afford the most expensive schools and the best teachers. Believe me, they are exceptionally well educated."

For the first time in her life, Flora was glad that she had studied English and French herself. "If you go out into the world, you have to speak its languages"—that was the motto of the seed traders.

Flora smiled as she addressed her new customer.

"*One* bouquet probably won't be enough to make the young woman notice you. You will have to let the flowers speak for you several times." She was already selecting flowers from the buckets. "We'll start with amaryllis. That will go in the middle, because it will tell her that you admire her proud demeanor. The three white calla lilies express admiration for her beauty." *This is going to be rather an expensive bouquet,* Flora thought. But one could not win a beautiful young woman for nothing.

"To that we'll add a little wolfsbane. They say, 'You are the personification of charm and beauty.'"

"That's exactly what she is!" the young Russian exclaimed. "But she doesn't see me like that . . ." He looked at Flora with concern. "And the flowers really speak for me? I would never dare address the young lady personally."

Flora struggled not to smile. "I'm afraid you will have to take that risk, once you have won her favor. But for the moment, just give her this bouquet and a copy of my *ABC of Flowers*. This flower, the iris, is the most important of all—it tells the recipient that she has stolen away any peace your heart had otherwise. And we'll go a step further and fill out the entire bouquet with chestnut." She had broken off an armful of young chestnut twigs on her morning walk, fortunately.

Igor nodded, impressed. "What does chestnut say?"

"'Gladly would I be with you!'"

Three days later, the young Russian returned.

Before Flora knew what had happened, he kissed her hand. A miracle had come to pass, he said, his eyes shining. The woman he was courting had smiled at him in the foyer of the theater! And there had been nothing arrogant about it at all. Now he needed more of Flora's magical flowers.

Soon, the door of the flower shop hardly closed. The Russian visitors threw themselves wholeheartedly into the new floral fashion. They already knew, only too well, the dancers turning tiptoed pirouettes during the hors d'oeuvres, the wise women who deciphered the future in coffee grounds after dinner, and the sopranos trilling arias in the afternoon. But flowers that could "speak" were something new, and the hostesses of Baden-Baden always had one eye open for something fresh for their parties, after all. Nor did they consider themselves above seeking Flora out in her flower shop—for them, the stroll along the street of tradesmen and simple workers was like going on a small adventure. And then the eye-opening conversations with their "flower girl." It all felt so *très chic.*

Kuno's regulars suddenly returned, too: Ernestine's friends, neighbors, acquaintances. As before, they bought mainly loose flowers and cheap bouquets, but they took a lot of pleasure in rubbing shoulders at the counter with the rich customers.

Ernestine missed no opportunity to emphasize that *Flora's ABC* had come to fruition only on her urging. Now, she sat behind the counter every day and watched in awe as works of art materialized beneath Flora's skillful hands: bouquets both lavish and delicate, corsages and flower baskets, garlands to be affixed to landau carriages, flower and fruit still lifes intended as table decorations—Flora's imagination was inexhaustible. Over time, her works grew more and more elaborate. And more expensive.

Her initial reluctance to charge high prices melted like ice cream in the sun. After the winter, with hunger knocking at the door, the family could use every mark. Finally, no more monotonous cabbage and turnip meals. No more thin soups or mushy oatmeal. Instead, they ate sausage, meats in aspic, pork, fish, eggs, and other delicacies.

The rich Russian visitors were certainly willing to pay a lot of money, but in return they demanded first-rate quality, as Flora discovered very quickly.

A single limp leaf in an arrangement, or a flower wilting in the heat from nearby candles, was all it took—then all goodwill ceased! Many of those who commissioned her work insisted that Flora be present at their festivities so that she could spray her handiwork with water whenever necessary, or tend to a drooping leaf or flower.

Flora was not bothered by the extra work she had to put in. For her, it was far more fun to watch over her floral decorations from a back door or a corner off to one side, and at the same time observe the festivities going on all around. She did her best to remember every detail so that she could tell Ernestine—who sucked up her stories like a sponge—about it the next morning.

Although Flora stayed in the background as inconspicuously as possible, it was common for a guest to come over and exchange a few words with her.

Konstantin Sokerov was present at almost every party Flora attended. Each time Flora saw him, she hoped that he might come a little closer to her. The thought excited her as much as it made her anxious. What was she supposed to say to the good-looking man? Should she curtsy as she did with the older guests? If she did, she knew she would feel strange, because he was, at most, just a few years older than she was. What would she talk about with him? No doubt he would find her terribly dull . . .

The chance that Konstantin Sokerov might make his way through the throng of guests at one of those events was slim. The moment he entered a room, he was surrounded by women who laughed too loudly at his jokes, flushing red and fanning themselves furiously. Usually, he had Princess Stropolski on his arm, and she laughed louder than anyone else at his humor.

How can anyone make such a fuss? Flora wondered.

Normally, it was well past midnight when Flora—with swollen feet and a sore back, but happy—made it home from one of those parties.

Even so, she was back on her feet again the next morning the moment it was light.

"I really don't know why you don't just give up picking flowers yourself and sleep a little longer," said Ernestine one morning, when Flora returned to the store with an armful of ferns. "Mr. Flumm will be coming soon. Why not just buy what you need from him?"

"Because the wildflowers have become something like my trademark," Flora replied. "Besides, many of them are important in the language of flowers. These ferns, for example—"

She did not finish her sentence, because the door to the store opened. It was not the expected nurseryman, however, but a man in uniform.

When Flora recognized the policeman that Else Walbusch had dragged into the store the previous year, she was momentarily taken aback. Then she recovered herself and said with a smile, "I haven't poisoned anybody this time. These ferns are completely harmless, I can assure you." She heaved the green bundle that she had cut in a clearing in the forest into a bucket of fresh water.

"Mrs. Sonnenschein, I have to inform you that we have received a complaint about you for vandalism of the woods and meadows along Lichtenthaler Allee. I have received a statement asserting that you cut rare plants there almost every day."

"Can you believe it? I can thank the women in Maison Kuttner for this, I'm sure of it," said Flora to Ernestine and Mr. Flumm, who had just arrived.

The store door had just closed behind the departing officer. He had informed Flora that she had to appear in person at the station sometime during the day, where her own statement would be taken. In a grave voice, he had added that a court appearance was not out of the question. Flora had felt quite ill at his words. This was all she needed now that business was going well! Why couldn't something just go along easily for once?

"What will they do to me? Will I have to go to prison?" She looked from one to the other despondently.

"And what will the people around here say when they get wind of this?" Ernestine chewed her bottom lip anxiously.

The elderly nurseryman lifted his hands dismissively. "Don't go getting yourselves worked up. The most you'll get is a fine. If it will help, I'll testify on your behalf and tell them how you buy large quantities of flowers from me every week. I don't think the vandalism charge will go very far."

"You'd do that for me?" Flora's heart was already a little lighter.

Flumm nodded. "But why is Josef Kuttner trying to blacken your name at all? That's not something I'd expect among comrades in this business."

"Comrades!" Ernestine spat the word. "He's never looked on us like that. And now that we're successful, he's suddenly burning with envy." Her face had flushed bright red. "What he has done is simply wrong. Oh, I'd like to give him a piece of my mind."

"Don't worry," said Flora grimly. "I have a much better idea." She seemed to hesitate for a moment longer, then took a deep breath.

"Mr. Flumm, I need yellow flowers. Roses, lilies, whatever you have. This very morning!"

The nurseryman did not have to be asked twice. He hurried out to his delivery wagon and trundled off.

Another yellow rose here, a handful of marigolds there—Flora's bouquet grew and grew. She stopped only when she could barely hold it in both hands. With a final flourish, she tucked half a dozen yellow silk ribbons among the flowers.

"Yellow, wherever you look! It's marvelous," Ernestine said reverently. She had sat and watched Flora assemble the entire thing. "But for whom is such a magnificent construction intended?"

When Flora told her, Ernestine could hardly believe her ears.

With the overflowing bouquet in her arms, Flora set off. When she arrived at Maison Kuttner, she noticed immediately that the shop seemed all but dead. One of the girls was dusting a shelf, and the rest were standing behind the counter looking bored. A pity—if it had been up to Flora, she would have wanted as many customers as possible to see her entrance.

As she stepped inside, a disbelieving murmur went through the room. The young woman dusting dropped her dustrag in astonishment.

Flora stifled a grin and let her eyes roam calmly around the room. "No esteemed clientele in sight?" She put on her sweetest smile. "I guess business isn't quite as good as it was not so very long ago. Well, the cake's been sliced differently this year, hasn't it? But perhaps I can cheer you good ladies up a little." In both hands, she held out her bouquet to the young women behind the counter. "A floral arrangement for a flower shop. At first glance, perhaps, a rather unusual choice." She giggled affectedly. "But believe me, this is a bouquet you have honestly earned."

The girls exchanged a mystified look.

"You know, in the language of flowers, yellow is the color of envy." Flora looked from one to the other. "And in my entire life, I have never come across more envious women than you. As for your complaint to the police, all I can say is shame on you!" Her head held high, she turned toward the door, but with the doorknob still in her hand, she swung back a final time.

"If it had been up to me, we could have gone on existing peacefully side by side. Baden-Baden is big enough for two florists. But you'd better get used to hard times. Believe me, I'm going to steal as many customers away from you as I possibly can."

The vandalism report went nowhere. Flora showed that no plant suffered any long-term detriment because of her, and the police dismissed the complaint.

Chapter Thirty-Eight

"Princess Gagarina came in this morning. Imagine that!" said Flora, looking across the lunch table to Friedrich and Ernestine.

It was the start of June. The season was in full swing, so sitting and eating lunch together had become a rare event. Flora had little appetite anyway. Oppressive humidity had been smothering the town for days, and on that particular day it was making her downright queasy. She had almost thrown up that very morning.

She picked at a piece of trout with her fork and acted as if she were lifting it to her mouth. It smelled very strong—had it gone off, perhaps?

"Princess Isabella Gagarina . . . It would not surprise me these days to hear that the Russian czar had come by," said Friedrich, jabbing his fork into a potato.

"What if he did?" Flora said. "Don't you think I could deal with him?"

"So, is it true that—" Ernestine began.

"Sabine! Where's the sauce? The fish is bone-dry," Flora shouted at the same moment.

Sabine came in with the *saucière* and a sour look on her face. She went around the table, but when she got to Flora, Flora held her hand over her plate. "I've changed my mind. In any case," she went on, ignoring Sabine entirely, "the princess wants to celebrate an Italian-themed summer party in two weeks, and it's my job to decorate her palace park for the occasion."

Friedrich let out a derisive snort. "Gagarin Palace! When I hear that name . . . you know, before the princess spent a fortune renovating it, it was just the old Schweiger mill. But a German name wasn't good enough for the Russkies, apparently."

"So what? What are you trying to say?"

"Children, now don't start fighting," Ernestine cut in as she dabbed the sweat from her brow with a small cloth. "Tell us about this Italian party. I can't imagine what she has in mind."

"Honestly, neither can I." Flora frowned. "What do I know about Italy?"

Friedrich shook his head and said, "Italy in Baden-Baden? I wouldn't put much past the Russians, but my Lord, what a mad idea that one is." He looked at his wife. "I hope you turned it down? You don't have to take every job that comes along anymore. Besides, I don't like it that you go running around town at night, alone. We should have agreed on a fixed time long ago when I can come and collect you from your parties."

Flora sniffed. "I wish it was as easy as that. Oh, Friedrich. Baden-Baden is a safe town. You worry too much."

"Just yesterday," Friedrich went on, "a vagrant began shouting abuse at a group of guests from the Holländer Hof. Particularly vile, I'm told. The man's been drifting around town for quite some time, they say, and several thefts have been ascribed to him, but so far the police haven't been able to collar him. I don't want him to cross your path one night."

"That's all well and good, but Princess Gagarina is not someone I can just cancel with. Her opinion counts for too much around here. If this commission goes well, then . . . but you don't understand that."

Friedrich could be impossible sometimes. Flora pushed her plate away angrily. What little appetite she'd had had vanished completely.

"Child, don't drive yourself mad. You're the darling of the season," said Ernestine, and she patted Flora's hand. "Oh, by the way. Josef Kuttner was in the Grüns' pharmacy the day before yesterday. He did not look good at all, Gretel said, and he wanted something to help him sleep. Your success is robbing him of his sleep, I'll wager." Ernestine told her story with so much zeal that a chunk of fish fell off her fork without her noticing.

At least my mother-in-law is happy, Flora thought, *unlike my husband.*

She had to swallow a sob and felt tears welling in her eyes. She glared furiously at Friedrich. "That's so typical of you. Now that the store is running well, it doesn't suit you. Instead of helping me come up with a few good ideas for the Italian party, all you do is grumble and groan." She let out a sob, then stood up abruptly and ran from the room.

"What was that all about?" Friedrich could only sit and watch helplessly as his wife ran out.

Ernestine pushed her own plate away. "Everything is simply too much for your wife right now. In winter, she was worried about the future, and now all the work and being afraid that she can't live up to the standards the Russians demand. It's no wonder she gets upset. And you really were not very helpful just now."

Friedrich put down his fork and sighed. "You're right, of course. Flora is completely overtaxed, and that's why I feel sorry for her. I know very well how it feels to be responsible for a thousand things at once. When everyone wants something from you at the same time and the day already didn't have enough hours in it . . . But how am I, of all people, supposed to help her with her Italian party?"

Sunflowers? Would they be the right thing for an Italian party? Or would she be better off with roses and—

Flora was halfway back into the store when Sabine grabbed her by the sleeve from behind.

"That fish was not dry in the slightest! And if you hiss at me like that one more time, I'll be out the door before you know it! I can find a job like this one anywhere."

Flora's brow furrowed. "It wasn't meant that way. I'm sorry, truly. But leave me alone now, I have to get back to work."

But Sabine pushed between Flora and the store, blocking the entrance. "Irritable, no appetite—I've seen that often enough before, with my own mother. How long do you think you can pull the wool over our eyes?"

"What? What are you talking about?" Flora shook her head in confusion.

Sabine laughed. "Now don't look at me all innocent like that. I've known for weeks that you're expecting, and you're already starting to show a little."

"Show what . . . ?" Flora looked down at her stomach, which had been feeling quite bloated in recent days. She had put her queasiness down to the sultry weather and having so much to do that she forgot to drink enough water.

"That you're pregnant. What else?" Sabine replied and rolled her eyes.

Flora collapsed against the wall. The nausea in the morning, and she had not had her period for two months—how could she have been so naïve?

"No, that can't be true!" She let out a sob and threw herself onto Sabine's shoulder.

"Now, now. Settle down," Sabine murmured, and she stroked Flora's head as if she were a small child. "You know, it's strange in a way. You are so clever, but sometimes, you don't have the faintest clue."

Of course, Friedrich and his mother were overjoyed when Flora haltingly told them she was pregnant. Friedrich kissed Flora and excused himself a thousand times for his behavior at lunchtime. Then he hurriedly fetched writing paper so that they could tell Flora's family the happy news right away.

"A grandchild! If only Kuno could have lived to see this," Ernestine said, and she wiped a few tears from her eyes.

"A child . . . ," said Flora.

Just two weeks until the Gagarins' Italian party, and now *I find out I'm pregnant . . .*

Flora did not get any sleep that night. Of course she was happy. But couldn't a child have waited a little while? In her mind, she calculated that the child would be born sometime in January or February. Maybe Sabine could give her a more accurate estimate; she seemed very well informed about such things.

That meant that she would be able to work through the rest of the season. But what would become of the seed trade in the winter?

She tossed and turned restlessly, pondering, preventing Friedrich from sleeping. He tried to take her in his arms, telling her that in her condition sleep was the best medicine, but Flora escaped his embrace. Finally, she climbed out of bed and went to pore over past issues of *Die Gartenlaube*, hoping to find something about Italy. But her efforts were in vain.

The following midday—Flora managed to eat a few noodles, but no more—Friedrich pushed a book across the table to her. "Goethe's *Italian Journey*. I borrowed it for you from the reading room."

Flora's brow creased. "What am I supposed to do with it?"

Friedrich opened the book to a marked page and, in a solemn voice, recited:

Know'st thou the land where lemon trees do grow?

And oranges 'midst dark leaves golden glow?

With gentle winds from deep blue heavens fanned

The myrtle hushed, the laurel tall doth stand?

Know'st thou this land?

"That's very pretty . . . but wait a moment. Oranges and lemons? Myrtle and laurel? That's it!" Flora's joyful whoop was so sudden that Friedrich and Ernestine jumped in surprise. Before Friedrich knew it, Flora had thrown her arms around his neck.

"I finally know the mood my flowers have to create. Oh, Friedrich, what would I do without you?"

The Italian summer party in the Gagarins' garden was Flora's greatest success. For the rest of the season, the guests raved about the lemon trees, about the silver plates on which she arranged oranges and white flowers into the most arresting still lifes, about the handwritten poems of Goethe that every guest was given, and about the water lilies drifting in enormous glass bowls filled with blue-tinted water.

Flora was made to feel like a celebrated artist, and from that night on no festivity or function was complete without her artfully conceived, lovingly executed arrangements.

Chapter Thirty-Nine

Now that Flora was expecting a baby, it was even more important to take some of the burden of running the shop off her. Ernestine was adamant about that, and after a few sleepless nights, she found a solution: Sabine would be her assistant. The maid would still be responsible for all the housework, but for the shopping and cooking a young widow from the neighborhood would come in every day to give Sabine the time she would need to help Flora in the shop.

Nobody asked Sabine's opinion, however. She would have been ten times happier to have someone come in to take over the drudgery of her housework and to let her continue her work in her beloved kitchen.

Flora was satisfied with the new arrangement. With Sabine's help, she would get through the season well enough. But as far as Friedrich was concerned, she still spent far too many hours in the shop.

"In this kind of muggy August heat, you should be sitting in the garden and putting your feet up," he said one evening when they went to bed. "My goodness, look at yourself!" He pointed at Flora's legs, which were so swollen that she winced and cried out a little when Friedrich touched them.

"It's just a little water in the legs. It's not so bad," she managed to say. "My mother wrote that it would go away again. I can't just sit around in the garden—what if someone important walked in just then?"

"Shall I?" Friedrich held up the bottle of medicinal alcohol, and then he heaved Flora's legs onto his lap to work the spirit in. "I wouldn't be surprised if our child came into the world behind the counter," he said.

Flora laughed. "Then I would certainly be very much like my mother. She gave birth to me while she was working out in the fields. Oh, Friedrich, I know you mean well, but I find the work so enjoyable. Oh, that feels good," she added with a sigh as he massaged her legs.

Friedrich smiled. He was happy that his wife managed everything so well and so uncomplainingly. He had not been able to find the time to be much help to her; in the evenings, he rarely returned home before nine.

"What a crazy summer it's been. I have never worked as many hours at the Trinkhalle as I have this year."

"I hope your hard work pays off one day," said Flora sleepily.

Friedrich hoped the same. If, at some point, the newly established Spa and Bath Administration took over the responsibility for the Trinkhalle, he wanted to be able to present himself as a keen and knowledgeable employee whom they could not overlook.

"Who knows, maybe I won't forever be the Trinkhalle manager, but will find a more important role in spa life here. As director of baths or something similar." Friedrich laughed, feeling a little embarrassed. "In the past, I never would have dared to set such lofty goals for myself, but now I know that you can go a long way if you only want to badly enough. Thanks to you."

Flora raised her head a little. "Is that meant to be a compliment?" She stroked his arm tenderly.

The rubbing alcohol irritated Friedrich's nose, and he had to sneeze. "Well, when I look at what you've done with the shop . . ."

"I had no one to get in my way—the shop belongs to us, after all. But you're an employee there. What would you like to achieve?"

"It's simple. I want to make it clear to as many people as possible how important and how beneficial a drinking regime can be. That's why I'm always running off to the library, and why I read everything about thermal waters that I can. One day, I want to deliver in-depth lectures about curative waters at the Trinkhalle. Wouldn't that be a fine thing?"

"Will many people want to hear about it?" Flora murmured, then let her head drop back onto the pillow and turned onto her side.

"Well, Lady O'Donegal is already a devotee. She peppers me with new questions about our waters every day." When Flora said nothing, Friedrich looked up from her legs. His wife was sleeping.

He would gladly have heard Flora's opinion about one of his presentations. Did he sound too much like a doctor or a chemist when he talked about spring water containing lithium and arsenic? Friedrich sighed softly.

How long has it been since we spent a pleasant evening with each other? he wondered as he lay down carefully beside Flora. A stroll along Lichtenthaler Allee, a concert in the park beside the Kurhaus, talking with one another . . . somehow, there was never any time for such things anymore. Instead, they were so exhausted in the evenings that all they could do was fall into bed and sleep.

"Artificial flowers are not welcome here. If you are serious about wanting artificial flowers for your birthday picnic, then you will have to seek out someone else to do the decorating for you." With her hands planted on her hips and an earnest expression on her face, Flora stood facing Princess Irina Komatschova.

Friedrich, the door handle in his hand, sighed. A customer this early? He had wanted to talk to Flora for a moment about something that had occurred to him the previous evening.

"The weather at the start of September can turn in the blink of an eye. If that happens, the picnic will have to be moved to the ballroom in the Hotel Stéphanie les Bains. Perhaps you are not familiar with how run-down that particular room is? Artificial flowers would distract my guests from that, at least a little. Even our esteemed kaiserin is considering gracing me with her presence. Is she supposed to look at crumbling plaster?" The Russian's brow furrowed.

"But artificial flowers!" Flora spat the word out in disgust. "I am sure that Kaiserin Augusta has little interest in that."

Ernestine, who sat behind the counter tying loops from a spool of white ribbon, nodded vigorously.

Friedrich looked from one woman to the other. Why was Flora assailing a customer so vehemently over such a trifle? If she absolutely wanted to have artificial flowers, then why not give her what she wanted?

For a moment, he was tempted to just leave the "tonic"—chocolate, in fact, that he had bought for Flora at the pharmacy—on the counter and walk back out. Then the anticipation of the look on Flora's face when she heard about his flash of inspiration kept him there, waiting patiently.

"Can you really afford to push your customers around like that?" he asked when the princess had finally left.

"Oh, if I don't get this particular job, it won't be any great loss," Flora said and laughed. "Princess Irina Komatschova is a miser. Besides, she's famous for paying her bills very late."

Friedrich cleared his throat. "The reason I'm here . . . Flora, it's been a long time since we spent a nice evening together, just the two of us, and so I'd like to invite you to a concert by the spa orchestra. Next Monday would be best—would you be able to find the time?" Automatically, he held his breath as Flora turned pages in her diary.

"I'm free that evening," she said. "But to be honest, I'd much rather go to a concert by the Waltz King. Everyone raves about his music, but we can't talk about it because we've never been to hear it. Who knows if Schani will even come back to Baden-Baden next year?"

Friedrich grimaced: *Schani*—Flora used Johann Strauss's nickname as if they were bosom friends.

"It would certainly be good for Flora to be seen on the social stage in *private* life for a change. A Strauss concert would be just the thing," Ernestine added.

"But those things are terribly expensive! I can get free tickets for the spa orchestra. I thought you'd like my idea, but if you don't want to . . ." And for this he'd made himself late for work!

"Friedrich, don't get in a huff. I'd be happy to go with you." She put her arms around his neck and looked into his eyes, smiling. "But there's another thing . . ."

Friedrich had to smile himself. They would not be able to hold each other like that much longer—Flora's belly would soon be too big for that.

"It's about the kaiserin's birthday," said Flora slowly. "They say she'll celebrate it here in Baden-Baden, as she does every year, on September thirtieth. That's still a good five weeks away."

"Are you doing her flowers, too?" Just the thought of it made Friedrich's heart skip a beat.

"No, and that's the problem." Flora stamped her foot. "And it would be my dearest wish. Friedrich, do you think you could put in a good word for me? I mean, you're an important man in the town; you know a lot of people. The mayor and—"

"Now that is something you could really do for Flora," Ernestine cut in.

"I'd love to," Friedrich replied. "When I drop by for tea with the kaiserin later, I'll put a word in her ear. I'm sure she'll listen to me." He set the chocolate on the counter and left.

Have you completely lost your mind? Six months ago, you would have been happy to tie a bouquet for the pharmacist's wife, and now it has to be for the kaiserin! I'm starting to believe you're suffering from delusions of greatness.

Friedrich kicked so hard at the white gravel that the little stones flew in the air.

Damn it, *that* was what he should have told his dear wife. And his mother, too! But instead he had left the shop and headed in the direction of the Trinkhalle, lost for any more than the few ironic words he'd managed to find.

Chapter Forty

So this is why I let Princess Irina haggle down the price so far, Flora thought angrily as she saw Kaiserin Augusta disappear through the door. The kaiserin had spent no more than five minutes at Irina Komatschova's birthday party. No doubt she had barely noticed Flora's elaborate re-creation of a picnic scene, complete with trees, a mossy forest floor, and dozens of rosebushes that she had had brought into the ballroom of the Hotel Stéphanie. It seemed Flora's plan to catch the kaiserin's eye had failed miserably.

What were you thinking, you silly creature! she berated herself as she tossed her rose shears and other tools into her basket. *Imagining the kaiserin would see your flowers and want you as her private florist from that moment on, ha!*

The dance floor, in the meantime, had filled. No one would notice if she disappeared now, so she seized the moment and hurried out in the direction of Lichtenthaler Allee. Maybe the fresh air would cure her of her arrogant notions.

On the bridge that crossed the Oos, she set her basket down briefly to rub her aching back. Gradually, her anger at her own impertinence faded and she relaxed a little.

How autumnal the night already was. And how the earthbound fog engulfed the river.

"Yer money, or you'll regret it!"

Before Flora knew what was happening, she felt a bony arm around her neck. She was yanked back so violently that it took her breath away. "You're that flower harlot," a male voice hissed in her right ear. The man's breath reeked, and Flora instinctively held her breath. "I've been watchin' you for a long time, seen you dancin' round the rich folk while the likes of us go hungry."

Friedrich! Help me! Someone, anyone, help! Flora wanted to scream, but she could not make a sound. She wanted to kick at the man behind her, to hurt him as he was hurting her, but she was paralyzed with fear. The arm around her neck was choking her.

"Give me yer money!" the man snarled and squeezed even harder. Flora whimpered, gurgled, and was on the verge of throwing up when the man loosened his grip. "Hand it over."

With trembling hands, Flora picked up her purse from the basket and handed it to the man, whose eyes sparked greedily. She gathered up her skirt to try to run, but before she could take a single step, he grabbed her by the chin with a dirty paw and turned her face to his.

"You're not bad lookin' at all. If you're good enough for the Russians, you're good enough for me." He let out a husky laugh, and a wave of bad breath washed over her.

"No, leave me alone, I—" Flora tried to break free, but he dragged her to the first bush behind the bridge and pushed her to the ground. Flora's knee slammed down on a stone, and the pain was so intense it made her dizzy.

My child! I have to protect my child! The thought shot through Flora like a bolt of lightning before she passed out.

Nine already! Irina's birthday party would already be in full swing. *But so what?* thought Konstantin as he strolled along Lichtenthaler Allee.

He had no interest in putting on a cheery face and bantering the evening away. Was it because the season was nearing its end and he did not know what was coming next? Or was the news he had heard earlier responsible for his frame of mind?

It looked as if the casino's days were truly numbered. Piotr had mentioned that afternoon that the silver ball would roll for the last time on October 31 . . . unbelievable!

One thing was certain: he had no interest in wasting his time in just any old spa town. He needed amusement, games, entertainment. And places that offered all those things were also to be found in other parts of the world.

The only question was whether he would ever get to see those parts of the world.

He had tried several times to pin Püppi down on where she would spend the winter, but she did not know where she wanted to go.

As he stepped onto the bridge that crossed the Oos to the Hotel Stéphanie, he spied the hazy outlines of two people. A man and a woman in a close embrace. The man was leading the woman off into the bushes.

Konstantin grinned. The passion of the lovers seemed to be a matter of urgency. He sighed deeply. It had been a long time since he had felt such feelings for a woman. To be so aroused as to be unable to think clearly, and only able to feel, taste, smell . . . skin, hair, feminine curves . . .

Should he take the next bridge and avoid disturbing the couple? Konstantin looked toward them again.

Strange . . . the woman seemed to be resisting. Yes, and the man was dragging her along! Something wasn't right.

Damn it, that was no couple. The woman needed help!

Konstantin broke into a run.

Shouting. Her head against the hard ground. Her knee, throbbing. The arms of the man, no longer so tightly around her, maybe she would manage it, to break free . . . Flora's eyelids fluttered. She tried feverishly to come to her senses, to breathe. Her child. She had to think of her child, to protect it.

She jerked her eyes open, started to beat the man wildly with her fists.

"Let me go! You filthy man!"

"Little flower girl! It's me, just me," she heard. A different voice, vaguely familiar.

"You?" When Flora saw who it was holding her in his arms, she almost fainted a second time from the shock.

"Yes, me. Everything is all right." Konstantin rocked her in his arms like a child, brushed the hair out of her face. "The man's gone. I sent him packing. Flora, that's your name, isn't it? Are you all right?"

Flora tried to nod, tried to thank the man for his kindness, but instead she burst into tears.

"If you hadn't come along, then . . . then . . . that beast would have—" Her words broke off into loud sobbing.

"Easy now, easy now. I'll look after you."

Flora sniffed and bawled. First that horrible man and now Konstantin Sokerov. She let out a wail, then could not catch her breath, could not compose herself.

The slap on her right cheek came without warning. The second on her left, too.

Flora instantly fell silent. She stared at Konstantin wide-eyed.

"I'm sorry. I had to bring you back to your senses somehow." A lopsided grin accompanied his words.

Flora was suddenly all too aware of how terrible she must look. The snot and the tears. Her disheveled hair, bleeding knee, rumpled skirt.

"Thank you for helping me," she murmured. She tried to stand up and wipe the mud from her skirt and—where was her basket? Her money? Was her baby unharmed?

She staggered, her head spinning, and sank to the ground again. "I don't know what's wrong with me."

"It's the shock. It's deep in you, down to your bones. Allow me." Before she knew it, Konstantin had taken out his handkerchief and with a light touch dabbed away her tears and the snot, wiped the spittle from the corners of her mouth. Then he tried to bring some order to her hair, combing it with his fingers, but they kept catching in the tangled mop. He laughed.

"You'll just have to live with being an untamed beauty! Shall I take you to the police so you can report the robbery? Or do you want to go home? Or . . . could you do with a vodka for the shock of it all, like me?"

"Could it be . . . a small schnapps?" Flora squeaked.

A short time later, they were sitting at a table in the back of a wine bar. The waiter had started momentarily at Flora's somewhat unkempt appearance, but then brought them their drinks without a word.

"I'm angriest at myself. Friedrich warned me that there'd been a vagrant around. I should have been more careful," said Flora. She had drained her schnapps in a single draft, and it ran hot and soothing down her throat. "Instead, I almost let that man defile me."

"He certainly defiled your dress," said Konstantin, pointing to Flora's soiled skirt.

Flora let out a laugh. "Thank you for reminding me how elegant I look."

"It's really not so bad. That pale lilac suits you, by the way," he said, picking a bit of moss from the sleeve of her dress.

Flora, abashed, took a sip of water. "It's the color of my favorite flower, the cuckooflower. In the language of flowers, it stands for charm and esprit." She shrugged. "I thought I could use a little of both this evening." At Konstantin's prompting, she began to tell him about Irina's party, and very soon about her failed expectations.

"I actually believed the kaiserin would see my flowers and jump for joy." Flora felt her face redden with her mortification. She sighed. "Florist to Her Imperial Highness—that would have been a dream. But dreams burst like bubbles, don't they? This evening, I also heard a rumor that the casino is closing its doors. If that's true, then I can forget a second dream, too. I would have loved to tie a few particularly beautiful bouquets for those elegant gaming rooms, just once." What was she prattling on about? She did not know this man at all or anything about him, except that he was Princess Stropolski's escort and that he had rescued Flora not so many minutes earlier. She had to be getting home. Friedrich was already waiting for her, no doubt. What was she supposed to say to him? Would he be angry that she allowed herself to be robbed? And the money . . . Thank God she had only a little change with her.

Konstantin's harsh laugh dragged her out of her brooding. "At least you have lofty dreams to forget! Lofty dreams . . . sometimes I wonder if I ever had any."

"But you want to be a famous painter, don't you? That is a tremendous dream!" Flora said. But he continued to look morosely at his drink, and Flora reached across the table spontaneously and pressed his hand encouragingly.

He shrugged. "If you say so. Oh, it's probably just the autumn fog that's making me so melancholy. Or how seriously you take your work. Whenever I see you at a party, surrounded by your flowers, I wonder how it must feel to have such passion."

Flora frowned. Konstantin was very different from what she knew him to be among the perfumed, powdered women who laughed loudly at his jokes. Was this change in him because of her? The magic of the moment, which had just felt so wonderfully warm, threatened to pop like a soap bubble.

"It's strange, isn't it? We see each other at almost every party, and until today we have not exchanged so much as a word," said Konstantin. "Apart from your talent for the language of flowers, I know nothing about you."

Now it was Flora's turn to shrug. "I'm sure you always had something better to do than spend time with the flower girl . . . ," Flora said. She held her breath instinctively. What a topsy-turvy evening it had been.

"Maybe I was just wasting my time," Konstantin said, looking at her hands.

She followed his eyes and saw that on her pinky, the nail had broken, but it had not given up without a fight and still held on valiantly. Flora's brow creased. How shabby her nails looked! As shabby as her whole hand with its nicks and calluses.

Konstantin plucked off the last of the broken nail and traced the side of her finger with his. The gesture was so intimate that Flora withdrew her hand, taken aback.

What was she doing there? Why hadn't she gone to the police long before to report the robbery?

"I . . . it's already so late and—" Flora wanted to stand up and leave, but could not. She felt almost glued to her seat.

"I'm worried about Püppi—Princess Stropolski," said Konstantin, out of nowhere. "She feels tired and drained. She is awake night after night, but instead of enjoying her waking hours, she sits in her room and gazes into the darkness, where the ghosts she fears so much are just waiting for her to fall asleep."

"Now that you mention it, I realize that the princess wasn't there this evening. She was the first one to commission my work."

Konstantin nodded.

Flora went on. "I'm sure the princess will be feeling better once she's home again. Travel for a woman her age must be . . . trying."

Konstantin laughed. "Home? Where is that supposed to be? I have no idea where we are going to end up when the season comes to an end. The Russians are plagued by homesickness for Mother Russia, but they don't want to go *home*."

Then why don't you stay here? What is better or more beautiful elsewhere? Flora wanted to ask him, but her own impudence frightened her. What business was it of hers where these people spent their winters?

Before she could do anything to stop him, Konstantin took her hand again. "You know what? Your dream shall come true. You will see your flowers in the casino. I'll come up with something, I promise you." He pressed a kiss to the back of her hand, then called for the waiter.

Chapter Forty-One

Of course, Flora's news about the late-night incident caused an uproar in the Sonnenschein household. Red blotches appeared on Ernestine's face, and she went down with a migraine. Friedrich was angry that Flora had not gone to the police immediately, and he insisted on accompanying her to the station that very minute. But he was angrier at himself. Why hadn't he asserted himself and collected his wife after the party?

As luck would have it, the vagrant was arrested the very next morning when he tried to steal a chicken from a woman at the market. The policeman to whom Friedrich and Flora reported her assault brought them the good news in person.

Flora heaved a sigh of relief. At lunch, in a long discussion with Friedrich, she managed to convince him that she would now be safe when she walked through the town. Friedrich and his mother were making a fuss, but Flora was decidedly cheerful. Nothing happened in the end! Konstantin had saved her.

She had just reopened the store after the midday break when her savior appeared in person, carrying a bowl of blueberries.

Flora felt momentarily dizzy at seeing him again.

When he asked how Flora was, she told him that the thug had been arrested. Glancing at her belly, he inquired after her baby, and she assured him that she and her baby, too, were fine.

"I can't do much after the fact to remove the bitter taste of what happened last night, but"—he handed her the bowl of berries—"perhaps you will still enjoy the fruit."

"I have to thank you a hundred times. No, thousands! If not for you . . ." Not wanting to linger too long on the thought, Flora popped one of the berries into her mouth. How sweet and juicy they were! She came around from behind the counter, grabbed a fat bundle of ferns and bellflowers out of the buckets, and began to tie them into a bouquet.

Konstantin smiled as he watched her work. "A bouquet for me? I guess in your famous flower language?"

Flora nodded. The bouquet was almost finished when she added a few blooms of morning glory.

"And what does this bouquet have to say?" Konstantin asked.

Sabine, who had come in with a cup of tea for Flora, whispered in her ear, "Is that the man who rescued you?"

Flora replied with a short nod, then elbowed Sabine aside.

"The bellflowers express deep gratitude. The ferns are meant to bring you luck in love and games."

"I can use both of those!" he replied with a laugh. "And what about these?" He touched the morning glory, and his eyes—smiling, full of interest—burned into Flora's.

Suddenly, she felt hot, feverish. Was she coming down with something? She cleared her throat abashedly.

"The morning glory? Oh, they're nothing special."

"I'd let a man like that rescue me any day." Sabine sighed as she watched Konstantin go. When she saw that Flora's gaze was also directed toward the door, she added, "I might be mistaken, but didn't I read in your book that morning glory is a symbol of affection?"

"What if it is? I think Konstantin is very nice. And I will never forget how he helped me yesterday."

"All right," Sabine said with a dismissive wave. "I just want to point out that a man like that can be risky for a woman."

"What kind of talk is that?" asked Flora, giving her friend a light rap on the head.

Konstantin kept his word: Flora got to dress the casino in her floral arrangements. The commission came formally from Princess Stropolski, and it was for the casino's final day of operation.

Flora considered it a twist of fate that she should get to decorate the elegant rooms on that particular day. With a heavy heart, she positioned her majestic arrangements of roses—half deep-red, half blackened with ink—beside the roulette table. Then she took a step back and watched the gamblers play.

How things had changed, she thought, since the rainy afternoon when she had gambled away the little money she had at this very table.

Usually, most of Baden-Baden's visitors would have been long gone this late in autumn, but on October 31 the roulette table was thronged with people. Russian mixed with English, and the guttural sound of Portuguese with various German dialects. Everyone knew the language of the ball that rattled as it jumped among the numbers and colors.

What a high-spirited atmosphere reigned in the room, even on that final day!

Princess Stropolski and Konstantin sat together at one of the roulette tables. The princess did not look well at all, Flora thought. Her face was deathly pale. She stroked her faithful little lapdog mechanically but took no notice of his playfulness.

Konstantin, however, seemed in the best of moods. He laughed as he embraced the man beside him. The man avenged himself with a hearty dig of his elbow into Konstantin's side. Flora smiled. Konstantin could really enjoy himself! And he was oblivious of everything around him, so involved was he in his game.

When was the last time she had felt so lighthearted? Perhaps when she had worked with Seraphine on the *ABC of Flowers*? Yes, there had been such moments then, playing with words and flowers and ideas.

Still, though, there had been the pressure of finishing the book in time for the start of the season. And whenever she devoted herself to her floral decorations, she was always painfully conscious of delivering only what fulfilled the wishes of whoever had commissioned her.

In contrast, the people around the tables seemed as carefree as children.

Konstantin looked up, waved to Flora, and mouthed a word that she understood as "later." She nodded happily.

Yes. Later. She wanted to ask him if her ferns had, in fact, brought him much luck in the game and—

"Last game, ladies and gentlemen!" the head croupier announced, at which a murmur rumbled through the room. Konstantin turned his attention back to the table.

On tiptoe, Flora watched as the wheel was set in motion a final time. The last fling of the ball . . . and it settled finally on the red nine. Flora did not see who the lucky winners were.

The croupier's final *"Rien ne va plus"* was still echoing in Flora's ears when half a dozen Conversationshaus staff stepped past Flora and began to roll up the huge carpet from the side. Other staff brought in ladders and extinguished the candles on the chandeliers for the last time, taking no notice of the guests still standing around, who slowly began to slink away like beaten dogs.

When Flora returned from a visit to Kuno's grave the next day—she had taken him a few roses—she was passed by a procession of carriages, riders on their horses, and piled-high wagons—all of them rolling out of town as if the plague had broken out in Baden-Baden.

Where were they going, now that the days were gray? What was better about Paris, London, or Monte Carlo? Who would tie their bouquets there?

The gravel crunched loudly underfoot as Flora walked along the lonely Promenade. The shop windows left and right were empty, the small tables and chairs at the cafés cleared away. No more coffee aroma in the air, nowhere the pop of a champagne cork.

"They're all gone!" Flora grumbled when she arrived at the store. "Who knows which of my customers I will even see next season? They will probably turn their backs on Baden-Baden forever. And not one of them came to tell me goodbye." *Not even Konstantin,* she added to herself.

"What did you expect?" Sabine said. "That our summer visitors would come one by one and say a personal adieu? You get some strange ideas in your head. Aren't you happy that things will be a bit quieter now? It will give you a chance to get ready for the baby."

"Of course." Flora bit her lip. Everyone must have been in a terrible hurry to leave. Because the Baden-Baden season had gone on so long, they must have postponed engagements and appointments. *Yes, that's how it must have been,* Flora thought to console herself. Princess Stropolski, Irina Komatschova, and a few others would certainly have come to say goodbye otherwise. And Konstantin Sokerov, too.

So there had been no "later" after all.

Would she ever see him again?

Chapter Forty-Two

"Today a year ago we danced at your wedding, and now look at you, a regular little family. Oh, I'm so happy I could cry!" Hannah clapped her hands together so loudly that the infant in his basket on the table opened his eyes wide and instantly began to wail, for which Hannah earned a disapproving look from Flora. "Sorry, darling. I'm not used to being around such little creatures anymore."

Flora picked up the baby. "It's not so bad. But I hope little Alexander goes back to sleep again soon. I'll take him to bed, and when I come back we'll have a glass of wine, all right? We've got our first wedding anniversary to celebrate, after all."

Shaking her head, Ernestine watched as her daughter-in-law left the room. "It's amazing how fast that girl recovered from the birth. I remember being so exhausted back then."

Hannah shrugged. "I guess we Kerner women are made of sterner stuff. Being pregnant is not a disease, after all."

"Well, now, I wouldn't be so sure. I had such a rumbling in my tummy, or a gurgle, no, it was really more like banging around, yes! Well, on some days . . ." While Ernestine went on about every little affliction that she suffered during her own pregnancies, Hannah's thoughts drifted back to her arrival in Baden-Baden just a few days ago.

She had arrived on January 2, one day before Alexander's unexpectedly early birth. It was as if she'd had a premonition. At the sight of her daughter, Hannah had gone rather weak at the knees. It was not just Flora's swollen belly, but her radiance and everything about her—she was so different from the Flora who had left Gönningen a year before as a newlywed. Flora exuded a self-confidence for which Hannah found herself actually envying her daughter.

Like a queen, she suddenly thought.

"The day before Christmas Eve, she was still standing in the shop," said Friedrich. "She'd been closing up very early the evenings before, at least, but we were desperately in need of a little peace and quiet when the season was over." Without a sound, he opened the bottle of sparkling wine that Sabine had brought in. "All of the running about was not good for her. Sometimes she was so jittery . . ." He waved one hand dismissively.

Hannah held out her glass to him. "Well, Gönningen women are just like that. Temperamental."

"You are certainly somehow . . . different," said Ernestine. Neither her voice nor her expression betrayed whether her words were meant as a compliment.

Flora returned, and all four raised their glasses to the young couple's first anniversary.

"Friedrich tends to exaggerate, you know. It wasn't nearly as bad as he says," said Flora. "But was I supposed to let Maison Kuttner have all the Christmas business?"

"By no means! After that complaint to the police they've not earned any clemency at all, though I do sometimes have a bad conscience because you've been working so hard," said Ernestine, with a fond look at Flora. "If my Kuno could see everything you've set in motion . . ."

Flora handed Ernestine a handkerchief, then said to Hannah, "I'll show you the shop tomorrow. Just before Christmas, I bought a lot of potted plants in bloom. Sabine has been watering them, but I'd still like to check on them. I thought a little color during the cold months couldn't hurt. The flowering violets and begonias will march out the door."

Friedrich raised his eyebrows. "It sounds as if you'd like to get back into the shop sooner rather than later. But you really need a little more time to rest."

"And Alexander needs his mother," Ernestine said emphatically. "When my Friedrich came into the world, I . . ."

When his mother was done rattling off her list of all the trouble he had caused her as a baby, Friedrich said to Hannah, "At least Flora is sensible enough to let you take over the seed trade."

"And thank God for that," said Hannah with a grin. "I'm very happy to get around and see our customers again. Helmut is off with Valentin, and Seraphine and I would have just been sitting around the house for the next few weeks anyway." Hannah told them how Seraphine would have loved to come back to Baden-Baden, but Hannah had convinced her that one of them had to stay at home and look after things there.

"By the way, Helmut asked if it would be possible to get another stack of your *ABC of Flowers*. A lot of his customers were so happy with it that they want a second copy."

Flora nodded. "I have to have more printed for the store in any case, so I'll order for you at the same time."

Hannah stifled a remark—so much for more time to rest. She turned to Friedrich.

"So tell me, how is work at the Trinkhalle?"

"Now that there's no more casino, the Trinkhalle falls under the auspices of the Spa and Bath Administration, which makes them my employer now."

"Flora mentioned that there were a lot of changes happening in Baden-Baden right now. Just yesterday, on the way to Flumm's Nursery, I passed a large construction site. What are they building out there?"

The sparkling wine tickled Hannah's tongue. She leaned back luxuriously in her armchair and looked expectantly at her son-in-law.

"You must mean the Friedrichsbad. They say it's going to be quite grand when it's finished. The site you're talking about is exactly where the Romans once had their thermal baths, and the old Trinkhalle used to be there, too. Fascinating, isn't it?"

"So they're naming a bathhouse after you!" said Hannah.

"Now that would be something, wouldn't it?" said Ernestine. "With all the hard work he's done, he deserves it. But the bathhouse is to honor Grand Duke Friedrich."

"A magnificent thermal bath. That will really be a dream come true for Baden-Baden." Friedrich took a deep breath and straightened up in his seat. "There's something else that's rather exciting: in March, I will be taking water and mud samples to Bad Ems, to the best chemists in the entire empire for a detailed analysis. Me, personally!"

A courier's job, then. Hannah did her best to look impressed. "Well, you've always had an interest in the curative waters, haven't you?"

"I feel deeply honored to have been asked. On the other hand, I don't have much travel experience at all. I'll probably end up on the wrong train." Friedrich had meant it as a joke, but there was a degree of uncertainty in his voice.

"My poor boy. The things they burden you with," said Ernestine, crumpling the handkerchief in distress.

"My goodness, it's not as if Friedrich is off to Tierra del Fuego! Everyone in the German Empire can speak the German language, so . . ." Flora shrugged as if to say, *Why all the fuss?*

Hannah cleared her throat. "We Gönningers are used to traveling, but I can imagine that it's a fearsome prospect for other people," she said to Flora. Turning to Friedrich, she added, "You'll manage it just fine. There is a reason that they have chosen you for this important task." It was really Flora's job to bolster her husband ahead of a journey like that, Hannah thought. Still, her words seemed to have an effect.

More confidently, Friedrich said, "Our waters here were tested many years ago, but the science has advanced, and we are hoping for more precise results from the new tests. And then there's the mud. I am convinced that it can be extremely beneficial for treating the sick. In the war, they used it to treat wounded soldiers, and it did them good. All that's missing is the scientific proof."

"There you are, Mother," said Flora. "Around here, the main subject is water, water, water. My husband can't think of anything else, although I prefer a glass of wine or champagne myself." Flora laughed, but Hannah clearly heard the tinge of criticism.

Friedrich looked across at his wife. "You and your rude remarks. These are serious matters. When we have people coming to Baden-Baden for the spas instead of the casino, then the shop will benefit, too." His eyes gleamed fervidly. He slid forward to the edge of his chair. "The changes we are going through in Baden-Baden are naturally making a lot of people anxious. Some hoteliers are even considering closing their doors, but if you ask me, that would be utterly the wrong thing to do."

Flora yawned.

Hannah looked from Flora to Friedrich to Ernestine and back. The Sonnenscheins made a strange family. None of them seemed to have much interest in the others at all. Friedrich had no head for Flora's love of flowers, and she did not understand his fascination with medicinal waters and belittled him for his interests and his fear of traveling. With her crumpled handkerchief, Ernestine stood somewhere in between.

Flora and Friedrich, because of their enthusiasm for their own work, seemed to have lost sight of each other.

In Hannah's mind appeared an image of two floating logs, drifting side by side in a swift current—that was how she saw Friedrich and Flora in that moment. With no log driver to make sure they did not drift too far apart . . .

Chapter Forty-Three

"If Candlemas be fair and bright, winter has another flight. If Candlemas brings snow and rain, winter will not come again." Flora turned around to her mother. "Isn't that how the old rhyme goes?"

It was February 2, and although it had been snowing since the evening before, Flora and Hannah had paid Kuno's grave a visit that morning, the anniversary of his death, and were on their way back to the shop. They had left an arrangement of fir sprigs for him. Ernestine wanted to wait until Friedrich was free in the afternoon before going out herself, hoping the weather would improve.

"Let's hope that old rhyme holds—you wouldn't wish this weather on a dog. I'll tell you this much: if Sabine hasn't got the fire going in the stove in the shop, I'm going straight back to the house. I can stand and watch you decorate a window display another time," said Hannah grumpily.

Flora laughed. "I never knew you to be so lily-livered, Mama. Whoops, I almost fell!" She latched on to her mother and held tight. It was certainly for the best that she had left Alexander with Sabine. The thought of slipping on the ice and falling with her Alexander, her one-and-only, in her arms . . .

In the iron stove in the shop, however, a crackling fire welcomed them. Sabine, who had looked after the shop and Alexander well, disappeared to the kitchen to make tea.

"The windows are completely fogged up again," said Flora. Still wearing her coat, she wiped briskly at the glass to clear it.

"Why go to the trouble? No one's going to be out on a day like today to look at your decorations anyway," said Hannah. "Maybe it would be better to shovel the snow off the footpath. If you've got a snow shovel here, I could—"

"Forget it. You sit in here with Alexander, and when Sabine comes back with the tea, you can make yourself as comfortable as you like," Flora said, interrupting her mother. As far as she was concerned, her mother already did far too much. In the end, they'd say that Flora would never have been able to stay on top of things by herself! Now that Hannah had visited all Baden-Baden's gardeners and her order book was full, she could focus on spending time with her grandson, nothing else.

Hannah sighed. "You really won't let anyone help you, child. Friedrich was right. You—"

Flora cut her off with a kiss to the cheek. "It is so lovely to have you here! If it were up to me, you could stay forever."

"Well, I think your father would have something to say about—" Hannah broke off when a shrill cry sounded just outside the shop door. Flora dropped the rag she was using on the window and ran out.

"That certainly could have been worse! Take my arm . . . and if I may be so bold, dear lady, you are as light as a feather."

Flora watched in disbelief as Konstantin Sokerov brushed snow from Gretel Grün's rear. For a moment, she thought he was some illusion caused by the driving snow, but it really was him.

His hair was longer than it had been in autumn, and he was tan. He wore a black fur coat, the likes of which Flora had never seen before.

It was probably the fashion abroad right now. And he looked good in it. Dashing, somehow.

Konstantin was back! And she had feared that she would never see him again.

What was he doing here in the middle of winter?

Still speechless with shock and joy, Flora finally held the door open for them.

Before the pharmacist's wife could launch into a tirade about the uncleared snow on the pavement, Konstantin picked up one of the potted violets. "Allow me, as your rescuer, to give you this?" He gave Gretel a conspiratorial wink. "I know that a stout-hearted woman such as yourself has earned some splendid roses, but . . ."

Flora watched with admiration as Konstantin chatted amicably and placatingly with Gretel until a hint of a smile appeared on her face. A short time later, she left the store with a flush in her cheeks and the potted violet in her hand.

Flora turned to Konstantin and shook his hand vigorously. "Thank you! Now you've rescued me again. If not for you, Gretel would have bitten my head off."

"I fear the lady's rear end will be about the same color as that violet by tomorrow," said Konstantin drily.

Flora laughed. In the same moment, she sensed her mother's eyes on her. She had completely forgotten Hannah was right there!

"Wouldn't you like to go into the kitchen with Alexander? It's sure to be warmer in there," said Flora, although the stove was almost glowing.

"No, thank you. We're quite comfortable where we are," said Hannah, leaning back in her chair with the infant in her arms. "I'm Flora's mother, by the way," she said to Konstantin. "And this is her son, Alexander."

"Charmed," said Konstantin. He flashed a smile and looked from Hannah to Flora and back as if comparing them.

"This is Konstantin Sokerov, the painter," said Flora. "I'm sure I've mentioned him," she added.

"Not that I recall," said Hannah, narrowing her eyes. "Oh, yes! You saved our Flora from that beastly man. Thank you," she said, although she did not sound particularly grateful.

"Don't get up," Konstantin said. He turned to Flora. "No need to wake your beautiful boy."

"Don't worry. We'll just sit here by the stove," said Hannah, wrapping her shawl closer around Alexander.

Flora shrugged, then turned back to Konstantin. "Can I help you? Would you like to buy flowers? And what brings you back to Baden-Baden in the middle of winter? When I saw you, I was . . . I was completely . . . speechless, and—" Flora broke off, abashed. She felt a strange prickling sensation in her belly.

How long had Konstantin been back in town? Had he perhaps come straight here to her?

Konstantin began to talk. "Once the casino closed, we followed the croupiers, so to speak. The climate of Monte Carlo was exceptionally good for Princess Stropolski's constitution last year. But this year . . . well, she was already rather weak before we left Baden-Baden, and then—" Konstantin bit on his bottom lip. "Do you remember Püppi's little dog?"

"Isa?" Flora gave her mother a quick sideways glance. Hannah sipped with exaggerated indifference at her cup of tea. Konstantin's story seemed not to interest her at all. *So why doesn't she go into the house?* Flora wondered in annoyance.

Konstantin was back! Would she see him often now? The idea made her heart beat faster.

"Isa, yes. The poor little beast was run over by a carriage on the very last day of the year. Püppi was inconsolable. I wanted to get her a new dog immediately, but she rejected the idea out of hand. She did not want to spend another day in Monte Carlo, but to travel back to the place where she had been so happy with Isa."

Flora frowned. So much fuss about a dog?

"She could not possibly travel alone, of course, so I came with her. But to be honest, I have no idea what we're supposed to do in Baden-Baden so early in the year." He raised his hands in a tragicomic gesture. "Püppi wants to take a course of baths. Is that even possible outside the season?"

"Oh, certainly. The healing waters here are sure to do the princess good," Flora replied hastily. "My husband always recommends the baths at the Hotel Marie-Eluise. I've never been there myself, but the woman who runs the place is said to be very careful and her place especially clean and tidy."

Konstantin nodded. "And what else is going on in Europe's summer capital in winter?" he asked, rubbing his arms as if he were chilled to the bone.

"Oh, there's quite a bit going on," Flora said, and she thought quickly about what Konstantin might find interesting. "The Hotel Stéphanie les Bains has been sold, and the new owner has plans for some magnificent renovations, I've heard. He believes quite firmly that enough people will come for the spas even without the casino. I'm a little skeptical myself," she said with a shrug.

"So the Stéphanie's been sold? Irina will be happy to hear that, I'm sure—no more cheap doss-house for her," Konstantin murmured as he glanced over the flowers on display.

Oh no. He must have seen flowers a thousand times more beautiful than what I can offer. Flora hurriedly drew several decorative panels—designs composed from dried flowers, stems, and seedpods—from beneath the counter and handed them to Konstantin. "In case you're looking for a gift for the princess, I have something brand-new. Here—my flower pictures." For a moment, their fingertips touched, and Flora flinched as if she'd laid her hand on a hotplate. What was going on with her? Why was she so animated? And why didn't Hannah just get up and leave? Sitting there like that with her ears pricked up—it was embarrassing. What must Konstantin think?

But Konstantin's eyes were on her pictures. Almost reverently, he traced one finger lightly over the dried petals that Flora had arranged on a thin wooden panel, just as he had traced the contour of her pinky, once, in the wine bar, after she had been attacked.

"They're beautiful. They remind me of my criminal neglect of my own art. Unfortunately, my obligations leave me with no time for that, if you know what I mean."

Flora nodded vigorously. Of course she understood. It was almost scandalous, the demands the old princess put on his time.

He chose one picture composed from red poppies. "I'd like to buy this one."

While Flora wrapped the picture, he asked, "So what do people do to pass the time in Baden-Baden now that the casino's closed?"

"Who says you can't gamble here anymore?" Flora looked up from her packing paper, and for a moment their eyes met. Then Flora began to tell him about a foggy November day she had spent at the Villa Menshikov.

"On that particular day, they founded the so-called International Club." Konstantin seemed to find her story fascinating, so Flora continued. "I was really quite dumbfounded to see all the landgraves and princes there to offer their future support to the racetrack in Iffezheim. The newspaper even reported on the gathering. I saved the article. Would you like to see it?"

"I don't have much time for horse racing," Konstantin said. "I went to that . . . Iffezheim with Irina once. So many people go there, but it's no more than your typical farming village. The Duke of Hamilton's horses won every race, so even the betting was boring."

"I can imagine what the horse lovers would say to that," said Flora, and she laughed. "Friedrich says the International Club wants to make sure that jockeys come from lots of different countries, to keep up the standards of the races. He says that even Kaiser Wilhelm is planning to come one day."

"Perhaps he'll bring his charming wife with him? And your dream will come true after all."

"Delivering the flowers for the kaiserin's birthday." Flora looked up and sighed. "I'm surprised you remember that."

Konstantin shrugged. "You remember things that impress you. But tell me, what were you going to say a moment ago, when you . . ." He trailed off, trying to find the right words.

Flora looked at him impishly. "You mean the gambling? Well, while I was decorating the Villa Menshikov with my flowers, I managed to pick up bits and pieces from various conversations." She lowered her voice. "Betting on horse races seems not to be the only way to try one's luck. There was talk of a hidden room somewhere."

Konstantin grinned. "And *you* remember my passion for taking a chance."

"There are some things you just don't forget," Flora replied, and they laughed together like old friends.

The next moment, Alexander began to wail.

"He 'followed the croupiers'—did you ever hear anything so affected in your life? Who the devil was that?" Hannah asked as soon as they were alone.

Flora stroked Alexander's head as he nursed and did not immediately reply. When he had drunk his fill, Flora put her son back in his crib, where he slept peacefully.

"Child, I'm talking to you! Who was that . . . self-important fellow?" Hannah was not far from physically shaking her daughter. The ruddy tinge on Flora's neck and cheeks was certainly not because of the hot oven! Add to that the blissful smile playing around her mouth, and the way she had laughed at every halfway funny remark the man had made in his broken German! Hannah did not like the look of any of it.

"Konstantin Sokerov is a Bulgarian painter. He was the one who saved me when that tramp attacked me—I know I wrote to you about that. He's also Princess Nadeshda Stropolski's companion. Everyone just calls her Püppi, though she's as old as the hills. You heard what he said: without him, she could no longer travel at all. It's really quite touching, the way he takes care of her. She was my first customer last year. I wrote to you about that, too, didn't I?" Flora's words came as breathlessly as if she'd just run up the steps to the market square.

Hannah waved off her daughter's explanations. Yes, yes, of course.

Flora looked at her triumphantly. "Hundreds of my lilies of the valley went into decorating the exhibition of his pictures. Later, he confided to me that he found the entire exhibition terribly embarrassing. He is not so far along with his painting that he feels ready to exhibit. He's just very modest."

"A customer, I see. Or rather, the companion of a customer—and yet you seem to be on quite familiar terms with him."

"I maintain a friendly relationship with all of my customers. Do you think I would have gotten as far as I have if I did not? Really, Mother, I don't know what you want to hear!" Her hands planted combatively on her hips, Flora stood and glared at her mother.

"All right, all right," said Hannah defensively. "What did the woman from the pharmacy want just now?"

"No idea!" Flora replied. "But maybe I'd better clear the snow before someone else falls on their rear."

Mother and daughter both laughed, but the laughter sounded strangely forced.

With the flower picture tucked under his arm, Konstantin stepped out of the shop.

How happy Flora had been to see him again, and she had been positively breathless when she told him all the news about Baden-Baden. She was a sweet thing, despite her dirty apron, despite her hair curling and tangled from the snow, despite her hands, with grime in the cracks in her skin. She was so full of enthusiasm for everything she did and said. Wasn't that what had caught his eye the year before, when he had taken her to the wine bar after she'd been attacked by that horrible tramp? He thought her appealing then, but now, without her pregnant belly, she was even more so.

The most beautiful flowers bloom in secret—Konstantin could not have said why that particular saying occurred to him just then.

Maybe it had not been such a bad idea after all to return to Baden-Baden.

Chapter Forty-Four

"A sleigh ride! How wonderful!" Püppi leaned against Konstantin beneath the heavy blanket. Her arms embraced his neck; her lips moved closer for a kiss . . .

Konstantin quickly leaned forward to the basket with the champagne and glasses.

"I'm glad I was able to surprise you." He opened a bottle with a loud pop, the cork flying over the side of the sleigh into the snow. One of the horses let out a nervous whinny and the other pranced a little. The driver spoke to them in a calming voice. It was rare for the horses to be fetched from the stables on a snowed-in February morning and harnessed to the sleigh, and the animals were skittish.

As the sleigh began to move, Konstantin poured the champagne. The bubbly liquid glittered in the sunlight and looked clear and pure. A sudden, unbounded joy gripped Konstantin and he let out a whoop.

"Let's drink!" He held out a glass of champagne for Püppi.

Püppi shook her head regretfully. "My stomach. The last thing it needs is more bubbles. You know I had such terrible wind yesterday."

Without another word, Konstantin tipped the contents of her glass over the side of the sleigh, then drained his own glass in a single draft.

"A sleigh ride." Püppi sighed. "Did I ever tell you about the time Josephina and I . . ."

Konstantin listened with feigned interest to Püppi's long story from her childhood in the palace at Tsarskoje Selo. God, it all happened more than fifty years ago, but Püppi was talking as if it had been yesterday.

The sleigh turned onto Lichtenthaler Allee. Seeing the long, straight way ahead of them, the horses automatically trotted a little faster.

"Then there was the fire! I remember how the flames swallowed up the house with Josephina still inside, because . . ." The more entangled Püppi became in her story, the more shrill her voice became.

Suddenly, Konstantin could not bear it another minute.

Stop! Shut up! Look around, life is still beautiful! he wanted to scream at her. But instead he leaned forward to the driver and said, "To the Hotel Marie-Eluise."

Then he turned to Püppi and said, "I fear our little outing has been too much for you, my dear. We'll go to the Marie-Eluise, where you can take your special bath in peace and quiet." He patted her bony bird's-claw hand.

"But why? I don't want that. The water is always so hot and it makes me dizzy. And there's never anyone else there. I always lie in one of the tubs all alone." Püppi's eyes grew watery. "Couldn't you at least keep me company for a little while?"

Konstantin ignored her plaintive tone. "The solitude will do you good," he said, and he sighed with relief when the small hotel came in sight.

"Where to now?" asked the sleigh driver when Konstantin stepped out of the Marie-Eluise.

Back to the Europäischer Hof? Konstantin dismissed the idea. He had been looking forward so much to a little excursion in the cold, crystalline air, to finally getting out of town, seeing and smelling something different. Maybe stopping in somewhere and having a bowl of hot soup instead of the usual five-course meal with the usual handful of faces at the Europäischer Hof.

When he had rented the sleigh for the entire day, Konstantin had hoped that a change of scenery would also do Püppi good. He had not, however, reckoned with how agitated and confused she seemed to be lately by anything that deviated from her normal routine. Sometimes just the face of a new chambermaid was enough to remind her of some long-past acquaintance, and off she went into her endless reminiscing, from which she only returned with great difficulty to the here and now. That a sleigh ride would trigger recollections of the Russian winters of her childhood . . . he should have expected something like that.

Poor Püppi. How long could things go on like this?

Konstantin, pondering, squinted toward the sun that was just starting to creep into the sky beyond a few naked trees. Soon, its light would transform the town into a glittering, snow-white winter fairy tale.

One of the horses scraped a hoof impatiently in the snow. "What's it to be?" the coachman asked again.

"I have an idea," Konstantin murmured. And with the first rays of sunlight, a smile stole over his face.

"To Princess Stropolski in the Europäischer Hof? Now?"

The messenger boy who had handed Flora the note and now stood waiting in hope of a tip shrugged uncertainly.

Flora frowned, then looked up from the note to the boy and then around her at the shop.

It was an exceptionally quiet morning, and Flora had so far spent it cleaning. Apart from Else Walbusch and Mr. Schierstiefel, no customers had come by. Ernestine was in the living room with Hannah and her embroidery, and both were keeping an eye on Alexander, who was sleeping soundly in his bassinet.

Flora pressed a coin into the palm of the boy's hand. "Run back and tell them I am on my way."

Then she trotted into the house to tell them that the princess had sent for her.

"Princess Stropolski? That could be a big order. Go. I'll take care of everything here," said Ernestine, while Hannah, at the mention of the princess's name, grimaced, which Flora did not understand.

Maybe Konstantin will be there with her, she thought, filled with hope, as she hung the "We'll Be Right Back" sign on the shop door.

"You are completely mad!" cried Flora half an hour later. "Kidnapping me in broad daylight for a jaunt in the snow . . . And then this!" She laughed and held up her champagne glass. What was she thinking, joining in willingly?

The clink of their glasses mixed with the tinkling of the tiny bells that hung on the sleigh and the horses' harnesses.

Flora had barely emptied her glass when Konstantin refilled it for her. "I hope you can find it in your heart to forgive my little subterfuge." He winked mischievously at her over the rim of his glass.

"I'm going to have to think long and hard about that," Flora replied with a giggle, and she sipped at her champagne. It tasted wonderful, and she was already a little dizzy from the first glass.

Although the chill winter air lay on her face like a film of ice, her cheeks were red and warm. But was that any surprise? There she was, in the middle of the day, sitting with a Bulgarian and drinking champagne in a horse-drawn sleigh hung with a hundred bells.

When she had seen Konstantin in front of the Europäischer Hof, her heart had skipped a beat. Where was the princess?

He had rented the sleigh for the entire day, but the princess did not feel like going out, Konstantin had told her. So he thought that Flora might like to go for a ride, and it would be a shame to shut the horses up in dim stables on such a beautiful winter's day.

Flora had shifted from one foot to the other doubtfully. How was she supposed to explain to Friedrich later that she had gone for a sleigh ride with a strange man?

She had been on the verge of turning Konstantin down when a load of snow from a low branch slipped and fell directly on her head. Puffing and laughing, she had shaken it off and swept her wet hair out of her face. From downturned eyes, she had looked up at Konstantin. He seemed to be waiting so yearningly for her reply.

A sleigh ride. Why not, then? No one at home needed to find out about the little adventure, anyway, did they?

"You are the only person I know who could come up with an idea like this," said Flora. "I'd like to know why you spoil me like this."

"Why?" Konstantin replied. "Because you're young, you're beautiful. Life is beautiful, too, and you and I have been chosen to revel in it!"

Flora reddened. *Young and beautiful*—no one had ever said anything like that to her.

"You don't know how happy you have made me by coming out with me now," Konstantin went on. "You have, in point of fact, saved my life, because I would otherwise have died of boredom. Thank you for accompanying me."

Flora gasped in surprise as he planted a kiss on her cheek. "Konstantin! How can you—" She broke off abruptly and pointed excitedly off to the right. "Look! Just there is where carpets of cowslips grow in March. And a little farther back you can find wonderful wild lilac." The impetuous kiss was forgotten as Flora's gaze wandered wistfully along the avenue. "If only spring were already here. I miss the colors and the scents, and I so want to go out and pick flowers again." She swallowed a large mouthful of champagne, and for a moment she thought she could smell the springtime in her glass.

Konstantin exhaled, a slow, deep sigh. "You live in time with the turn of the seasons. You live so close to the natural world, and I admire how . . . immediately you experience everything. You are actually part of it all, one could say. I guess that is what they call home. It's strange, but when I'm around you, I am reminded of what I myself have lost. I can't feel any roots in me, not anymore. I can't sense 'home' anywhere. The most I could tell you is when the opera season starts in a certain city, or if there's a premiere at the theater, or when and where everyone is meeting for a hunt."

Flora looked at him sideways. "What you call 'home' is nothing special. Can't one also long for the unknown?" Just then, she ducked beneath low-hanging fir branches. At the same moment, one of the horses snapped at some of the fir sprigs in passing and munched on them happily as it trotted on. Konstantin and Flora both had to laugh.

"When I began to travel, I thought that the exotic was worth striving for, and more than anything else that having nowhere to call home meant having my freedom." Konstantin swung his arms out wide. "I wanted to cast off the bonds of my old home and follow untrodden paths. But I have come to wonder, sometimes, if I am walking into a cul-de-sac."

The bitter tone of his words surprised Flora. He usually seemed so sure of himself. His face was only inches from hers. She could see the flecks of gold in his dark eyes, glittering in the pale sunlight. The urge to take him in her arms and cheer him up with a thousand tiny kisses was suddenly overwhelming.

"Don't you carry your home in your heart?" she asked quietly. "And can't a person put down new roots in a foreign land? Perhaps you should really start painting again."

"There is nothing I'd like more. In your presence, I feel so inspired, as if your creativity were infectious. But then there's Püppi. She's getting stranger every day. And sicker, too. Day in, day out, everything revolves around the state of her health. What she can eat, what she can't, when she can sleep, and when she can only rest. No one asks how *I* am. Baden-Baden, in the season, is an entertaining place, but now that winter is here, there are only a few of us in the hotels, and all the sitting around drives me mad."

What kind of fool am I? Flora chided herself silently. How was he supposed to start painting again if the princess monopolized all his time?

Konstantin went on. "Forget my stupid remarks. Maybe I'm feeling so melancholy just now because coming out with you has made me so happy. Maybe we humans are doomed to yearn for the one thing we cannot have." He looked her roguishly in the eye.

Flora laughed. "I'm sure I've heard that before, but I can't remember from whom. Maybe you're right." At least Konstantin's expression had brightened.

"You long for your meadow flowers, and I long for our Russian friends. I've been so bored lately that I've even started to miss old Popo, and Irina's constant complaints about how terribly expensive life has become." He shook his head. "Püppi writes letters back and forth with many of them, so I know that the Gagarins and Anna and perhaps Matriona and her sons will return at the start of the season. Then we'll have a little more variety, at least, and it will do Püppi good, too."

"They are really planning to come back? Even with the casino closed?" Flora asked, her voice trembling a little. That was more than she had dared hope for. She could hardly wait to tell Friedrich!

Konstantin grinned. "Who needs a casino to spin a ball? And as long as the ante's right, one can always find someone for a hand of cards. Oh, look!" He laid one arm across her shoulders and pointed off to the right, where two deer had just appeared from a copse.

"Just like at home in the Swabian Mountains," Flora whispered, and leaned into Konstantin's arm.

Just before they reached the Lichtenthal nunnery, Konstantin asked the driver to stop. He jumped out of the sleigh and held out his hand to help Flora down.

"Shall we stretch our legs a little?"

They walked off into the snow while the driver hung feed bags for the horses.

"Winter smells so lovely. A little like freshly washed clothes," said Flora, lifting her face to the sun. *How late is it?* she wondered. *Not yet midday, surely.* She jumped over a small snowdrift. And so what if it was? It made no difference now. She was allowed an occasional bit of lunacy, wasn't she? Still, after a few steps, she turned around. It wasn't necessary to drag out their stroll unduly.

"And the contours of the trees and houses are razor-sharp. No color anywhere, everything black and white, like a pencil drawing, don't you think?" said Konstantin, and he lifted a branch for Flora to pass underneath.

"Or like a silhouette cut from paper. But at least we are not as motionless as that," said Flora, scooping up a handful of snow. She formed it into a snowball, then laughed as she threw it at Konstantin.

It took Konstantin a moment to realize that the snow had not fallen from one of the trees.

"Now you're in trouble!" he said, already crouching and scraping together a snowball of his own. But Flora had her second snowball ready to go and hurled it at him mercilessly.

They romped in the snow, and Flora's stomach hurt from laughing. She could not remember the last time she had been so carefree.

Tears of laughter streamed down Konstantin's face, too, as he tried to swat a handful of snow on her head, but she kept twisting free of his grip.

They both saw the group of nuns moving past the sleigh on their way to a barn outside the nunnery walls, but they paid them little attention.

Soon after, loaded with bales of hay and straw, the nuns returned, watching the young couple curiously in passing.

Chapter Forty-Five

Two days later, Ernestine received a letter from Sybille. Strange . . . it was neither Christmas nor Easter. For a moment, she thought about opening it at the dinner table and reading it aloud to the others. A letter from the nunnery was something special, after all. Hannah would certainly be impressed. But then her curiosity got the better of her, and she tore the envelope open.

"The girl's gone completely out of her mind now," she murmured to herself when she had reached the end of the letter. To claim that she had seen Flora in the company of an unknown man close to the nunnery! How would Sybille even have recognized her sister-in-law? She had only ever met Flora once, although Ernestine knew that Sybille also possessed a wedding photograph of Flora and Friedrich.

She had written something about a snowball fight right outside the nunnery walls, but part of her text was all but illegible. Sybille had written the words very small and tightly spaced to save room on the side for a Bible passage.

Ernestine glanced toward the door. Flora and her mother were both in the store, thank God!

Sybille wrote that she had seen Flora on Tuesday, and Ernestine knew perfectly well that Flora had gone to visit Princess Stropolski at the

Europäischer Hof on Tuesday. Flora had been delighted to go and visit her very first customer so early in the year, and she had spent almost half the day with her. In the end, however, the princess had been unable to decide what kind of party she wanted and what kind of floral arrangements she would therefore need. Well, that's how rich people were, sometimes.

Ernestine shook her head. What had driven Sybille to write such a confused missive? Did she envy Flora? Was she jealous because of everything Flora had done for the family? Or was it perhaps a moment of religious mania?

The child had always been a little strange. Ernestine only had to recall the penetrating gaze that Sybille liked to put on, as if she were trying to read her thoughts. It was downright spooky at times.

Sending her off to the nunnery had been the right decision, at least, Ernestine thought as she threw the letter into the stove, where it flared brightly and disappeared into a thousand tiny grains of ash. It really would not do to have Friedrich or someone else stumble across Sybille's muddled lines. She would do best to forget all about it herself, and the sooner the better.

Despite her resolution, however, Ernestine could not drive Sybille's words out of her mind; come evening, she could no longer stand it. She thought it was only right to tell Flora about it—at some future point, the two young women would certainly cross paths again, and Flora would be better prepared if Sybille began espousing her confused imaginings.

"Now don't go looking so shocked," she said to Flora, after telling her in minute detail about the contents of the letter. "Sybille must be jealous because of your good fortune. In the past, you could see the envy on her face if I so much as picked up Friedrich in my arms, as if I were not allowed to do that!"

Flora grasped her mother-in-law's arm. "Ernestine, on that day, well, there was—"

Ernestine interrupted her with a sad voice. "You don't have to say a word, dear child. It is abundantly clear that the signs of delusion Sybille exhibits in her letter have upset you, and I feel just the same, which is why I understand you without you having to say a word. But with my own daughter, well, we never really got on. It is so good to have you here!" She embraced Flora so tightly that Flora could hardly breathe.

The old proverb that Flora had quoted on that stormy, snowy Candlemas Day, February 2, 1873, turned out to be true: old man winter faded fast, and when the first violets showed their pretty faces through the previous year's leaves, no one shed a tear for him.

"My two months here have passed in the blink of an eye. Where have the days gone? And why are we Gönningers always saying good-bye?" Hannah said, and she sighed so dramatically that Flora almost laughed out loud, although she felt more like bursting into tears.

Her mother was going home, and later the same day Friedrich would also be setting off on his own journey. Flora did not know exactly when his train would leave for Bad Ems.

"Come back soon," she urged her mother as the two held each other and rocked back and forth.

Sabine stood beside them on the platform, holding Alexander in her arms. Hannah looked yearningly at her grandson. "If it were up to me, I'd be on my way back tomorrow. It almost breaks my heart to leave the little boy."

"I'll write you every week, and next time you visit, bring Papa along, too. And Seraphine. And Valentin, too, of course. Oh, bring everyone!" said Flora. She sniffed, teary-eyed.

Flora did not have much more time to digest the painful farewell. Hardly had she arrived back in the shop when a widower from the neighborhood appeared, wanting to use the language of flowers to turn down a woman who was getting a touch too persistent.

"It's the wrong time of year for goosefoot," Flora told him regretfully. But she could offer him dried autumn asters. Together with *Flora's ABC*, the woman would certainly get his message—namely, goodbye. The man left with a basketful of the dried flowers.

Sabine, who had brought Alexander in to be fed and who had observed the exchange, shook her head.

"People are cowards," she said. "They need your flowers to express if something annoys them or pleases them."

Flora laughed. "Does it matter? If everyone could say what they felt as beautifully as the poets, *I* would be out of work. Give me the boy before my breasts explode!"

"Say hello to the princess for me."

"And don't forget your promise, all right?"

"We'll see," Flora said with a smile.

Friedrich watched his wife wave after the departing man, and his forehead rumpled.

"That was that Konstantin Sokerov, wasn't it? What was he doing here? Wasn't he here just yesterday? And what was that about a promise?"

As if she had only just noticed him, Flora turned to Friedrich. "He's a good customer. Didn't you see the enormous bouquet of daffodils he bought for the princess?" Her eyes were shining, and her cheeks were as red as if she'd just been out for a brisk walk in the fresh March air. *My wife is so beautiful,* Friedrich suddenly thought.

Then he screwed up his nose again. "In the past, someone like him would have been called *un gigolo*. Letting an old, sick woman keep him . . ." A small porcelain butterfly sitting on the edge of the counter caught his eye. "What's that?"

"Konstantin Sokerov gave it to me as a mark of gratitude . . . because the bouquets I tie for him are always so beautiful."

"A mark of gratitude, uh-huh . . ." Friedrich found the gift excessive. But what did he care about the man? "I'm on my way to the station and came in to say adieu—"

Flora threw herself so unexpectedly at his chest that he had to stagger back a step.

"Flora!"

"Why can't I come with you? We haven't been away together anywhere since our wedding in Gönningen. I'm sure I would like Bad Ems. And it would be wonderful if we finally had some time alone together again. Just you and me—"

"What do you mean? With my schedule, I wouldn't have any time for you at all."

"But we'd still have the evenings. We could go out for dinner and . . ." She shrugged helplessly. "I just feel that it isn't good if you go away, and I'm left behind all alone. Just the thought of it almost scares me."

"Oh, Flora." He released himself gently from her embrace. "I would like nothing more than to have you at my side. But what about Alexander? And the shop? Is Mother supposed to look after everything by herself? She would not manage that."

Friedrich sighed and took out his pocket watch. He was late. The train would leave in just under an hour. He also had to make sure that he got his visit to Bad Ems over with as quickly as possible—the Baden-Baden season would open again in just a few weeks. He had mud and water samples to deliver and results to wait for, but he did not expect to learn anything particularly new on his trip to Bad Ems, unlike the bigwigs in the Spa and Bath Administration. He was certainly interested in the inhalation regime that had been introduced in Bad Ems some twenty years earlier. At least there the people had not set everything on the casino and had promoted the region's curative advantages far earlier.

"It's only for a week," Flora pleaded. "We can just take Alexander along with us. I'd be so happy to see something new for a change. For inspiration . . ."

Friedrich put his watch away in his pocket, took out his train ticket, and glanced absently at it. "You're talking as if I am off on a pleasure cruise," he said.

Flora turned away from him. "Your objections are justified, I know," she said softly. "But how many times have you told me that I can't think of anything but the shop? Now here I am thinking about both of us, and that doesn't suit you, either. I just think a little time together would do us both good."

"Yes. No." Friedrich gave an agonized sigh. "If you'd said all this earlier, we might have been able to think about it, but like this?" He saw Flora's disappointment and felt a silent anger rise inside him. He had come to get a kiss goodbye and good wishes for his journey. Instead, he now felt queasy about going at all. "Why are you making it so hard for me?" he blurted. "Can't you be content with what you have for once? Can't you just be a . . . a normal, everyday woman, and not always looking for whatever comes next?"

Flora stepped away sharply, as if he had slapped her.

Friedrich wanted to take back his words instantly, to find appeasing words to make up for the hurt he'd caused. He did not want their farewell to end on a discordant note, not like this. But nothing came to him.

The watch in his pocket ticked.

"Adieu," he finally said, and left.

"Püppi was overjoyed at the daffodils. She even recited a poem by a German poet—Goethe, I think," Konstantin said to Flora as they strode along Lichtenthaler Allee in the damp, misty morning air.

Then his companion, in a dramatic voice, began to recite:

Thus the early sprung narcissi,

Bloom in trim rows in the garden

Well may one imagine that they

Know for whom they wait so smartly.

"That's exactly the poem! Where do you know that from?" As they walked, Konstantin took a bundle of twigs from her. They were not blooming like the other bundle that Flora carried, but their leaves had a silvery sheen. With his free hand, he wiped away the droplets of morning dew.

The bundle soon grew heavy in his arms. What did Flora want with all the greenery? And what was he thinking, coming out with her on one of her early-morning wanderings? She was a pretty thing, admittedly, and there was something in her passion for flowers that he found entertaining. And her admiration of him felt good. In the last few weeks, he had caught himself often imagining her as his lover. Just once to trace the lines of her slender neck with his finger, to feel her young, tender skin beneath his, to probe beneath the many layers of fabric of her skirt for the most feminine part of her body . . . maybe then he would better ride out the times with Püppi. My God, a little pleasure ought to be granted to him!

His train of thought was abruptly interrupted as he stepped in a puddle with his right foot. Damn it! Hadn't he promised himself to stay away from married women? What was he doing out here at the crack of dawn?

Flora beamed at him. "Johann Wolfgang von Goethe. Every child in Germany learns his poems." She scratched her nose. "There's another verse, something about lilies, but I've forgotten how it goes, I'm sorry." With her hand holding her gardening shears already reaching out toward a blooming almond tree, she paused. "How nice to hear that the princess liked them. Some people would be a little put out, because in the language of flowers, the daffodil, or narcissus, stands for self-centeredness."

Konstantin waved it off. "I sometimes wonder how much of any of it she really understands. She lives almost entirely in the past these days. Flora, if it weren't for you, I think I would already have gone mad." He realized as he said it that it was no glib compliment, but the truth, and the thought frightened him. He hoped he was not falling in love with the girl. It could not just be physical desire that kept him going back to her shop, because their meetings with one another were invariably demure. And in that respect, he was not suffering much. He was almost always able to find a chambermaid somewhere who was willing to give herself to him in a dark corner.

"I do wonder what could be so exciting about a stroll through wet fields, but if I can keep your boredom at bay for a while like this, then I'm happy." She laid a second bundle of blooming branches in his arms, then put the shears away and crouched down.

"It's strange, somehow," she murmured to herself. "Wherever there are cowslips, cuckooflowers are not far away. But daisies are usually to be found in the company of violets and forget-me-nots. White, purple, and that beautiful blue . . . everything in nature grows in complete harmony." She straightened up with her head tilted to one side and one hand shielding her eyes from the morning sun. As they walked on, she looked at Konstantin. "And then I come along and mess everything up."

Konstantin shook his head vehemently. "That isn't true. Your bouquets show a wonderful harmony themselves."

Instead of responding to his compliment, she cleared her throat. "Konstantin, what I wanted to say to you . . . I look forward to you coming to the flower shop, truly, every time. But you can't come out picking flowers with me again. And you can't give me anything else. I know you only mean well, but I'm a married woman, and the people around here love to work things out for themselves. Do you understand?"

He shook his head. "No. I don't understand that at all. We're just going for a walk. There's nothing indecent about that!" *Unfortunately,* he added silently. He stopped, one hand holding her sleeve. He lifted her chin so that she had to look him in the eye. "Flora, now don't be so terribly stern. Enjoy the moment."

"Enjoy . . . but it isn't about enjoyment!" she replied. "It is about doing your daily work. About attending to one's duties, and about being someone that others can rely on. Isn't it?"

Konstantin dropped the branches and flowers and all his reservations about married women.

He took Flora in his arms and kissed her. Kissed her and kissed her and kissed her.

Chapter Forty-Six

As soon as Friedrich returned from Bad Ems, he threw himself back into his work at the Trinkhalle, making repairs and tending the property from first thing in the morning until late in the evening. Friedrich was still holding the broom he used to clear away cobwebs from the walls when the first spa guests came strolling along the paths.

What everyone in Baden-Baden had hoped for—but few believed would happen after the closure of the casino—came to pass: the streets filled with visitors, and the 1873 season began.

On the one hand, everything seemed as it always had been. But on the other, nothing was.

"It's the middle of May already, and I still can't find many familiar names in the guest lists. Where are my customers?" Flora leafed frantically through the *Badeblatt*, then looked over at Friedrich. "No sign of Matriona Schikanova. And it doesn't look as if Piotr Vjazemskij has turned up, either."

"Vjazemskij was only here for the casino—Baden-Baden isn't interesting for someone like him anymore," said Friedrich, dipping his spoon into the marmalade pot.

It was a rainy morning with low-hanging clouds and an unpleasant, gusty wind. The guests would mostly still be in bed, so he allowed himself the rare luxury of a leisurely start to the day.

The evening before, they had heated the dining room, and a little of the warmth remained. Even Alexander was sleeping soundly, although he usually woke very early—a tendency that he had indisputably inherited from his mother. Friedrich looked over to the cradle by the window and smiled. Ernestine stepped into the room.

"What a miserable day!" Cocooned in a heavy knitted cardigan, she joined them at the table. When Sabine had poured her coffee, she wrapped her hands around the cup as tightly as if her life depended on it. "Flora, am I mistaken, or did I hear you rumbling through the house before it was even light?"

"I . . . yes, I was out picking flowers," said Flora, trying to concentrate on the guest lists. "Finally! Princess Irina Komatschova, Count Popo, and there are the Gagarins and the Menshikovs! Konstantin was right: almost all of them have come back."

Friedrich laughed. "I could have told you they'd be back. With their International Club, no doubt they have big plans for the Iffezheim racetrack this season. Who knows, maybe you'll get to make the laurel wreath for a winning horse."

Flora smiled, but it was a pained smile.

"You were out picking flowers so early? It was hardly even light!" Ernestine said.

Flora frowned at her mother-in-law. "Now that spring is here, I find it easy to get up early. Besides, I can get a lot more done during the day this way."

Was she supposed to say that it was Konstantin who made her get out of bed so early every morning? That is was because of him that she went creeping through the meadows and fields in the dawn twilight? That she did not want to run the risk of meeting him outside ever again?

Flora stared absently at her hands. That kiss . . . what a sheer delight! She had flushed hot and cold, tremors running through her, warm, exciting—

Done. A slip, one time, never to be repeated. She would make sure of that.

Of course Konstantin had apologized to her. He had been carried away by the radiance of the morning, by the bounty of nature around them, by the feeling of having discovered in Flora a kind of kindred soul.

Kindred souls—what a lovely notion.

Flora pulled herself together and tapped on the list of names of newly arrived guests. "I don't know most of the names here. Who are these people?"

Friedrich leaned over the *Badeblatt*, and for a moment she thought she smelled not his scent, but Konstantin's. Leather and tobacco and cognac and . . . but it was just the odor of the tincture that Friedrich applied to the small nicks when he shaved.

"Most of the men and women here are connected to the music world or some other side of cultural life. Really, Flora, you must know some of them from last year."

She shrugged. Last year? She was having enough trouble with this year, with trying to act as if everything were normal, with living every day as if it were everyday.

And all the while, deep inside, an unease roiled. She often found herself unable to concentrate on her work. When was Konstantin coming? Would he come to buy flowers at all? And then she scolded herself for thinking about him so much.

"But what's this?" Friedrich's eyes widened. "There are also the names of several high-ranking statesmen here, from Karlsruhe and Stuttgart, even Berlin. Baron von Schimmel from Schwedhausen with his family, Count Volkhard von Fürstenweiler and his wife. And that one, too! Look at that—it's a veritable gaggle of nobles and diplomats." He shook his head. "It's one of fate's ironies, I think, that the men who had a hand in the war with France—the same men who are to blame for the French not being here—are now coming here themselves."

"Maybe they're trying to make up for some of Baden-Baden's lost trade," said Ernestine.

Friedrich snorted. "You don't believe that. These men are coming here for the same reason as all the other guests: because Baden-Baden has something to offer them!" He nodded toward the sideboard, where a small pile of freshly printed programs for the new season lay.

Flora's own eyes turned automatically to the stack of programs, each of which listed the attractions organized by the spa committee under the leadership of their newly appointed director. There were chamber music soirees, matinees, military concerts, galas, and symphonies—and the town's own orchestra was playing three times a day with more than forty musicians. The Grand-Ducal Court Theater of Karlsruhe was appearing in the theater, and other German ensembles were coming to perform.

Konstantin had said that the Baden-Baden theater could stand up to the most splendid in Europe, and that she should absolutely go with him to see a performance. It would be his treat, and after the show he would take her for hot chocolate with a shot of rum. He made it sound so easy—the two of them, in public, in Baden-Baden.

He'd crept back into her thoughts again, when she should really have her mind on Friedrich, her husband, the father of her son, to whom she had sworn herself until death did them part.

"So many wonderful performances—wouldn't you like to take me out to the theater or a concert, too?" she asked with deliberate gaiety. "Why should we leave all the nice things to the tourists?"

Friedrich drank a swig of coffee. "Because all the nice things are put on for them?" His voice was heavy with irony. "Frankly, I think the program is too much. When are the guests supposed to take the waters or bathe? Between performances?"

That was so typical of Friedrich. All he ever thought about was his precious water! Flora didn't know whether to feel sad or angry.

"Don't you think, Flora?" said Ernestine. Then she shook Flora's arm. "Child, are you even listening to me? I said that theater people would certainly have a sense for flowers. With your *ABC*, you might be able to win over some of them as customers."

Flora looked at her mother-in-law uncomprehendingly.

"Honestly, sometimes you're more absentminded than me. You know what? I'm going to go to the theater myself and ask the dressing-room girls if they'd be prepared to hand out your little booklet to the guests." Smiling kindly, she patted Flora's hand.

"You could also count the smaller hotels this year when you print more of the *ABC*, and not only the big, fancy places," Friedrich added. "The big hotels spare no effort as it is in making their guests' stay as comfortable as possible, and the smaller places have a very hard time competing. Gustav Körner, for example—the owner of the Hotel Marie-Eluise—was complaining to me about it just yesterday. Your *ABC* would be a small gift he could pass on to his guests."

Flora frowned. "What guests? Princess Stropolski, whom I advised to take her curative baths at the Marie-Eluise, mentioned that when she went she was almost always the only guest there. My booklets would not be seen."

"No guests? I'm not surprised," Ernestine said. "Gustav Körner's wife ran off with a man from Milan, you know!" She opened her eyes wide at the horror of it.

"I haven't heard that story yet," said Flora as she lifted Alexander, who had just woken up, from his crib.

Friedrich nodded. "It happened last autumn. And without a woman in the house, Gustav probably won't be able to run the hotel much longer. Marie-Eluise was the one who took care of everything. When she was there, the place was always spic-and-span. It's a shame that the hotel is going downhill. Especially because the spring that flows through its cellars is one of the best in town. You should see the water analysis I had done for Gustav. It—"

"Everyone has their burden to bear," Flora interrupted him. If she listened to Friedrich's water stories one moment longer, she would go mad. She folded the *Badeblatt* together with her free hand and looked across the table at Friedrich and Ernestine. "Theater people, writers, politicians—it seems to me the guests who've come this year are as mixed a crowd as we had before. And the stage itself hasn't changed . . ."

Chapter Forty-Seven

Baden-Baden, June 9, 1873

Dearest Mama, dearest Papa,
I hope my letter finds you well. The new season is in full
swing here. Does that count as an excuse for not writing
to you in so long? Mama, Papa, though I may not write
as often as I should, I think of you all the time.

The days are busy here. I have a lot of new customers,
mostly people who work in the theater: actors, dancers,
and I've even got a real opera diva who comes in. She
only ever wants orchids, as if those are easy to come by!

All the prominent statesmen from Berlin that Fried-
rich is so happy to see here, on the other hand, are rather
thrifty gentlemen when it comes to flowers. But what is it
Father always says? Every little bit helps.

"Is too much information about the business in a letter boring?"

Sabine finished mopping the floor, then looked up. Flora had put down her pen. "No idea. I'm not the one to ask." Sabine tipped the sudsy water down the drain. The shop floor practically gleamed, and now she could tackle the next task. The Monday morning rush of customers had abated, and before the next ones came in the early afternoon, she wanted to get things cleaned up.

Flora had also wanted to make the most of the brief respite to write her letter to Gönningen. But instead of continuing to write, she gazed absentmindedly out the window, as she had so often recently.

Sabine sighed. Where was her friend's mind wandering? She hoped it wasn't to—

"When I popped off to the kitchen earlier, did Konstantin Sokerov happen to come by?" Flora asked.

"No. He hasn't been here since Friday. It's almost insane how much money he spends on flowers."

"Then he probably went away with friends over the weekend," said Flora, with feigned indifference. "Although he normally tells me if he's doing something like that."

"The man doesn't owe you any explanations, you know," said Sabine.

"I know that. And I'll see him on Wednesday at Irina Komatschova's reception or Thursday at the Gagarins' garden party. Konstantin is a welcome guest wherever he goes, but that's no surprise. He's so charming."

"And you are still just the woman who brings the flowers. You're not one of them!" said Sabine grumpily. She did not like the way Flora talked about the man one little bit, nor did she like the way he seemed to haunt Flora's thoughts. Was she in love with him? Good heavens, anything but that!

"Sabine, don't start acting like my governess," Flora said irritably. "There's really nothing wrong if I exchange a few pleasantries with Konstantin at one of the parties. That's all there is to it. Nothing has happened since that one kiss when we were out walking. He's an honorable man, after all." When Sabine continued to look skeptically at her, Flora muttered, "I knew I shouldn't have told you anything about the kiss." But her face brightened a moment later. "You should see how the women latch on to Konstantin at those parties! Sometimes it's almost impossible for him to get free just to come and have a chat with me, and yet he's always in a good mood. Sometimes he gives me a wink over the heads of the others, or he screws up his face like he's sucked on a lemon. Oh, he's so funny!" Flora sighed deeply.

She sounded so wistful. Even worse than Minka, who was head over heels in love with the head chef at the Englischer Hof. Sabine could hardly put up with their ravings anymore, particularly because she no longer had anything of her own to rave about. Moritz, the apprentice at the gentlemen's tailor, had gone back to the family farm after the death of his father, and instead of wielding needles and a tape measure, he was wielding a pitchfork in the Black Forest. So much for their future together.

Men! Sabine glared at her washrag. The way things looked, she'd be cleaning for strangers for the rest of her life.

Flora, however, had a good husband, a lovely home, and a successful shop. What more could she want? Sabine felt like giving her a good talking-to. She would bet everything she had that Flora had fallen for that . . . good-for-nothing, even if she denied it a thousand times.

But Sabine did not trust herself to do it. Friendship aside, Flora was the woman of the house these days, and she was the one who paid Sabine. It was not necessary to tell her what she thought.

"Should I change the water in all the buckets, or just for the peonies?" she asked.

"What kind of question is that? All the flowers get fresh water, of course!" Flora looked at the freshly mopped floor with narrowed eyes. "Back in the corner there . . . run the washrag over that again. And then fill up the basket with the binding things."

"With cord? Or do you want the heavy string?"

"Some of everything, so I can choose. And where's the binding wire gone now? Why must you all make my work so hard?" Flora dipped her pen back into the inkwell. A fat drop of ink splattered onto the letter paper. She hastily dabbed at it with a cloth. "Damn it. Everything's going wrong today."

Sabine rolled her eyes. Lately, Flora had often berated those closest to her, only to feel sorry a short time later and apologize for taking out her bad mood on someone else.

When Flora finally spoke again, Sabine was counting on another apology, but Flora said, "You know, Konstantin really doesn't have an easy time of it. All those nights spent awake at Püppi's side, nights filled with pain and tears. The princess's fears are draining him completely. I would like so much to help him."

"What are you talking about? It's not as if he's with her just for fun," Sabine said, planting her hands on her hips and glaring at Flora. "The old lady pays for everything, right? That makes Konstantin no more than a paid laborer, which is no reason to feel sorry for him. Do you feel sorry for me because I'm your maid?"

"What kind of comparison is that? As if we'd put the same kind of demands on you that the old princess makes of Konstantin. She's almost certainly the reason that he still hasn't been in today. I'd like to go and give her a piece of my mind."

I'm starting to think you've taken leave of your senses, Sabine thought. Just then, she noticed a shadow by the back door—Ernestine and Alexander.

Flora jumped up, took the child from Ernestine's arms, and kissed and hugged him. "My little darling."

Sabine and Ernestine had to smile at the endearing scene. "I'm off now," said Ernestine. "I'm meeting Gretel in the café. Alexander can stay with you until I'm back."

Flora abruptly pushed her son back into his grandmother's arms. "No. I slave away in here all day—is it too much to ask you to look after the child?"

"A baby needs his mother!"

Flora sniffed. "Tell it to the Gönninger seed women! When they go off traveling in autumn, they leave their children with a grandmother or great-aunt. No one cares if it makes their heart break."

Flora, what is going on? Sabine asked herself silently, while Ernestine slunk away like a whipped dog, holding the baby.

"Do you know our little country place behind the Conversationshaus?" Princess Markova fanned herself gracefully as she spoke. A thunderstorm had struck at midday—now the streets were steaming and it was almost tropically humid.

"Not yet, I'm afraid, but I will stop by this afternoon when I go for a walk," said Flora. When someone like Princess Sophia Markova talked about a "little country place," then it was probably an enormous villa.

"There will certainly be some questions asked about why we are not celebrating our daughter's engagement in one of the hotels." The princess lowered her fan. "But Elena has expressly requested a more subdued affair. No formal six-course dinner for her, oh no. And we'll only be serving two or three wines. If it had been up to me . . ."

Flora glanced surreptitiously to Sabine, who rolled her eyes. As the princess droned on about how "meager" the planned engagement party would be, Flora looked out along the street, where passersby dodged the deep puddles.

Still no sign of Konstantin. And it was already three in the afternoon.

"And no red roses, not under any circumstances! Elena's first fiancé died tragically in a fall from a horse. He crashed into a rose hedge— can you believe it!—and the roses were bright red, the same color as his blood. So it's no wonder that Elena avoids even the sight of red roses whenever she can." The princess's voice, which was already high-pitched, had become shrill as she spoke her last sentences.

The next moment, the shop door was thrown open with such force that the little bell above the door tinkled wildly.

"Konstantin!" As she called his name, a wave of warm joy broke over Flora. She returned her attention quickly to the princess, took her by the hand, and maneuvered her toward the exit. "Let me surprise you. I will come up with something extra special for your daughter's engagement."

"My dear Sophia, what's that I hear?" Konstantin sighed. "The prettiest of all young girls is getting married? Sometimes I wonder what purpose life still has."

Flora frowned.

"Well, Konstantin Sokerov, you are quite the Prince Charming, aren't you? But you are right, of course. A pearl like our Elena is truly one of a kind. I hope I'll be seeing you and Püppi next Sunday, too?"

Konstantin shrugged. "The princess is not at her best. I don't know if she—"

Sophia Markova patted his hand. "In your good hands, I'm sure Püppi will be up and about again in no time." Satisfied with herself and her world, the princess strutted out of the shop and away.

Konstantin watched after her for a moment. Then he murmured, "Elena's dowry must be remarkably high if it keeps her fiancé distracted from her long, pointy nose."

"Konstantin!" Flora let out an almost hysterical laugh, and instantly felt Sabine's glare. There was nothing unseemly about a little chat, for God's sake. Flora really did not understand what Sabine was constantly inferring. She was probably just jealous—especially since her Moritz had left town—because a man like Konstantin had no interest in her.

Who did Sabine think she was? Was she paid for her work, or to stand around gawking?

"Nothing to do?" Flora snapped at her. "Are you just going to let the trash overflow? On the compost heap with it, and make it fast!"

The moment they were alone, Konstantin took Flora's hand. "I've missed you so much! The weekend seemed endless without you." As he spoke, he stroked the underside of her wrist with one finger. Flora felt her pulse quicken beneath his touch.

"It was a boat cruise on the Rhine. Popo invited the usual crew. I all but died of boredom." He twisted his face as if he were describing an excursion through hell itself.

"What can I say?" Flora replied. "I spent all of Sunday dealing with my son's stomachache." She breathed in the scent of his shaving lotion, headier and spicier than all the flowers and herbs in the shop together.

As usual, when Flora talked about her son and her family, a shadow crossed Konstantin's face, as if it pained him that Flora lived in a world to which he had no access. Flora chastised herself silently for even mentioning Alexander.

A moment later, Konstantin was beaming again. He took a scarf from his pocket; it was pink and white with long fringe and decorated with flowers.

"The flowers reminded me of you . . . If I was not always thinking about you, my life would be easier." He moved behind her and tied the scarf, and when he took his hands away, he let his fingers trail over her slender waist.

"You mustn't do that," Flora said, her voice hoarse. She turned to face him and touched the silky fabric of the scarf.

"Whether or not I give something to the most beautiful flower girl in the city is up to me," Konstantin replied, his eyes flashing.

They chatted while Flora tied a bouquet of peonies, and when Konstantin left the shop fifteen minutes later, Flora's fingers roamed over the fringe of the scarf as she watched him go. For the rest of the day, she was in the best of moods.

"I'm going to come up with something especially nice for Princess Markova," she said to Sabine, when she returned from the garden. "Or did she already have something special in mind?"

"She said something about red roses. I didn't hear it exactly, because you shooed me out of the shop," Sabine replied curtly.

Chapter Forty-Eight

Püppi's leather-bound diary was in her line of sight. If she was reading the numbers correctly in the low light of the sitting room, today was June 15.

Wasn't Elena—Sophia and Tabor's daughter—getting engaged later that day? Konstantin had said something about it.

Püppi felt her head tipping to one side. Don't fall asleep! She stood up and tottered out onto the balcony. It was three o'clock in the morning. It would not be much longer before the sky began to lighten, the nightingales began to sing, and she could finally go to bed. Püppi loved the summer months, when the nights were so short and the days long and filled with sunshine. She had already changed into her nightdress. Soon she would slide beneath the cool covers. She was so tired.

The fifteenth of June. Wasn't that one of the so-called "black" days? *Dies atri* she recalled her mother calling these ill-starred days—days on which one should not start anything new. No travel. No signing contracts. And certainly no doctors letting blood. Her mother's superstition about those days was strong—she had gone so far as to hang dark curtains over the windows. "It was on one such day that Christ was nailed to the cross. Do we need any greater proof of how fateful these days can be?"

A weak smile crept over Püppi's face as she recalled her mother's hands folded in prayer. Her mother had liked to pray. Often, long, and wherever the urge took her. But in the end it had not done her much good. Together with her husband, Püppi's father, she was murdered in an attack on their isolated summer palace. Püppi and her siblings were away in Tsarskoje Selo at the time. Their parents were murdered on the first of April, the day on which Judas was born. Also a *dies ater*, as Püppi discovered much later.

And Elena wanted to get engaged today, of all days. But days like today were more suited to farewells!

Püppi's eye fell on the bouquet, from which more and more petals had fallen. She had had to say farewell to so many, many people over the years . . .

Her parents had been the first, then Josephina in the fire, then her sons. Both had perished in the war. Then Stepan had left her, although he had not been a bad husband. And her own youth had slipped away so mysteriously that Püppi had not even been able to give it a decent send-off. Then, slowly, day by day, year by year, her beauty had slunk off into the background. And now, last of all, her health was gone.

Püppi tried in vain to take a deep breath, trying to break through the constricting ring that seemed coiled around her chest. She padded back into the room. She was not sure that all the therapeutic baths she took in that terribly hot water were as beneficial as Konstantin seemed to believe. They seemed, if anything, to make her weaker and more tired. But every day, he insisted on them. Why did she let him persuade her?

Stealthily, one day, her love of parties had also disappeared—Püppi no longer wanted to celebrate through the nights, as she had done for decades. She preferred to spend her time alone, as now.

She turned her watch a little so that the glimmer of the candle fell on its mother-of-pearl face. Fifteen minutes past three. Konstantin would come back from his card game soon. She would ask him to take her to Sophia's house late in the morning—perhaps the engagement planned for that evening could yet be postponed. No girl should get engaged on one of the black days.

You and your superstitions, she heard Konstantin say in her mind, mocking her. *Why don't you just stay in the hotel and rest? A party at the Markovs would be too strenuous anyway,* he would say. She would nod, and he would go without her.

The mother-of-pearl watch face showed eighteen minutes past three.

It was still dark outside.

Püppi's eyes closed.

Flora had decorated the entire house. A dozen enormous flower-pots stood around the bronze statue beside the entrance to the Villa Markov, while in the house itself a veritable sea of flowers would greet the guests. The balustrade up to the second floor, the stairs and land-ing, the large portrait on the wall that depicted the master and mistress of the house—Flora had decorated all of it with her arrangements. On a table along one wall stood polished crystal glasses beside dozens of bottles of champagne in buckets of ice, and Flora had covered it with an embroidered tablecloth, while in the center of the table stood a magnificent porcelain jardinière overflowing with blooms.

Although her hands were cut and sore from the arduous work on the garlands and spectacular arrangements, Flora was satisfied with what she had achieved. It would take a visitor hours to discover every single flower, if they were so inclined.

The family and the guests were still out enjoying a walk along Lichtenthaler Allee. Until the first of them arrived, Flora had nothing to do. Later, if the princess wanted her to, she would help pour drinks for the guests.

Flora stepped out the back door into the expansive gardens. They could just as well have served the champagne out there, she thought. Why hadn't she noticed how picturesque the gardens were during her first visit?

Because you haven't been able to concentrate on anything at all this week, again!

Konstantin had not shown his face in the shop for a week. What was so much more important than being "kindred souls" that he simply forgot about her like this? Had she only imagined the bond between them? And why did it all affect her so deeply?

Flora sighed and sat down on a stone bench. Maybe she would feel better if she could find a little time to rest.

What is going on with me? she asked herself, not for the first time, as she absentmindedly picked a lonely daisy beside the bench. It was all she could do to get through her daily work. She was tetchy with Friedrich, and even Alexander had suffered her impatience that week.

He'll come, he won't, he'll come, he—

Flora looked at the daisy in her hand, plucked bare.

She had never in her life called on the power of the flower oracle for herself. She threw the remains of the flower away in disgust and wiped her hands on her skirt as if they were soiled.

The woman on the floor was surrounded by a crowd of people. They were standing or kneeling, some on her dress, ignoring the quality of the fabric. One was waving a fan, another held a bottle of smelling salts under her nose, and a younger man—probably the fiancé—dabbed at her temples with chilled champagne. But Elena had fainted so deeply that nothing seemed able to wake her.

"How *could* you?" Princess Markova shrieked at Flora. The bride-to-be's mother was trembling with fury.

"I . . . I don't know how—" Flora began, but at the look on the princess's face, she fell silent. All she saw was abhorrence and horror.

"You could have brought anything, any flower in the world! Anything but red roses!" The princess looked as if she might spit on Flora at any moment. "I will never, never forgive you for this!"

Flora's apology was not accepted. Nor was her offer to somehow make good for her terrible error. Beneath an onslaught of Russian curses, she packed all the red roses onto the handcart, out of Sophia's and Elena's sight.

Flora held her head high as she left the house, just as the doctor that had been called arrived. But the moment she was outside, the first tears came. And when she reached Lichtenthaler Allee, nothing could hold back the flood.

How could she have made a mistake like that? The princess had said something about red roses. She remembered that. But she had utterly forgotten the "under no circumstances" part. Why hadn't she written herself a note at the time?

She left the handcart standing and ran away from the path, out into the meadows, the same meadows where she picked flowers every morning. She wanted to be alone, somewhere no one would find her. Her skirt caught in the high grass, and low-hanging branches whipped her face. Once, she tripped over a root. But Flora felt none of it. Beneath an ancient oak, she finally sank to the ground wailing.

She had never in her life been so muddled. She lamented ever meeting Konstantin, because meeting him meant she thought of him constantly, wherever she was. Being in love like that was dreadful, just dreadful!

Flora's body heaved with her crying, and behind her hands thrown over her face, her tears would not stop.

"Flora! For God's sake! What's the matter? I saw your cart over on the path."

She looked up in astonishment and squinted against the sun. She had not heard anyone approach.

"You? Why *you?*" she cried when she realized she was looking at Konstantin. "What do you want?" She let out a sob. "I . . . I want to be alone. Leave! Go away!" When he did not do as she said, she lashed out at him with her fists. "You . . . you terrible man! If only I'd never met you, you . . . you bring me nothing but trouble and more trouble." With every word, drops of spittle hit Konstantin's face. Flora did not care. "You don't show your face for a week, so why now? I hate you!"

"Püppi is dead."

Flora stopped crying in a heartbeat.

Konstantin sat down beside her in the grass. "I've been sitting with her since early this morning, keeping vigil. I came out briefly because I needed some fresh air."

"When . . . when did it happen? Oh, not—" Flora, who knew about Püppi's fear of dying at night, broke off at the look in Konstantin's eyes. "Oh no."

"Püppi feared nothing more than the reaper coming for her at night. If only I'd been there with her! But I was away, at a card game. When I returned, she was in the armchair. Dead." Konstantin's eyes were wet with tears. "I was taken completely unawares. I never would have thought that she could just . . . die, just like that. She was weak, but we all thought that after her bath treatment she would start to improve. She wanted to go to Elena's party."

Elena's party . . . Flora bit down on her lip. Set beside Konstantin's grief, her own disaster counted for little.

"I'm so sorry . . ." She stroked his cheek, but he took hold of her hand, kissed it. His eyes peered into hers, hungry, avid, yearning.

"Flora, don't send me away now. You and I . . ." He drew her to him, and his words caught in her hair. "I have never needed anyone as much as I need you now."

And then she was lying in his arms. His full lips found hers and he kissed her deeply, nibbling, tasting. She responded with small, frantic kisses as she pressed against his chest. She felt his tongue in her mouth, started, then opened her lips wider, wanting more from him, everything from him, wanted to feel him deep inside her.

A loud clinking beside Konstantin's leg startled them both.

Konstantin lifted the linen sack that had fallen out of his pocket. It was clearly heavy. "Püppi's jewelry," he said. "And some of her money. I had to secure both before I left the room. The staff steal like ravens, you know," he said. He dropped the sack on the grass beside him.

Flora nodded, and lifted her skirts.

Chapter Forty-Nine

Looking back, Flora could not have said how she made it home that evening. Or how she managed to lie down next to Friedrich in bed as if nothing had happened.

Konstantin . . .

Early the next morning, she woke to Alexander's happy babbling. She wandered into the kitchen like a sleepwalker, made some milky porridge, and fed her son. Friedrich had already left, and had left a note for her saying that he had been invited to a sitting of the spa committee that evening. Thank God.

As on every Monday morning, the street was filled with wagons, all of them in a hurry. Pedestrians had their work cut out trying to navigate among the horses and drays. In front of the printer's shop stood one particularly large wagon stacked high with boxes. Flora wound her way past it and along the crowded footpath, careful not to bump anything or anyone with the bouquet of sunflowers she was carrying. As she walked past the Promenade boutiques, she glanced covertly across to Maison Kuttner, as she normally would. Today the flower shop did not interest her, and the other pretty shops just as little. She wanted nothing more than to deliver her bouquet as quickly as possible and then to be alone. So far, she had managed to suppress every thought that had entered her head. She did not know how long that would continue to be possible, or what would happen when it was not.

Don't think. Don't feel. Don't think. Don't feel.

Normally, Flora would have looked forward to a visit to the Mallebrein family. She would be met by Marie Mallebrein and invited in for a cup of coffee. After a little gossip, Flora's bouquets would be praised. Sometimes, Flora would even talk with the senior judge himself. Franz Mallebrein was an amiable man who spoke wisely and also radiated a human warmth that Flora would not have expected in someone of his profession. He respected the fine arts at least as much as he did the law, he once confided to Flora. He used the little free time that his profession and his ever-growing family allowed him to delve into the mythology surrounding Baden-Baden. He wrote poetry and short stories, and had once recited a few of his own verses for Flora.

On that Monday morning, Flora was relieved to find that no one besides the maid who answered the door seemed to be at home. Marie would be at the market, most likely, and the children probably off playing. Flora sighed with relief. Gossip was the last thing she felt like sharing just then.

"The sunflowers for the lady of the house," she said, handing the large bouquet to the maid. "And here is the bill. Mrs. Mallebrein can—" Flora broke off abruptly when a door on her right opened.

"The flower girl! My ears do not deceive me." With ruddy cheeks and a piece of paper in his hand, the judge stood in front of her. "What a beautiful bouquet! You are a true artist."

Flora gave him a small curtsy. "Judge Mallebrein, you are too kind."

The judge took a step toward her and pointed to the paper in his hand. "It occurs to me that just recently you were happy to listen to some of my verses. This is my latest attempt. Would you like to hear it?"

Flora had no choice but to nod.

"Do you know the legend of Merline, the nymph of the pond? I've been trying to put the story into verse. Listen:

> *By the lake in the woods so high,*
>
> *the nymph 'mongst the mosses abides*
>
> *her golden lyre by her side,*
>
> *her deer a-frolic nearby.*
>
> *Oh Mother, let me go to her.*
>
> *Trust her I never will do,*
>
> *I will watch from afar and be true*
>
> *but can no longer bear to stay here . . ."*

Flora staggered back a step as if she'd been slapped in the face. Merline, the nymph! The personification of temptation, today of all days. She pressed herself against the wood-paneled wall of the stairwell and sighed deeply.

The judge lowered the page. "What do you think?"

Flora felt the man's expectant gaze on her. *Say something! Something friendly and harmless, you can do that. Just don't start bawling!* she told herself.

She felt tears rising and fluttered her hands in front of her face as if she had to sneeze at any moment. But the judge was not to be deceived.

"Young lady, why are you crying?"

Flora turned and ran out the door.

"Why are you running away?" he called after her. "Stay, please. I still have to pay for the flowers and . . ." Perplexed, the judge looked at the paper in his hand. "The poem wasn't *that* bad, I'm sure."

Out! Out of town! Away from the staring people. Flora took the first bridge she came to that crossed the Oos. But she had not considered that her route would take her past the Trinkhalle.

At the sight of its columns, she burst out sobbing again.

Merline, the embodiment of temptation.

What had she done?

When she had first come to Baden-Baden, Friedrich had been quick to take her to visit his sacred place. Flora remembered it as if it were yesterday—the sun on her back, his laughter in her ear. He had enjoyed playing the city guide for her. And what had she said to him, when he told her the legend of the nymph in the pond?

"Merline wouldn't get anywhere with us."

What a joke! What had she done?

She had given in to temptation more easily than any goatherd, had given herself over to desires that she had not even known existed.

She blushed with shame when she thought about how she had pressed herself to Konstantin. She had practically thrown herself at him! She was no better than the cocottes for whom Friedrich had nothing but contempt.

And there had been no need for it to happen. For weeks, she had sensed the threat that Konstantin Sokerov represented for her. Every accidental touch, every feather-light kiss of her hand by Konstantin had burned on her skin. Even Sabine had suspected something, and had tried to warn her. But Flora had preferred to close her eyes and ears and give in to the pleasant tingling in her belly.

Flora came to a standstill and gazed at the elongated building, toward which—now, late in the morning—more and more people were making their way on foot. Should she go to Friedrich and confess everything to him, now, on the spot?

The terrible scene in Villa Markov, and then the news of Püppi's death—she had not been in her right mind the day before. She had not been herself at all.

How was she supposed to explain to Friedrich something that was unexplainable even to herself? What did she hope a confession would bring? That the burden on her heart would ease? That Friedrich would forgive her? What kind of man would ever forgive something like that? And if she were not mistaken, adultery carried a prison sentence, didn't it? Ha! She could have asked the judge about that just now. People would point their fingers at her, and would ostracize her as they had Marie-Eluise, the wife of the hotelier that Friedrich had told her about.

Flora walked stiffly alongside the river. She breathed deeply, wiped the tears and snot away, swept the hair out of her face.

She could never, ever breathe a word to anyone about what had happened the day before. She had to blot it from her memory forever. Deep inside, deep in her heart, she would carry this sin with her. And the memory . . .

※

Konstantin whistled over one of the carriages for hire waiting for passengers at the Baden-Baden train station, and a minute later he leaned back in the plush upholstery. Now that he had returned, he would do all he could to stay in Baden-Baden until the end of the season.

Karlsruhe had been an impressive city, but he found all the hustle and bustle of the place too strenuous. He was obviously not used to that kind of turmoil anymore.

He patted the leather bag on the seat beside him. At least the journey had been worth it. The jeweler had paid well for Püppi's strings of pearls, sapphire rings, and emerald necklaces. His mouth had watered at the sight of several of the pieces, and small bubbles of spittle had appeared at the corners of his mouth. Konstantin knew such signs of greed well and had pushed the price higher accordingly.

The money that he had gotten for the baubles would make his remaining weeks in the summer capital of Europe particularly comfortable. He did not need to worry about the ensuing months, either. Monte Carlo? Paris? Or perhaps a cruise across to America? He could go wherever he pleased.

He had never in his life had so much money at his disposal. Perhaps he should try his luck at the racetrack in Iffezheim? And he would certainly do his best to increase his pot at card tables—he was a good player, after all.

The carriage turned in the direction of the Europäischer Hof hotel, and for a moment Konstantin felt a pang of regret that the drive would soon be over. It had been so nice just to sit and think such delicious thoughts.

Püppi's funeral would take place in two days. She had no close relatives, so Konstantin had managed all the arrangements. Nadeshda Stropolski—like so many other Russians—would be laid to rest in Baden-Baden, the place she had spent so many happy hours on earth. After the funeral, there would be a small reception. Irina and Count Popo had both nodded their agreement when he told them of his plans.

Two more days and he would finally be free!

Today, he would leave the Europäischer Hof. He had had enough of that gilded cage. A cheap hotel would meet his needs—life was far too exciting to spend it in a room.

The move would proceed quickly. He had packed most of his things the evening before in Püppi's luggage. Of her things he would take the valuable furs and the box of hand-painted fans. The silver cutlery was also too valuable to leave to the chambermaid. He would pack the gold toiletries kit away with the furs—for a rainy day, so to speak. A rainy day he hoped would never come.

He did not care who would take care of the rest of her things.

Konstantin tipped the driver well. For the rest of his life, the poor man would be dependent on passengers, good weather, and healthy horses. But from that day forward, he, Konstantin Sokerov, would no longer depend on anyone.

He had dismissed Püppi's staff the previous day. She had made no provisions for them in case of her death, so why should they concern him? Still, he had given each of them a little money and wished them luck. He had also given Püppi's maid all the bright-pink, lurid-green, and too-youthful-looking dresses, all of which smelled of Püppi.

He shuddered. He still had the smell in his nose—the odor of fear and loneliness, of age and decay.

She had a will, Popo informed him. Püppi had been a rich woman with extensive lands not far from Saint Petersburg. The count had promised to take care of those, and had added that it would probably take quite a while. Konstantin was indifferent to Püppi's will. As far as he knew, Püppi had not seen a lawyer in the last one and a half years, so how was *his* name supposed to appear in her will?

No, for him, the last Püppi chapter would come to an end with her funeral.

No more dependency. No more flaccid skin, no more sagging breasts, no more sniveling old affections.

From today, he could pick and choose women to suit his personal taste, and not because of how well supplied they were with money. And for the weeks and months ahead, all he had in mind was to enjoy himself.

Of course, at some point, he would have to seek out a new bene-factress. Why should he spend his own money if there was always a woman to be found who was willing to pay his bills for him? But that could wait—he would not let himself get tied down to another old widow right away.

The flower girl, however, was a nice change, and he saw signifi-cance in the fact that he had taken her on the day of Püppi's death. Hadn't Püppi been the one to introduce them? If he looked at it like that, Flora was a "bequest" from Püppi in death . . .

And how willingly she had given herself up to him! He had stopped believing that he would ever reach his goal with her, and he could not adequately explain to himself why he continued to visit Flora in her flower shop almost every day. It probably had to do with how very few young people he knew in Baden-Baden, and Flora not only was young and pretty, but had spirit, courage, and imagination. It was fun to talk to her! That, and Konstantin also envied her a little for how she threw herself into her work. After talking to her, he always felt full of energy, as if her own drive rubbed off on him.

The eager little bouquet binder . . . he would never have guessed the passion she had in her. Konstantin smiled to himself.

He would visit her later that day; he had to order flowers for Püppi's funeral.

Should he arrange another tryst? Why not? Once he was settled in his new hotel that afternoon, he would have time for a little love.

Chapter Fifty

"I was thinking of brightly colored flowers, many different kinds. Püppi loved variety."

"I know." From the corner of her eye, Flora glanced toward the back door of the shop. Everything was quiet. Ernestine was taking a midday nap with Alexander, and Sabine and the kitchen maid were making strawberry marmalade.

With trembling hands, she opened her order book and noted Konstantin's request. As if she would have forgotten a single one of his words. But occupying herself with pencil and book gave her the moment she needed to gather herself.

So far, Konstantin had not breathed a word about their encounter the previous day. Was he an honorable man, or did it simply show that he attached far less significance to it than she did?

She cleared her throat, counted to three, and spoke aloud the sentence she had spent the entire morning practicing in her mind.

"It is an honor for me to be able to provide the flowers for the princess's funeral." She flinched, however, when Konstantin took her hand and squeezed it gently. "Konstantin, why . . . why do you make this so hard for me? I am a married woman. What happened was a mistake, that's all. It's over. That it even happened is unforgivable." Flora was surprised at the determination in her voice. It felt good. She took another breath. "Maybe it is for the best if you buy flowers elsewhere in the future." She pulled her hand away from him and rubbed it as if she had just been burned by nettles.

When Konstantin laughed, small lines appeared as they always did around his mouth. Flora managed to withstand her urge to smother them with a thousand kisses, but it was not easy.

"And if I don't want to buy my flowers somewhere else?" He gazed at her so insistently, so intimately, that she felt dizzy and had to hold on to the shop counter. Then he leaned across and whispered with his hot breath in her ear, "Flora, darling, in your arms I can forget my pain for a little while. I know I will never call you mine, but I beg you not to kick me away like some troublesome dog." He took her hand again, kissed each finger, one at a time.

Flora groaned when he told her the name of his new hotel and the room number.

"I'll wait for you . . ."

Hardly had Konstantin left when Flora grabbed a handful of flowers and trotted to the kitchen door.

"I have to make a delivery. Keep an eye on the shop while I'm out, please. And tell Ernestine that she should feed Alexander after his nap," she called to Sabine. Then she hurried off.

Looking neither left nor right, Flora ran in the direction of the Trinkhalle. *What am I doing here?* she asked herself when she finally stood, out of breath, in front of the long building. It was not Friedrich she was going to see. She wanted to be alone with her unworthy thoughts and emotions.

Tears trickled over her cheeks as she crept past the Trinkhalle like a thief and tramped up Michaelsberg, the hill that formed part of the parklands beyond. Although the sun was shining, it was uncommonly quiet. Only here and there did she see an occasional walker among the trees. Most of the visitors were probably down on the Promenade or wandering along Lichtenthaler Allee, as usual. That was fine with Flora. Her legs trembled as she climbed the hill.

This bench . . . she and Friedrich had sat there often in their first summer together. And here, on these paths, they had gone strolling on many an evening. Why didn't those memories make her feel anything?

Had her heart beat faster back then? Had she felt that strange feeling in her belly? She could not remember.

Flora blinked as the dome atop the Stourdza Chapel appeared between the trees. A Romanian count had had it built to honor his deceased son, Friedrich had once explained to her.

Oh, Friedrich . . .

Why did her heart not beat any faster when she thought of him now?

And why did it begin to pound when Konstantin flitted through her mind? She only had to look at *him* to forget everything around her. Earlier, too, she had almost succumbed, had wanted nothing more than to press against him, feel his powerful torso against her breasts, his hand wandering up her thighs.

She reached the chapel and, sobbing, dropped to her knees. She beat the stone with her fists, as if like that she could destroy her love for Konstantin.

Love? Was it really love?

Or was it just desire? A kind of disease?

Flora hoped so fervidly that the latter was true, because a disease could be cured, couldn't it?

"Dear God, let me be strong! I beg you. I will do penance. Give me back my peace. I promise I will be a good wife and mother . . ."

Her words echoed in the high, domed building, her voice sounding strangely hollow.

Should she go back to Gönningen? Would she be cured there? No. She had to find her strength alone, here. She could not let herself be so easily seduced, like a whore. She would go home to her husband and child, right now.

Yes. She would do that.

Perhaps, if she tried hard to be a good wife, she could one day look Friedrich in the eye again. Perhaps, if she truly stayed strong, she could one day look at herself in the mirror without feeling wretched and ashamed.

Flora looked around the chapel one last time.

Please, dear God, give me the strength and the courage.

Then she stood up, wiped her face, and brushed the dust from her skirt.

In the distance, from town, church bells chimed four times.

"Really, your customers are becoming more and more outrageous, putting demands on your time like this. Why, it's almost seven o'clock!" Ernestine shook her head so violently that one of her hairpins flew out and fell on the floor.

Flora crouched to pick it up. "Did you manage all right without me?" From the corner of her eye, she saw Sabine standing in the doorway, eyebrows raised, watching her critically.

Flora handed the hairpin to Ernestine, then stepped back before Sabine caught the scent of lovemaking that wafted around Flora like the sweetest perfume. *Stop accusing me like that!* she felt like screaming at the maid. *I know very well that what I'm doing is not right. I know I'm playing with fire. But it's . . . just playing. And I simply can't do anything else.*

Chapter Fifty-One

Her eyes closed tightly, Flora moved to the left to make room on the cool sheets for Konstantin. With a sure hand, he undid the buttons on her blouse, slid it over her shoulders, and caressed her breasts as if he were handling a precious treasure. His lips were warm and experienced, encircling her nipples, promising intimacies to come.

Flora instinctively opened her legs. She wanted her lover closer to her, to feel him inside her, to take him in. She was not used to a man taking so much time . . .

But Konstantin pushed her legs together again gently. "We have all the time in the world. You are so lovely. I could lie here and look at you for hours."

A shiver went through Flora as she felt Konstantin's tongue on her breasts again—small, firm motions that made them burn with passion. Forgotten was the sinfulness, forgotten her bad conscience. More. She wanted more!

Konstantin's lips had left her breasts, and his hands traced the curves of her waist, moving a little deeper, deeper.

The tremor that began between her legs and rippled outward, down to the tips of her toes . . . up to the end of every strand of her hair! To each fingertip . . . Could one lose one's mind from sheer desire?

"Flora, dear Flora . . . will you look at me, too? Or . . . touch me?

Flora opened her eyes abruptly and blinked several times. What did he mean by "*look at me*"? He was naked! And touch him? Wasn't she doing that the whole time?

He took her hand and guided it down between them, placing it around his sex. "Like that . . . you can make a man very happy."

It took a moment for Flora to recover from her shock. Friedrich never would have thought to ask something like that of her.

Her eyelids almost closed, she peeked downward. She had never in her life touched a man there. The delicate skin was so wonderfully tensed, and how yearningly his shaft throbbed, as if it had a life of its own. Was that caused by her touch? Was she doing it right? Wasn't she hurting him? Uncertainly, her fingers closed around him a little tighter, and she smiled as she heard Konstantin's groans. She seemed to be doing something right . . .

But the next moment he pulled free of her. "Slowly, my darling. You're going too fast. Love is something to be enjoyed like champagne, not to gulp down like a glass of spa water."

"It's already after two. I should have been back in the shop long ago." With a sigh of pleasure, Flora rolled onto her back and gazed around Konstantin's room.

He had certainly made it his own. His clothes were everywhere, his boots and shoes scattered on the floor. On the small table by the window stood a bottle of port, and beside it a jar of something Flora had not immediately recognized. "Preserved walnuts. Püppi hated them," Konstantin had explained before eating one of the nuts himself and popping one in Flora's mouth. The delicacy had an unusual flavor, salty and sweet and sharp. The entire room smelled of the preserved walnuts and of Konstantin, of his masculinity.

"Always in a hurry, my little businesswoman. Does a fire break out in the shop whenever you're not there? Do the flowers transform into ghastly ghosts while you're lying in my arms? Are your violets being stolen by a horde of robbers as we speak?"

Flora had to laugh at the image of robbers fleeing through the streets of Baden-Baden with her potted violets.

"My customers like to discuss their special requests with me, not Sabine." Ernestine would also be wondering where she was all this time, Flora thought as she kissed the hollow between Konstantin's shoulder blades. And there would be hardly any time left to spend with Alexander that afternoon. But not even the thought of her son made her get out of bed, get dressed, and leave.

How perfectly their bodies nestled into one another, as if they were fashioned for nothing else. Flora cradled her cheek in the curve of Konstantin's neck, enjoying the warm, moist cocoon of sweat and love in which their lovemaking had swathed them. Like Adam and Eve. Like the Garden of Eden . . .

The hairs on her salty skin were beginning to prickle with desire again when Konstantin abruptly sat up.

"I don't like to throw you out of my bed, but we have to get up. They'll be laying Püppi to rest very soon."

For Flora, the summer of 1873 passed in a state of exhilaration, with Konstantin as both her poison and antidote. They met in his hotel, where Flora always used the back entrance, and they met out in the meadows, too. Of course, they saw each other at the parties for which Flora arranged the floral décor and to which Konstantin was invited as a guest, but for Flora such evenings were more anguished affairs than joyful. She wanted to drive away all the cackling chickens that gathered around Konstantin the moment he entered the room. Konstantin, who was well aware of her jealous eye, flirted all the more with his admirers.

He did not ignore Flora, though, and when he talked with her the women who so gladly kept him in their midst looked on with a critical eye. He would return to them after a whispered pledge of affection or two, and Flora was left to console herself in the knowledge that there were hours in which he belonged to her alone.

Her talent for coming up with excuses and rationales for leaving the house and shop developed rapidly, and also for her occasionally disheveled appearance when she returned home with her skirt grass-stained or her arms scratched.

"Blackberries," Flora said then, or "I slipped and fell; I'm so clumsy!" But the truth was that she had lain voluntarily among the nettles and thorns.

As soon as she was home, and with a heavy heart, she washed away the perfume of love that clung to her body.

You're a sinner! You are not worthy of being the wife of a good and loyal man like Friedrich.

A thousand times she made up her mind never to see Konstantin again. But she returned to him. Again and again. How was she supposed to leave him? How would she ever again be able to do without what only he could give her?

What her family and her customers saw of her was only an imperfect thing. It was Konstantin who . . . completed her. Never was she in higher spirits than with him. With him she laughed until tears ran down her face, and sometimes he was sillier even than she. In his arms, the carping of customers was a distant memory, and there was no talk of healing waters, oh no—they had champagne instead!

But when the rendezvous was over and Flora trotted breathlessly home again, the burden weighed heavily on her shoulders. Alexander. Ernestine. Friedrich. And there was always the work: bouquets to be made, orders to be placed, invoices to be written. She had to get home. She did not have another valuable minute to waste!

There were moments when she stood at the counter in the shop and her floral arrangements came to her with uncommon ease—when every movement flowed into the next, when erotic desire inspired every deft motion, when she scooped her creativity from the cornucopia of love. But most of the time she kept her passion for Konstantin separate.

If she had not been able to do that, she would have gone utterly insane.

Chapter Fifty-Two

Nine o'clock. He should have been at the Trinkhalle long ago. Friedrich walked faster. It was not that the guests necessarily had a glass of healing water in mind so early in the morning, but before the first of the ladies and gentlemen arrived he had to sweep the floor, empty the trash, wipe the glass panels of the doors clean of yesterday's fingerprints.

You're no more than a lackey, you know, he thought, as he had many times before.

His presentations on the benefits of taking the waters were poorly attended. Not many wanted to hear about his conviction that a drinking regime was best undertaken along with a course of curative baths. Friedrich was coming to doubt whether the members of the spa committee were serious in their efforts to turn Baden-Baden into a true spa town. No one seemed to have much interest at all in the ideas about healing spas and water cures that he had put forward during the year. He had been hoping, because of those ideas, to be called to join the committee and to obtain a better position. But the way things looked, he would forever be no more than a page boy to the rich at the Trinkhalle.

As he passed by the theater, Friedrich ran into the owner of the Hotel Marie-Eluise, Gustav Körner. He paused and greeted the hotelier with a friendly nod and was about to continue on his way when Körner held him back.

"You know a lot of people here in town, don't you? And quite a few of the guests, too, I'll wager."

Friedrich frowned. "That's true."

"I thought . . . well, I wanted to ask you . . . would you happen to know someone who would like to buy my hotel?"

Friedrich sighed. "So you've really decided to sell it?"

The older man laughed bitterly. "I have no choice. In the last year, I've lost not only my wife, but gradually also my guests."

Friedrich shook his head. "It's a disgrace. You've got one of the best springs in Germany flowing under the place."

"Please make sure my future buyer hears that. Unfortunately, so far, I've had no success in finding one. Before the war, when we still had the casino and the French came in droves, it would probably have been child's play to sell my hotel, but now?" Körner tilted his head to one side, and for the first time a smile appeared on his pinched face. "What about you, Mr. Sonnenschein? Wouldn't the Marie-Eluise be something for you?" When he saw the look of disbelief on Friedrich's face, he added, "You know our springs better than anyone in this town. It was from you that I learned just how good our own spring is. Frankly, I believe you could turn my hotel into a destination for those who come here in search of a good spa."

Friedrich laughed. "Now you're exaggerating."

Körner nodded. "I'll probably never get rid of the old box. You know, I'd get out of Baden-Baden tomorrow if I could. I'd move to my sister's place in Munich . . . just to finally get away from the place where everything reminds me of Marie-Eluise."

With a smile, Friedrich marched on toward the Trinkhalle. Old Körner had some ideas! He, Friedrich, as the proprietor of a hotel, and Flora as proprietress—ha! As if she didn't have enough to do in the flower shop. And as a mother? She'd hold Alexander in one arm and use her free hand to set tables, and be thinking about whether candelabra were appropriate during the week or should be reserved for Sundays!

His mother could work there, too. It could be a family affair. The thought of Ernestine wearing a small white apron and setting tables in a banquet hall made Friedrich laugh out loud.

She probably wouldn't do a bad job of it. His mother understood how to run a household in an orderly, efficient way. Flora was good at dealing with people, and he certainly understood the Baden-Baden springs.

Apart from the fact that they would never be able to scrape together the money for the purchase, it would mean he and Flora working side by side—could that go well?

Friedrich's expression grew serious.

Flora had been so . . . changed lately. He could think of no other way to describe it. She constantly overreacted to things. If she made a joke, she was too jolly about it. When she talked, or sang Alexander a song, or discussed something with a customer, she was always a touch too loud. And there were many times she was *too* loving! Some evenings, she threw her arms around him and squeezed so hard he could barely breathe.

There was the opposite, too. Days on which she hardly spoke a word and she sat and stared out the window with an absent look on her face, as if . . . as if what?

None of it could be put down to normal moodiness, could it? But when he broached the subject with her, all she said in reply was that he was imagining things.

Friedrich would gladly have talked to someone about his concerns, about how, at times, he felt as if he did not really know who his wife was anymore. But Ernestine was out of the question; she would have gotten too upset. Besides, more often than not, his mother was on Flora's side.

"You are becoming more and more like your father. All he ever wanted was his peace and quiet, too," she had said to him just a few days earlier when Flora had asked him if they couldn't perhaps all go off on a cruise along the Rhine one day. It would be wonderful fun, she had added, as if to pressure him.

A cruise, in the middle of the season? Flora and his mother knew perfectly well that he could not tear himself away from the Trinkhalle for an entire day. And then there was the cost.

He would have preferred to talk to Hannah. No one knew a child like their mother did. Hannah would perhaps have an explanation for Flora's behavior, and might have been able to give him some advice about how to respond. Maybe she would have commiserated with him and said something along the lines of "Changes like this are like measles, which means all you can do is wait for them pass."

Friedrich abruptly stopped. And what if they did not pass? Wasn't it possible for measles to kill you?

Maybe it was time for him to sit down and have a long talk with Flora, and not make do with her excuses.

Should he talk to her about the Marie-Eluise as well? Just to see how she reacted? He pictured her overflowing with enthusiasm about the idea—with Flora, anything was possible.

She would be a good proprietress for a hotel, he was certain of it. A new task for both of them. Together. No more separate roads, and the spa management could go to hell.

He laughed—what a mad idea it was. It really was not like him to drift off into dreams like that. Even if it was only a dream, it was a pretty one. He would have loved to dream it with his wife.

He had just set foot on the top step of the Trinkhalle when he bumped into Lady Lucretia.

Of all people! thought Friedrich with an inward smile. He was certainly not the kind of man to give much credence to omens, good or bad, but that he should run into the health-conscious Englishwoman now was a pleasant coincidence.

"You look very excited, I must say," she said, after they had wished each other good morning.

With a jug of Trinkhalle water and two glasses, they sat together on one of the benches. "I ran into the owner of the Hotel Marie-Eluise earlier. He's come up with a completely crazy idea," said Friedrich with a shake of his head. "If it were up to him, I would soon be buying his hotel." Lady Lucretia seemed interested, so he told her briefly about the encounter with the hotelier.

"The rooms are certainly a little run-down, but some paint would work wonders," he said.

Lady Lucretia emptied her glass in one draft. "With a little money and a measure of goodwill, one can move mountains. I've had that experience many times in my life. And your Mr. Körner rightly saw that you are a man who can get things done. Personally, I would trust you with an enterprise like that tomorrow."

"Really?" Friedrich was honestly surprised.

The Englishwoman nodded. "How many rooms does the hotel have?"

"Twenty, I believe."

Friedrich refilled her glass while she took out a leather-bound notebook and scribbled something.

"And how many baths? Six. All in good condition? I see. And its own spring that flows beneath the hotel? How very interesting . . ." She pursed her lips, which made her chin appear even longer than usual.

"The location is excellent. From the Marie-Eluise, you can reach the Conversationshaus on foot in less than five minutes. But it's still doubtful that Gustav Körner will find a buyer. Men with vision are few and far between."

Lady Lucretia took a swig of her water.

"Granted," she said. "But let's not forget that there are also women with vision." She broke out in a braying laugh. "I think I have an idea, but . . . My God, it's almost ten!" She stood up so quickly that the bench wobbled. "My treatments are waiting for me. I fear, my dear Mr. Sunshine, that we have to postpone our discussion. What about tomorrow morning, first thing? But no, I'm already meeting Ingrid to go for a walk in the woods. Dr. Green comes at twelve and, wait . . ."

"What discussion? What idea? I didn't know—"

Lady Lucretia interrupted his objection with a wave of her hand. "Why don't you just come to visit me this Sunday afternoon in my hotel? Sunday is the only day I have no baths or treatments scheduled. So I would have time for visions, you see."

Chapter Fifty-Three

It had been a good idea to choose a different destination for the engagement party, thought Irina Komatschova, looking out the window. Meadows, floodplain, the trout ponds—all very attractive.

In Baden-Baden, all the talk was about which rooms were the most exclusive, and Irina wanted no part of that game. She considered it a stroke of luck that the head waiter at her hotel had told her about his aunt's inn, the Forellenhof. It was not far away, the man had said—one only had to travel along Lichtenthaler Allee to the nunnery, from where it was just a little farther to the newly opened inn, which was tucked away in a small hamlet called Gaisbach in the beautiful Oos Valley.

Why not? Irina had thought, and she had moved her engagement party to the country. A farmhouse lunch, a little music to celebrate the day, returning to Baden-Baden proper in the evening. Her fiancé had agreed to the idea.

Admittedly, the Forellenhof Inn was not the most elegant of destinations; the atmosphere, however, was intimate. The proprietress and her three daughters served the dishes and drinks. At Irina's request, they had assembled a troupe of young women in colorful costumes who performed local dances. Irina smiled to herself. A good idea.

In short, the party in the Forellenhof had been the right decision, and was affordable to boot.

Unlike the flower arrangements! Flora Sonnenschein had charged a considerable fee for producing her baskets filled with sunflowers and all sorts of other bits and pieces that were supposed to look rustic, Irina thought with annoyance. Just then, two arms wrapped lovingly around her waist from behind.

"Irinotschka, darling—are you happy?" a deep voice whispered in her ear, and Irina nodded.

Happy? If I died today, would I die a happy woman? she wondered as she and her fiancé enjoyed an intimate moment at the window. Then his arms loosened again.

"Darling, why don't you go back to the ballroom? Our guests must be missing you by now. I'd like to practice my speech one more time." He waved a handful of paper.

"You and your speech," said Irina with a smile as she left him alone in the room.

Were reason and good sense important when it came to happiness? It was probably not a question one could answer with a yes or a no. All Irina knew was that she wanted to believe they were. Her wealth combining with Popo's inexhaustible riches . . . Security could mean happiness, too.

On the way back to the ballroom, she encountered two of the dancers. Püppi would have loved the colorful outfits, she was certain.

Püppi . . . Her old companion seemed to have chosen that day of all days to appear in Irina's mind. What would she have said about Irina's engagement to Popo? Or about Konstantin's dalliance with the flower girl?

At one time, Irina had believed that Konstantin had felt something for her, Irina. Deep feelings, true feelings, like what she had felt for him. What people called love.

Love! Irina sniffed at the thought. Konstantin Sokerov knew only one form of love, and that was for himself. And yet, how good his intimate embraces had felt.

Now he was squandering his attention on Flora. And look there! Once again, he was with her, standing together by the back door.

The way she drew closer to him, as if she wanted to creep inside him. How shameless it all was. Did they think the world around them was blind?

"You ordered a room for us? Now? Are you out of your mind? What will Princess Irina say if I disappear? I'm supposed to be keeping an eye on the flower arrangements." Although Flora tried to sound stern, she could not hide her pleasure at his audacity.

An hour of happiness, perhaps even two. She smiled in blissful anticipation.

Konstantin took her hand and kissed her palm. "Come, let us not waste any time. I'm as hungry for your body as a starving man for bread." He tried to lead her through the door to the back of the hotel, but Flora resisted.

"Wait. The princess is coming." She nodded toward the dining room, from which Irina Komatschova was heading in their direction, her expression stony.

"Hmm, our fiancée does not look to be in a particularly happy mood," Konstantin murmured. He smiled radiantly and waved to Irina, then turned quickly toward the back door. "I'm going!" he whispered breathlessly to Flora. "I do *not* have the energy for Irina's mood. Room nine, the first door on the right, got it? And don't wait too long, because I have quite a bit of energy for you."

"Rascal!" said Flora with a giggle. As soon as he was gone, she straightened her shoulders. "Princess Komatschova, I hope you like my flower baskets?"

Irina flicked one hand impatiently. "Yes, yes, the flower baskets. But don't try to distract me. Do you think I didn't see how Kostia and you . . . how you've been acting? It's worse than an Italian opera. All the flirting and fooling around. I've known for a long time that Konstantin possesses no decency whatsoever, but I would have expected more from you. As a businesswoman, you are normally so much smarter!"

Flora felt as if she'd been slapped in the face. "I don't understand—"

"You understand perfectly well!" Irina looked at her furiously. "Did you think we were all so blind and stupid that we would not notice that Kostia had his eye on you? Konstantin Sokerov is arrogant, self-absorbed, and lazy—and *those* are his good qualities! On top of that, he's a master at getting whatever he wants. What do you think you are to him? A tawdry little affair, that's all." The princess gathered her skirts, turned on her heel, and stalked off.

Flora could only stand and stare. Konstantin was lazy and self-absorbed? How could the princess insult him like that? If she despised him that much, why did she invite him? She usually behaved as if she and Konstantin shared one heart and soul.

A tawdry little affair—it sounded so dirty, and it had nothing to do with the great love she and Konstantin shared.

She would not say a word about this to Konstantin, Flora decided, as she climbed on trembling legs to the first floor. The old princess was probably just jealous.

Room nine. Flora shook her head as if trying to shake out Irina's harsh words, then put on her best smile.

"Flora, finally! I could not have stood another minute without you."

At the sight of Konstantin, Flora's anger at Irina evaporated. She would not let Irina or anyone else in this world take away the magic of this day. She would enjoy herself and be happy.

Resolved, she slammed the door behind her so hard that the topmost of the two tacks holding the brass "9" in place on the door came loose.

"Now it's just the two of us," said Flora.

Outside, on the front of the door, the "9" turned into a "6."

What had he gotten himself into? On a hot Sunday afternoon like this, he would have much rather been sitting in the shade in the garden at home.

Friedrich took a deep breath, wiped the sweat from his forehead, and returned his handkerchief to his pocket. It was typical of Lady Lucretia to choose a place so far out of town to stay. The air was probably much fresher in the forest than in town. When he had asked her if the location of the Forellenhof Inn was perhaps less than ideal, she had said, "The daily walk into town is good for one's physical fitness!"

Physical fitness. That sounded more like a soldier's lot than that of an English lady.

He had briefly crossed paths with Lady Lucretia once more after their previous conversation, and instead of repeating her offer to continue their discussion, she said she wanted to meet him to discuss a "business proposal." He had agreed only because Flora's work meant she was also away from home, and Friedrich had had no great desire to spend a long Sunday afternoon with only his mother and baby Alexander for company.

What did the Englishwoman want from him? He had asked her, but she had merely hemmed and hawed and asked him if he might possibly imagine some other line of work than what he did at the Trinkhalle.

Did she think . . . ?

He knew from Gustav Körner that she had, in fact, been to look at the Hotel Marie-Eluise. The hotelier had thanked Friedrich effusively for sending a potential buyer to him. So far, the lady was keeping her cards close to her chest, but he believed he would soon be in serious negotiations with her. The bath area, in particular, had appealed to her very much, and she had personally measured the cellar rooms to see if two additional tubs would fit.

Potential buyer? Serious negotiations? More tubs? Friedrich had nodded, but in truth he thought he must have misheard. He knew that Lady Lucretia was a little . . . different from other women, that she had a serious interest in hydrotherapy, and that she loved Baden-Baden. But to buy a hotel because of that?

"My dear Mr. Sunshine! Here you are at last!" The Englishwoman strode toward him, red-cheeked and energized. "Did you know there's a celebration going on right now in the Forellenhof? A Russian princess is throwing quite a party, it seems—which is rather unfortunate for us, considering that we need peace and quiet for our deliberations."

"Should we simply ignore the party and find a place for ourselves here?" he asked in a hopeful voice. Although the terrace was busy, he would have enjoyed nothing more, just then, than a cool pitcher of beer, and the wonderful smell of smoked fish made his mouth water.

The Englishwoman shook her head. "I've prepared documents, plans, drawings! Am I supposed to spread that out in the middle of all these people? No, that won't do." She looked away and seemed to be struggling inwardly. "I think I might have an idea, but please don't misunderstand me . . . Do you think you might come to my room for our discussion? It has large windows, and we'd have the peace and quiet we need. I'll order a pitcher of beer for us. A bracing drink has never done anyone any harm, has it?"

Friedrich suppressed a smile. Misunderstand her? Lady Lucretia? He could imagine many things, but that she might want to lure him away to a lovers' tryst was not one of them.

"I'd be happy to," he said. A serving girl walked past, carrying plates of golden fried trout to a table. "If it is not too much to ask, I wouldn't say no to a bite to eat, either."

"Of course, of course. A decent meal certainly couldn't hurt." Lady Lucretia clapped him solidly on the shoulder and handed him a key. "Room six. You go ahead—I'll go put our order in."

Whistling happily to himself, Friedrich climbed the stairs to the first floor of the hotel. He was, quite frankly, excited at the prospect of hearing Lady Lucretia's revelations and looking over her documents and drawings. Her plans for the Hotel Marie-Eluise appeared to have moved along more rapidly than he'd thought.

When he reached the landing, Friedrich paused for a moment to orient himself. There were four or five doors along each side of the corridor, with "6" right at the head of the stairs. Was he mistaken, or was that a male voice he heard coming from beyond the door? No, the man's voice must have been coming from the next room.

He swung the door open.

The punch to his gut came without warning. A hand clenched painfully around his heart, and from one moment to the next, he could not catch his breath.

He stared in disbelief at the scene before him.

"Flora . . . ?"

Chapter Fifty-Four

Her nightdresses and undergarments. A whore's laundry! Handkerchiefs. Blouses. Wool vests. And what was this? Friedrich dragged a roll of fabric out of the cupboard. Ha, as if Flora would ever have found the time to make anything with it. His wife preferred other entertainments.

He threw the fabric into a linen sack along with everything else. Flora's smell soon penetrated the linen, a mixture of seeds, rosewater, and sun-warmed apples. And it made Friedrich choke.

"Friedrich, my one-and-only. Talk to me. Why are you packing Flora's clothes?" A tear-soaked handkerchief in her hand, Ernestine tugged at his arm. "Where is she? What's happened? I don't understand what's going on . . ."

Her words were swallowed by a tremendous thunderclap. Alexander's heartrending cries pealed from the next room, and he heard Sabine running up the stairs.

Friedrich glared at his mother. "See to the boy and leave me alone!"

"What's the matter?" said Sabine, appearing at the door with Alexander in her arms. The infant's eyes were wide with fear.

"Get out of here before I throw you out, too!" Friedrich screamed at her, hating himself for it as he said it. Blind with anger, he turned to his mother again. "Flora this and Flora that—the way you toadied up to her was disgusting. You backed every stupid word she ever said!" Friedrich shook off his mother's hand like an annoying fly, then jerked open the next cupboard door. The shoes. "All I was for both of you was the simpleton with his water. Look at this!" He held up a flowered scarf. "This is not from me. And there, the fan! See the Russian inscription on it? Oh, look closely, take your time! She took gifts like a whore, your *wonderful* Flora."

"Friedrich, for heaven's sake!" With one hand at her throat, Ernestine stared at him as if she had the devil himself in front of her. Her mouth opened and closed, opened and closed, but no words—no sound at all—came out.

Her damned flower books—away with them! The amber necklace. Her hair bands. And this . . . Friedrich gazed at the glittering *F* in his hand.

The brooch he had given Flora on their wedding day.

Again and again, he had the feeling that an abyss had opened beneath him. He shifted his weight from one foot to the other, then tossed the brooch aside in disgust.

No. It could not be. A nightmare. A case of mistaken identity! Someone who looked like Flora. Who laughed like her. It was not his wife at all who he had seen in that room.

His feelings were racing ahead of any understanding of what he'd seen. Hot, salty tears came to his eyes, ran down his cheeks, and gathered at the corners of his mouth. He tasted something foul, like spoiled food. He gagged and swallowed, closed his eyes, groped blindly for the water bowl on the chest of drawers. Then he vomited.

"Friedrich . . ." He felt his mother's hands, clopping him helplessly on the back as if he'd choked on a fish bone and had to get it out.

Fish bones. Fish. Smoked fish. As long as he lived, he would never forget the smell of smoked fish. He would always connect it with this day, with the Forellenhof Inn. With the laughter and gaiety he'd heard coming from the ballroom. With the corridor, the doors left and right, all dark and gloomy. The door to the room. And on the other side, Flora and—

And the man, that Bulgarian . . .

He threw himself onto the bed and beat at the pillow with his fists with all his strength, until the seams burst and clouds of feathers flew into the air.

Outside, it had begun to rain.

Flora had never dressed so quickly in her life. Underwear, underskirt, bodice, her lilac-colored dress. She slipped her shoes onto her bare feet and flew down the stairs.

"Friedrich!" she cried. Over and over: "Friedrich!"

At the bottom of the stairs, she ran past Lady Lucretia. What was the Englishwoman doing there? Flora ran past her and outside without a word of greeting.

A cloud of dust hung over the road. Flora could make out the vague form of a carriage through the haze, driving off as if Satan himself were after it. "Friedrich!"

Flora ran. The sky, earlier a magnificent blue marred by only a few wispy clouds, was now gray and blotchy. Soon, the breeze strengthened and grew gusty, swirling the first tired leaves from the trees. The chill of it made Flora shudder, and gooseflesh crept over her sweaty back and breasts.

Why had he suddenly been standing in the doorway? Who had told him that she—no! Don't think. Just go. Run! Don't think about it.

If she were able to make it back to town without stopping . . .

Please, dear God. Please.

The closer she got to Baden-Baden, the darker the sky overhead became. The last of the sunlight faded away, and thunder roared.

Flora was just turning into Stephanienstrasse when the first raindrops splattered onto the cobblestones. When the flower shop came in sight, the heavens opened their floodgates as if the storm were following some secret dramaturgy.

The house door was bolted from inside; Flora's key rattled in the lock in vain. She stared uncomprehendingly at the mountain of bags and bundles tossed like trash outside the door. The rain had soaked through everything, and the beige linen of her seed sack had darkened to a muddy brown.

"Friedrich! Please, I'm begging you!" She pounded her fist on the door over and over, wailing and screaming. Shadows appeared behind the curtains in neighboring houses, and here and there a curious head popped out of a window to watch the spectacle.

Flora was drenched, and her dress hung heavily. She sat on the sidewalk outside the shop, exhausted, drew her shaking knees up to her chest, wrapped her arms around them, and laid her head there. Just then, a window opened above her.

"Friedrich." Flora, her neck stiff, looked up. The next moment, a bundle smacked her heavily on the head.

"Take your damned *ABCs*! To hell with them. And to hell with you!" Friedrich shouted at her before slamming the window shut again with all his strength.

Mad weather! The storm had come from nowhere. Konstantin pulled his hat deeper over his eyes while Matriona Schikanova's pony cart turned off Lichtenthaler Allee toward town. The fat pony snuffled and puffed and, despite the streaming rain, stopped every few leisurely steps to tear off a tuft of juicy grass. Matriona, who was never one to expend energy unnecessarily, did not try even once to inspire the beast to go any faster.

Konstantin sighed. He knew how miserly Irina could be and should have known that not all the guests would have a decent means of transport at their disposal. While Matriona went on at length about the engagement party and about how everything looked so cheap and shabby, Konstantin put on his most interested face and made appropriate comments in the appropriate places. In reality, his mind was miles away.

Poor Flora. Caught in flagrante by her husband—he would much rather have spared her a scene like that. He did not like to think what awaited her at home.

How had her husband even been able to find her? Who the devil had talked? Who even knew about their little rendezvous? He and Flora had been exceptionally discreet. Had it simply been an accident? Konstantin shook his head. He could not imagine that that was possible.

Of course, Irina and several of her guests had noticed the incident with Flora's husband: the man had run out through the ballroom as if a horde of howling Cossacks were after him.

"A furious husband and a distraught wife. Count yourself lucky that the man's a coward. Another would have challenged you to a duel," Irina had hissed at him afterward. "Konstantin, you are and will always be a rogue." She had slapped him on the back of his head as if he were a recalcitrant schoolboy, but the next moment had hooked one hand in the crook of his elbow and said that after a shock like that, they could both do with a good glass of schnapps. Popo—who had, in fact, seen nothing of the incident—was more than happy to join them for a drink.

After half a bottle of plum brandy, Konstantin could no longer see why he had broken his old and fundamental rule, never to get involved with a married woman.

"Will you be at Iwan's tonight?" Matriona asked as the pony cart finally pulled up in front of Konstantin's hotel. "He tells me it's about time he finally teaches us how to play cards. Funny man . . ."

"Probably later," Konstantin replied. He yawned lavishly. "Somehow, the afternoon's events have made me very tired." He grabbed the bottle of champagne he'd picked up before leaving the Forellenhof and jumped down from the cart.

What a day. Grinning to himself, Konstantin took the stairs up to his room two at a time. Maybe he'd go to bed, drink the champagne, and fall asleep. On the other hand, a round or two of cards with Iwan was not something to scoff at. The players there were all experienced old foxes, and the vodka flowed freely. The bets, however, were high, so he—

"Flora! What are you doing here?" He stopped in the doorway, shocked.

"Konstantin, finally!" Drenched and shivering, Flora threw herself into his arms, burst into tears, and was not to be consoled at all. Konstantin looked over her head at the bags piled beside the bed. That did not look good . . . Was this the bill for a bit of fun?

Damn it, what was the porter thinking, letting her into his room?

The way she clung to him and expected him to make everything right again, blathering on so fast that he had trouble following her words!

"The door was locked . . . not even allowed to see Alexander . . . so angry . . . how did he even find us? . . . never felt so miserable . . ."

"My poor little flower girl." Konstantin tried to look sympathetic as he held Flora in his arms. "Easy now. Your husband is sure to calm down soon. Everything will be all right. But you need to get out of those wet things. It won't help anyone if you come down with pneumonia now, on top of everything else." With experienced hands, he went to work on the tight knots holding her skirt in place. Beneath the cold, wet fabric, Flora's body was encouragingly warm. Like a ripe peach. Her nipples were pink and firm, her body pressing against his . . .

Suddenly, the game of cards was forgotten.

Chapter Fifty-Five

On Tuesday, Siegfried Flumm's wagon pulled up as usual in front of the store. He had known, of course, that Flora would not be there. Gossip and rumors spread on the wind in Baden-Baden, as they always had, but he preferred to feign obliviousness. The Sonnenscheins were good customers, and he would do what he could not to ruin his relationship with the family by talking badly about Flora in her absence. In the end, everything would probably straighten itself out, and anyone who'd grumbled about husband or wife would end up the fool. He arranged his flowers prettily in their buckets and prepared to extol them profusely. Ernestine Sonnenschein and the housemaid were already standing around the wagon, looking rather lost.

Sabine frowned. Calendula, rudbeckia, phlox . . . what was Mr. Flumm talking about? And why didn't Mrs. Sonnenschein simply send the nurseryman away again? She shifted Alexander from her left hip to her right. What did Mrs. Sonnenschein think she was doing? Did *she* want to take over Flora's work? Before she could answer her own questions, the first customers marched into the store.

The nurseryman, who had followed Sabine's gaze, cleared his throat. "I'd recommend some of the early asters and a dozen or two of these gorgeous sunflowers and a few bundles of greenery. Nothing complicated."

"I don't know . . . Maybe we should fetch Friedrich and ask his advice?" Ernestine looked wide-eyed from the gardener to Sabine, while Else Walbusch stood in the doorway and tried to catch their attention, which they studiously ignored. "Sabine?"

"The master . . ." *has been lying in bed dead drunk since Sunday afternoon*, Sabine came very close to saying. "The master has another commitment, I'm afraid," she said instead. "Madam, do you really think we should try to run the store in Flora's absence? I mean, we really have no idea . . ."

"I don't know," Ernestine said nervously. "I don't know anything at all." Her voice was on the verge of cracking, and her eyes were suspiciously moist. "Things have to go on somehow, don't they? And don't we owe it to Flora to at least try?"

Sabine shrugged noncommittally.

"Excuse me? Could I perhaps get my flowers here, or do I have to go to the market?" said a voice from the front of the shop. Else Walbusch, of course. Sabine was certain a little bird had twittered in Else's ear about things going on in the Sonnenschein house, and now she'd come to delight in the misery of others.

Sabine glared angrily at her.

"Would madam not like at least to try?" said Mr. Flumm. "I'd be glad to put my own modest expertise at your disposal."

"Sabine?" Ernestine looked at the maid uncertainly. "What do you think?"

Sabine sighed. "How hard can it be? I think we'll muddle through."

Ernestine smiled bravely at Mr. Flumm. "Let me have a bucket of each kind, and as much greenery as you think necessary."

"But you'll have to give us especially good prices today," Sabine added quickly, ignoring the nurseryman's look of disapproval.

"I also have these beautiful sunflowers. Or would you prefer the asters?" Ernestine held up both varieties for comparison.

"The sunflowers, yes," said Else Walbusch. Then she leaned over the counter and acted as though she did not want Sabine to hear, though her voice was as loud as a siren. "Is it true, what they're saying out on the streets? That your Friedrich threw his wife out of the house?"

Ernestine jumped back as if she'd been bitten.

Well, aren't we off to a promising start, Sabine thought grimly.

"If anyone asks you about Flora, tell them she's gone to Gönningen," Ernestine had told her early on Monday. Sabine knew from the start that they would not get far with that tactic.

"My Otto's asking whether Friedrich has already filed for divorce. You Lutherans can do that, can't you?" Else asked.

Ernestine's hand flew to her throat as if she were suddenly unable to catch her breath. "Heaven help us, I hadn't even thought about that."

Else nodded self-importantly. "Remember the old carpenter up past the market? When his Margret ran off with the son of Schwarz, the forest ranger, he swore out a complaint against his wife before you could blink. Your son's probably planning something like that, too.

"I'll say this much: the poor child!" Else looked at Alexander, who lay in a basket and chewed gummily at a twig. "I always suspected Flora was not to be trusted. I only have to think back to the incident with the poisonous plants—I almost died!" She looked around at Luise Schierstiefel, who had just come in. "You weren't much better off than me, were you?"

"It wasn't that bad, though, looking back," said the tailor's wife. "Personally, I thought Flora was very nice."

"Nice, ha! Those Württembergers all think they're a cut above the rest of us."

What a terrible pair, thought Sabine in disgust. Sitting with Ernestine in the garden week after week, drinking coffee and eating cake until they were fit to burst, and now that madam could use a little help, just once, they had nothing better to do than come into the store and act like . . . like . . . Sabine could not even find the words she wanted.

"Did you come here to buy flowers, or not?" she barked at Else. "And what about you? Usually, it's your husband who comes to get your carnations," she said to Luise.

Both women gasped. They had never known a maid to snap at them like that.

Just then, the doorbell tinkled again.

"Gretel. You, too," said Ernestine, her face deathly pale.

Sabine moved protectively in front of her mistress.

In her zeal, Else Walbusch's cheeks had turned bright red. She looked around at the women. "The way that girl threw herself at your Friedrich certainly looked questionable to me. Not even two years have passed and she's gone and cuckolded him."

"So what I heard at the market just now is true," said Gretel. "I hoped so much that it was just someone talking nonsense. You poor thing!" She stroked Ernestine's hand. "Anyway, can I have a dozen of these pretty purple flowers? Asters, aren't they, Ernestine?"

Ernestine let out a sob. She had given up hope of at least one of her friends standing by her.

"Of course, madam!" Sabine dipped in a hurried curtsy, then wrapped the flowers in newspaper.

"What are you staring at like dumbstruck geese?" the pharmacist's wife growled at Else and Luise. "What happened to poor Friedrich could happen to anyone. Oh, it's a terrible tragedy, certainly. A sin! But who can claim to be immune to the power of love?"

Her argument was lost in the general uproar that ensued.

In the days that followed, the doorbell tinkled constantly, but few of those who came in were there to buy flowers. Luise Schierstiefel had heard from someone that Flora had fled with her lover and that they were headed for Bulgaria. This was contradicted by another neighbor, whose sister was a chambermaid in one of the smaller hotels, who reported that Flora was living with the Bulgarian in "depraved circumstances" in a single room. The shoemaker's wife, by contrast, claimed to have seen Flora wearing a dancing outfit and escorted by two men at once—and drunk!

It was only with a great effort that Sabine managed to choke back the tears of her anger, and she stayed even closer to Ernestine in support.

For a week, they did their best together to withstand the barrage of rumormongering and sensationalism.

Regardless of how other people vilified and censured her daughter-in-law, Ernestine never took part in their spiteful talk. Just once, when she was finally alone with Sabine as they were closing up after a particularly bad day, did she open up. "When I think what Flora did to my one-and-only boy, I feel so angry and let down I could burst into tears. I could slap her face, too. Left and right, left and right! But who would it help?" She slumped dejectedly onto the chair behind the counter.

Sabine, who was in the process of locking the front door, merely shrugged. *A slap on the face never did anyone much damage, and Flora has certainly earned it,* she thought. But she kept the thought to herself—as open as her madam might be in that moment, she certainly did not want to hear Sabine's opinion.

"I keep asking myself how someone could be so stupid, so ungrateful," Ernestine muttered. "She really had everything. A lovely home, a good husband, a healthy child. And then she throws it all away for a . . . a nobody who just happens along!"

Sabine jumped when Ernestine suddenly banged her fist on the counter.

"How is anyone supposed to understand that? My poor Friedrich."

Sabine sighed. She asked herself constantly how Flora could ever have fallen for Sokerov. You could see from a mile away that he was a wolf. Hadn't she tried to warn Flora about him many times?

Oh, Flora, what were you thinking?

Ernestine took a deep breath. "And still it isn't right for people to talk about Flora the way they are. There's a great deal she has to answer for, I know that as well as anyone. But what business is it of anyone else? Why is everyone suddenly acting like judge and jury?"

Sabine handed Ernestine the key to the store and said, "The women who are screaming the loudest are the same ones who giggled most at Sokerov's jokes and compliments. There were customers here who would not leave when he was in the shop. I saw for myself how expertly he flirted. He probably had Flora so deeply under his spell that she couldn't break free anymore."

Ernestine's face brightened a little. "So deeply under his spell, you say? I never thought of it like that before . . ." She threw her arms around Sabine tightly for a moment, then turned away again almost immediately, as if the gesture were embarrassing. "Heavens above, why did a mishap like this have to happen in my family? Everything had been going so well."

※

In the second week, the neighborhood slowly began to calm down again. This, in turn, meant that many customers simply did not come to the store. Among the spa guests, too, word had quickly gotten around that Flora was no longer at the shop, and they went instead to the market or to Maison Kuttner for their flowers.

Sabine managed to keep the shop open for several hours a day, while Ernestine mostly hid herself away in the front room, where no one could talk to her about Friedrich, Flora, or "*depraved circumstances.*"

In the third week, the store stayed closed. Sabine saw no reason to sit in an empty shop when all the housework was waiting to be done. The wilted flowers went onto the compost heap in the garden, the stale water in the flower buckets went down the drain, and the buckets themselves were stacked and stowed behind the counter.

No one thought to hang a "Closed" sign on the door. But anyone passing could tell at a glance that there were no flowers there anymore.

Chapter Fifty-Six

Konstantin's hand slid along the inside of her thigh, pausing at the hem of her underwear. Flora sighed with pleasure and raised her body slightly. His hand moved on, gliding over her mons veneris, then caressing her most intimate bud, moist with her own nectar.

Flora responded to Konstantin's touch with growing intensity. Her body lifted, writhed, pressed against his hand. She wanted to have him inside her, all of him.

She felt his hardness, but the next moment he pulled away again playfully, though her desire was like a whirlpool—she wanted to swirl herself around him, to hold him tight. She groaned loudly.

How could a woman want a man so much?

Flora leaped from the bed, reaching for a washcloth with one hand and her stockings with the other.

It's almost time! She felt like laughing out loud in her anticipation.

"Flora, darling, what is it? Where are you going? Why don't you stay with me?"

You know what I've got planned for today, Flora thought, but as she opened her mouth to reply, she heard a soft snore. Konstantin had fallen asleep again.

Flora rarely left the hotel so early in the morning, but when she did, she was enveloped in the smell of freshly baked bread from the bakery next door. Every time, she felt a pang in her belly.

But it was not hunger. It was Friedrich and herself at the breakfast table. Ernestine joining them, her hair disheveled, spilling her coffee when she sat down. Sabine bringing fresh marmalade to the table. Alexander, his mouth smeared with raspberries.

Don't think! Over. Done . . .

With a headscarf pulled low over her eyes, Flora hurried from the hotel in the direction of Lichtenthaler Allee. Although it was only the end of August, the first chill of autumn was in the air. It had rained in the night and the streets gleamed wetly. One had to take care not to slip.

Flora looked stubbornly at the ground. She did not want to see anyone, or be seen. Still, she did not fail to notice a large shadow slide past her. She raised her eyes and saw the pair of storks from the nest atop the church tower. They circled overhead, their wings pounding the air loudly.

Flora watched the birds wistfully. Where did their travels take them? Wasn't it true that many birds flew off to warmer places to spend the winter?

The storks would be the first to go. Soon, however, the tourists and spa guests would follow. To Nice, Monte Carlo, Paris.

And then?

What would become of her and Konstantin?

He still had not said a word about his plans for the winter, and Flora did not want to ask him. Would he take her with him? Or would she end up on the street like a wretched tramp, homeless?

Flora ripped all thoughts from her mind like weeds from a flower bed. Woe betide her if weeds like that once began to thrive . . .

Sabine had not even brought the baby carriage to a standstill when Flora darted out from her hiding place behind a rosebush. "My boy! My dear, darling Alexander! My one-and-only." She lifted her son from the carriage and cuddled and kissed him, barely keeping back the tears of joy that sprang to her eyes. Lord, that one person could miss another so much.

"Is it just me, or has our little man grown a bit just since last week?" Motherly pride shone in Flora's eyes. For a moment, she forgot everything else around her.

"I don't know." Sabine looked around uneasily, then pushed the baby carriage a short way into the meadow. "Let's get a little off the path."

"There's hardly a soul out this early. In this weather, they'll all be lying in bed or dawdling over breakfast," Flora murmured. She had noticed Sabine's uneasiness.

"Well, you'd know about that. I don't have time to dawdle over anything. We've got a pile of wood coming soon, and I'll be stacking it all morning. I can't stay long."

Flora nodded ruefully. "I'll never forget you bringing Alexander out here every week like this." A lump formed in her throat, but she swallowed it down.

"I don't mind, but we should be cautious. If someone sees me with you and tells your husband about it, then God have mercy on me."

Flora instinctively pulled her headscarf a little lower over her eyes. She felt like an outcast, a leper. Someone no one wanted to be seen with.

The meadows along Lichtenthaler Allee were covered with tens of thousands of glittering cobwebs, and the grass was so wet that there was nowhere they could spread a blanket and sit. Sabine turned the carriage toward a bench beneath a weeping willow. "We'll be safe from any curious eyes here," she said, sitting down. "So? How's the sweet life now?"

"The sweet life . . ." Flora laughed joylessly.

What was she supposed to say? That she was almost dying of boredom? That every passing day felt like a year? That she spent most of her time sitting in a hotel room, hidden away like something to be ashamed of? Even among Konstantin's Russian friends.

From the start Konstantin had told her his friends would not accept it if they came out as a couple so soon after Püppi's death. "Besides," he added, "as enlightened as they might seem, deep in their hearts they still cling to the belief that marriage is sacred, and that a man and woman can only be together under its protections. How do you think they will look at us as two adulterers? They'd hound us out of town like rabid dogs."

Flora could not believe what she was hearing. "But . . . your friend Irina . . . wasn't she involved with Count Popo for months before their engagement? And didn't you tell me that Matriona Schikanova was always off trysting with Sergej Lubelev? And—"

Konstantin had interrupted her objections with a laugh. "You are so naïve sometimes. Do you really think you can put yourself on the same level as society women like them? The rules that apply to them certainly don't apply to you. Believe me, there's nothing I'd like more than to show up at a party with you and announce to the whole world: this is my flower girl, my Flora! But for now it is really for the best if we aren't seen together in public." Of course, he promised he would tell her at length about every party he attended. And he suggested more than once that some peace and quiet would help her forget that little incident in the Forellenhof.

That little incident . . .

Stop! Don't think about it!

Alexander began to squirm restlessly on her lap.

"If you don't want to say anything, then don't." Sabine took out a bag of large wooden balls, and all three of them rolled them around together on the damp bench.

In any case, Flora did not understand why Konstantin was constantly out and about. He had her now!

"Should I pick you flowers?" she said to her son, holding out a pale-blue bellflower that Alexander immediately reached for. "How is Friedrich?" she asked then, and held her breath. At the same time, she had no idea what she wanted to hear—that he was well? That he missed her terribly?

Sabine looked away. "He hardly talks, not with his mother, never with me. What can I tell you? He comes home, bounces Alexander on his lap for a minute or two, then vanishes into his room. Next morning, I get to clear away the empty schnapps bottles."

"He's drinking? He never touched schnapps before," said Flora.

"It's horrible stuff. I tried the last few sips from a bottle, once, and even that little bit made me dizzy. I'd like to know who turned him onto that stuff." Sabine shuddered.

"You're impossible!" Flora dug her friend in the ribs.

Sabine's joking mood had already passed. "You can't imagine how much you're missed. Madam hardly leaves the front room anymore. It's like the time after Kuno died. Remember that? It troubles her terribly that we've had to close the shop. She never smiles. Just gloom and sighing, all the time. I've caught myself sighing out loud like your mother-in-law, but it's really no surprise. The household money is tight again, and I'm having a hard job making it stretch."

Money was running short? Hadn't they had enough in reserve? She'd earned so much through the flower shop.

"I'd like to start looking for a new position," Sabine went on, "but if I go now, madam will probably be lost once and for all. And she can't look after Alexander by herself." She smiled sadly and stroked Alexander's hair.

"Thank you," said Flora. She laid her arm across Sabine's shoulders, but Sabine moved away and cleared her throat. "There's another thing I wanted to mention. There's been a woman coming to the house quite a lot lately. A foreigner. I don't know where she's from, but she's certainly not Russian. Not very good-looking, either. Tall and as skinny as a starving goat. When she laughs, it's like a donkey braying."

Flora smiled. "That sounds like Lady Lucretia. She's an old friend of Friedrich's. She's from England, and she's been coming to Baden-Baden for years." Flora absently plucked a few more bellflowers. Wet from the rain, they felt so delicate. With a few blades of grass, they made a nice little bouquet . . .

"You know her? In any case, whenever she comes, the young master pulls himself together, and sometimes I even hear them laughing. They talk about curative waters and chemical stuff. Don't you think that's strange?"

"Sabine, you really are impossible. Do you honestly think the Englishwoman has her eye on Friedrich? No, you're imagining things again."

"What's that supposed to mean? Haven't I almost always been right in the past?"

Flora shrugged. "And even if she *did* have her eye on him, Friedrich has every right in the world to find himself a new, better woman. I can be happy that he hasn't already filed for divorce . . . or had me thrown in jail. He's a good man. Maybe he'll find a wife who makes him as happy as he deserves to be. It doesn't look as if I was the right one." As glibly as the words tripped off her tongue, her heart felt as heavy as lead.

Try as she might to banish all thoughts of her and Friedrich's life together in Stephanienstrasse, they roiled up again and again. She missed Friedrich.

His serious eyes whenever she announced another idea for the shop. His skeptical questions. His grumbling about how she was never satisfied, about how she always wanted more. But in the end, he had always supported her. He had trusted her, and trusted that she would make it all work.

And what had she done in return? She had destroyed the lives of everyone in the Sonnenschein family. *Oh, Friedrich. Forgive me. I was so foolish . . .*

The two women sat in silence for a long moment while Alexander crawled around on Flora's lap, babbling away.

"The Englishwoman . . . Friedrich might be able to talk to her about curative waters and such," Sabine said slowly. "But he certainly doesn't seem happier for it."

Konstantin had already had breakfast when Flora returned to the hotel. He sat at the dressing table, tying his long hair back into a tight braid.

He's so handsome, Flora thought. A tray with empty plates and bowls caught her eye. It stood on the small table by the window and smelled of caviar and onion.

"Did you have something brought in from the *épicerie* again? Starting the day with caviar . . . that's not a proper breakfast." Flora's own stomach growled; she'd assumed that they would have breakfast together.

"Who's to say what a proper breakfast is? You, my dear?" Konstantin murmured as he plucked nose hairs in front of the mirror.

Flora stepped up behind him and tickled him on the nose with her makeshift bellflower bouquet, still damp from the meadows.

"Wouldn't today be a good day to start painting again? If you like, I'll model for you. Perhaps naked, with nothing but the flowers in my hand?" The idea was enough to put a blush into her cheeks.

He pushed the hand holding the bouquet away roughly. "Do you know how late I was up last night?"

"No one forced you to stay out late playing cards," she replied archly, and she sat on the bed. She would pick flowers, and Konstantin would paint them—that was how she had daydreamed their life together.

"One has to be in the right mood to paint. It certainly doesn't help to have you pushing me all the time," he said as he polished his cuff links.

For a moment the previous night, her fingers had suddenly been so eager to try painting that she had been on the verge of taking out Konstantin's supplies. Oh, to finally do something with her own hands again! Add red to white, swirl together some shades of blue, and be happy with whatever came out. But painting was his art form, not hers. She had forfeited hers, along with everything else.

"When Püppi was still alive, you were always complaining about how much you missed painting. Now that you have the time, you're no longer interested," she said, her voice cool. "You've always got a thousand reasons not to get started, and yet it's a gift to dedicate yourself to something so beautiful."

"I honestly don't know why you're getting so worked up about it." Konstantin kissed her lips fleetingly, then peered around the room, looking for something. "My hat?" he asked.

Creases appeared on Flora's forehead. "You're going off again? Weren't we going to go up to the Altes Schloss? The weather would be perfect today."

"I'm sure it would be, but the Altes Schloss isn't going anywhere," he replied. "In Iffezheim, however, there's a very special horse race on today—a race just for German officers. Not that I'm particularly interested in horses, but Popo persuaded me to come along. He says it will be interesting to see how good the German horses are."

"When are you coming back?" Flora could do nothing about the disappointment in her voice.

"I don't know yet. Why don't you get yourself dressed up and go to a café or take a stroll along the Promenade?" He pressed some money into her hand. "What do you think? Should we go back to that little wine bar this evening?" Without waiting for Flora to reply, he tapped his hat and blew her a farewell kiss from the door. "Go out and have some fun! I promise I'll do the same."

"I don't doubt it for a second," Flora murmured to herself. Go to a café? Take a stroll? Did Konstantin have any idea what he was suggesting? Either one would be like running the gauntlet.

Listlessly, she went down to the kitchen, where she could at least talk the cook into a cup of coffee and a sweet roll.

Chapter Fifty-Seven

Work like that is not seemly *for a woman!*

With trembling hands, Ernestine wiped the sweat from her brow. Had there really been a time in which she had believed that to be true? Foolishness, that's all it was. And was it not *done* for one to keep their things in order? For one to take care of what was necessary? What other choice did she have, when Friedrich chose to hide away and perpetually lick his wounds? She had asked him at least three times to turn the compost heap, and what had happened? Nothing. She felt sorry for her one-and-only, of course, but she was starting to sense another emotion rising in her. Was it annoyance? Disillusion? Anger? Ernestine did not know.

Anger at her son . . . no, that was not possible. Not with him suffering. But good heavens, what was she supposed to do to ease his misery? She had Sabine prepare his favorite meals, opened the newspaper for him when he got home from work, endeavored to keep a merry tone in her voice when she told him about her day with Alexander. Friedrich didn't seem to appreciate her efforts in the slightest.

Ernestine looked up to the second floor. The shutters were closed over his window, which meant he was probably sleeping off last night's indulgences, as he did so often. The only thing that surprised Ernestine was that his late appearance at the Trinkhalle morning after morning had not had consequences. *My God, what if he loses his job on top of everything else?*

Although her arms were sore from the unaccustomed work, Ernestine went on with it. All her neighbors were busy that early in the morning, so it was unlikely that any of them would see her slaving away in her garden like a common farm girl.

So what if they did see! Ernestine snorted contemptuously. She didn't really care what her neighbors thought anymore.

What Sabine had seen, however, mattered far more. Sabine believed she had seen a rat on the compost heap, which was why she refused to do the job herself. Neither cajoling nor threats had been able to change her mind.

Ernestine kept peering at the mountain of kitchen waste, decaying flowers, leaves, and earth. She hoped Sabine had been mistaken and that the alleged rat was a little mouse.

Had Flora had any fear of rodents when she worked in the garden? Ernestine had never asked her. When it came down to it, no one had ever asked Flora how she was.

And what had she herself done to help Flora with the thousand tasks she did? It was not the first time the question had appeared in Ernestine's head, and the answer was invariably devastating: not very much at all.

No, for Ernestine it had always been Friedrich this, Friedrich that. Always her one-and-only son.

"Every third thing you say is about your son and his heroic deeds at the Trinkhalle," Gretel Grün once had chided her. "I have to say, his work there isn't really that interesting." Ernestine had been horrified. Why could her friends not understand that Friedrich's happiness and contentment were her heart?

Friedrich this, Friedrich that. Just as it always had been Kuno this, Kuno that in the years before he passed away. And what thanks had he given her for *that*?

If only she had paid a little more attention to Flora. Maybe then she would have noticed that someone else had lured the girl astray, and maybe then she could have saved Flora from this terrible turn of events.

"Mother?" she heard directly behind her. Ernestine wheeled around and let out a cry.

"Good heavens, Friedrich, do you have to creep up like that?" He looked so grim and dismal: dark shadows around his eyes, empty gaze, stooped posture.

"Mother, what are you doing here?"

"I'm doing your job and turning the compost heap," she snapped. Was he blind?

Friedrich frowned. "I would have taken care of the garden, but it looks as if you could not wait." He shrugged. "You should stop. This work isn't for you—you're already red in the face."

Ernestine was momentarily struck speechless. She had a red face? Is that all that occurred to Friedrich to say?

She was seized by such a fit of anger that she almost slapped her son's face.

"Nothing matters to you anymore! How much longer are you going to continue like this?"

"I don't know what you're talking about," he said cautiously.

"Oh, you do, my boy. It's been almost two months since Flora left us. Eight weeks in which you've barely taken part in the life of this household. Do you really think you're the only one who's suffering? Do you really believe Alexander doesn't miss his mother? Do you think *I* don't miss her? Flora was like a daughter to me. I can't stop thinking about her . . ." Ernestine's anger dissipated. She blinked several times, and a muscle beneath her right eye began to twitch nervously. "I want to know how she is."

"How nice of you to think about *her*," Friedrich replied drily. "Just to remind you: she's an adulteress."

"Oh, Friedrich. Of course I know that Flora is guilty of a great deal. But does that make the rest of us innocent?" Ernestine leaned heavily on the rake. Sadness ran through her like poison, robbing her suddenly of her strength.

Friedrich let out a bitter laugh. "Your wise words come a little late. If you'd told me about Sybille's letter when it came and not just recently, then things might never have come this far." He turned on his heel and marched away.

Ernestine stayed behind, trembling and cold. It was all she could do to stay on her feet.

※

"Here, in the fourteen frescoes along the arcade, you see depictions of the legends and stories woven around our lovely Baden-Baden." Friedrich went from one picture to the next, rattling off his usual presentation without going into any details about the stories themselves. He was listening with one ear to the tolling of the church bell . . . nine, ten, eleven. Thank God. Just one hour until he could take a break. With any luck, the visiting group from Heilbronn would be gone. He had no intention of missing his midday nap for the sake of a few old women. And there would be trouble if his mother came at him with her words of wisdom again.

Friedrich managed to force a cramped smile. A few of the women held elaborate glasses at the ready, so he said, "You will find the drinking fountain inside the Trinkhalle." He indicated to the group that they should go into the hall, then nodded, turned, and walked away.

Just then, he saw Lady O'Donegal striding toward him.

Oh, wonderful. The last thing he wanted to talk about were her plans for the Hotel Marie-Eluise. According to Gustav Körner, they were on the verge of signing a contract of sale. The man had once again thanked Friedrich effusively for putting him in touch with the Englishwoman. Friedrich could still hardly believe that Lady O'Donegal was going ahead with it. Just because someone liked Baden-Baden was no reason to buy a hotel there. Some people in town thought she was not right in the head.

Far worse, however, was the fact that she wanted to persuade him to be the director. What was he supposed to do in the Marie-Eluise by himself? She knew the reason that Gustav Körner had been forced to sell the place, and she also knew about Friedrich's own family situation. She had, after all, been present on the day when his entire world fell apart out at the Forellenhof. He had been utterly stunned when, sometime later, she had suggested it to him again. She could buy ten hotels if she wanted, but she should leave him in peace.

If he'd been able, he would have ducked away and pretended he had not seen her, but the next moment, she was on him.

"Mr. Sunshine! Have you already heard that I—" She fell silent instantly when she saw his face. "My God, you are a sight! Pale as death warmed up and ready to drop. Simply terrible, if I may say so."

A pained smile crept across Friedrich's face. Lady Lucretia certainly was not the kind to beat around the bush. He shrugged. "One tires toward the end of the season."

"You can't fool me. Your cares come from somewhere else entirely." She peered at him intently for a moment, then let out a deep sigh. "My dear Mr. Sunshine, I believe you and I need to have a chat, and the sooner the better. Come with me!"

"I can't just leave. I'm needed here!" he protested.

"The way you look right now, you are certainly *not* needed here," she replied, and she pushed Friedrich in the direction of the Conversationshaus, ignoring his protests.

They took seats at one of the small tables in front of the Conversationshaus. A waiter came, and the Englishwoman ordered tea and brandy for them.

As soon as the waiter was gone, Lady Lucretia picked up where she'd left off. "Do you imagine you're the only man in the world whose wife ran off and left him? It happens all the time, I'm sad to say. I may be getting on, but I've learned a thing or two in my time, and I can tell you this: a rift like this in a marriage is never the fault of just one."

Friedrich let out a harsh laugh. "Now you sound like my mother. In her eyes, I should have *saved* Flora from that bastard. She acts as if he's the devil incarnate and Flora is at his mercy. When I saw her in the Forellenhof, she looked anything but helpless." He pushed his chair back to stand up, but Lady Lucretia grabbed his wrist.

"Now pull yourself together! I haven't done anything to hurt you, so you've no cause to attack me like that. I harbor no ill will toward you. So sit." She released his hand.

Friedrich chewed his lip for a moment before speaking. "Excuse me. I don't know what came over me." The argument with his mother that morning, and now this. He seemed to have forgotten who his friends were.

The waiter brought their drinks, and Lady Lucretia lifted her brandy glass. "Let's drink. Cheers!"

The red-gold liquid trickled warmly down Friedrich's throat and settled in his stomach. Chastened, he looked across at the Englishwoman. "Sometimes, I don't know who I am anymore. The whole affair with Flora . . . I feel as if someone has jerked a rug out from under my feet. I still can't really believe what's happened. We were so happy! She with her flowers and I . . ." He waved vaguely in the direction of the Trinkhalle. "When Alexander was born, my happiness was complete. Where did we go wrong?" A despairing sob escaped his breast.

Lady Lucretia raised an eyebrow while she poured the tea.

God, what had gotten into him? Airing his troubles to a complete stranger. As embarrassed as Friedrich was, he could not stop. The words welled up inside him and overflowed. "I've asked myself the same questions a thousand times: When did our marriage go wrong? Why didn't I notice anything? I mean, Flora is not naturally a scheming liar. There must have been signs of what she was doing, but I did not see them. Nor did my mother. She didn't have the slightest idea, either, not even when—" He broke off. Enough. What sense did it make to burden Lady Lucretia with Sybille's letter?

Lady Lucretia shrugged. "When it comes to oneself or one's own family, it is not hard to be blind. But we see the mistakes of others so much more easily for that."

Friedrich's eyes widened. Had the Englishwoman also been deceived, as he had?

He lifted his hands helplessly. "What am I saying? Why am I blaming myself at all? *I* certainly haven't made any mistakes."

The older woman sighed. "One does not necessarily have to make mistakes to court disaster. Sometimes it's enough to do nothing at all. Or, to put it another way, to refrain from doing something."

"What am I supposed to have refrained from doing? *Ach*, this talk makes no sense. I repeat: Flora is an adulteress! And a mother who abandoned her son." Friedrich looked in disgust at the tea the Englishwoman had poured for him. He would have preferred another brandy.

Lady Lucretia turned her head slightly and looked at him sideways. "Wait just a moment. Didn't you say that *you* had thrown your wife out of the house?"

Friedrich glared at her angrily. "What if I did? What difference does it make? She should have reckoned with that! Was I supposed to forgive her?"

Lady Lucretia held his gaze. "Only you can answer that."

Chapter Fifty-Eight

The woman stood on tiptoe and peered over the heads of the waiting crowds along Lichtenthaler Allee.

"Not a high-society face in sight." She turned around to her husband in annoyance, and seemed not to notice that she elbowed Flora in the ribs as she did so. "I don't care if it's the last hunt of the season, if they don't show up soon, I'm going home and getting started with the cooking. Seppi, stop that!" She reached down and slapped the hand of her little boy, maybe three years old, who was tugging wildly at her skirt. The little boy let out an outraged howl.

Her husband smiled. "Maybe you're right. So what are you putting on the table today?" He lifted the boy onto his shoulders, and the howling ceased.

Flora smiled at the boy, who had his hands clenched tightly in his father's tangled curls.

"Steak, mashed potatoes, and gravy."

"With onions?"

"Of course with onions. I know how much you like them." The woman looked fondly at her husband.

Flora turned away abruptly.

Was Friedrich perhaps standing there somewhere with Alexander? Or were they at home with his mother, already tucking into the Sunday lunch that Sabine had cooked?

Flora felt herself on the verge of tears, as she always did when she thought of her son. But she forced herself to push the thought aside, and craned her neck with all the others there to catch a glimpse of the hunting party.

Oh, Konstantin, you always leave me alone.

In truth, Flora had not wanted to come out here today at all, but sheer boredom had driven her out of their hotel room. When she finally reached Lichtenthaler Allee, the best viewing spots had already been taken. The Sunday hunts in autumn were a spectacle, and many came to see the hunters riding by.

With her headscarf pulled low over her eyes, Flora moved into the middle of the crowd.

A leaf drifted down and settled on Flora's shoulder. She picked it off and held it delicately in her hand.

Autumn leaves . . . The sight of the first colored leaves of autumn had always made her heart leap. As a child, she had loved to collect the largest and most colorful leaves with her brothers. Later, she had incorporated the leaves into her autumn bouquets. The year before, she had even decorated their front window with them—much to Ernestine's displeasure! "Child, it looks as if the wind blew the leaves into the store and you're too lazy to sweep them out again," she had said.

Ernestine, I miss you so much. You and Mother and everyone else.

Flora closed her eyes, as if like that she could flee from her memories. She had not written home to Gönningen for months. What was she supposed to put into a letter? Lies? Or the truth, one so terrible that Flora preferred to say nothing at all? She imagined her parents' hand-wringing if they knew . . . But then, maybe they already did know. Maybe Friedrich had written to them. Or Ernestine. Perhaps that was it; otherwise, wouldn't her mother at least have come for her?

Flora inhaled the clear air deeply. It smelled of leaves and horse manure, of the wood of freshly felled birches, of the fires burning in the potato fields.

Intoxicated by the spicy mix of aromas, Flora tore off her headscarf and turned her face up to the autumn sun, falling in streams of light through the colorful canopy of leaves. If someone recognized her, she no longer cared.

What a gorgeous day it was!

The perfect day to gather chestnuts, or to tie a wreath. To dry flowers and weave garlands. A day for purple bouquets and aromatic herb bundles, for silver thistles and the first sprigs of fir. And—

Over! Done! Don't cry, don't cry . . .

Konstantin would come soon, and then she would smile. He hated it when she was feeling weepy. He did not want to carry the burden of her sadness; he wanted things to celebrate, wanted gaiety and high spirits.

Flora had become a good actress. Hardly a sigh escaped her anymore, nor did her eyes brim with tears. She could laugh out loud when she felt like nothing more than bawling.

Shielding her eyes from the sun with one hand, Flora looked off into the distance. Maybe Konstantin would go out for a walk with her later? If they walked a short way off the paths, they could go hand in hand, collect leaves, fashion pipes from acorns and twigs, as she had as a child in Gönningen.

Flora's spirits brightened at the thought. She was sure that such a playful idea would appeal to Konstantin.

Yes, Konstantin liked her cheerfulness. He would not have asked her to go with him otherwise. "Paris is an exciting city," he'd said when he'd told her about his plan to leave at the end of the coming week. He had not asked about what she might like to do.

An exciting city. Was that reason enough to leave behind everything one held dear? A shadow crossed Flora's face. She could not leave. Whatever happened, she had to stay close to her son.

But Konstantin never considered things like that. He'd been so excited when he'd said to her, "Come with me and we'll spend a glorious time together! Dear Anna tells me there is more than enough entertainment in Paris right now."

For whom? she had thought about asking. *For you and "dear Anna"? While I get left behind in some hotel room like a forgotten toy? I'm good enough for you at night, but during the day you'd rather adorn yourself with Russian royalty.*

Flora could not imagine that Konstantin would be any more willing to show himself in public with her in Paris than he was in Baden-Baden. From what he'd told her, almost the entire Russian circle of friends was planning to spend the winter there.

"*Dear Anna . . .*" Her name had come up more and more, lately. Did she have her eye on Konstantin? Was she the one who paid his bills now, the one who found a horse for him to ride today?

It struck Flora as strange that she felt no fear or worry at the thought. Strange, too, that she hardly cared at all with whom he spent his time when he was not with her. She could not change anything about it in any case. Besides, Konstantin assured her constantly that he would only ever love her, Flora.

Love . . . Flora knew less than ever what that was.

Suddenly, a tremor of unrest ran through the crowd around her.

"Look! There they are!"

"What a beautiful coach."

"Look at the wonderful horses!" Fingers pointed, necks stretched. Flora received another jab in the ribs, and someone trod painfully on her right foot.

The twenty-member orchestra specially assembled to mark the occasion broke into a brisk marching tune when the first carriage—an open landau decorated with garlands of fir—rolled past. Count Popo held the reins of the two black horses that slung strands of saliva with every snort onto the crowds that lined the way. Behind him on the wagon, on a bed of greenery, lay the body of a huge wild boar, a bright-red apple wedged between its jaws. The dead beast drew admiring comments from the crowd.

Where is Princess Irina? Flora wondered. Had Popo wanted to go to the hunt alone? Ha! As if the princess would let anybody forbid her to ride with them. The thought was so comical that Flora had to smile.

More carriages followed, all magnificently polished and outfitted for the big day. Then, finally, the riders came into view.

There! There was Konstantin! Flora jumped high and cried out his name, waving her hand, trying to catch his attention from the tumult around her.

He looked so smart on his brown steed. Like a pirate on horseback. How admiringly the people around her looked at him, and how the women lowered their eyes, and yet covertly looked at his thighs, his broad shoulders, his broad smile.

Flora let out a short, sad laugh. People were so easily deceived. Did they really believe that a noble shell contained a noble soul? Or did they simply not care?

As she did not care?

Konstantin. Her adventurer. Wild and turbulent. And beneath his noble shell . . .

Now he had caught sight of her, and he waved his hat merrily, signaling to her that he would meet her farther ahead. Flora hurriedly attempted to break free of the crowd.

"Flora, dear Anna has invited me and a few others for a drink. You won't be upset if I stop by for a glass or two, will you? I promise you I'll be there tonight, just for you." His smile was seductive, full of promise, but also unbending.

Flora sighed. Today it was a successful hunt that had to be celebrated. Tomorrow it would be something else, the day after that, something else again. As it probably always would be.

His horse had already started off again when Konstantin turned around in the saddle. "Think about tonight, just you and me." He winked at her once more.

Flora nodded dumbly.

For that wink, I've thrown away everything I loved and held dear.

The realization soaked into Flora like a stain into cloth, deeper and deeper with every step that Konstantin's horse took away from her.

Konstantin. A heartbreaker whose greatest possession was his smile. A noble shell with very little underneath.

Incapable of any other thought, Flora stood there among the apple cores, horse dung, and trash while the crowd around her dispersed.

Was she doing Konstantin an injustice, being angry at him because he constantly left her alone? He had, after all, never promised her anything, had never pretended to be anything other than he was.

All lost. For nothing. Not a damned thing.

If she peered deep down inside, all she found was infinite emptiness. Everything else was used up. Her great love, or what she thought had been her great love, was a straw fire. Extinguished. Where had the rising breeze suddenly blown her yearning, her passions, her emotions?

All at once, she felt more powerless than she had ever felt in her life. Mechanically, she set one foot in front of the other and did her best to breathe calmly. But her throat felt tied closed.

Where now? Back to the hotel? Everything in her bristled at the thought. No! Never again! She did not want to wait any longer.

Then out of Baden-Baden? Back to Gönningen? They would have to take her in there. It was her home, even if she had brought shame on the family.

And what about Alexander, then? Could she bring herself to leave him behind? There were others here who loved him . . .

She needed to sit and think.

Flora had not reached the park bench when her legs failed and she collapsed on the grass.

Chapter Fifty-Nine

At five in the afternoon, Friedrich slipped on his jacket and took a final look around the Trinkhalle. Not a soul in sight. The spa guests were either off somewhere celebrating their departure or were already packing their bags.

Anybody who came in now could damn well fill their own glass.

What's changed this year, apart from the loss of the casino? he wondered, threading a path through the throng of well-dressed people outside the Conversationshaus. Parties, outings, champagne—keeping the spa guests amused had come first, as it always had, and the Spa and Bath Administration had not gone to any great pains to change that.

"You're too impatient. Our guests' habits have developed over many years, and you can't change them overnight. Be happy that they still come here. Once the Friedrichsbad opens its doors, the real spa guests will also arrive," the director himself had told him just a few days before.

Friedrich snorted derisively. How many years would that still take?

He abruptly stopped. He had been so deeply buried in his ruminations that he had actually walked right past the turn into Stephanienstrasse.

Then again, no one was expecting him home so early anyway. Sabine had a day off, and hadn't Mother mentioned that she wanted to make waffles herself that evening? For Alexander and him.

As was true so often lately, he had not been hungry during the day and had eaten nothing for lunch. A brazen ray of sunlight fell through the canopy of leaves over Lichtenthaler Allee, and Friedrich felt it warm his nose. Maybe a stroll would bring back his appetite?

He had gone only a few steps when a mountain of construction materials, piled high along the facade of the Hotel Stéphanie, caught his eye. Wood, stone, then more wood, and . . . stone statues? The new owner seemed to have big plans for the old place.

Just like Lady Lucretia with the Hotel Marie-Eluise. "The contract of sale has been signed, the architect has drawn up the plans, and as soon as the building authorities give their blessing to my alterations, we'll be ready to go," she had said to him that morning. "I would like to stay in my own hotel next season, after all, and welcome the spa guests in person!" Even on the last day of her stay, she had insisted on enjoying the benefits of taking the waters.

Lady Lucretia was certainly serious about her new undertaking. For a long time, Friedrich had harbored his doubts. People could talk a great deal and have nothing to show for it in the end.

But Lucretia O'Donegal was different. She did not do things halfway. Zealously, she had told him all about her various ideas for the Marie-Eluise. "The new bath area will have ten tubs, one of which will be fed only with cold water, for those who prefer a course of cold baths. You with your technical knowledge would be just the right man to introduce all this to the guests. I also believe that a new job would divert you a little from . . . well, you know what." Lady Lucretia had then clapped him on the shoulder in her usual hefty manner. "I await your final decision this evening at six, no later. In case you turn me down, then for better or worse I shall need to look for someone else."

One hour. Friedrich's gaze drifted back in the direction of the town. Should he go to the Marie-Eluise now and take a final, undisturbed look at the tubs? One last chance to dream about the enormous job being offered to him on a plate?

With a wife at his side, he probably would not have hesitated for a moment. He would have accepted the Englishwoman's offer days ago. But alone, it made little sense.

No, at six on the dot, he would go to the hotel and tell Lady O'Donegal that—

His thoughts were interrupted when he saw a miserable-looking figure slumped in the grass.

Flora!

His first impulse was to turn away before she noticed him and act as if he had not seen her. No, he couldn't leave her on the ground like that. As he helped her onto the bench, he saw that her eyes were red and she clearly had been crying. She looked at him in disbelief.

"Friedrich?"

He straightened his shoulders automatically and nodded to her. His jaw was clenched so tightly that he could not even say her name.

"Friedrich . . ."

The way she said his name. It sounded like a sigh, and a shudder ran down Friedrich's spine.

"How is Alexander? Is he well? And you? You—" She broke off and slapped one hand to her mouth. "Forgive me. I have no right to ask something like that."

"Alexander is fine, as if you didn't already know. Did you think I hadn't noticed that Sabine takes the boy out to see you every week? Do you really believe I'm that stupid?" He felt a roaring in his head, as if a thousand wild bees were buzzing in there.

For several seconds, neither said a word.

She was pale. And she was so thin, no more than skin and bone.

Could it be that the sweet life did not taste so sweet after all?

Friedrich sniffed churlishly. Served her right. This woman—who seemed so delicate and fragile, no longer the strong and vibrant Flora he'd known—was no concern of his anymore.

The bees buzzed on in Friedrich's head, and his heart beat so hard it felt as if it would burst out of his chest at any moment. Flora . . .

"How are you?" he said. The words flew from his mouth so suddenly that he could not stop them.

"How am I supposed to be . . . ?" She scratched a small circle in the gravel with the toe of her shoe. "I'm going to leave Baden-Baden."

Friedrich had not reckoned with the impact of her words. But it was obvious: the season was over, and new adventures waited elsewhere. Of course she would leave on her lover's arm. A wave of heat washed over him. He heard her words as if they came through fog from a long way off.

"Gönningen . . . my family . . . can only hope and pray that they take me in . . ."

Friedrich frowned. What was she talking about?

"Maybe, if I come back to Baden-Baden in winter to sell seeds . . . would you allow me to see Alexander? I know I have no right to that, but it would make me very happy. If you would let me."

What was he supposed to allow? Friedrich understood nothing. What about the Bulgarian painter? Was it over?

Flora looked at him with eyes red from crying. "Oh, Friedrich, what have I done? I've done everything wrong. When I think about what I did to you . . . and our son. Your mother . . ." She threw her hands over her face and her body heaved, racked with sobbing. "I'd give anything to be able to turn things back again. But there are mistakes in life that can't be reversed, can't be made up for. What have I done!" she repeated, and she looked up at him, her cheeks wet with tears.

Friedrich took out his handkerchief and handed it to her. His knees felt weak as he sat beside her on the cold bench and struggled with the impulse to take her in his arms. *Are you mad?* he reproved himself in silence.

"Your realization comes a little late, I'm afraid," he said stiffly.

It was too late for so many things. *Even for Lady Lucretia and her hotel,* he thought as he heard the church bell strike six in the distance.

Flora blew her nose, then crumpled the handkerchief into a ball. "I've said sorry to you a thousand times in my mind—a thousand times I've rehearsed the words. And now? Now I can't think what to say at all. Friedrich, I miss you all so terribly! I think of you every day, so much that it hurts." She sobbed silently and turned away.

He nodded tiredly. What could he say? That he missed her, too? Every day, over and over? That he hated himself for it and did everything he could to suppress his feelings for her? And that it did not work?

She touched his sleeve. He jumped as if he'd been burned.

"Remember the first day you showed me the Trinkhalle?"

A gust of wind chilled Friedrich. Why did he not just stand up and leave?

"The picture of Merline. You told me about how she lured the goatherds with her songs, and how, despite all the warnings they were given, they followed her into the depths." Flora laughed bitterly. "Back then, I could not understand how anyone could be so stupid that they would leave everything behind and go into the water. Today . . ." She twisted the handkerchief with both hands. "Today, I know how tempting it can be to dive into unknown waters. At the start, you dip in just the tip of your toe. It feels good, and you think that nothing can happen. Then the song comes again, so filled with promise, and the thought that you might never hear it again is suddenly too terrible to contemplate. You stop thinking, and you dive in headfirst." She twisted her mouth and spat out the next words like spoiled fruit. "For nothing but a fear I would miss out, for nothing but lust for life."

"But what would you have missed out on? Why were Alexander and I not enough for you? Why did you lust for another life?" Friedrich asked. He felt like taking her by the shoulders and shaking her. "You sit here, cry your eyes out, and feel sorry for yourself. You don't seem to care how I am at all! And yet . . ." Again, a shudder ran through him. This time it settled like frost on his skin.

"What?" she asked quietly.

He looked at her sideways. "When I told you the story back then, do you remember how you asked me about the goats? You wanted to know what became of them after their goatherd abandoned them." His brow furrowed before he went on. "At the time, I could not give you an answer. Today, I can tell you what became of them, left alone," he said in a gloomy voice. "They were lost, all of them. They went astray, with no one to stop them or guide them. A shadow hung over their lives, darkening everything, and they could not escape it." Without warning, a sob escaped him, and he cried, "How could you do that to me?" Tears flowed over his face, and he banged his fist angrily on the bench.

Friedrich remembered clearly the last time he had wept, at home, after he had discovered Flora's betrayal. He had been so furious and hurt that he felt he would never stop weeping. Now the hurt returned. The salty flood chose its unstoppable path, taking with it all his pent-up rage, his hate, his sadness and incomprehension. With no will of his own, he let Flora take him in her arms and rock him like a child. Together they wept for what they had lost.

Chapter Sixty

At some point, all their tears had been cried. Flora let go of Friedrich and wrapped her arms around her own body, meager protection against the rising wind. Exhausted and awkward, they sat side by side on the bench as the setting sun weakened.

And now? What would happen now? Would each go their own way? Where would her road lead her? Now that she had encountered Friedrich out here, the thought of returning to the hotel was even less imaginable than before. Of course, she had to go back to collect her things, but . . .

Flora sought nervously for something to say. She glanced surreptitiously at Friedrich from downturned eyes.

That she had met him today, the very day on which her feelings for Konstantin had died . . . All her feelings, all at once. Was it only a coincidence?

Friedrich cleared his throat. "It is like this: I have to go. I should have been on my way long ago. I have a pressing appointment." He turned in the direction of the town.

A sadness stronger than any before came over Flora. He had to go. He had a pressing appointment on Sunday evening. Of course.

She sprang to her feet. "I'm sorry I held you up. I . . . I needed to be getting along anyway."

His "No!" came as sharp as the crack of a whip, and made her jump.

"Don't go," he said softly. "I . . . would like to show you something." He stood and offered her his hand. "Come."

"You were to meet Lady Lucretia here? She owns the Marie-Eluise now?" Flora turned to Friedrich in disbelief. Her voice resounded in the vaulted cellar, through the length of which water rushed inside a heavy pipe.

Flora heard a rush in her own ears, and for a moment she had to hold herself upright on one of the iron tubs arranged on both sides.

Friedrich nodded. "She's probably left already and forgot to lock up. We'd agreed to meet at six."

Flora raised her eyebrows. The regret in Friedrich's voice was clear. What was this all about? And why had he brought her here? Did he want to introduce Lady Lucretia as the new woman in his life? Hadn't Sabine said that the Englishwoman had even visited Friedrich at home? So many questions shooting through her mind. She had to keep them all in check.

She looked around the cellar. The rust-red brick walls, the tubs in which a few spiders scrabbled, a shelf of dusty towels, a rolled carpet leaning against the wall—everything left the impression that the proprietress had stepped out briefly, and would return any minute to resume her cleaning. It did not smell stale or musty at all, as such vaults often did, but of camphor, and also a little like the inside of Friedrich's Trinkhalle. What an unusual space. In all her time in Baden-Baden, she had never been in a bathhouse quite like it.

Flora frowned. She was slowly starting to feel as if she were inside a peculiar dream.

"It's strange. Everything has been abandoned, but it doesn't really feel like it. I feel much more as if I can hear the happy sounds of women laughing," she said in amazement.

Friedrich nodded. "I also feel a very special, very pleasant atmosphere down here." He twisted his mouth to one side. "I hope that Lady Lucretia manages to maintain that. If it were up to me, the first thing I would do would be to have a branch pipe installed to feed a drinking fountain." He pointed to the water pipe. "The water in that pipe is also good drinking water. The guests could enjoy a hot bath and take the water in sips at the same time. They'd get the benefit on the inside, too. And then I think it would be important to . . ."

Flora listened to Friedrich attentively. She did not understand everything he said, but his enthusiasm was infectious. How he gesticulated! And how he strode through the room like a field marshal! He was clearly very certain about what he wanted.

Lady Lucretia had asked Friedrich to be the manager of her hotel? She would not have thought he could even imagine taking on such a role. What about the Trinkhalle?

What do you really know about this man, so familiar and yet so unknown?

Leaning against a wall, she said, "You're so exhilarated. It all sounds so exciting!"

He laughed harshly. "Really? Suddenly? For you, I was always boring old Friedrich with his waters."

"That's not true," she said feebly.

"Oh, yes it is! For you, every Russian coffee circle was more interesting than what I could offer. You wanted champagne, and all I could give you was water."

Flora looked at the floor. What could she say to that? "Friedrich, I know I've made a thousand mistakes. And yes, I really did not show enough interest in your work. But I always had the feeling that your Trinkhalle was none of my business, as little as the flower shop interested you." She swept aside a small spider that dropped on a web in front of her just then. "Maybe we should have talked to each other more than we did. Like at the start."

Friedrich laughed. "Talk! For you, that's always a cure-all. My parents did not talk to each other all the time, and they stayed together until my father's death."

"And? Were they happy like that?"

Friedrich waved it off. For several moments, the only sound was the rushing of the water in its pipe.

"When do you start as the new manager, then?" Flora finally asked, to break the silence.

"I won't be."

"But why not?" Flora asked uncomprehendingly. "Just now, your plans, your enthusiasm. I thought . . ." *I thought you wanted to show me that you could get along just fine without me.*

Friedrich sat on the edge of one of the tubs, propped his elbows on his knees, and shrugged helplessly. "You know, there was a time when I could well have imagined taking on something like this with you. Me down here in the bathhouse, you looking after the guests. Your flowers in the breakfast room and the sitting room." He looked up and smiled at her. "I thought that we would make a good team."

The two of us in a hotel? What a mad, thrilling notion! Flora thought.

Flora smiled, too. "You were always the more . . . measured of us. I was the one with the overflowing imagination." She shook her head. "Oh, Friedrich, I'm such a fool. If only you'd married someone smarter."

"But I didn't want anyone else," Friedrich replied, and his expression grew a little defiant. "Flora, life without you . . . I miss you more than I can say."

She looked at him wide-eyed. "Really? I thought you hated me."

"In the first weeks, I did. But now I've come to see that love and hate are perhaps not so far apart after all."

Friedrich stood up, went to the window, checked that it was latched. Without turning around, he said, "You and I . . . that we met at all, back then, well, I always considered it somehow fated, as if fate made the two of us for each other. Which was why I simply could not understand it when you—" He stopped abruptly and turned around. "Damn it! I still don't understand what got into you. I also don't know if I can ever forget what I saw in the Forellenhof. You and that man. That image will be burned into my memory forever."

"Friedrich . . ." Why did he have to start with that? Her conscience was already as black as a raven.

"Even if we both try as hard as we can, I don't have the slightest idea if things can ever be the way they were."

"The way they were? You mean, you in one place, me in another?" she asked softly. "This hotel"—she opened her arms to include everything around them—"maybe it stands for what we were missing. What did we have in common? What aims and plans and tasks did we share?"

Her knees trembling, she went to him, hesitated for a moment, then took his hand and laid it against her cheek.

"Friedrich, if you really believe that we can still have a future together, I would do everything I can to make you happy. Of course I can't turn back time or undo everything that's been done. You would have to take me back with all the terrible mistakes I've made. You would have to be able to forget."

"Forgetting is one thing, but there is also forgiveness," Friedrich murmured. He stroked her hair tenderly. "Maybe I will do a better job of that."

A sudden loud sound made both of them flinch, and it was a moment before Flora realized that it was her own stomach rumbling in discontent. Abashed, she pressed her hand to her stomach. "I'm sorry, I . . . I haven't had anything to eat since this morning."

Friedrich laughed. "Neither have I. And now I'm as hungry as a bear." He took Flora's hand and led her toward the exit. "What do you think? Could you eat a few fresh waffles?"

"Waffles? I love waffles!" Flora laughed in confusion.

"Then come with me. Sabine has the day off, so my mother will be wielding the waffle iron herself."

"You want me to . . . come *home*? As simple as that?" Flora felt as if all the blood were draining out of her face. Her eyes wide, she stopped and looked at Friedrich.

He nodded. "I don't know if it will be quite so 'simple.' But we'll soon see."

"What about Lady Lucretia? The hotel? Didn't you want to—"

He waved it off. "None of that matters now."

Without another word, they climbed the stairs and left the vault behind.

Flora's ABC of Flowers

Flowers from A to Z	Their Meaning
Acacia	"Friendship is the best medicine."
Adonis	"Your words hurt me."
Almond flower	Symbolizes resurrection and reawakening love
Amaryllis	"How proud and splendid you look!"
Anemone	Its name stems from the Greek anémos, meaning "wind." It is considered a symbol of endangered love and unfulfilled hope and a sign of departure and transience; anemones are said to have been created from the tears of Aphrodite, which fell in mourning after the death of her beloved Adonis.
Angelica	"My heart has made its choice!"
Apple branch	"Why don't you return my love?"
Aspen branch	"I'm frightened!"
Aspen leaf	"Will you protect me from my fears?"
Aster	"Are you also true to me?"

Autumn aster	Give these to bid someone farewell in a most elegant way
Bellflower	Express deep gratitude
Birch leaf	"Don't take your game too far!"
Boxwood	"Can I take hope from your behavior?"
Broom	Symbolizes modesty
Burdock	Represents affection and devotion
Buttercup	Give buttercups if you can recognize beauty even in old age, and if you love change
Cabbage rose	Stands for opulence
Calla	Symbolizes beauty and vitality
Caltha	Attributed with magical powers
Camellia	Symbolizes perfect proportions, beauty, and a desire for harmony
Carnation	A sign of piety, pure and deep love, true heartedness, friendship, and esteem
Centaury	"I cannot satisfy your desire."
Chamomile	"I wish you only the best."
Cherry blossom	Symbolizes inner beauty
Chervil	Represents honesty and uprightness of character
Chestnut leaf	"Gladly would I be with you."
China pink	"You are one of a kind!"
Christmas rose	Symbolizes a long, fulfilled life, and protection for those in love
Chrysanthemum, red	Represents being in love
Chrysanthemum, white	Symbolizes truth and truthfulness
Cinnamon Rose	"I owe what I am to your love."
Cinquefoil	A gift for a beloved child, as a symbol of motherly love
Clematis	Symbolizes security and peace of mind
Clover flower	A sign of luck in love and a promise given

Clover leaf	Give to wish someone luck
Columbine	"Can I put any credence in your words?"
Cornflower	Symbolizes loyalty, modesty, and lifelong love
Cowslip	"How dearly I wish for the key to your heart." Also, "I'm in the mood for something new!" This early sign of spring is considered a symbol of optimism and zest for life.
Crocus	Symbolizes the greatest virtue and pure love
Crown imperial	Symbolizes power and sublime strength
Cuckooflower	Give these to a woman blessed with a wealth of humor, joie de vivre, and fire
Cyclamen	A gift for someone timid, modest, and compassionate
Cypress	Symbolizes despair and mourning
Daffodil	Symbolizes yearning, unrequited love, and vanity
Dahlia	Represents coldness and lost feelings
Daisy	Symbolizes virtuous friendship
Damask rose	Its luminous beauty is short-lived, like many a flirtation
Dandelion	"Your rejection cuts me to the quick!"
Dead nettle	"I don't want anything to do with you again."
Elderberry	Give these if you feel you have been misunderstood
English daisy	Stands for the innocence of childhood, and is commonly used as a love oracle
English violet	Symbolizes modesty
Erica	"We cannot elude fate!" Or, "This separation is final!"
Fern	An old-world magical plant; a gift for someone who needs luck in gambling and love
Fir branch	"Don't be so grumpy!"

Fir tree	Symbolizes endurance and growth
Forget-me-not	"Remember me always!" Also, "I will never forget you!"
Gentian	Symbolizes unspoken love and fidelity, and a romantic nature; also stands for uprightness and honesty
Goat's rue	Stands for reason and good sense
Golden rain	Considered a sign of melancholy beauty
Goosefoot	"I can't bear your courting anymore!"
Guelder rose	Symbolizes old age
Hawthorn	Represents hope and happiness in marriage
Heliotrope	Symbolizes devotion and deep admiration
Hibiscus	Symbolizes tender beauty
Honesty	Represents integrity and uprightness
Hyacinth, blue	Symbolic of friendship and steadfastness, loyalty, goodness, and benevolence; also a sign for the annual reawakening of nature
Hyacinth, white	A gift for someone beguilingly beautiful
Hydrangea	A sign of true and constant love; also given as a reminder of the days in which one first fell in love
Impatiens	Represents impatience
Iris	A symbol of unrequited love: "I think of you day and night!"; also symbolizes imperturbability and strength
Italian honeysuckle	"The bonds of our love will grow stronger and dearer every day."
Ivy	Stands for eternal loyalty and love that blooms forever; also symbolizes immortality
Jasmine	A gift for an exceptionally captivating and sensual woman

Juniper	Considered a provider of comfort in times of great need
Larkspur	A particularly potent symbol of eternal fidelity and constancy
Laurel	Considered a symbol of eternal renown; give it if you want to swear perpetual loyalty
Lavender	Symbolizes love and devotion
Lemon balm	Represents cheerfulness and love in one's heart
Lilac, purple	Symbolizes budding love
Lilac, white	Symbolizes praise of youth; during the period of his engagement, a groom should take white lilac to his fiancée's house every day
Lily	The flower of kings; considered the symbol of majesty and of innocence, purity, and humility
Lily of the valley	Stands for recurring joy; a symbol of spring and new beginnings
Linden flower	"Have you understood me now?"
Love-in-a-mist	"I do not want to suffer your courtship."
Magnolia	Represents pure, feminine beauty
Mallow	Give these to someone you regard as kindness personified
Marigold	Symbolizes jealousy
Marsh marigold	"Please don't spurn my love."
Mexican aster	Symbolizes tender yearning
Milkwort	"I have to forget you, though it breaks my heart in two."
Morning glory	Give as a sign of affection
Mugwort	Represents satisfaction, calm, and reflection

Mullein	"For me, you are the most precious in the world."
Myrtle	Represents innocence, but is also a gift for a virgin who will soon wear the bridal wreath
Oak leaf	Symbolizes eternity, because an oak tree will outlive thirty generations
Oleander	Give as a warning
Olive branch	Considered the most beautiful symbol of peace
Orchid	Considered the loveliest of all flowers
Pansy	"I think about you all the time." Or, "Your body is beautiful, but your heart is not."
Peach blossom	A promise of sensual eroticism
Peony	The rose without thorns stands for a happy marriage; it is also said to drive out melancholy and restore good cheer
Peppermint	Stands for hospitality, but also passionate love and curative power
Pomegranate	Symbolizes sensual love and passion
Poppy	A dangerous flower with two sides: a symbol of sensuality and superficial love. Also, "No minute with you is forgotten." Considered a magical plant, uniting both healing and ruin in its blossoms.
Pot marigold	Symbolizes immortality—blooms all summer long
Quaking grass	Symbolizes the transience of life
Quince blossom	Symbolizes happiness, delight, and fertility
Robinia	"I will love you beyond the grave!"
Rose	The classic symbol of love, admiration, reverence, and pure beauty

Rosebuds, red	Give to your first love
Rosebuds, white	Give to someone chaste and pure
Rose hip	"I don't understand you anymore."
Rosemary	Symbolizes eternal fidelity and fellowship
Rowan branch	Expresses courage and aid in difficult times
Sage	A symbol of high regard
Snapdragon	Symbolizes sweet revenge
Snowdrop	Symbolizes consolation and hope, and love and innocence
Spearmint	"Without you, my life has no meaning."
Stinging nettle	"Watch out! Don't let your high spirits get you stung!"
St.-John's-wort	Considered a love oracle; it is also said that the red color obtained from the buds is the spilled blood of Christ
Stock	Stands for eternal grace
Strawberry flower	"You are still too immature for me!"
Sunflower	A symbol of summer; also an expression of strength and boundless love
Sweetvetch	Give to a country beauty
Thistle	Symbolizes inner strength, but also inflexibility, hard-heartedness, and mocked love
Touch-me-not (mimosa)	Symbolizes femininity, sensitivity, and untouchability
Tulip	Symbolizes renown, wealth, and the transience of earthly things
Tulip, bright red	Represents the all-consuming fire of love
Verbena	Considered to ward off the devil; give to someone in need of protection
Vetch	Symbolizes affection and love
Violet	Symbolic of a secret love, but also of youthful innocence

Wallflower	Give when you want to express true, unwavering love, or hope in difficult times
Wax flower	Give to a woman with a soft heart
White clover	Symbolizes ease and freedom from care
Wolfsbane	"You are the embodiment of charm."
Woodruff	Considered to have magical properties; a reminder of the merry sides of life
Yarrow	A magical plant and an oracle; do not give yarrow to someone thoughtlessly
Zinnia	Give these to a happy woman with a zest for life

Acknowledgments

My gratitude goes to all who helped me bring this book into existence. Special thanks are owed to one wonderful Baden-Baden woman who was enormously generous with her extensive knowledge.

About the Author

Photo © Privat

Petra Durst-Benning is one of Germany's most successful and prominent authors. For more than twenty years, her books have invited readers along on adventures with courageous female characters, through rich and engaging detail. Petra has written more than a dozen historical novels, many of which have gone on to be bestsellers and be adapted for television. She's enjoyed immense international success and has developed a loyal following of fans. She lives with her husband in Stuttgart, Germany.

About the Translator

Photo © Dagmar Jordan

Australian-born and widely traveled, Edwin Miles has been working as a translator for fifteen years.

From the town of Perth in Western Australia, Edwin completed an MFA in fiction writing at the University of Oregon in 1995. While there, he spent a year working as a fiction editor on the literary magazine *Northwest Review*. In 1996, he was shortlisted for the prestigious Australian/Vogel's Literary Award for young writers for a collection of short stories.

After many years living and working in Australia, Japan, and the United States, he currently resides in his "second home" in Cologne, Germany, with his wife, Dagmar, and two very clever children.